Incomplete

A Novel

J.D. LEVIN

INCOMPLETE

A NOVEL

J.D. LEVIN

NOT-SO-SILENT LIBRARIAN BOOKS

Not-So-Silent Librarian Books
Ventura, CA 93003
www.notsosilentlibrarian.com

This is a work of fiction, obviously. References to real people, events, establishments, organizations, products, bands, brands, or locales are intended only to provide a sense of authenticity, and are used to advance the narrative. All other characters, and all incidents and dialogue, are drawn from the author's imagination and are not to be construed as real.

Apart from well-known historical figures (I'm looking at you, Brian Wilson and the Beach Boys), any resemblance to actual persons, living or dead, businesses, companies, events, or locales is entirely coincidental.

This book is not authorized, approved, licensed, or otherwise endorsed by Brian Wilson, Mike Love, the Beach Boys, or the Brother Records Inc. (BRI) corporate entity. Buy their music and support the band. Please don't sue me.

Library of Congress *Cataloging-in-Publication* Data
Levin, J.D. (Joel David)
Incomplete: a novel / J.D. Levin
p.   cm.
ISBN 978-0-578-73852-9 (pbk.)
ISBN 978-0-578-73853-6 (ebook)
  1. Adolescence — Fiction. 2. Popular Music — Fiction. 3. Rock groups — Fiction. 4. Composers — Fiction. 5. High school students — Fiction. 813'.54 — DC23

Book design and layout by J.D. Levin

Printed in the United States of America
DOC 10 9 8 7 6 5 4 3 2 1 (Counting is fun!)

For my daughters,
Alexandra and Charlotte.
Without you, my life would truly be incomplete.

INTRO RIFF

PROLOGUE
"Sail On, Sailor"

The dusty CD bins at used record stores are filled with the ghosts of one-hit wonders.

As anyone who has watched VH1's *Behind the Music* can attest, the music industry is a fickle mistress, a siren luring you into her trap with temptations of fame and fortune. However, like the sailors in Greek myths, countless bands meet their doom when the shifting tides lead them not to everlasting treasure – but to a shipwreck.

I was once one of these musical sailors, though I was forced off the vessel before the band met its inevitable demise. Just as things were starting to gain momentum, as the ship was heading towards that mythical island oasis, populated by unfathomable beauty and riches…

I quit.

But this isn't so much the story of a band as it is a tale about sailing those turbulent tides and treading water in the years after. Self-absorbed and egocentric as that might sound, it's true: what you're reading isn't a rock star's autobiography as much as it is a memoir by a pop music has-been. I promise that I will tell you all about my personal history in due time, but (more importantly) I'm going to present you with an atypical tale.

This, dear reader, is something different.

This is the story of a song.

Now, as you're holding this stack of several hundred pages in your hands, you obviously recognize that this tale stretches beyond the confines of a three-and-a-half-minute pop song; as with everything else in life, there is always a backstory, an event, and an aftermath that's much bigger and broader than the original piece of music that I wrote two decades ago. Additionally, there's a whole cast of characters – probably not unlike people you've known in your own life. This is a story about my father and my wife and my daughter and my students and the members of the band that I used to be in.

And, yes, it's about the Beach Boys.

You don't know me, but I'm the guy who wrote Call Field's "Incomplete (Just Like Your Smile)," a song that peaked at Billboard's #19 spot for three short weeks in the summer of 2000. Although the name might not ring a bell, the melody probably sounds familiar: as soon as anyone starts singing the chorus (*"I get lost sometimes..."*), it tends to spark a personal recollection – perhaps lounging by the lake at summer camp or driving three hundred miles on a college road trip or hitting blackjack three times straight at a table in Vegas on your 21st birthday. In some crazy, metaphysical way, I was there with you – or, at the very least, my song was.

My band's last album, the only one we ever professionally recorded, earned pretty good reviews: *Rolling Stone* magazine called my songwriting "exemplary" and *Alternative Press* said that the world should "expect big things from this ex-punk quartet."

But those days are far behind me now.

When I think about my tenure in Call Field, it feels like another lifetime, like watching a made-for-TV movie from the comfort of your living room couch. The world is full of bands and singers and songwriters who have had "one-hit wonders" on the radio... but what happens to those musicians when the spotlight fades and the fickle fan base dwindles?

I'll tell you what I did.

I became a high school English teacher.

There are actually a few of us now who have traded our guitars for podiums: Peter Tork from the Monkees, Blake Schwarzenbach from Jawbreaker, John Hampson from Nine Days, Eric Axelson from The Dismemberment Plan, Frank Koroshec from The Autumns – and yours truly, Brian Richard Smith.

Where do all the rock stars go when the lights die out? They grow up, they get jobs, and they try to live normal lives in the aftermath of a truly surreal experience. In my case, I traded an enthusiastic audience of admiring music fans for a tolerant audience of captive high school students. However, I can honestly say that I am happier now than I ever was thumping the strings of a bass guitar on a darkened stage. It's hard to believe, but it's true: high school teachers live more spiritually fulfilling lives than mid-level, major-label musicians.

Plus, the paychecks are more consistent.

While public school teachers are not paid as much as legendary rock stars, we earn a decent middle-class salary. More importantly, though, it's what we *do* with our lives that makes the job so rewarding. My entire existence these days is dedicated to helping young men and women and non-binary folks follow their passions. I already had my chance to dream the impossible dream, like Don Quixote charging at windmills; unfortunately, I got knocked off my horse before I actually battled any dragons. But none of that matters anymore. My life now is in service of others. And I wouldn't want it any other way.

The tricky part is when the past comes back to haunt you. The Byrds' "So You Want to Be a Rock 'n' Roll Star" provides a pretty concise outline for how to pursue a career in music: you buy an instrument, spend countless hours practicing and refining your craft, then let the good times roll. However, Roger McGuinn and company never prepared a follow-up song about the aftermath of fame. [**Side-note:** I doubt that a tune entitled "So You *Used to Be* a Rock 'n' Roll Star" would have been a smash success. Just an observation.]

So, what do you do when the past and present meet head-on? Suddenly, your worlds have collided, and you're faced with a difficult choice. Do you maintain your sense of normalcy with your safe, secure, and comfortable life? Or do you embrace the punk-rock unpredictability that comes with the career of a professional musician?

But I'm getting ahead of myself. All you really need to know right now is that I'm a semi-typical, white-collar suburbanite with a regular job. The rest will be revealed shortly. You might have heard some rumors about what happened to our band, about why I left and how things fell apart. I'm here to set the record straight.

Let me leave you with one final thought before we start. What I believe is this: like the beating organ in Edgar Allan Poe's "Tell-Tale Heart," rock 'n' roll will haunt you until the day you die. It just sounds more like a metronome than a heartbeat.

FIRST VERSE

California can be cruel in the summer –
the girls will give you sunburns with a grin,
and the gray skies can be colder than December
when all you want is sunshine on your skin.

CHAPTER ONE

"We'll Run Away"

I t's just one step at a time.
Right foot. Left foot.
Right foot. Left foot.
Repeat for an hour.

Three days a week, I step onto the treadmill in my garage and run for sixty minutes straight. When I first started running twenty years ago (on doctor's orders, I might add), I could only jog for a mile or so before I needed to walk the rest of the way. These days, I'm able to squeeze six or seven miles into each workout session.

I suppose much of my existence is a treadmill these days. Over the last few years, I've fallen into a very comfortable pattern with my job and my life, a regimented routine that looks something like the following:

5:00 AM-7:30 AM	Wake up, get ready, eat breakfast, and drive to work.
7:30 AM-3:30 PM	Teach English at a public high school in Oxnard, CA.
3:30 PM-4:30 PM	Prep for the next day of work and drive home.
4:30 PM-5:30 PM	Grade papers (T/TH) *OR* run on the treadmill (M/W/F).
5:30 PM-6:00 PM	Eat dinner.

6:00 PM-6:30 PM	Do dishes, clean up, and prepare lunches for the next day.
6:30 PM-7:00 PM	Help my daughter with her homework.
7:00 PM-8:00 PM	Get my daughter ready for bed and read her bedtime stories.
8:00 PM-9:30 PM	Finalize my lesson plans, read a book, and get ready for bed.
9:30 PM-5:00 AM	Sleep. Or *try* to sleep, at least.

This schedule, stagnant and robotic as it might seem, comprises the vast majority of my life these days. Of course, there are always deviations from the routine – extracurricular events, dinners at local restaurants, etc. – so it's not immaculately etched in stone. However, I have found comfort in the ritualistic nature of the working week, a way to stave off the unpredictable darkness of living.

And, as I mentioned before, there's the treadmill.

Right foot. Left foot.

Right foot. Left foot.

Repeat for an hour.

While this mechanical lifestyle might be too cold and inflexible for some, it's the only way I've found to maintain my sanity as a teacher.

People always joke about how easy it must be to teach: *After all,* the public thinks, *you only work from 8:00-3:00. You get summers off. And then there are all those holidays. It's a cushy job, right?*

If you've ever had this thought, then you're misinformed or just plain ignorant. Non-teachers always forget about the long nights spent planning lessons and grading papers and calling parents and e-mailing students and creating assignment sheets and writing tests and...

You get the idea.

Even those precious weekends, though *technically* student-free zones, are still dedicated to grading essay after essay after essay – albeit from the comfort of your own coffee table, couch, or bed. I would estimate that I spend an average of 60 hours a week working, from mid-August through mid-June. While the month of July is a glorious oasis of relaxation, the other eleven months of the year are a stressful, nightmare-inducing marathon.

Right foot. Left foot.

Right foot. Left foot.

Repeat for an hour.

So much of youth is spent sprinting from one milestone to another, straining to cross finish line after finish line in a *Chariots of Fire*-worthy race. Yet, after you reach adulthood, the rules change and you can no longer maintain a never-ending sprint; instead, as your body and heart slowly age, you learn to find a relaxed pace that you will repeatedly run for the next few decades. Literally and figuratively, I've found my rhythm, my pace. I can comfortably continue moving at this speed for the next decade or two.

And I will be content with what I have moving forward.

Though I did my fair share of sprinting in my younger days, I find security and solace now in the steady pace of the treadmill. There is something reassuring about running countless miles on a contraption in my garage – moving constantly, but going nowhere.

I might not be participating in any kind of race, but I am hitting my stride from the comfort of my own home. This, my friends, is the beauty of living your life on a treadmill.

Right foot. Left foot.

Right foot. Left foot.

Repeat for an hour.

CHAPTER TWO

"Disney Girls"

E nough exposition.

This story *really* begins with Veronica. She's part of the reason that things have been so busy these last few months: she lit the match that started the fire that crawled along the fuse until the inevitable conflagration consumed my life.

But we'll get there soon enough.

In any case, Veronica is one of *those* girls, the unbelievably perfect kid from the perfect family, with the perfect GPA and the perfect brag sheet. Of course, she was popular in school (ASB president and "most likely to succeed") and well-rounded (an Honors student, volleyball team captain, and lead actress). The year before last, when Veronica was a junior at Oxnard Shores High School, she was the shining star student in my Advanced Placement English Language and Composition class. Somewhere along the line, between homework assignments and in-class essays, we bonded over our mutual love of indie rock bands and *Wonder Years* reruns. So, it was no surprise when she asked to be my TA this year.

Awesome, I thought to myself, *another smart kid whom I can trust to proofread papers and help run Socratic seminars.* To be fair, she wasn't the first "super-TA" that I've had, and she certainly won't be the last; however, she's the only one who could've set things in motion to the extent that she has. As this story unfolds, you'll see that she's already had a profound effect on my life in a very limited amount of time – and she's not even out of her teenage years yet.

One of the most endearing things about Veronica is that she has impeccable taste in music. As she proudly proclaimed in her first writing assignment for my AP English class during her junior year, her top-five all-time favorite bands are (listed alphabetically):

* The Beatles
* blink-182
* The Civil Wars
* Death Cab for Cutie
  AND
* Fleetwood Mac

Obviously, as her musical palate implies, Veronica is not the stereotypical caricature of a teenage girl. Of course, she *does* have a soft spot for Britney Spears... But, hey, nobody's perfect.

When we initially crossed paths almost exactly two years ago, it was the first day of school. As students filed into the classroom, many with the sullen look of defeat that accompanies the end of summer vacation, Veronica bounced into the classroom with a swarm of girls in her company. Even at first glance, I could tell that there was something unique about her – she had the kind of magnetic personality that captivated and enchanted the people around her. Of course, the best part of teaching AP English is that you find yourself surrounded by dozens of fascinating, engaging kids; yet, even amid such remarkable company, Veronica distinguished herself as the queen bee of the room. Unlike Regina George from *Mean Girls*, however, there was something serene and unthreatening about Veronica. Even from our first encounter, she exuded kindness and intuitiveness and honesty and authenticity.

I'll interject here with a side-note. I shouldn't have to make a disclaimer, but I will: this is NOT one of *those* stories, the unsettling *Lolita* tale with a Humbert Humbert narrator. Veronica and I have a purely platonic relationship that does not cross any inappropriate boundaries; rather, she's almost become like an adopted daughter to me. One of the sad facts of the teaching profession is that you often hear sensationalized stories of improprieties committed by predatory adults with doe-eyed victims. To make matters even more challenging, young male teachers have historically been some of the worst culprits. So, as a young-ish male teacher surrounded by high school girls, I have to be *extra* diligent in my efforts to maintain appropriate boundaries and borders with my students. It's heartbreaking that dynamics in the teaching profession have come to such a sad state of affairs, but it's one of the challenging rivers that every educator must navigate in his or her career.

That being said, what first impressed me about Veronica was her musical pedigree. On the first day of class, I always ask my students for a mnemonic device to help me remember their names. Most of Veronica's classmates came up with uninspired phrases ("Claire with brown hair" or "Charlie owns a Harley" or similarly sterile rhymes), but when the kindly queen bee introduced herself, she provided a little anecdotal background information.

"You see," she began, "I'm *technically* named after my grandma, but my dad also has a soft spot for this New Wave singer, Elvis Costello. So, my parents named me after my grandma *and* after this song about a woman with Alzheimer's who is fighting for her memory."

Elvis Costello? I wondered to myself. *Really?*

"Basically," she laughed, "my name implies that I'm a little old lady."

The class giggled at their queen's commentary.

"I know, I know," she continued, "it's kind of strange. But that's my story."

I chuckled aloud and impulsively plunged into my best Elvis Costello impression: *"You can call me anything you like…"*

"…but my name is Veronica," she finished, with an impressive vocal delivery. She gave me a quizzical smile as she sang, though, seemingly surprised that I knew her musical birthright. After a second, however, she turned back to the rest of the class and finished her introduction. "My last name, however, is much less unique," she explained. "It's Jones. Like Indiana."

The class giggled good-naturedly at their queen bee, and we moved on to the next student. I knew right then and there, though, that I would enjoy having this Veronica Jones girl in my English class. Not only was she equally well-versed in Elvis Costello's music and George Lucas's films, but she could also sing. And sing *well*, I might add. Any of these traits in isolation is enough to make a high school kid memorable in my book; when combined, however, it's clear that the student in question is destined to be unforgettably unique.

The rest of the school year with Veronica's AP English class was smooth sailing. The queen bee and her acolytes, including the aforementioned Claire and Charlie, had wonderful chemistry – the right combination of studiousness and enthusiasm that make the year truly rewarding for students and teachers alike. For all the grumbling talk of millennials ruining the world, these bright, good-natured students will restore your faith in humanity.

When the year was over, after seemingly endless hours of essays and novels and expository articles, Veronica's parents wrote me an incredibly kind, thoughtful note about how special my class had been for their daughter and how much growth they had seen in her writing over the course of the school year. As a small token of appreciation, Mr. and Mrs. Jones invited us over for dinner that summer. I should note that, in my eighteen years of teaching, I have only been invited to a student's house for dinner a handful of times; as much success as I've had in the classroom, the barriers between students and teachers are typically too rigid and awkward to overcome.

The Jones family, however, was anything *but* typical.

During our delightful summer dinner at their house, Mr. and Mrs. Jones thanked me for being such a positive presence in their daughter's life. Of course, as I explained to them that evening, my relationship with Veronica was a symbiotic one: it's easy to be a good teacher when you have such wonderful students in your classroom.

"If I could have thirty-five students like Veronica in every class," I explained, "I could lead a happy, fulfilling career for years to come."

Alternately, while Mr. and Mrs. Jones were full of praise and kind words for me, I also saw firsthand how such a wonderful household could foster greatness in a remarkable young lady like Veronica. After spending a year with her in class, I assumed (correctly) that she must have come from a good family; little did I realize, however, just how compassionate and sweet-natured her parents were.

As I learned over the course of our first dinner together, Veronica's mother was an elementary school teacher (just like my mom had been), and her father was an oral and maxillofacial surgeon (essentially a "dental surgeon," as he explained). As I saw it, both of her parents were in the "smile" business: her mother helping to empower little children and her father literally working on the physiological smiles of patients.

My wife, Mel, was enchanting during the dinner (as always), but the real star of the evening was my eight-year-old daughter, Samantha. Every comment that Sam uttered, every gesture that she made elicited sighs and grins and laughs from the adults in the room.

Sam, it seemed to me, was also in the smile business.

During our dinner, Veronica became increasingly smitten with Samantha. Though she had seen Sam's picture on my cluttered classroom desk, there was undoubtedly something extra charming about spending time with my daughter in the flesh. I might be biased, but I think that Samantha is a truly remarkable kid; and, while she's not immune to tantrums and outbursts and other childish behavior, she has a naturally sweet disposition. Plus, with her mother's good genetics, Sam is simply a breathtakingly beautiful little girl. At least I think so.

As the evening progressed, Samantha politely asked the adults at the table if she could be excused – so that she could play with Veronica. We all laughed, and Veronica volunteered to occupy Sam while the adults stayed behind in the dining room. As Sam scooted down from her chair, she shoved her oversized sketchbook into her backpack and pulled out a handful of little plastic Disney princesses.

After taking her dinner plate to the kitchen, Veronica kneeled down on the carpet next to Sam's diminutive figure. Each of my daughter's little hands grasped a Disney princess, Aurora in her left hand and Cinderella in her right. From across the room, the two dolls looked like miniature bouquets of pink and blue.

"What are we playing, Samantha?" Veronica asked in a genuine, earnest voice.

"We're playing princesses," Sam responded enthusiastically. "Cinderella and Aurora are going camping, but they don't want to go by themselves."

"That sounds like fun!" Veronica exclaimed. "Who do I get to be?"

"You can be Belle," Sam decided, gleaming up at her new friend.

Veronica picked up the little yellow *Beauty and the Beast* doll from Sam's backpack and posed her upright on the coffee table that occupied the center space of the living room. "Belle is my *favorite* princess," Veronica said. "Do you know why she's my favorite?"

Sam smiled up at the young Miss Jones, eyes bright with wonder. "Why, Veronica?"

"Because she *loves to read*. I love to read, too, and I wish I had a library as big as the one in the Beast's castle."

"I have a really big library in my room," Sam responded gleefully. "It takes up a whole bookshelf! You need to come see it!"

In addition to her multitudinous academic attributes, Veronica was a natural with Sam. And, fortunately, Sam seemed to adore Veronica, too.

Although teachers are probably supposed to avoid having favorite students, it was hard not to feel a special kinship with a wholesome, well-rounded kid like Veronica. She was brilliant, kind, thoughtful, respectful, and well-adjusted. In short, she was *exactly* the kind of young lady that I want Samantha to become in the next few years.

Not only were we well-fed at the end of the evening, but we also had a built-in babysitter for the next year. Veronica volunteered to watch Sam for free, and Mr. Jones insisted that it was the least their family could do, considering all the help that I had given his daughter in my English class. We thanked the Jones family profusely for their offers and for their hospitality, and we promised to utilize Veronica in the near future.

As we left the Jones house that evening, a full moon illuminated the sky. The world seemed full of good people with good intentions, and I felt serenely at peace as we walked to our car, my wife holding one of my hands and my daughter holding the other. In the soft haze of the moonlight, our evening seemed like the prologue to a lovely summer – one in which I would be able to spend time with my family without the distractions of grading and lesson planning. Of course, if we needed some time alone, Mel and I could now rely upon Veronica to babysit Samantha for a few hours here and there – and that provided no small relief. Watching these two Disney girls playing sweet, innocent games in a safe, warm home lifted my spirits.

It's hard to feel weighed down by the ghosts of the past when you see the spirits of the present laughing and grinning.

CHAPTER THREE

"In My Room"

When the kitchen table is too noisy to grade papers, when the buzz of the television set is too loud to concentrate, I retreat to the upstairs of our house and plant myself in my office.

This personal *Fortress of Solitude* is *exactly* the kind of place that Brian Wilson sings about in the Beach Boys' classic 1963 song, "In My Room." Though I am far beyond my teenage years, the lyrics still resonate strongly with me: whether I'm doing my "dreaming" or my "scheming," this office provides me with the peace and quiet that I need to simply *get things done.*

I have made this miniature kingdom my own, with an assortment of tchotchkes and mementos decorating the room. The walls are adorned with a variety of rock and roll posters, including a lithograph of the Brian Wilson concert at the Hollywood Bowl that Mel and I attended a few summers ago. On either side of the wall, Brian's image is flanked by posters of Bob Dylan and John Steinbeck; elsewhere, posters of the Grateful Dead, Jack Kerouac, and Neil Young adorn the azure walls, like little vertical ships on a muted sea.

I also have an overcrowded CD library situated along the east wall, a cluttered collection that begins with AC/DC and stretches along the wall to The Zombies, with a wide array of artists sandwiched in-between. Of course, the albums are all meticulously organized: alphabetically by artist/band, then chronologically by album release date. Yes, I am *that* much of a music geek.

While some artists occupy more space than others, the band that takes up the biggest section of my collection is The Beach Boys. I have all

29 studio albums from the band, from 1962's *Surfin' Safari* to 2012's *That's Why God Made the Radio*, in addition to live records, compilations, box sets, and a handful of bootlegs.

The Grateful Dead have Deadheads. Jimmy Buffett has Parrotheads. Phish has Phish Heads. Neil Diamond has Diamond Heads.

By that logic, I am an unapologetic *Beach Head.*

When I tell people that the Beach Boys are my all-time favorite band, I get some amusing reactions. There's often the initial, knee-jerk response: "Oh, I love them! They're so fun!" or "[*Insert name of radio-friendly 1960s pop hit*] is one of my favorite songs!" However, when I ask a more probing follow-up question, I rarely get anything more than an admission that *Endless Summer* or *Sounds of Summer* is the only Beach Boys album in this person's record collection. Disappointment ensues.

Other folks, however, seem incredulous. Less-educated hipsters have a hard time seeing past the "beaches and babes" iconography of the band, and I am sure that I must come across as incredibly square to anyone who attempts to judge me by my favorite musical act.

The truth, of course, is much more complicated than that.

The Beach Boys were always in the background of my childhood, like nondescript drapes on a theater stage. My dad was so obsessed with the band, in fact, that he even named me after their leader, Brian Wilson. Whether my father was listening to L.A.'s K-EARTH 101 or playing scratchy vinyl LPs on his ancient record player, the band's music became the soundtrack of my youth. And, thanks to Dad's retelling of stories from David Leaf's *The Beach Boys and the California Myth*, I also learned about the rich, tragic history of the band.

Most bands, like many families, are dysfunctional in some way. The Beach Boys, however, were both a family and a band – and, thus, they have taken dysfunction to a whole new level of sophistication.

For the casual listener, the Beach Boys narrative might go something like this: the group starts off as a novelty act in the early sixties, rivals the Beatles for a few years, reaches pop music perfection with *Pet Sounds*, then disappears until "Kokomo" in the 1980s. While this is a conveniently concise (and not entirely incorrect) overview, it neglects to address some key questions: What happened to the band from 1966 to 1988? Why did they lose their "musical arms race" with the Beatles? How could a band create a masterpiece like *Pet Sounds* and then subsequently fail to create anything else of substantial merit? Is the current incarnation of the band that plays the county fair circuit the same band from the 1960s, or is it a bastardized reincarnation solely intent on making a few cheap dollars by peddling nostalgia to aging baby boomers?

In reality, the Beach Boys story is hotly debated and nearly impossible to canonize. In the most commonly accepted versions of the narrative (such as the one presented in the film *Love & Mercy*), Brian Wilson was the tortured genius behind the band, the solitary guiding force whose sheer force of will and talent propelled the band to the apex of mainstream American popular culture. When Brian seemingly imploded in the late 1960s after the aborted *Smile* album, his absence created a vacuum that needed to be filled. What most people don't know (or don't remember) is that the Beach Boys consistently pumped out albums through the 1970s *and* 1980s, some of which are pretty incredible records. Yes, they did have their biggest hit in 1988 with the unbearably dated "Kokomo," as well as a successful 50th-anniversary reunion tour in 2012 that ended acrimoniously; that being said, their most recent release (and swan song?), *That's Why God Made the Radio*, has some really impressive, breathtaking moments. This album alone could stand as proof that the band is a living, breathing organism – and should serve as a symbolic victory lap for the not-always-victorious Brian Wilson.

Unlike Bob Dylan or Johnny Cash, who have had remarkable late-career renaissances, the Beach Boys have struggled to stay relevant in the last few years. To be fair, though, how many mortals can maintain a superhuman sprint throughout their entire lives? Most of us learn how to find a pace that allows us to persevere through the later, slower years of existence, as we continue on the winding mountain passes that lead us towards our eminent ends.

Right foot. Left foot.

Right foot. Left foot.

Repeat for the rest of your career.

You've gotta' love the music industry.

Apart from the Beach Boys memorabilia, the bookshelves, and my oversized CD collection, there is one key item that has made its home in my office: my father's old acoustic guitar. For the six-string aficionados out there, this isn't just any guitar – it's a 1961 Martin D-21 that my dad bought on his fifteenth birthday, right after he started playing guitar. At the time, he was just a regular high school kid who wanted to look cool like Elvis Presley or Johnny Cash, both of whom played Martins. These days, however, his guitar sits in the corner of my office, accumulating a fine layer of dust on its strings and frets.

Occasionally, I'll look up from my stacks of essays and see the Martin stationed stiff and upright on its guitar stand, as if it's settled into a state of refined rigor mortis. Of course, I do get a nagging feeling when I glance at the corner of my room and see my father's old guitar. Time coats all things in layers of dust – including our memories – and I can't help but think I should pick up the guitar, clean it off, and strum… if only for a few minutes.

Unfortunately, I rarely do.

So, the Martin sits in its station, resting and waiting for the day in which I will bring it back to life, save it from its catatonic state, and wring some music from its strings. Most of the time, though, I simply turn back to my stacks of essays, pen clenched firmly between my fingers, and I grade one paper after another…

And the guitar patiently waits in silence.

CHAPTER FOUR

"Good Timin'"

Everybody wants to be the lead singer in the band. Or snag the starring role in the school play. Or serve as the starting quarterback on the football team. The problem, though, is that there can only be a handful of lead actors and actresses in every realm; and, while many can dream of these roles, only a small, select group will ever be able to attain them.

Veronica, the Queen Bee of English AP, was one of the lucky ones. Before playing princesses with Samantha sporadically in the summer of 2019, Veronica had actually earned her royal status when she was cast as Cinderella in the Oxnard Shores production of Rodgers and Hammerstein's musical. It seemed appropriate enough: as in the Cinderella fairy tale, Veronica's hard work in every facet of her life would soon be rewarded (albeit with scholarships and entry to topnotch colleges, not with shiny crowns and breakable footwear). Plus, Veronica already had experience ruling the school with a gentle hand, as evidenced by her flock of sidekicks in my AP English class the previous year. With a little luck – and a lot of preparation – she was hoping to use some academic magic to recreate herself as a college student with glass slippers.

Before she could make her great escape in a transformed pumpkin coach, however, Veronica had to tackle the most dreaded teenage rite of passage, the strangest of all high school rituals: the college application essay. And, as she engaged with this task, I was to play the role of the fairy godmother – or god*father*, technically (even if the title makes me sound like I'm part of the Italian mafia). Having lived a very sheltered life (and I mean that in the nicest way possible), Veronica had not encountered any traumatic personal tragedies or revolutionary transformative experiences. Because of this, she had to draw upon her talents and skills to flesh out her essays – specifically, her experiences in theater. Of course, to really make her words sparkle and shine, she had to find some way to connect her drama experiences with her intended future profession…

Dentistry.

Yes, Veronica was the odd duck who wanted to pursue the family business in dental health and become a DDS/DMD. How many popular high school girls want to become dentists? In almost two decades of teaching, I can tell you exactly how many: one.

Veronica knew how challenging it would be to piece all of this together, so she enlisted my help to brainstorm and develop ideas for her essay. And, being the overachiever that she is, Veronica asked if we could meet over the *summer* to start work on her essays. That's right: the young Miss Jones wanted to use her well-earned vacation time to start working on her college applications – which wouldn't be due for almost four months.

Did I mention that Veronica is a workaholic? I think describing Veronica as "Type A" might be an understatement for a girl like her… Is there a "Type A+" description out there? If not, we should coin the term to accurately describe folks like this gal.

So, in early July, Veronica and I met up at the local Barnes & Noble to begin work on what she hoped would be her masterpiece of an admissions essay. Mel and Samantha planned on attending a *Star Wars*-themed story-time in the children's section upstairs, so Veronica and I were free to work uninterrupted in the downstairs café. After exchanging princess-related pleasantries with Sam, Veronica settled into a cozy chocolate-colored chair at one of the circular café tables and started to unpack her backpack. Like a warrior nerd, Veronica withdrew an armory's worth of pencils, pens, highlighters, and sticky notes, placing them delicately on the oaken table in front of her. The centerpiece, however – the crown jewel of her display – was the multipage essay that she had freshly printed out and which she proceeded to place in the exact geometric center of her makeshift workstation.

Unlike other students, who might show up with a few scribbled bullet points, Veronica already had a solid rough draft of her essay completed. Within those eloquent paragraphs, she discussed at great length how much her experiences in theater had meant to her and how much she had grown in confidence since immersing herself in high school drama productions. However, like many of her teenage peers, Veronica had a tendency to *tell* – rather than *show* – her experiences. This, I pointed out to her, was going to be the most important part of her essay. After all, a powerful "picture" within a narrative can speak volumes more than a paragraph pontificating about the merits of hard work.

"But how do I start something like that?" she asked me, concern etched in the creases of her forehead. "What does that even look like?"

"Let's try a little visualization exercise," I told her. "Close your eyes."

"Do I *really* have to close my eyes?" she asked skeptically. "Is this necessary?"

"Yes," I sighed. "You trust me, right?"

"Of course," she replied, rolling her eyes.

"Okay. Then close your eyes, nerd."

"No need to get mean," she said with a squint. "Fine. I'll just try not to fall asleep."

After she begrudgingly shut her eyelids, I began.

"Picture yourself on the stage," I commanded gently. "It's opening night. You're in your costume, and you step downstage-center. What do you see?"

"Well," she said, bunching up her cheeks, "I see the bright lights."

"What else do you see?"

She paused. "I see the dark silhouettes of people in the audience."

"Let's focus on some details," I told her. "You look down at the floorboards in front of you. What do you notice about them? What color are they? Are they new or antiquated?"

"Hmmm…" she started cautiously. "Our theater is really ancient and it's in really bad shape. I guess the floorboards must be a few decades old, and they're definitely in need of repair. They're chipped and peeling and they creak loudly when you step on the wrong sections of the stage."

"What about the wings or the orchestra pit?" I prodded gently.

"Ugh. They're in even worse condition than the main stage."

"Bummer," I responded. "Let's talk about the curtains then."

"What *about* them?" she asked.

"Well," I said, "think about all of the curtains you see in the theater: the cyc, the grand drape, the scrims, anything that might be dangling from the proscenium…"

Though her eyes were closed, she seemed to be gazing thoughtfully over my shoulder, visualizing the Oxnard Shores auditorium in all of its dilapidated splendor. With her eyelids clenched shut and mouth slightly agape, she inhaled a slow, deep breath.

"The grand drape is an obnoxious Smurf-blue color," she exhaled. "It's almost like a bunch of blueberries vomited all over the front of our poor stage and someone used the grand drape to mop it up. Apparently, it's been there since the school opened in the 1960s. Gross, huh?"

"Yuck," I agreed. Blueberry Smurf vomit, while cleverly described and easy to visualize, was definitely not an image I wanted to dwell on at that precise moment. "And you said it's not in the best shape, either?"

"It's all scratched up," she replied. "There are a bunch of slits and tears all over. I mean, the curtains have been patched up and stitched back together like rag dolls, but it all looks so ugly. When you touch them, they have this velour kind of fuzz, but it actually rubs off onto your hands, like the drapes are molting or shedding skin. And they smell like old people or moth balls or something."

I snickered and tapped the table, amused by her impression of our aging school's decrepit facilities.

"That's a really good start," I told her. "Let's change gears… What about the audience? What can you tell me about them?"

Even though her eyes were closed, Veronica squinted tightly as she tried to envision the scene. "I can't see many of their faces, because the spotlight is so blinding… it's even brighter than the overhead light above a dentist's chair…"

Suddenly, she had an epiphany.

"HEY!" she exclaimed as her eyes popped open. "Can I use that in my essay? The fact that there are these bright lights in a dentist's office, kind of like the lights on the stage?"

I smiled, feeling that swelling sense of pride that teachers get when students start to connect the dots and form their own shapes. She got it. Now, she just needed to make those connections more explicit.

"You can *definitely* make that comparison later in your essay," I told her. "Your job for this kind of writing is to look at all of the little stars in your life and explain how they form constellations. And *that* is what's going to set you apart from the throngs of high-achieving high school kids applying for the same high-profile schools."

Veronica smiled, then slowly un-squinted, opening her eyes precisely and resolutely. "Okay," she said. "This is starting to make sense. So... I just give this detailed description of an acting experience and make it sound original. Then what?"

"Then, your job becomes twofold. You need to explain why this experience is an important one to you, why it's worth writing about. And then you need to find a way to connect it to your career in dentistry."

"How the heck am I going to do that?" she asked. "Dentistry is *nothing* like acting."

I paused for a second, thinking about how I could encourage her for this more challenging aspect of her essay. "A wise man once told me that a great writer can make *anything* a metaphor, with enough effort and creativity. That's the beauty of clever writing: you can find original ways to say something that has already been said a million times before by a million different writers. When you stretch your wings a little bit, when you create new constellations for your readers, you leave an indelible mark on your audience."

Veronica gave me that familiar skeptical stare that said, with its non-verbal prompting, *get on with the show.*

"So, what *do* actresses and dentists have in common?" I asked her.

Veronica thought for a second, and then beamed with an idea.

"They both make people smile," she said.

And there it was: the key to her essay.

For a good two hours, we talked about acting and dentistry and singing and princesses and college. Veronica, being the sharp girl that she was, picked up on a few personal details I had let slip during the conversation. The wheels were turning, and she was making her own mental connections, homing in on clues that I had unintentionally revealed.

"Did you do drama in high school?" she asked tentatively.

"*Me...?*" I laughed. "Definitely not. I didn't have the nerve back then to get up and recite lines in a play." I shifted uncomfortably in my seat. "Why do you ask?"

"Well, you know an awful lot about theater stages. You've clearly studied theater or spent a good deal of time onstage or *something*. If you weren't an actor, you must have done *some* performing..." She paused, gears grinding in that brilliant brain of hers. "Were you in orchestra or marching band or...?"

My face flushed involuntarily. "Something like that," I muttered in a clipped tone.

Right about then, Mel walked up with Sam, bags of recently purchased books weighing down their arms like anchors. "Why don't you tell her about the band?" Mel suggested nonchalantly.

Veronica's ears perked up. "*Band...?* What band...?"

"There's a band?" Sam asked, echoing her babysitter.

"It's nothing," I hurriedly told them. "Just something that I used to do once upon a time. In a former life." I shot Mel a desperate, pleading look.

Mel stiffened, her languid posture abruptly transformed into stoic silence.

Despite my noncommittal answers, Veronica wasn't ready to let the subject drop. "I didn't know you played an instrument! Why have you never mentioned this before? Let me guess... Were you in jazz band back in high school?"

"Actually, I *was* in jazz band back in the day," I admitted, hoping my answer would be enough to quench her curiosity.

Though I was *technically* telling the truth, I was also neglecting to mention the bigger part of my musical experience: the punk-rock ensemble that defined my life for so many years.

"I played the bass," I confessed, "and it was a really great experience. In any case, it was a long time ago…" Changing the subject, I shifted the conversation back to Veronica. "Anyway, *you* have these wonderful theater experiences to draw upon, these memories that you can utilize to create a memorable narrative for your college essays."

"I think things are starting to make a lot more sense now," Veronica said methodically, concentration seeping through each saturated word. "The picture is really starting to come into focus…" Then she looked at me funny, a hint of suspicion in her expression as she studied my face. Suddenly, the alarm on her phone started to chime, and Veronica snapped out of her trance.

"Oh, shoot! I have to head off to volleyball practice. But thank you *sooooo* much, Mr. Smith," she said as she packed up her things. "I really appreciate you spending some of your summer to help me with this college essay stuff. I owe you big time. And not just babysitting hours, either! If you ever need any favors from me, just say the word!"

"That won't be necessary, Veronica," I told her. "But thank you for the offer."

With that, Veronica waved goodbye, bounced out the front doors of Barnes & Noble, and headed out to her black Range Rover. Before she got in, though, she snuck one more investigative look back at me.

Her detective work had begun.

CHAPTER FIVE

"Wonderful"

L ater that afternoon, while I was sorting through tax documents in the filing cabinet of my office, I was still stewing on the uncomfortable café conversation I had endured with Veronica. It wasn't until dinnertime that I surreptitiously snapped out of my trance. As I passed by the living room on my way towards the kitchen, I heard my daughter carrying on a playful conversation with herself. Casually, I leaned against the white-trimmed doorframe of the room and paused to eavesdrop. From her spot on the floor, adjacent to the pink Disney Princess Castle that rested against the wall, Samantha spoke in the hushed, private tones of playtime – something about Aurora and Cinderella helping Princess Leia blow up the Death Star.

I envied Sam's ability to effortlessly blend disparate realms and universes. In her sweet world of make-believe, Disney princesses and *Star Wars* space-opera heroes can coexist on the same plane of imagination. I only wished that it was as easy for me to blend the different departmentalized components of my own life.

Escapism is a powerful tool in the heuristic arsenal. Of course, the same holds true for adults, as well as children: whether it's a sci-fi popcorn flick or a beer-soaked football game, adults crave an escape from their lives – if only for a temporary reprieve from the sheer ordinariness of adulthood.

Though I might not play dress up in ball gowns or cosplay with a lightsaber in hand, I suppose I'm guilty of indulging in my own kind of suburban fantasies with my Beach Boys obsession. After all, escapism was one of the most valuable tools in the Beach Boys' arsenal: conjuring images of fast cars, challenging waves, summer fun, and beautiful bikini-clad babes, the band capitalized on a very specific caricature of California life. How appealing must the band have been to kids in landlocked suburban towns across the country? After all, who wouldn't want to have "Fun, Fun, Fun" with flawless surfer girls in such a gorgeous locale?

The truth of the matter is that California is just as much a land of make-believe as any imaginary Disney kingdom. Anyone who lives by the beach will tell you that days without offshore flow are bound to be dark and dreary; however, while magic spells can be dispelled with the right wand, you can't *un*-cast an overcast sky. For all the talk of endless summers, Californians still contend with more "May gray" and "June gloom" than outsiders would ever anticipate.

While Sam, in her childish wonder, seems to live in a world of sunshine and warmth, her parents know all too well about the darkness that can seep into carefree summer days. For Samantha (and even Veronica), charcoal clouds are only a temporary distraction from the promise of never-ending August afternoons. These Disney girls reside in a world of silver linings, while their mothers and fathers live in a photonegative realm that recognizes the inevitability of leaden gray days.

After a few minutes of spying on Sam, I straightened up from the doorframe and walked towards the kitchen. Just down the hall, Mel was busy prepping dinner on our freshly cleaned dishes. Though we're not gluten-free vegan health-food nuts, we do our best to live a healthy, balanced life – especially because of our respective family medical histories. Even from the hallway, I could hear Mel humming a Taylor Swift song while she chopped a variety of vegetables for our evening salad. As I approached her from behind, I slyly slipped my arms around her waist and pulled her close.

"Hey, stranger," she said with a smirk, never lifting her eyes from the task in front of her.

"Hey, *Beautiful*." I nuzzled my face into her neck. "Do you need help with anything?"

She pointed her kitchen knife towards the refrigerator. "Do you mind grating some cheese while I prep the veggies?"

I pulled my arms away from her waist and strolled to the fridge, removing a chilled block of cheddar cheese.

"I didn't get to ask you earlier," Mel said apologetically, "but how did everything go with Veronica?"

"I think it went well," I said. "She's such a bright kid, and I think she's on the right track using her theater experience as the focal point of her college admissions essay."

I looked down at the kitchen counter as my hands moved in a quick succession of rhythmic motions. With each slice, I left a series of vertical scars on the block of cheese that I was grating.

Slice. Reposition.

Slice. Reposition.

Repeat until finished.

"Do you think she'll get into UCLA?" Mel asked.

"*Well...*" I responded with a mock-serious tone, "I think she's a shoe-in, but UCLA *is* the best school in the world. I mean, they took us, right? Obviously, the admissions department has *incredibly* high standards."

She let a subdued snicker escape under her breath. It's nice to know that I can still make her smile with stupid jokes and moderately amusing commentary, even after more than a decade and a half of marriage.

Working side-by-side, we made small talk – about the article she was editing that afternoon, about Sam's elementary school, and about her parents – all while edging and slicing and chopping through the fixings on the counter.

After a pregnant pause in the conversation, she broached the topic that I dreaded, the punk-rock elephant in the room that's stalked me everywhere I've gone in the last two decades.

"You didn't tell Veronica about the band," she said cautiously. "It's been what...? Nineteen years now? I know things were rough for a while, but a *long time* has passed." She paused, sizing up my stilted, silent response. "You still don't want to talk about it...?"

I didn't answer at first, and the hushed room was suddenly filled with a vacuum of voices. In sharp contrast to the absence of our conversation, every deft movement of my hands as I cut away at the block of cheese seemed to fill the kitchen with an unnecessarily loud clatter of metal and rhythmic thumping on the countertop.

"I just don't want to go back there," I told her. I stopped and set the block of cheese back on the counter, leaning forward onto the granite surface and refusing to look up at her. "It took long enough to get past that, and I'm too happy now to dredge up old memories for the sake of some misbegotten nostalgia." I returned to the cheddar on the counter and continued my food preparation.

Slice. Reposition.

Slice. Reposition.

Repeat until finished.

A few seconds passed before she said anything, the rhythmic motions of our hands marking every unspoken moment. "Okay," she sighed in defeat. "But are you just going to lie to Veronica?"

"I don't want to *lie* to her, per se..." I explained. "I'm just going to avoid talking about it. It's more like *deception by withholding information.* For all she knows, I just played in my high school jazz band and that was the end of it. She doesn't need to know my whole sordid backstory."

"It's not *sordid*," Mel sighed in exasperation. "It's just *something that happened.* And one day you're going to have to tell Samantha about those years with the band, right? She deserves to know her father's history, when she's old enough to understand."

"I know, I know..." I murmured, slightly exhausted by the conversation. "I just want to put it off as long as possible. I feel like I've exorcised those spirits, and the last thing I want is to end up haunted by ghosts again."

"Fair enough," Mel conceded, nodding her head in agreement. "When you *are* ready, though, maybe you should consider writing it all down. It might make for an interesting book."

I continued to mechanically grate the cheese in front of me until the block was reduced to a large pile of thin, delicate strips. After a few minutes of slicing, the scars that had been etched into the side of the block were gone – along with the block itself. It had all been transformed into something entirely different, as if the spirit had been released from the shell. I collected all the shredded scraps of cheddar, put them into a plastic bag, and handed them over to Mel.

"Maybe one day in the distant future, I'll give it a shot," I said finally, admitting partial defeat. "You know, Frank McCourt didn't start writing until after he retired from teaching. Maybe I'll write *Brian's Rock 'n' Roll Ashes* or something when I'm finally done with my teaching career."

"Or maybe you'll get inspired and write your story before then. We'll just have to see."

"You're right," I echoed back sullenly. "We'll see."

Considering the fact that you're holding this book in your hands, you obviously know that I didn't wait until after I retired. Clearly, the events of the last year have inspired me to write it out much earlier than I anticipated.

Don't tell my wife, but she was right.

Again.

CHAPTER SIX

"You're So Good to Me"

I've neglected to speak much about Mel thus far, but I promise that we'll get to her story soon enough. In many ways, she's the light to my dark, the yin to my yang. She's too impossibly good to be true, and yet she's here, in this home that we've built together, doing the lion's share of work raising our daughter – all while patiently putting up with me and my idiotic idiosyncrasies.

I'm sure that we look like an odd couple to the random strangers we encounter in the streets: I'm a pretty ordinary-looking fellow without any especially handsome qualities, but Mel is a bronze beauty who turns heads everywhere she goes.

People must wonder, *how did such a normal guy catch such a gorgeous wife?*

Perhaps people just assume that I've held her captive too long and she's developed a case of Patty Hearst syndrome. Or, perhaps, they think I've put Mel under a magic spell to capture her heart.

The truth, however, is something far less mystical.

I wrote her a really good song.

Yes, my wife is gorgeous. But, more importantly, she's also smart and kind and thoughtful and loving. After all, a woman's worth is more than the slope of her curves and the subtleties of her skin. I'm just grateful that I get to spend the rest of my life with this brilliant *Beautiful Girl* that caught my eye so many years ago.

That's what I call her: *Beautiful*. It's no longer just an adjective, a word with a lowercase "b" at its forefront; instead, it's become a title, a proper noun with a capital "B" that captures her essence more accurately.

With her darker Polynesian features, she's a sharp contrast to the pasty white blandness that I exude (courtesy of my Russian ancestors). I'm boring white bread, and she's an elegant pastry. And, no matter how old she gets, she will always be my *Beautiful Girl*.

Of course, we're both aging. Mel's not the young college girl that she once was, with an ocean of pure raven hair cascading down her shoulders; these days, she finds herself plagued with rogue strands of silver in her silken tresses, and it infuriates her to no end. Likewise, I can't ignore the fact that my own copper-colored hair is slowly thinning out, more resembling a porcupine's back than a lion's mane. And my defining facial features – the asymmetrical trio of moles that subtly form a Bermuda Triangle of birthmarks on my face – now appear even *more* profound and pronounced on the slightly sagging skin of my cheeks. We're slowly suffering the wear and tear of age – but at least we're facing the inevitable aging process *together.*

Those telltale signs of age – the crow's feet and wrinkled frown lines – have been creeping up on us gradually, like waves at high tide sneaking up on the smooth surface of the sandy shore. Mel also contends with the curse of varicose veins, which she half-jokingly blames on Samantha: when Mel was pregnant with our daughter, she started noticing the dark blue marks creeping up to the surface of her legs. The swollen, twisted cords of cobalt never disappeared, never retreated back beneath the surface of her supple skin; instead, the demarcations have left roadmaps between the freckles and scars on her thighs and calves. Though Mel can be incredibly self-conscious about this (she never wears shorts or skirts in public anymore), it doesn't detract from the majesty of her beauty: these small flaws are like the creased corners of a stunning photograph, only highlighting the value and preciousness of the contents within. Mel is a masterpiece, from silver-streaked head to varicose-veined toe.

If we are all Polaroids, destined to bleach and fade in the recesses of old age, Mel is the *Mona Lisa.*

And I will always hold her picture close to my heart.

CHAPTER SEVEN

"Salt Lake City"

T he rest of summer floated by on the gentle wings of July and into the anxious arms of August. Mel, Sam, and I made the most of our precious weeks together, squeezing in day trips to Malibu, Santa Monica, and Santa Barbara. Of course, Mel still had to balance our summer excursions with her year-round job editing for the *Oxnard Breeze* newspaper, but Sam and I were free to explore and adventure during Daddy-daughter outings. Slowly, though, the days slipped away from us, and I could feel the impending invasion of the fall semester on the horizon.

Though Mel and I had never relied upon regularly scheduled babysitters for our daughter, we felt confident enough to leave Sam in Veronica's care on a weekly basis that summer. In fact, when I stepped foot on campus for the first day of the 2019-2020 school year, only a few days had passed since the last time that I had seen Veronica. Of course, being the Type A+ overachiever that she is, Veronica had spent some of *her* precious summer solace writing several revisions of her college essays – all of which she brought with her on her return from vacation.

Before school on that first day, she strolled confidently into my classroom with an envelope that had been stuffed with stacks of printed pages. "I know that it's really early, but I wanted to give you my updated drafts, along with the prompts for a bunch of schools and scholarships. Oh, and I spoke with my counselor. I'm going to be your first-period TA this year. You can thank me later, when I have officially earned the title, *Best TA in the History of Mankind*."

How can you *not* appreciate this kind of go-getter attitude, especially when it comes from a seventeen-year-old high school kid? Dutifully, I extended my arm to Veronica for a handshake.

"Welcome aboard, sailor," I greeted her with a smile.

Veronica grinned, put her fingers to her forehead, and saluted me.

"Aye, aye, Captain," she said with a twinkle in her blue eyes.

In the following weeks, Veronica did her best to win that *Best TA in the History of Mankind* award: she kept my otherwise-messy desk meticulously organized, she served as my dramatic foil for class discussions, and she helped provide written feedback on the stacks of essays that quickly piled up in my inbox. While some TAs are not much more than human stapler-operators, Veronica was more like a *student teacher* than a student. The young Miss Jones had a skillset far too broad to waste on mere secretarial tasks, and I quickly caught on to her natural teaching abilities; in fact, every time that I was out sick, I trusted Veronica to teach my AP classes in my stead, rather than rely upon a mysterious substitute teacher of unknown origins. At the age of 17, Veronica was already wise beyond her years – and I was wise to utilize her talents for the benefit of my AP English students.

During a random day in the first week of September, when my AP kiddos were attending a career education session with their counselors, Veronica and I were left alone in the classroom – each with a pile of essays to read and critique. After working my way through half a dozen timed responses on a passage from Mark Twain's *Roughing It*, I leaned back in my chair, took off my glasses, and rubbed my temples.

"Tired of grading already?" Veronica asked with a competitive hint in her voice.

I squeezed my eyes tightly and scratched the back of my head. "Just taking a short breather before I plunge back into battle," I told her.

"Good call," she responded. "Do you mind if I take a quick stretch break?" Without waiting for a response, she jumped up from her desk, stretched out her arms, and popped her knuckles.

Not ready to resume my grading, I did what all teachers do to procrastinate: I made small talk instead.

"So, Miss Jones... how are you doing with your college essays?" I asked, an irrepressible yawn escaping my lips.

"Remarkably well, thank you," she said. "Your advice about using specific details really helped. The only part I'm still struggling with is making the dentistry career thing fit."

"It'll come eventually," I reassured her. "Just keep working on it."

I got up from my chair, walked over to the small refrigerator behind my desk, and grabbed a can of Coca-Cola. "I would offer you one," I told her, "but you don't drink this stuff, right?"

"No, thank you," she responded. "We don't drink any caffeine in my house, and my dad is a stickler about sugar. Plus, what kind of a future dentist would I be if I indulged in the kinds of syrupy treats that ruin your teeth?" She paused, then provided an addendum. "No offense, of course."

"None taken," I told her. "I keep meaning to ask you, though... Why dentistry? I mean, I understand that it's the family business and all, but is there more to it than that?"

She grinned, showing off her own perfect pearly white teeth. "It's pretty simple, actually," she explained. "Nothing is more beautiful than seeing someone smile."

"That's your motivation?" I asked with a raised eyebrow. "You make it sound... I don't know, kind of spiritual or something."

"Well, it's not like going to *church*," she laughed. "I realize that it seems like a purely cosmetic kind of thing, but it goes deeper than that."

"How so?" I probed, squinting my eyes.

"People always say that the *'eyes are the windows to the soul,'*" she explained to me, "but I think that your smile is the doorway – not just to your soul, but also to your voice."

Veronica's comment stunned me with its succinct poetry. "That's a really profound statement," I told her. "And I think that it's the thesis statement for your college admissions essay."

Her face lit up brighter than the Fourth of July. "You really think so? Is it that simple?"

"It *is* that simple," I said with my own toothy grin. "So, you've clearly got your whole career planned out, but what schools are you aiming for?"

"Well, my dad went to UCLA and my mom went to BYU. If everything goes according to plan, my guess is that I'll end up in Los Angeles or Utah. But I'm kind of leaning towards UCLA at this point..."

"It *is* the best school in the world," I interrupted with a wink, pointing to the Bruins pennant on my classroom wall.

She chuckled. "As I was saying *before I was rudely interrupted*," Veronica stressed the second half of her preface with a mock-serious tone, "UCLA has one of the best dental programs in the country. Plus, I'd kind of like to explore the Los Angeles entertainment scene a little bit."

"Really? I didn't realize you were that serious about theater..."

"It's not just theater," she explained. "I mean, I enjoy acting and all, but my heart is really in *singing*." She paused and blushed. "Of course, I know that it's not realistic to pursue a career as a professional singer, but I think it would be fun to just play a coffeehouse gig or something. How cool would that be?"

If you only knew, kiddo, I thought to myself.

"I think you're making the right decision," I told her. "Pursue a realistic and pragmatic career, but follow through with your passions, too. You're absolutely correct: it *is* hard to break into the music business. But if you're playing music for yourself – and not a paycheck – then you can have the best of both worlds."

"Is that what *you* did?" she asked me with squinted eyes – and just a hint of interrogation in her voice.

"I became a professional *teacher*, didn't I?" I gave Veronica a shrug, intentionally leaving a significant part of her question unanswered. "And, speaking of which, we should probably get back to these essays..."

I had successfully changed the subject – or so I thought. But, when I glanced up at Veronica, she was eyeing me suspiciously. When our lines of vision met, however, she quickly redirected her attention to the pile of papers in front of her.

We spent the rest of the period grading in silence.

CHAPTER EIGHT

"God Only Knows"

A few days after that essay-grading session, Mel and I enlisted Veronica for babysitting duties. Of course, it wasn't just for a simple dinner date or a night out at the movies: Mel and I had tickets to see Brian Wilson and his band performing with The Zombies at the Arlington Theatre in Santa Barbara. As a self-professed Beach Head, I can't pass on any opportunity to see the legendary Brian Wilson in a live setting; the fact that he was sharing the bill with a reunited incarnation of The Zombies made this musical event even more monumental in my eyes.

Though Mel might not share my religious fervor when it comes to the Beach Boys, she tolerates my fanaticism. So, like any good spouse, she begrudgingly promised to be my date for the evening. Of course, while we joined the throngs of folks flocking to Santa Barbara to see Brian Wilson – the man, the myth, the legend – perform less than an hour away from home, we needed someone to watch Samantha. Luckily, we now had a built-in babysitter. Thank goodness for Veronica Jones.

True to form, Veronica showed up early with a flurry of questions about her duties. Even though she had watched Sam half a dozen times by that point, this would be our first late-evening outing with Veronica babysitting. And, being the nerdy teacher that I am, I had prepared a detailed lesson plan of activities and instructions – just as I would for a substitute teacher in my own classroom.

As Mel likes to point out, I might have some control issues that I need to work out. Maybe.

The minute that Veronica stepped onto the porch, Sam fluttered excitedly to the front door to meet her babysitter, the delicate trim of her little pink and purple dress wavering behind her.

"Are you ready to play princesses, Veronica?" Sam asked, barely able to contain her excitement. Her eyes were open wide with anticipation and her chipmunk cheeks quivered eagerly.

"Why do you think I came here?" Veronica answered, grinning broadly and kneeling down to Sam's eye level.

Before the girls got started, Mel and I showed Veronica the printed bullet-point outline of the evening's schedule.

Like I said, I'm a nerd. With control issues. It's a dubious combination.

Despite my litany of requests and directions, Veronica didn't seem threatened or overwhelmed. "Don't worry," she assured us. "I've got half a dozen nieces and nephews, so I've spent more than my fair share of late evenings with little rug-rats."

While Mel and I chatted with Veronica in the kitchen, the sounds of our voices reverberating through the open spaces of the tiled room, Sam anxiously waited for her chance to steal her babysitter back for playtime. While she listened, she perched her little arms on the side of the living room couch and tapped her fingers impatiently against the faded green cushions.

"So, who are you going to see tonight?" Veronica asked. "Anyone I know?"

"The Beach Boys," Mel responded casually, stifling a sigh.

"The *Beach Boys?*" Veronica yelped. "I love them! They're like the soundtrack to my childhood."

"Well, it's not *technically* the Beach Boys," I clarified.

Veronica shot me an inquisitive look. "Wait... is it the Beach Boys or *not* the Beach Boys?" she asked.

Mel laughed, knowing exactly where this conversation was headed. Lord knows, she's heard me ramble about the band for more than two decades now, so she's become very well-versed in the group's colorful history.

"What do you know about the history of the Beach Boys...?" I asked Veronica cautiously.

"Uhhh..." she murmured. "They were big in the 1960s? And they play the Ventura County Fair every few years? And they love the sand and surfing and girls in bikinis?" She scrunched up her mouth into a sideways grimace. "Gosh... that's really about it."

My eyes gleamed with fire, ready to proselytize to a potential convert. I rubbed my hands together like a silent movie villain, prepared to pounce on the ignorant soul in my kitchen.

"How much do you *want* to know?" I asked.

"Pardon my husband's obsessiveness," Mel interrupted, shielding Veronica with a wave of her arm. "Just give her the *Reader's Digest* version, Brian," Mel suggested, roguishly rolling her eyes before walking to the other side of the kitchen.

"Okay, okay," I said, throwing my hands up defensively. "Geez... where do I begin?"

"From the beginning," Mel said (with more sass than necessary, I might add). "It's usually the best place to start."

"Here's the scoop," I said. "Almost sixty years ago, there were three musically inclined brothers growing up in Hawthorne, California: Brian, Carl, and Dennis Wilson. The three boys had a tumultuous childhood with a controlling, abusive father. But, despite their traumatic environment, they all took solace in music."

"Wow," Veronica interjected, surprise etched into her furrowed brow. "That's not what I expected at all. I thought everything was all sunshine and surfboards."

"Most people think the same thing," I told her. "Anyway, Brian was the oldest brother and the de facto leader of the group. Though he was a troubled kid, he was also a musical prodigy. In fact, he used to force his mother and siblings to sing harmonies with him when the three brothers were little. Shortly after Brian finished high school, the Wilson brothers joined up with their cousin, Mike Love, and a couple of neighborhood friends, Alan Jardine and David Marks..."

Mel cut me off with a raised eyebrow and a caustic tone. "I thought I said the *brief* version of their history, Bri…"

"I'm *getting* there," I reassured her, scowling from across the kitchen.

Veronica simply snickered at our marital bickering.

"So, anyway," I continued, "they started off as a very derivative surf-music group. During the early 1960s, they had a bunch of hits about cars and girls and surfing. But in 1966, Brian elevated their status and made the greatest album of all time, *Pet Sounds*."

"Tonight," Mel interrupted again, "we're going to see Brian Wilson and his band, including a few ex-Beach Boys, play live in Santa Barbara." Mel turned to me and tenderly wrapped her fingers around my arm. "And my husband is going to pee his pants with excitement."

I nudged her with my elbow – lovingly, of course. "Jerk," I muttered playfully, my lips pursed in a faux-hurt expression.

"That's funny…" Veronica observed. "Your first name is Brian, Mr. Smith. And you're going to see *Brian* Wilson."

Once again, Mel chimed in. "It's not a coincidence. My dear husband, Brian, is named after Brian Wilson."

"*Kind of…*" I reminded Mel.

"Kind of," she echoed.

Veronica's forehead crinkled with confusion. "Wait… So why won't it be a Beach Boys show? Didn't they just get back together a few years ago or something?"

I sighed. "Let's just say that Brian Wilson had some mental health and drug addiction issues after *Pet Sounds*. And things got contentious and weird between the band members for a couple decades."

"Two of them died," Sam cheerily contributed with an ironic brightness, showing off her knowledge. "The guitarist had cancer and the drummer drowned."

"Wow," Veronica mumbled. "That's sad."

"It is," I reiterated somberly. "Dennis Wilson drowned in 1983 and Carl Wilson died of lung cancer in 1998. And Mike Love, Brian's cousin, has been touring under the 'Beach Boys' name with his own band – even though he only has one other official Beach Boy, Bruce Johnston, in the group."

Veronica looked like she was still processing the facts of the story, taking in all of the drama that I had attempted to distill into a few rushed sentences.

"You're right, though," I added. "All of the surviving members got back together in 2012 to celebrate the fiftieth anniversary of the band. They played some pretty big venues and received a lot of great press. Unfortunately, in the end, it wasn't enough to placate the egos of all the various parties involved. Mike Love and Bruce Johnston continued touring by themselves as 'The Beach Boys,' but Brian Wilson, Al Jardine, and David Marks got left in the dust. Or sand, as it were."

"Gosh," Veronica sighed. "Who knew that the *'Fun, Fun, Fun'* band was filled with so much *drama, drama, drama?*"

Mel and I chuckled at Veronica's joke. Even Sam laughed a little, though she obviously didn't appreciate the gravity and darkness of the conversation.

"Do you think they'll ever get back together?" Veronica asked.

"I don't know," I pondered. "Some wounds run pretty deep. Not even the best of circumstances can heal longstanding scars like those."

"But *anything* is possible," Veronica added.

"You're right," I conceded. "Anything is possible."

My words dangled there in the air, taking on an unintended weight… until our little daughter tugged on my faded gray *Surf's Up* t-shirt.

"*Daddy*…" Sam whined. "When can I get my babysitter back…?"

Mel and I laughed, leaned over, and kissed our little princess.

"And on that note," Mel said, "it's time for us to *go, go, go.*"

The drive to the Arlington Theatre was fairly smooth. Santa Barbara traffic is always hit-or-miss, so a half-hour drive through Carpinteria and Montecito can easily double (or triple) in time with the wrong traffic conditions. Fortunately for us, the rock and roll gods must have been smiling down from heaven: we made it through the unpredictable lanes of the northbound 101 without too much congestion.

By the time that we arrived at the Arlington, hordes of people of all ages and backgrounds were filtering slowly through the old movie theater doors. We saw hippies and hipsters alongside high school seniors and senior citizens, all of whom were here for the same singular purpose: to see the living legend, Brian Wilson, live onstage.

Though attending a concert might seem like a pleasant way for adults to occupy a few hours of an evening, it's something more akin to a religious experience for me. It's hard to explain how this kind of event empowers music obsessives like myself… I reckon that it's similar to a child's reaction when she visits Disneyland: there's sheer glee and wonder and excitement, something earnest and honest that can't be contained or replicated.

Sure, for some people a concert is *just a concert*. For some of us, though, a live performance can feel more like a transformative experience at church. It's history in the making, a moment that many of us will cherish indefinitely and to which we might ascribe almost mythical qualities. Heck, a great enough concert might wedge itself into the narratives of our youth that we will one day recount to our children and grandchildren. Or into the book that you're writing about your life.

There's something uniquely unifying about attending a live show. Music, even in its most primitive states, can be evocative and emotional – and seeing a truly legendary figure like Brian Wilson amplifies that experience tenfold.

As Mel and I found our assigned spots in the sixth row, sliding into those old movie theater seats from the early twentieth century, we talked casually – mostly about Sam and our families, but also about the past, present, and future. Small talk, big talk, and medium-sized talk flowed from us inconspicuously in that effortless manner married couples cultivate. It's one of the comfortable benefits that comes with familiarity and deep-rooted love.

"Just think," Mel said, "one day, Sam will grow up and go off to college and we can do this kind of thing, go out on dates, without having to hire a babysitter."

I nodded casually as my eyes scanned the empty perimeter of the stage. "It's so hard to envision that, though," I told her. "It's hard for me to see Samantha as anything other than a little girl right now. It's bizarre to think that she'll be a confused middle schooler one day and then an annoying teenager…"

"And then a brilliant UCLA student who will become a professional journalist…?" Mel suggested with a grin.

"I always imagined her as an elementary school teacher, like her grandmothers," I said, stroking the stubble on my chin.

Mel chuckled. "Like you said earlier," she reminded me, "*anything is possible*, right?"

"Right," I agreed.

Mel and I talked and held hands through the flawless September evening, listening attentively to the opening set – performed by a reunited incarnation of The Zombies – and watching the spectrum of passersby who made their way through the aisles in front of us. We had good seats for the show – which, for a theater as intimate as the Arlington, felt unbelievably close to the stage. The Zombies' set was impressive, beginning with their second hit, "Tell Her No," and segueing into a performance of the entire *Odessey & Oracle* album. Even Mel, who tends to listen primarily to modern pop country music, found herself drawn in by their elaborate British Invasion sounds.

Early in their set, Mel leaned over to me and put her lips up to my ear. "So, Mr. Rock Encyclopedia," she said, "what's the deal with these guys on stage?"

The keyboardist for the band, Rod Argent, was describing something about the band's lineup and gesticulating wildly with his arms, so there was a temporary lull in the venue's volume.

"I'm glad you asked," I said, perking up and sitting upright in my seat. "Way back in 1968, The Zombies recorded this masterpiece of an album called *Odessey & Oracle*. However, before their record label released the album, the band broke up. The following year, while the band was kaput, their song 'Time of the Season' became a smash hit. The only bummer is that the band wasn't around to enjoy the fruits of their labor."

Mel eyed me whimsically. "That storyline sounds vaguely familiar," she said, raising a sardonic eyebrow.

I glared at her, ignoring her comment. "Anyway," I continued explaining, "*Odessey & Oracle* developed this huge cult following over the next few decades, but the band never got to bask in the glow of their posthumous success."

"*Posthumous…*" Mel snickered. "That's funny for a band named *The Zombies.*"

"I know, right?" I said, lifting my arms like a penitent man in church. "Now, though, the remaining members of the band are reuniting for this tour to celebrate the fiftieth anniversary of the album. It's kind of like a belated victory lap." I gestured towards the stage. "But, you know, half a century later."

Mel's eyebrows crinkled adorably. "Wait, wait, wait..." she said. "A band called *The Zombies* came back from the dead...? That's too rich."

"Never underestimate the power of nostalgia," I told her. "Especially at a Beach Boys concert."

"You mean *kind of* a Beach Boys concert," she corrected me.

I shrugged and rolled my eyes. The band onstage was gearing up to start their next song, but Mel wasn't done with her questions yet.

"So, why'd The Zombies break up?" she asked over the rising din of the theater.

"I'm not entirely sure," I told her. "I have a feeling that it had to do with egos and conflicting personalities." I pointed up at the curly-haired figure at the center of the stage. "The lead singer, Colin Blunstone, has this amazing, distinctive voice, right? But he didn't write *any* of the band's songs."

"Really?" Mel asked.

"Yup. It was Rod Argent, the keyboard player," I said, pointing to the figure behind a Mellotron on stage right, "and Chris White, the bass player. Those two guys wrote just about everything for the band, but I don't think they ever got the full credit they deserved."

Mel's eyes narrowed conspicuously. "So, let me get this straight," she said, raising up her left hand, "the bass player and the keyboardist wrote all the songs, but hide in the shadows while the lead singer gets all the glory...?"

I nodded, my eyes darting back and forth between the figures onstage.

"Now, *that* sounds r-e-a-l-l-y familiar," Mel laughed. "Were you *trying* to model your life on this band, or was that just an uncanny cosmic coincidence?"

I scowled at her, trying my best to suppress the grin that threatened to expose me. "You can be a real jerk, you know that?"

"That's why you love me," Mel laughed, shirking her bare shoulders melodramatically.

I scrunched my lips up into an exhausted expression. "But, seriously, I have to admit that I didn't discover *Odessey & Oracle* until I was scavenging through my dad's record collection after…" I paused, unable to complete the sentence. "Well, you know."

Mel nodded sympathetically, her wicked tongue withering into something softer, more forgiving. She didn't speak. She just grabbed my hand and squeezed my fingers tightly.

By the time that The Zombies finished their gorgeous set (which concluded with a rousing "Time of the Season" that had everyone on their feet dancing), I was ready for a stretch break. As the lights in the venue went up, Mel and I strolled through the lobby of the Arlington, examining the theater's old *Gone with the Wind* artifacts and the early-twentieth-century décor. During the intermission, I perused the merchandise booth, buying a variety of Zombies posters, records, and t-shirts. Mel might have disapproved of my salacious spending, but she didn't harass me about it. I think she knew I needed this rock 'n' roll retail therapy.

Plus, who can predict how many opportunities I'll have to see the band play again in my lifetime? For all I knew, this might be my only chance. I didn't want to regret thrifty pocketbooks if this singular experience was whisked away on the winds of time, never to be grasped again.

Nothing is promised. Nothing is guaranteed.

After half an hour of waiting anxiously, the lights dimmed again. As a flurry of new musicians took the stage, the Arlington Theatre's crowd of 2,000 people applauded wildly. There was an undeniable sense of energy, a kinetic force propelling the night forward into history. The band sauntered over to their respective positions onstage, picking up their instruments and playing an immediately recognizable succession of notes in unison.

The swirling, orchestral opening melody of "California Girls" poured forth from the massive speakers. A frail, ghostly, familiar-looking figure shuffled uncomfortably towards the middle of the stage, aided by a rolling metallic medical walker; two stagehands gently guided him to the

pearlescent piano that sat centerstage. Once there, the man of the hour –
Brian Wilson – was able to swing the microphone up to his lips just in
time for the first few lyrics of the song.

Mel leaned over to me and cupped her fingers around my ear. "It
looks like The Zombies aren't the only zombies onstage tonight."

Ouch.

"Be nice," I said, reaching over and giving her hand a gentle,
disapproving squeeze. "This is an important night for me."

Mel sank back into her seat, her thumb caressing the palm of my
left hand. She might not have been as enchanted by the experience as I
was, but she was kind enough to humor me. God bless her for that.

As the bouncing initial verse of "California Girls" segued into the
first chorus of the song, the voices of Brian and his backing band
coalesced into a soaring, heavenly choir. There, under the lights of the
Arlington Theatre, the angelic vocals of the dozen or so performers
onstage melded seamlessly into one flawless wave of transcendent
harmony, each singer an individual crest in the movement that propelled
sound forward from the stage out into the wondrous night. For that one
song, the magic was there. It was, in my eyes, perfection.

What happens to Beach Boys when they grow up and grow old?
That question was answered for me as I perched in my seat, anticipating
what would happen over the next ninety minutes of the concert.

It was heartbreaking.

It was beautiful.

And I was grateful for the chance to see Brian Wilson alive.

From the opening salvo of "California Girls" into "I Get Around"
and "Don't Worry, Baby," the concert started out as a Beach Head's dream
come true. A few songs in, though, Brian and his band were mixing
effervescent classics like "Wouldn't It Be Nice" and "Sloop John B" with
less-obvious selections like Al Jardine's "Wake the World" and Blondie
Chaplin's thrilling rendition of "Sail On, Sailor." 1973's live double-
album, *The Beach Boys in Concert*, was the album my dad seemed to play

the most throughout my childhood, and seeing Blondie rip through "Sail On, Sailor" was basically Beach Boys bliss.

A third of the way through the set, as the introductory strains of "Wouldn't It Be Nice" resonated from a guitar onstage, I squeezed Mel's hand gently, her caramel fingers intertwined delicately with mine. With Mel, every kiss *is* never-ending – no wishes needed – and each time I hear the song, I can't help but think of her and our decades-long romance. I held her hand tightly as the song twisted and turned through its celebration of young love. Even though we were only college students when we first met, I can still remember the longing I felt whenever we shared a goodbye kiss, whenever we were forced to say goodnight after an evening together. Though a multitude of Brian's songs reverberate for me for a variety of reasons, "Wouldn't It Be Nice" will always be the soundtrack to our resilient, weathered romance.

I'll level with you. The Arlington show wasn't the greatest concert in the history of mankind. Heck, it wasn't even the best Brian Wilson performance I've seen. At times, Brian seemed to withdraw onstage, and his bone-white piano seemed bleached and sepulchral – like a tomb waiting to swallow a long-suffering soul. But, periodically throughout the evening, a glimmering revelation of Brian would reappear and we would see a glimpse of the magic that brought us – the musical pilgrims from far and wide – here to this beachside town on a Sunday night in September.

It wasn't until midway through the set, though, that we were treated to the apex of the evening: "God Only Knows."

There's a reason that Paul McCartney has called "God Only Knows" his favorite song. It's an honest, almost desperate, supplication – a prayer of peace from someone who understands how much his life has been defined by the presence of his loved one. While the original *Pet Sounds* recording (featuring a teenage Carl on lead vocals) was a sweetly innocent invocation of love, hearing a 77-year-old Brian intone the melody was nothing short of heartbreaking. Brian's voice was tender, vulnerable – the wizened words of a musical wizard. When the band's harmonizing vocals intertwined during the coda of "God Only Knows," I slipped my arm around Mel, her bare shoulders melting into my chest. The melodies coursed in and out of the nighttime atmosphere, dissolving into intangible majesty and breathtaking beauty.

It was exactly the kind of religious experience that I had hoped for.

The first time that I saw Brian Wilson live, twenty-one years ago, I stood side-by-side my father, both of us hanging on every magical phrase and turn of the tune. We knew that we were witnessing something special, so tender and delicate that it was too good for this world.

As Brian and his band navigated their way through "God Only Knows" at the Arlington, I could feel the sting of my eyelids and the damp trails that were forming down the sides of my cheeks. Mel, in her infinite kindness, reached out for my hand and nuzzled her face into my shoulder. To the cynics watching, we must have seemed like an overly emotional couple of forty-year-olds, too sensitive to make it through a rock concert without crying.

But that's because they don't know the full story.

Of course, as I looked around the theater, I saw that I wasn't alone. A middle-aged woman a row behind us was sobbing, tears streaming down her face like an unburdened waterfall. In front of me, an elderly gentleman was curled up with his salt-and-pepper-haired wife, the two of them gently swaying in time with the music. Throughout the Arlington, this perfect song with its imperfect performance was moving inside the chests and hearts and minds of the audience.

When the song ended, concluding Brian's earnestly quivering lead vocal and the gorgeous waves of harmony from the rest of the band, every single person in that theater stood up and celebrated the deeply flawed musician who slumped behind his snowy white piano. Even though he struggled to simply walk across stage, Brian moved us all to a standing ovation.

Brian Wilson is a man brought back from the dead, resurrected from the depths of hell and navigating through the world of the living. It can't be easy, but there's something incredibly noble about the mere attempt. As we stood there and clapped in the darkened rows of the theater, we recognized the vitality and value of this remarkable man.

And we considered ourselves lucky to simply see him alive.

As I know all too well, not everyone is lucky enough to defy the indiscriminate hand of Death for as long as Brian has. I can only pray that he survives for many more years to come.

Nothing is promised. Nothing is guaranteed.

The rest of the set was filled with deep cuts from the Beach Boys catalog, including songs that Brian's brothers, Carl and Dennis, had written in the 1970s. Towards the end of the show, the band manically worked through a half-dozen glorious selections of Beach Boys hits, from "Good Vibrations" through Al's triumphant turn on "Help Me, Rhonda" and the concluding trifecta of "Barbara Ann," "Surfin' USA," and "Fun, Fun, Fun." Immediately after that final tune, the band huddled around Brian for a victorious bow.

Everyone was on their feet, applauding and celebrating and hooting and hollering for the ninety minutes of nostalgic magic we had just witnessed at the Arlington Theatre.

Everyone, of course, except Brian Wilson.

While the band members bowed behind him, Brian sat stiff and uncomfortable, waiting to be helped offstage – where he would undoubtedly breathe easier without the stifling torment of an audience studying his every move. The houselights went up, the spotlights dimmed, and the band sauntered off into the wings.

And just like that, the show was over.

As Mel and I made our way out of the theater and into the simmering September darkness, I dried my cheeks, wiping away the tears of the past and present with my humble hands. Mel and I held each other closely, just one more married couple standing upright in the smoldering summer night, watching the crowd slowly disperse into the evening air like itinerant leaves from an ancient tree. Eventually, we joined the thousands of other concertgoers, maneuvering our way through the exits and back to our car.

It was time to go home.

The drive back to Oxnard was relatively smooth sailing – rather unusual for a Sunday night in Santa Barbara and Ventura Counties. As we made our way through the lanes of southbound traffic on the 101, Mel and I talked about various pieces of our shared history. Eventually, she broached the topic of the band.

And the song.

Our song.

"Do you think Brian Wilson has ever heard 'Incomplete' somehow?" she asked.

"I doubt it," I told her, my eyes never leaving the darkened lanes of the highway ahead of us. "I read somewhere that he doesn't listen to any music made after the 1970s. Most of the time, he listens to the 'Malt Shop Oldies' channel on satellite radio or recordings of the Four Freshmen."

"You never know…" Mel trailed off.

"I won't get my hopes up," I told her, grinning contentedly.

Mel stared off into the distance, her eyes studying the ink-black ocean that lazily shifted and ambled to the west, reflecting the hazy moon that hung in the sky like a docile angel.

"What did you think of the concert?" I asked her.

She angled her body back towards me, her fingers tracing lines along the seatbelt that ran the length of her torso. "Honestly?" she asked.

"Honestly."

"It was okay."

"Just *okay*…?"

Mel shifted again in her seat, rigidly propping up her body. "I feel like I spent the evening watching the world's best Beach Boys cover band. They just happened to have three real Beach Boys onstage."

"Ouch." I clutched my heart melodramatically with my right hand while my left remained glued to the wheel.

"I'm not trying to be a *jerk*," Mel explained. "I mean, it's just kind of heartbreaking to watch rock stars get old, you know? We grow up listening to their songs, those little musical time capsules, thinking that they'll stay young forever. But the singers just keep aging. Like our parents…"

I winced. My fingers gripped the wheel so tightly that my knuckles bleached white.

Mel hastily added an addendum to her argument: "Or grandparents, for that matter."

"True," I conceded, my fingers relaxing on the wheel. "But that's part of the reason I like seeing musicians in their winter years. They change, but so do their songs. Like when Brian sang 'God Only Knows' tonight. It wasn't a puppy dog with fluttering eyelids naïvely professing his love. It was a weathered man admitting his fragility and gratitude for the lover who has stuck by his side, through better *and* worse."

"I think you're reading too deeply into things," she sighed.

"I'm an English teacher," I said. "It's an occupational hazard."

Once again, Mel's eyes turned to the dark and undulating waves beyond her window. Though my sight was fixed firmly on the road ahead, I could tell by Mel's posture that she was distracted, contemplating something important behind those chestnut-brown eyes. That's one of the side-effects of marriage: you become acutely aware of your spouse's subtle movements, their poker faces and tells.

"I've been thinking…" she began tentatively. "Brian Wilson and a couple of other Beach Boys have reunited. And that opening band, The Zombies, came back from the dead." She exhaled a tired laugh at her own little joke.

"That's right…" I said, scrutinizing the shadowy lanes of the road ahead.

Mel turned back to face the capricious coastline and the swelling waves of ink that shifted against the shore. Without looking at me, she asked that fateful, ineluctable question. "So… what would it take for Call Field to get back together?"

"That would require one helluva' catalyst, Mel," I said.

"Really?" she asked. "Even after all these years, it would still take something dramatic for you to resurrect the band?"

"Nothing short of a miracle," I told her. And I meant it.

In the end, though, it didn't take a miracle.

Just one incredibly determined person.

By the time that we made it back to Oxnard, it was creeping close to midnight. As we pulled into the garage, Mel and I felt guilty that we had kept our babysitter out so late on a Sunday night; but, when we opened the front door, we found Veronica inside, quietly reading a battered copy of *Catcher in the Rye*.

"So, how was it?" Veronica asked, yawning away her fatigue.

"Unbelievable," I whispered. "It was like witnessing a piece of history. There were two thousand people at the Arlington Theatre, and they were all there for Brian Wilson."

"Wow," she nodded. "That's impressive."

"How was Sam?" Mel asked, taking off her lacy black shawl and placing it daintily on a hanger in our front closet.

"Sam was *wonderful*," Veronica assured us. "She really is a sweet girl. She ate all her dinner, cleaned up, took a bath by herself, brushed her teeth, and went to bed without a hassle. We pretty much played princesses the whole night."

"Oh, geez," Mel sighed. "Did she make you pull out the Disney Halloween costumes?"

Veronica laughed unassumingly. "Yup. We went from Cinderella to Sleeping Beauty to Elsa. It made me feel like a little kid all over again." She yawned once more. "As silly as it was, it was a nice break from being a teenager."

"And then you started rereading *Catcher in the Rye*," I noted dryly, "so you didn't get *too* far from adolescent drama."

"Oh, yeah," she nodded, "I browsed through your bookshelf and grabbed a copy to keep myself awake."

"You didn't get enough of Holden with my nerdy husband in AP English last year?" Mel asked puckishly.

"Not at all," Veronica grinned. "I skipped to the second-to-last chapter and reread the carousel scene. It makes me cry every time."

Mel mischievously squinted her eyes at our babysitter. "You should ask Brian about *Call Field* one of these days," she grinned.

"What about Caulfield?" Veronica asked, a perplexed look in her eyes.

I could feel the crimson rising to my cheeks. "Nothing," I said, rushing out the words as I gave Mel a bitter glance. "It's *nothing*."

"Okay…" Veronica yawned once more, stretching out her arms and sauntering over to the light of the kitchen. "Anyway, I'm jealous that you got to see the Beach Boys tonight."

I shot Veronica a disapproving look. "Did you learn *nothing* from my musical history lecture earlier?" I asked, mock-exasperated.

"Sorry," she apologized sleepily, collecting her jangling car keys from the granite countertop. "I'm jealous that you got to see *some* of the Beach Boys tonight. I've always wanted to see them in concert."

"You and everyone else," Mel chimed in, discreetly slipping Veronica a wad of cash as payment for her hours of babysitting. "It's like a rite of passage for all Californians, I think."

Veronica grabbed her Kate Spade purse from the kitchen counter and sidled over to the front door. "You said there were two thousand people there tonight?" she asked.

I nodded, my face revealing equal parts wonder and exhaustion.

"Wow," she said with a heavy breath. "Can you imagine what that must feel like? To have so many people there to love you and support you and cheer you on? That must be incredible."

"I can only imagine," I told her, shooting a firm glance in Mel's direction.

"But you never know, Mr. Smith," Veronica said, smiling as she wearily walked out to her car. "Like I said earlier… Anything is possible."

She was right about that.

CHAPTER NINE

"Spirit of America"

In a sense, teachers are a little like the Beach Boys: while we spend our lives diligently toiling away at respectable jobs, believing wholeheartedly in the golden promise of summer, we battle indifferent crowds in a valiant attempt to try and prove our worth. All the while, we constantly fight against the perception that we are caricatures, two-dimensional beings who fit snugly into unattractive stereotypes. It's hard for people to acknowledge, but teachers are actually *real* human beings with emotions, feelings, and dreams.

Bruce Johnston once claimed that the fickle public pigeonholed his Beach Boys bandmates as "surfing Doris Days" – previously attractive figures who now appear awkwardly out of place in popular culture. The same holds true for teachers. No matter what we do, we will always be viewed as "tragically unhip," as if our glasses and ties and skirts and suits are the defining aspects of our identities. If only the skeptical public knew our true histories, the stories we lived unapologetically in previous lives; perhaps then (and only then), our students and communities would view us as the rock stars that we truly are.

Despite all of the punditry and debates about redeeming qualities, there's something distinctly *American* about the teaching profession. Like Lewis and Clark, we brave the wilderness of adolescent drama, trying to forge a path that will lead future generations towards beautiful coastlines of growth. The forests and jungles might be dangerous along the way, but we do our best to navigate these dangerous trails for the betterment of mankind. In that regard, teachers are trailblazers, constantly facing overwhelming odds. Somehow, though, we persevere – even in the face of the most disastrous circumstances.

And that, my friends, is why teaching is the most punk rock profession in the world.

We might not appear dangerous with our pleated pants and ironed shirts, but we're here to transform society – one classroom at a time. And though we look like the candy-stripe-wearing Beach Boys of 1962, we are, in fact, the Ramones of 1977. Of course, while I have always felt a certain kinship with Brian Wilson, my first (and only) band was a punk-rock band – at least in the beginning. In my teen years, I was a punk rocker... but now I'm a balding, aging father with never-ending responsibilities and obligations. And, despite my rebellious spirit and my love of loud music, even I have to admit that it's not very punk to wear a tie to work.

These days, though, I can't help but think that teaching high school is a lot like playing a punk show. Of course, no one associates Mohawks and distorted guitars with podiums and dictionaries, but they should: in both circumstances, you stand in front of a cynical crowd, armed only with your words and voice, aiming to convince your audience that they should listen to what you have to say.

That's me: mild-mannered English teacher by day... mild-mannered ex-rock and roller by night.

CHAPTER TEN

"Don't Back Down"

T his is where all the trouble started.

A few weeks after the Brian Wilson concert, right before our school's weeklong October break, Veronica stormed into my classroom at lunchtime with an unusually aggressive gait. During her early-morning TA period at the beginning of the day, Veronica had seemed distant, standoffish – like she was processing some sort of unspoken trauma. I chalked it up to typical teenage drama and didn't think much of it. Now, hours later, she had returned to my classroom unannounced with a self-righteous sense of vindication. Rather than her standard irrepressible smile, Veronica's countenance exposed a sense of heretofore unseen urgency, and the creases around her eyes insinuated something else... a hint of betrayal, perhaps?

"Can I show you something?" she asked in an unusually terse manner.

"Sure..." I replied nervously, feeling the palpable tension in the recycled air of my classroom.

Before I could add anything to my awkward reply, Veronica marched over to the computer on my desk, stretched out her arms to the mouse and keyboard, brought up a new web browser, and went straight to YouTube. As she click-clacked the keys, her hands were trembling slightly. Something was clearly amiss with the Queen Bee.

I immediately felt anxious, and my fight-or-flight impulse kicked in. Instinctively, I got up from my desk, walked across the room, and grabbed a stack of handouts that needed to be stapled together. As I've learned over the years, physical distance in the classroom is sometimes the best tactic to defuse tense situations. I hoped that my simple solution would help ease the uncomfortable energy – the "bad vibrations," if you will – that I was feeling.

Veronica continued her diatribe, her voice intermittently crackling with nervous energy. "So, when we were driving to Seminary this morning, we were listening to the 90s channel on satellite radio and this old song came on," she explained. "My mom immediately cranked up the volume and plunged into this whole story about how this was her favorite song from when my oldest brother was a toddler. She told me that when Dad was finishing one of his DDS specialty certifications, she used to listen to this song every day, right when she woke up, in order to 'start her morning right.' She thinks this song might even have been playing in the background when she drove me to preschool for the first time."

"It sounds like you and your mom must have a pretty close relationsh—" I started to say.

Veronica cut me off mid-sentence and continued with her story. "Obviously, my mom has blasted the song a million times in our car, so it's not like it was my first time hearing it or anything. But, this time, Mom was going on and on about how much she *loved* the music video. So, she asked me if I could look it up for her on YouTube."

"YouTube?" I asked.

For a brief second, she pulled her shoulders back stiffly and looked up, her eyes creased and intently focused in my direction. "Whatever," she mumbled, dismissing her own story.

These kinds of conversations with Veronica were not uncommon – minus her visible sense of discomfort, of course. We talk all the time about intriguing bands and our favorite albums, about binge-worthy television shows and unputdownable books. Still, I could sense something peculiar in the tone of her voice, like she was reciting a joke that required the perfect delivery of its punch line.

"Anyway, we get to Seminary about ten minutes early, because my mom is *always* early," she continued, "and I take out my iPhone and go to YouTube. I hit play, and I watch the video with my mom standing over my shoulder. And this was the song."

As the music began playing through my tinny set of classroom speakers, I almost didn't recognize the song... It was a familiar guitar riff, repeating over fuzzy, distorted power chords – basically the sonic template for every 90s alternative rock song. But then the vocals kicked in:

"California can be cruel in the summer..."

I felt a sense of terror welling up inside of me, and my breath caught on the end of the song's first line. A chill swept up from the center of my chest; as it did so, I could feel myself blush uncontrollably. Though I was turned away from Veronica, I sensed that she could see the goosebumps forming on my forearms and the back of my neck turning crimson.

I knew right away that I was in trouble.

I had been found out.

In retrospect, I suppose it was a bit naïve of me to assume that the past wouldn't catch up with me eventually. In many ways, I'm surprised that it took as long as it did for someone to embrace their inner Sherlock Holmes, connect the dots, and uncover the precious secrets of my previous life. In this era of Twitter, Facebook, Wikipedia, and Google, it's impossible to remain anonymous for very long. I'm just lucky that I was able to keep my past and present as separate, distinct entities for almost two decades.

While Veronica was unveiling the fruits of her detective work, I was too stunned to do much of anything. I was a deer in headlights – albeit a deer wearing a silk tie and horn-rimmed glasses. Veronica let the song play, expecting me to have some grand reaction to her dramatic revelation. Despite her best efforts to out me, however, I wasn't giving in so easily: I kept a sturdy poker face as I stood across the classroom, keeping my gaze focused on the papers in front of me while the repetitive snap of the stapler kept time with the whole-note beats of the song.

Suddenly, Veronica paused the video and flipped the computer monitor around so that it was facing in my direction. On the screen, frozen in mid-jam, was a very familiar set of faces: four young kids in blue jeans and unkempt t-shirts, each of whom posed awkwardly with an instrument in hand. One face, in particular, haunted me – a slightly overweight kid with shaggy, shoulder-length hair, slouching in the still-frame with a bass guitar clutched in his hands. The one with the distinctive Bermuda Triangle of birthmarks on his face.

Veronica pointed to the same image that was sending chills up my spine, and then looked up at me.

"It's *you*, isn't it?" she asked tensely.

I didn't answer.

"I mean, you look different now – you've got glasses, you're a lot skinnier, and you've lost most of your hair." She caught herself, then immediately apologized. "No offense," she added quickly.

I stood stock-still, listening and ruminating without uttering a single word.

"But the resemblance is uncanny," she continued, tracing her fingers across the computer screen as she spoke. "Look at the hair – that copper-brown color isn't all that common. And those cheekbones. And that nose. And those eyes are *clearly* the same shade of hazel as yours. But the real giveaway is those three moles on your face – the top of your right cheek, the middle of your left cheek, and on the bridge of your nose."

Unconsciously, I reached up and stroked my cheeks, tracing the lines between that asymmetrical Bermuda Triangle of moles. I still didn't answer.

Undeterred, Veronica soldiered on. "I clearly remember your wife mentioning something about *'the band'* when we were going over my college essays at Barnes & Noble this summer. That was my first clue. And then when I went to your house to babysit Sam the night of the Brian Wilson concert, your wife said to ask you about *Call Field*. I thought she meant Holden *Caulfield*, but she was *really* telling me to ask you about your band."

She paused, still waiting for me to respond. I didn't.

"And when I looked online," she continued, "I saw your name. Kind of. Wikipedia lists your name as *Rick* Smith, but Richard is your middle name, right?" With a few more deft movements, Veronica brought up a new browser with a brief Wikipedia article on Call Field. "I know you go by Brian now," she said, "but it's you. It *has to be* you."

Call Field was an American pop-punk band from Ojai, California. The band was formed in 1995 by Steve Öken and his classmates at Sespe Creek High School, where the group attended school. The band independently released *The Bookhouse EP* in 1998, followed two years later by their major-label debut album, *A Different Slant of Light*. The band scored a hit with their single, "Incomplete (Just Like Your Smile)", which peaked at number 19 on the Billboard charts in the summer of 2000.[1] Although they never officially disbanded, they have been on hiatus since 2001.

Contents [hide]

History

Early years (1995–1998)

The band formed in the summer of 1995, after bass player Rick "Brick" Smith heard lead vocalist Steve Öken singing a Social Distortion song in the locker room after football practice. Their first gig was the fifteenth birthday party of Öken's high school girlfriend, after which the band adopted the name Caulfield, in tribute to Holden Caulfield from J.D. Salinger's *Catcher in the Rye*.[2]

Bookhouse EP (1998–2000)

After several months of recording at a local Ojai studio, the band released the seven-track *Bookhouse EP* in June of 1998. After opening for blink-182 the following month, the band was discovered by a representative from Lowercase Records, who offered to sign the band if they could produce a viable single. The band spent the next year submitting demos to the record label, finally striking gold with "Incomplete (Just Like Your Smile)," a song that ultimately led them to a major label deal and later became their only radio hit. At the suggestion of the record label, the group changed its name from Caulfield to Call Field, in order to avoid confusion with other similarly named bands.[3]

A Different Slant of Light (2000–2001)

Call Field's major label album, *A Different Slant of Light*, departed dramatically from their punk rock roots, embracing a sound that fit more seamlessly with the pop radio mold of the era. The album garnered mixed but moderately favorable reviews, including a three-star review from *Rolling Stone*. [4] Call Field embarked on its first headlining tour in the summer of 2000, just as "Incomplete" was starting to gain traction on the radio. However, after a contentious opening night gig at the Fillmore in San Francisco, half of the band quit. The following day, Öken announced that the former band members left "for personal reasons," but stated that Call Field would finish the tour with substitute musicians. That winter, the band released a follow-up single, "Stars," but the song failed to chart. After completing a second, less-successful headlining tour, Call Field was dropped from its label.[5]

Discography

- *The Bookhouse EP* (1998)
- *A Different Slant of Light* (2000)

References

I opened my mouth to speak, but nothing came out. I was literally speechless.

When confronted with this kind of situation, what do you do? As tempted as I was to lie about the band, Veronica was too good of a kid for me to feed her falsehoods or fabrications. Here was a girl who had been a model student, a leader in the classroom – and, over the past year, she had become almost like an adopted daughter to me. If nothing else, she was Sam's favorite babysitter, and that had to count for something. My devious ploy – *deception by withholding information* – had completely failed.

I sighed aloud. For a brief second, I scanned the classroom, even considering the open door as a possible escape route before I inevitably acknowledged defeat.

"Yes," I admitted sheepishly, "It's me."

For a split second, I thought Veronica was going to explode. Though normally a sweet, enthusiastic girl, something about this revelation had clearly bothered her – and that, in turn, had festered into a throbbing emotional wound.

"WHAT! THE! HECK!" she exclaimed, more of an accusation than a question. Her eyes were seething, a stew of honest anger and confusion and vindication. *"WHY HAVE YOU NEVER TOLD ME ABOUT THIS?"*

It's funny now to think that hiding something so seemingly trivial from those close to you can have such profound repercussions. I never anticipated that my personal history could affect a student like Veronica, a girl whose attention was usually focused on humanitarian efforts or church activities. Yet, despite my underestimation, here she was – ready to interrogate me about my past life.

I stayed calm, doing my best to retain my professional demeanor, and gave her the educator's equivalent of a brushoff. "To be honest," I told her, "I really don't like talking about it. It was a different time in my life, and it didn't end very well."

"But you were famous!" she interjected. "You were a rock star! Shouldn't you be rich? How did you go from being a punk-rock Superman to a Clark Kent English teacher?"

Then her eyelids vaulted open in mortified horror.

"Oh, my gosh…" she muttered breathlessly. "Did you blow all your money on drugs? Did you go to jail? Are you in rehab now?"

I couldn't help but laugh – at Veronica's discomfort *and* the absurdity of her questions. "No," I chuckled. "I'm not Johnny Cash, Veronica. Although I did write a song about him once." I took an uneasy breath and squinted my eyes. "I just… it didn't work out. I was in a band, we played together for a few years, and I quit right as we were about to hit it big."

Veronica eyes were wide open in wonder, as if she'd just discovered an archaeological goldmine buried in her backyard.

I glanced up at the clock. "In any case," I told her, "I have to get ready for my next class. It's kind of a long story, and I don't think my AP kids would appreciate me starting class late because I was too busy recounting my not-so-glorious glory days."

Veronica didn't move until I looked straight at her, my eyes glistening and welling with the threat of tears. My forehead creased in concern and little beads of sweat formed on my temples.

"You understand, right?" I asked, my voice trembling slightly.

A look of disappointment darkened Veronica's demeanor. "Sure," she murmured despondently. "I understand."

"Thanks," I sighed, dabbing my eyes with the phalanxes of my fingers. "I knew you would."

As I grabbed my messenger bag, packed to the gills with essays that awaited grading, I turned to Veronica. "Look… I hate to ask this, because it sounds creepy to be so secretive, but can you please not tell anyone? Not even your mom? I'm still not comfortable talking about all of this, and the last thing I want is for the rest of my students to start freaking out over something silly like a band I used to be in."

"Fine," she said dismissively, the resignation on her face fading into a steely expression. "On one condition."

"What's that?" I asked.

"That you tell me the full story, sparing no gory details, in the very near future. Like tomorrow. Or the next day."

I sighed again dejectedly. "Let me think about it," I negotiated. "Okay?"

"It's a deal," she said, a victorious smirk overtaking the dark disappointment on her face.

There are a handful of times in your teaching career when you are literally saved by the bell – when the obnoxious, dreaded din of a buzzer actually comes in handy. Fortunately for me, this was one of those days. The buzzer rang, my fifth-period students began to file into my classroom, and Veronica waltzed off to her next class.

Thank goodness for the life-saving bell schedules of public high schools.

CHAPTER ELEVEN

"Darlin'"

When I got home that afternoon, Mel was sitting on the green living room couch with Sam, the two of them planted like delicate flowers on a bed of tender grass. Samantha was in the process of identifying "sight words" from her third-grade homework list, and she was struggling with one item in particular, a troublesome piece of vocabulary that she had yet to master.

I stood in the doorway, watching my two favorite girls huddled over homework, and I couldn't help but smile as Samantha scaled the building blocks of literacy. I think that's every English teacher's not-so-secret dream: to propagate the world with avid readers.

"Ummm... *Fff...ahhh...ttt...eee...* Is it '*fought*?'" she guessed uncertainly. Her cheeks anxiously scrunched up.

"Try again, sweetie," Mel encouraged her. "This time, remember that the word has the '*bossy e*' at the end, so the vowel is actually making a long '*a*' sound. Like with the word '*plate*.'"

Once again, Sam phonetically spelled out the word, "*Fff...aaa...ttt...eee...*" Her little eyes squinted in intense concentration. "Is the word '*fate*?'" Sam conjectured, equally uncertain.

"Nice work, *keiki!*" Mel gently exclaimed to our daughter, pressing her forehead against Sam's and tapping her on the nose.

As Sam turned her head and giggled, she spotted me in the doorway. "Daddy's home!" she squealed, jumping up from the couch and running towards me, arms outstretched. I dropped my sagging messenger bag and empty coffee tumbler, and I wrapped my arms around Sam's eighty-pound frame.

"*Fate?*" I asked, delivering a quick succession of kisses on her cheek. "That's a mighty big word for such a little girl."

"*Daaaaaaddd*," she protested in a singsong voice, "I'm in *third grade* now. I'm *not* little."

Mel and I shared a laugh, while Sam stuck out a pouting lower lip.

"My mistake," I told Sam, as I gently eased her back down to the tile floor. "You're entirely right. In fact, I think you're going to knock me to the ground the next time that you tackle me like that."

I arched my back and stretched my spine to compensate.

"*Sorry, Daddy*," Sam said in a facetious voice, clearly indicating that she was, indeed, not sorry at all.

"Tell Daddy about your day," Mel encouraged her.

"It was great!" Sam exclaimed. "We read a chapter of *Charlotte's Web* at school and I finished all my math homework in class and Mommy took me to the library to get a book for independent reading. And now you're home!" Sam threw her arms around my waist and squeezed snugly.

No matter how difficult your afternoon has been, everything feels perfect (or, at the very least, palatable) when your child wraps her arms tightly around you and rhapsodizes about her day.

I kneeled down to look Sam in the eyes. "Did you make anything cool for today's art project?" I asked.

"I did!" she exclaimed. "But it's a surprise. I'm going to get it from my backpack." She promptly turned around and bolted away towards her bedroom.

As Sam scampered down the hallway, I picked up my bags and headed towards the living room, where Mel was stretching out on the couch. Though it was October, Oxnard was in the midst of an abnormally hot extended summer, and the open windows were all that kept the oppressive heat at bay. Even with the cool ocean breeze casually wafting through the windows, the house felt uncomfortably warm, especially since I still had a silk tie coiled around my neck. In sharp contrast to my formal apparel, however, Mel was clad in shorts and a tank top, looking nonchalantly gorgeous. Even with varicose veins slowly creeping down the sides of her thighs, she still had incredible legs. I was a lucky man, indeed.

I slid my hands along the smooth curve of her shoulders and started to massage her back. "How's everything going, *Beautiful*?"

She yawned and answered with an escaping breath. "*Goooood*," she sighed. "This weather is killing me, though. I feel like I need another shower, and all I've done today is sit at a computer and proofread second-rate news articles." She reached her arms forward, shoulder blades protruding delicately from her back. "How was *your* day?" she asked.

"Oh, man..." I started. "Veronica figured it out. She pulled a Nancy Drew and figured it all out." Though I took off my glasses with a dramatic flourish and rubbed my temples despondently, Mel just laughed.

"It looks like she's even smarter than you thought, huh?" Mel said with a smirk. "What are you going to do now that your secret identity has been revealed, Bruce Wayne?"

I sighed and kicked my legs out onto the couch. "I don't know," I mumbled. "I... I just don't know what I'm going to do."

"You can always go the easy route and just tell Veronica the *truth*," she suggested softly.

"You're right," I started to say, "but..."

"I'm *always* right," she interrupted. "And that's why you married me. Because I'm so perfect." She cocked her head to the side and raised her eyebrows flirtatiously.

I slowly leaned towards her and grinned. "And because you're *so* humble..."

Of course, before our tantalizingly brief moment of intimacy could continue, Sam darted back into the room with a large piece of butcher paper flailing around in her small hands. "Look, Daddy!" she commanded, shoving the paper unceremoniously in my lap. "It's a quilt!"

As I investigated the Crayola-colored patches in front of me, I could make out a series of smiling faces protruding from the vaguely cartoonish, human-shaped designs. "Who did you draw in these frames?" I asked her.

Sam pointed to the first image, with a trio of figures. "That one's you and Mommy and me at the park. See, Daddy, you're wearing a tie!" She moved her delicate little fingers to the adjacent picture and described the next scene in the sequence. "And this one's me and Grandma at the beach. And that one's me and *Tūtū* and *Tūtū Kane* watering flowers in their garden." Sam beamed with pride as her fingers traced out each of the not-so-expertly wrought details in her illustrated images.

I pointed at the next square, which had a few circles scattered around an amorphous, oblong, amoeba-like shape that was colored in brown and black. "What's this one, sweetheart?" I asked.

"That's you and me in your office," Sam explained. She pointed to the mysterious brown shape. "And that's Grandpa's guitar."

I got a little choked up then. A sharp sting hit me in the edges of my eyelids, and I could feel my eyes starting to moisten.

"And, one day," I told her with a cracked voice, "that will be *your* guitar, Sam."

Her face brightened up. "*Really?*" she asked, her mouth agape.

"*Really.* Your grandpa gave it to me and someday I'll give to you. And you can play it and sing songs to Mommy and Daddy."

Sam clapped her hands, jumped down from the couch, and started doing a celebratory bit of choreography on the gray carpet of our living room floor. Truthfully, it was more of a bouncing-stomping hybrid, but you get the idea: it was the triumphant dance of children who suddenly feel empowered and grown-up, the kind of unfettered rhythmic shaking that makes you laugh and eases all your heartache.

And that's exactly what it did for me.

Later that evening, though, I got to thinking about Veronica and the tenuous bridge between childhood and adulthood. Like Sam trying to sound out the word "fate" on her homework vocabulary list, I was struggling with the lines that connected my past to my present and my future. I had done my best over the years to maintain a sense of anonymity, to move beyond the cage of my history and keep looking outward. It was inevitable, obviously, that my worlds would collide, but I naïvely held out hope that I would be able to keep the past at bay indefinitely.

It was foolish of me to believe that I could avoid the legacy of my youth forever. For the last two decades, I have had a visceral reaction, a painful feeling that is akin to a kick in the gut, every single time that "Incomplete" comes on the radio. If I'm in the car, I will quickly change the channel; however, when the song appears in a public setting like the supermarket or the mall, I usually have to bite my lip, close my eyes, and practice breathing exercises until the three and a half minutes have lapsed.

Rock and roll PTSD is a strange thing.

Though nothing had happened yet as a result of Veronica's detective work, I could sense that a train was approaching from just over the horizon. It wouldn't arrive for a few more months, mind you, but Veronica's revelation was like the lonesome strain of a train whistle, a harbinger of things to come and a forewarning of my fate. The thin line of railroad track had been laid with Veronica's discovery, and I was powerless to stop the impending arrival of that powerful locomotive – the transport that would bridge my past and my future, inextricably connecting the two.

CHAPTER TWELVE

"Be True to Your School"

As a teacher, your public identity gets stripped from you like used sheets from a hotel bed. For most of us, "Mister/Miss/Mrs./Ms." becomes a first name, while our surnames – oftentimes foreign and exotic to our students – merely serve to illustrate the distance between "us" and "them." Of course, no one sets out to be the type of teacher who erects a barrier between adults and students… it just kind of happens.

However, while many struggle with this awkward metamorphosis, the twenty-two-year-old version of myself saw it as an opportunity for reinvention. I was no longer going to be "Brian" or "Junior" or "Richard" or "Brick" (we'll revisit my ridiculous nickname soon enough, I promise). No, I was going to be *"Mister Smith"* – just like my father had been during his teaching career. And, more importantly, I was going to find comfort in my anonymity. I wouldn't be the has-been bass player for a one-hit-wonder rock band: I would be *Mr. Smith, Super-Teacher!*

For the last eighteen years, I've taught high school English, and it's hard to imagine sometimes what my existence was like before I became a teacher – before the long nights of lesson planning and the never-ending, Sisyphean task of grading essays that dooms my existence from August through June. The days of playing bass in a raucous rock band and writing songs late at night in my bedroom seem like distant dreams, half-forgotten memories of someone else's life.

Of course, it's hard to dwell on the past when the present consumes so much of your attention. For all their confidence and structure, teachers are essentially tightrope walkers, and this career can frequently feel like an overwhelming balancing act. The high wire that we walk as educators is a fine, taut line – one that requires us to maintain a semblance of balance over every aspect of our lives. It means sacrificing time with your spouse, with your children, with your friends. It also means working ten-hour days, Monday through Friday, with work-from-home weekend shifts, too. Maintaining equilibrium above the crowds is rarely an easy task – a simple shift of the wind can be threatening for some of us, while others thrive on the thrill of the exhilarating unknown. Yet, despite our fears, we anticipate the breeze and we adjust accordingly, hoping to maintain our firm footing on the high wire that suspends us in the air, visible to all below us.

What makes the circus-like work of our profession palatable, though, are the human connections that we forge with kids – especially the rare superstars like Veronica Jones. As a high school teacher, you have the opportunity to meet and foster relationships with hundreds (perhaps even *thousands*) of students over the course of your career. Watching these young humans blossom and grow is akin to raising temporarily adopted children with whom you've spent short, intense bursts of time. For someone like Veronica, the bond you develop can be even more tightly-knit: it extends beyond the four walls of the classroom and into the unconfined lives of your families. As much as I was tempted to distance myself from Veronica, to do so would mean sacrificing the relationship that she and Samantha had forged that summer… and my devotion to Sam superseded all other facets of my life.

So, what happens when the tightrope that you delicately walk is suddenly jolted by a student, especially one with whom you have cultivated such a personal relationship? What happens when the Veronicas in your life threaten to expose your secrets to the world at large?

When these opposing magnetic forces come together, you better be prepared to clear your mind and stay poised on your tightrope. In that circumstance, you can only do what you have been trained to do: keep walking forward, one foot in front of the other, maintaining your balance and composure to the best of your abilities.

Right foot. Left foot.
Right foot. Left foot.
Repeat indefinitely.

CHAPTER THIRTEEN

"The Trader"

E xactly one week after the big revelation, Veronica found her way into my classroom after school and waited patiently while I helped a frustrated freshman revise his thesis statement for an assigned essay on *The Outsiders*. After the young fellow left, Veronica clutched her books tightly in her arms and tentatively approached my desk.

"Hi, Mr. Smith," she said with some out-of-character restraint in her voice.

"Hey, Veronica," I cautiously answered. "How can I help you this afternoon?"

Veronica stared intently at the space immediately in front of her Converse-covered feet, exhaling loudly before looking up at me with a nervous, enigmatic expression. "I have a favor to ask you," she said.

"Okay," I responded noncommittally. "Go ahead."

"So… we have this project for AP Econ," she explained, "and I was hoping that you could help me out."

"I'm not sure that I'd be much help," I told her, "I haven't taken an economics class since *my* senior year of high school. What's the assignment?"

"Well," Veronica clarified, "we have to find someone with a 'professional job' and interview them about the career path they took to find their current occupation." She paused again, drawing a deep breath from the wells of her lungs. "And I'm hoping to interview you. You know, how you went from being a rock star to an English teacher."

"Well, I wasn't really a *rock star*, per se…"

"You know what I mean," she said emphatically. She took the textbooks from her arms and set them down gingerly on a nearby desk, waiting for my response.

I paused. This was the moment I had been dreading: the reexamination of old wounds and battle scars. I had no desire to casually discuss the phantom limbs of my past, fearing that I might start to feel something moving in the space where that piece of my soul had been amputated.

"I don't know, Veronica," I said with deliberate hesitation. "It's kind of a long story. And it's kind of personal."

Without missing a beat, she asked a familiar, pointed question: "Do you trust me?"

It was the same question, delivered with the same tone, that I had asked her several times over the course of the year that we had known each other. I had asked Veronica to trust me when we worked on her class assignments and college essays – and now, she had turned the tables, asking *me* to trust *her* with something so personal and penetrating that I couldn't bear to discuss it with anyone other than my wife.

"Do I trust you, Veronica? Of course," I sighed. "You babysit Samantha. And there are *very* few people whom I trust enough to tackle that very precious job."

"If you trust me with your daughter," she inquired, "why can't you trust me with a story?"

She had me there. Still, I didn't quite feel ready to revisit that period of my life. Not yet.

Veronica must have sensed my trepidation. "I'll sweeten the deal," she said. "Agree to this interview, and I'll babysit Sam for free next weekend."

Despite my misgivings and fears about entering that torturous time machine and confronting my own history, it was hard to say no to Veronica. With a deep, unsteady sigh, I closed my eyes.

"Fine," I yielded, my eyes still scrunched closed. "It's a deal."

"YES!" she yelled, her voice echoing through my empty classroom as she hopped up and down. "Thank you, thank you, THANK YOU! You are *not* going to regret this! I promise you!" With a huge, irrepressible grin, Veronica grabbed her books and disappeared through the classroom door into the afternoon sun.

Despite Veronica Jones's naïvely earnest reassurances, I already regretted it.

CHAPTER FOURTEEN
"Child Is the Father of the Man"

A few years back, Oxnard Shores High School adopted a new school calendar that moved the start of the school year up a week in August – but provided a week off in October, right after the completion of the first quarter. Basically, it ended up serving as an "autumn break" right before Halloween. Though there was initially some rumbling and grumbling from staff members, the last decade has seen the teachers on campus embracing this weeklong vacation and welcoming the seasonal respite from the daily routine of school. For the AP teachers like myself, however, this vacation is a gift to be cherished – not for extra time off from work, mind you, but for the buffer zone to catch up on our Sisyphean stacks of essays. Before I begin my grading bonanza, though, I usually take the first weekend of October break to relax and avoid any work-related tasks.

This year, however, would be different. On the first day of October vacation – when I should have been lounging around the house in my pajamas and binge-watching a *Star Wars* marathon with Sam all day – I put on a plaid button-down shirt and blue jeans, and I drove to Veronica's house for our scheduled interview. While I'm not *usually* prone to panic attacks anymore, I could feel a sense of anxiety growing in my chest during the entire commute to the Jones household. By the time that I parked, I could feel my heart palpitating and my pulse throbbing in my forehead. With a deep breath and methodical exhalation, I warily exited my car and began the slow, deliberate walk up the driveway.

I realize it's *incredibly* melodramatic to say so, but I have to admit that I felt like a death row prisoner walking towards his own execution.

Right foot. Left foot.

Right foot. Left foot.

Repeat until you reach the front door.

When I finally gathered the courage to knock, Veronica's mother answered the door wearing faded denim overalls, a dirt-smudged t-shirt, and an oversized straw hat. As the heavy door creaked open, I thought to myself that the smiling Mrs. Jones actually looked more like a farmer than a Southern California supermom, like a countrified version of June Cleaver in blue jeans. Apparently, the ghost of Doris Day is alive and well in the suburbs of Southern California – she just likes to spend her spare time gardening.

"Good afternoon, Mr. Smith," she greeted me, smiling earnestly. "Please come in."

Veronica's mother led me through the spacious living room and ushered me to the dining room table, which was covered in an avalanche of textbooks and homework. Clearly, this was Veronica's workstation (even during the promised respite of vacation) and ground zero for my dreaded interview.

The dining room table was the only slightly disheveled location in an otherwise beautifully decorated and immaculately tidy house. Were it not for the sheer sweetness of Veronica's mother and her soil-stained gardening clothes, I would have felt eerily out of place – like I had stepped out of the real world and into the movie *Pleasantville*.

Keep it together, Brian, I thought to myself. *Keep it together.*

"Would you care for some water or some day-old lemonade?" Mrs. Jones asked. "I can't offer you coffee or soda, sadly, because I'm afraid we don't have any in the house."

"Actually," I replied with a deep breath as I tried to conceal my anxiety, "lemonade sounds wonderful. Thank you."

"Of course," she said, smiling back at me reassuringly before heading to the kitchen. "Veronica will be out momentarily. She's looking for a tape recorder for your interview."

"*A tape recorder!*" I snorted. "This all sounds so formal. Is this secretly a deposition?"

Mrs. Jones chuckled as she returned to the living room, surreptitiously balancing a tray of lemonade in her hands. "Hopefully, there won't be any lawsuits," she said. "Of course, you can always invoke the Fifth Amendment, if you need to." She smiled kindly, handing me a cool glass of lemonade and placing a second glass on the opposite side of the table, where I assumed Veronica would be sitting.

"Thank you for your hospitality," I replied feebly. "You're very thoughtful."

"We do what we can," she responded with a grin. "If you need me, I'll be outside tending to my garden. I have some hydrangeas and chrysanthemums that need my utmost attention. But if you get hungry, please don't hesitate to ask for anything."

"I will. Thank you, Mrs. Jones," I said.

From down the hallway, I could hear the quick pace of bare feet on tile. The footsteps grew louder and louder, until Veronica emerged in jeans and a BYU sweater. "Sorry to keep you waiting, Mr. Smith," she said, plopping down in the seat directly across from my own. "I just wanted to make sure that I had all of the proper materials for my interview with the *rock star*." She winked at me wickedly from across the table.

I sighed.

You know that feeling you get when you go to the dentist for a filling or a root canal? While you intellectually acknowledge and understand that the temporary discomfort you face in the presence of the dentist will only improve your smile, you *still* can't help but dread the encounter. Sometimes, the fear of discomfort is more powerful than the discomfort itself, but you can't escape the sense of terror in the pit of your stomach.

That's exactly how I felt at this moment in time: like I had an impending root canal that I could no longer avoid. And the dentist was going to be a seventeen-year-old girl.

"Before we start," I prefaced, "you should know that it's been a long time since all of this happened. Examining the past is a lot like looking through a filthy windshield. While images and shapes are still visible in your mind's eye, the fine details are often difficult to discern. I can't promise you that all of my memories are perfectly accurate. I might very well be an unreliable narrator for this story."

Veronica gave me a knowing smile as she clicked the little red button on her tape recorder. "You might be an unreliable narrator," she said, "but you have a story that I need to hear. And that's more important than the accuracy of every microscopic detail."

"Fair enough," I said. My eyebrows arched nervously, and I could feel my jaw clenching tighter and tighter. "So, where do we begin?"

Veronica's eyes opened wider, like tiny crystal balls eager to echo a dancing fire. "From the beginning, I suppose. As your wife likes to say, *it's usually the best place to start.*"

"Alright," I said. "Let's get started…"

FIRST CHORUS

I get lost sometimes in the melodies of my mind,
where I've tried to find what I need.
But the crashing tide has swept me off my feet,
and left me incomplete for a while...
And it's just like your smile.

CHAPTER FIFTEEN

"Their Hearts Were Full of Spring"

If you really want to hear about it, the first thing you'll probably want to know is where I was born, and what inspired me to start playing music, and how my parents turned me into a tortured artist, and all that *Catcher in the Rye* kind of stuff... but there's just one problem: I actually had a pretty decent childhood. I wasn't scarred for life by the loss of a sibling or traumatized by boarding school or faced with prematurely graying hair like a certain beloved literary character – though Holden will pop up again later, I promise. My story is clearly another entry in the *Bildungsroman* tradition, but most of my true transformation didn't happen until I was in my late teens and early twenties. For that reason, I'll try to keep this synopsis of my childhood as brief as possible. Otherwise, like a tie-dye jam band at a punk show, I might overstay my welcome.

By the time that I was born, on the first day of summer in 1979 (June 21st, to be exact), my parents were childrearing experts. My older sister, Marina, three years my senior, was a rambunctious child, so my mom and dad learned how to handle dirty diapers, toddler tantrums, and potty training through trial and error; in fact, they used to joke that my sister was their human guinea pig, so they made all their lab-test mistakes on her. Once I arrived, my folks were lean, mean parenting machines – and, as a result, they ensured that my sister and I were both incredibly well-behaved little children.

One might argue that my mom and dad lucked out with two "easy" kids, but I think that their so-called "luck" was actually just *good parenting*. Of course, it didn't hurt that both of them were public school teachers: in the grand scheme of things, teaching might be the world's best training program for would-be parents. I know for a fact that I'm a better parent because I was a teacher first; after all, if you're used to dealing with dozens of children in the sterile confines of a classroom, focusing your attention on one or two kids in the comfort of your own home seems less of a monumental challenge and more of a respite.

In any case, my musical story really begins before I was born. When my dad was growing up in Southern California during the 1960s, he had one singular musical obsession...

The Beach Boys.

Of course, "obsessed" might be putting it lightly. My father was the biggest *Beach Head* that I've ever met, and he never faltered in his support for the band – even when they lost their way and ended up wandering in the wilderness of the late twentieth century. To be fair, though, my dad converted to Beach Boys fanaticism at the very beginning: my parents were both sixteen years old when the band's first album, *Surfin' Safari*, was released in 1962 and – as SoCal kids from a coastal community – they were the target demographic for this teen-oriented Capitol Records musical group. Though the "surf music" fad seems quaint and irreverent by today's standards, the Beach Boys were edgy in their own safe and tender way. With the exception of Dennis (whom my mother used to fawn over), there was no hunky pinup boy; rather, these were a bunch of high school would-be-misfits and boys-next-door, the kind you might see on the football field or in Calculus class. The mop-topped Beatles or iconoclastic Bob Dylan, they were not.

My parents loved to retell the story that their first slow dance, at a senior prom in spring of 1964, was to a cover band's rendition of "Surfer Girl." By the time that the song was over, they were officially high school sweethearts (back when that mythical kind of thing still existed), with the deal officially sealed by a shy peck on the lips. Despite the fact that my parents came from very different worlds – my dad was a pale Jewish boy from an impoverished family, while my mom was a tan Catholic girl with middle-class roots – they somehow found a way to meld their two lives together in the sunshine of Southern California. Though my mother wasn't a surfer, my dad would call her his "little surfer girl" for decades, even when Mom had clearly outgrown this nickname. Still, there's something sweet about that kind of romance: two people loving each other for decades without ever conceding that time has swept away their youth like sea foam on the sandy shore.

It didn't hurt that my dad, Brian Richard Smith (later Brian Richard Smith, *Senior*), had the same first name as the leader of the Beach Boys, Brian Wilson. Somewhere along the line, with their shared given name and mutual passion for the trappings of SoCal beach-bum culture, my dad developed a kinship to the oldest Wilson brother – and he never outgrew that emotional attachment, even during the band's negligent nadirs and pits in popularity. In fact, my dad was so smitten with the band that he used to joke with me throughout my childhood about the significance of my given name.

"You know, son," he would tell me, "your mother thinks that you're named after me, but I'll let you in on a secret. You're actually named after Brian Wilson. You might be Brian Richard Smith, *Junior*, but don't ever forget that the *Brian* in your name comes from him."

Of course, I would usually listen disinterestedly or roll my eyes, but the message clearly stuck with me.

"Just don't tell your mom," he would add, with a mischievous wink of his eye.

For the sake of preventing confusion, though, my parents decided to call me "Richard" or "Junior" throughout my childhood. While my *real* name was "Brian," I kept it tucked away, like a secret identity or a spandex superhero suit in a darkened closet. The only time that anyone ever called me Brian was on the first day of school each year, and I was quick to correct my teachers that "Brian" was my *dad's* name, and they should call me *Richard* or *Rick*. Though this inevitably raised eyebrows year after tedious year, my teachers all kindly complied with my request and my classmates became accustomed to this annual rite of passage.

This early practice with name-swapping taught me very early about the importance of maintaining separate identities for different segments of my life. While the name *Brian* found a perpetual spot hanging in my closet, I stuffed the title *Junior* into my backpack every day when I left for school, and I wore the nickname *Rick* for all my peers and teachers. Regardless of what this forced identity crisis might have done to my splintered preadolescent ego, I never had difficulty reconciling these various titles in my life. I wore these different names like clothes, interchangeably shifting and discarding for the sake of my overall presentation. In my heart and my core, though, I have always been (and will always be) *Brian*.

It just took me a while to figure that out.

My father might have gifted me his love of the Beach Boys by modeling me after my namesake, Brian Wilson, but it was also something that I deflected, avoided, and buried for years and years. Nevertheless, I guess it was inevitable that my existence would be inextricably connected with that of the Beach Boys from the moment I was born. Whether I liked it or not, I was destined to be a Beach Head.

Apart from the sun-kissed soundtrack of my youth, I lived a very normal, uneventful, suburban life – perhaps not unlike your own. My childhood was filled with *Star Wars* action figures, Marvel comic books, family barbecues, and lots of time with my kinfolk. Not only were my sister and I close enough in age to play together regularly (though I did tire of having to be the "bad guy" in all our games and play-acting), but I also had the added luxury of living only a few blocks from my first cousin, Charles. In addition to being a blood relative, Charles was almost my doppelgänger: we had the same last name, we were the same age, we ended up in many of the same classes at school, *and* we shared a love of all things nerdy. Heck, we even looked alike, with our thick, curly hair and overabundance of baby fat.

Because my Uncle Jeff and Aunt Alyssa used to come over with Charles on a weekly basis, he felt more like a brother than a cousin. Though we did have our occasional arguments (usually over who got to be Luke Skywalker and who had to be Darth Vader), Charles became my best friend and partner-in-crime, like the Sodapop to my Ponyboy or the Jem to my Scout. I was a lucky child to have such a mundane life with such a normal family – and, as a result, I think I turned out pretty well-adjusted. I'm sure my wife can point out a wide variety of flaws and neuroses that stem from my childhood, but she's a bit too sweet to publicly report all of my weaknesses. Thank goodness for that.

In any case, my childhood zoomed along as normal, as smooth as the Millennium Falcon cruising through hyperspace. And, while I always enjoyed listening to the Beach Boys (as well as the other classic rock bands that my dad played on his Technics SP-10 turntable), I never thought twice about playing music myself... until the day of my dad's fortieth birthday party.

At the time, I was an awkward seven-year-old kid. To be fair, *most* seven-year-old children are awkward, but I also suffered from an undiagnosed social anxiety disorder that haunted me for years. To make matters worse, I was even more self-consciously awkward and uncomfortable because of my weight. I come from a line of big men: my dad hovered around the 270-pound mark for most of my childhood, and Uncle Jeff was the same way. Consequently, both Charles and I were very chubby little boys. In fact, poor Charles was even christened "Chunk" (lovingly, mind you) by our family, because of his resemblance to the infamous "truffle-shuffle" dancer from *The Goonies*. Years later, when I was in high school, my football coach provided me with a similarly unwelcome nickname: "Brick." Though my sister was always slender and athletic, taking after my mom's side of the family, Charles and I (or "Chunk" and "Brick," as we became known) felt uncomfortable in our less-than-petite frames.

This was our inherited legacy: we were heirs to a dynasty of big children who grew into big men. I only saw my paternal grandfather a handful of times in my life, but his specter loomed large in my dad's life, even larger than the 300 pounds that Grandpa Smith carried with him until his fatal heart attack at the age of 55. These three forefathers – my father, uncle, and grandfather – were large men with large personalities and large appetites. When they entered a room, they commanded attention, as if they feasted and grew confident from the audience they received. This even manifested itself in their career choices: Dad was a high school English teacher and Uncle Jeff was a professional musician (though he did run a pizza parlor during the day). Each of these roles required a large stage presence, but Dad and Jeff were large enough – physically and socially – to captivate any crowd.

In sharp contrast, I always felt my persona was inversely proportional to my physical appearance. For whatever reason, my weight forced me to implode emotionally, to withdraw from the world outside and turn inward. Mind you, I wasn't morbidly obese as a little kid, but I was noticeably heavier than my peers in elementary school. However, if you remember how cruel elementary kids can be, you can imagine how being "the fat kid" or "the chubby guy" might have shaped my sense of self as a child – and Charles's, too. As you know by now, I'm not one for dwelling in the past. I'd rather not spend any more time recounting those experiences... but you can fill in the blanks yourself.

All of this changed for me during one beautiful August evening in the summer of 1986, on the day that my father turned forty years old. My dad used to joke that my June birthday ushered in the summer, while his mid-August birthday brought the season to an end. Together, we were the alpha and omega of summer, the beginning and the end of vacation season. Seeing as how my dad's birthday coincided with the end of our two-month break from school, he decided to go all-out and celebrate his fortieth birthday in style: he invited fifty or so friends and relatives over to our modestly sized Ojai house, paid for professional caterers, and hired a band to play in our backyard.

Of course, this wasn't just *any* band. It was *Uncle Jeff's* band, the Stuttering Surfers. For those of you not from the Ventura County area, the Stuttering Surfers is the best surf-rock cover band this side of the Mississippi. Since 1963, they've been playing every kind of venue around – from bars to bar mitzvahs, restaurants to rest homes. Their crowning achievement, however, was opening for The Beach Boys at the Ventura County Fairgrounds on October 6th, 1984; though it was well after the band's heyday (and before its miraculous resurgence with 1988's "Kokomo"), it was a dream come true for my uncle and his bandmates. What Southern California musician of that era *wouldn't* want to meet – and play a show with – the Beach Boys?

It was August 14th of 1986, though, that I got to see my all-time favorite performance of the Stuttering Surfers – in my own backyard. Literally. It's been over thirty years now, but I still vividly remember that sun-drenched, hazy afternoon. The entire house was decorated like Disneyland's Enchanted Tiki Room attraction, and the property was aflutter with guests wearing flower-print Hawaiian shirts and plastic leis. My family even got in on the action: Marina wore a grass hula skirt, my mom sported a loose-fitting muumuu, and Charles adorned an *aloha* shirt that barely covered his robust stomach. Of course, while the Kahlua pulled pork and freshly cut pineapple were scrumptious, what really stands out in my memory is the Stuttering Surfers.

That afternoon was a clear turning point in my life.

It was the day I decided that I wanted to be a musician.

Throughout the evening, I shyly peeked out from behind the flickering light of a decorative tiki torch, absolutely mesmerized by the band's set. While Charles and Marina and the other little kids at the party galloped around and chased each other in some juvenile endeavor, I stood perfectly still behind the cheap imitation Hawaiian decorations, entranced by the music. For most of their performance, the Stuttering Surfers covered popular hits associated with the early "surf rock" era of popular music: Jan & Dean's "Surf City," Dick Dale's "Misirlou," The Surfaris'

"Wipeout," The Chantays' "Pipeline," and a healthy serving of songs from the Beach Boys catalog. My uncle, Jeffrey Alan Smith, was (and still is) an *incredible* guitar player, a musician whose raw talent and hard work have served him well for the last half-century. Throughout that whole performance, I couldn't pry my eyes away from his sunburst-colored Fender Stratocaster; watching his fingers fly across the dark brown slots of the fretboard was simply captivating. Though the vocals for the band weren't full of death-defying acrobatics, their musicianship was breathtaking. It was, in a word, inspiring.

In my seven-year-old mind, though, I had only one humble observation: Uncle Jeff's guitar made him look *cool*.

About an hour into their set, my uncle took off his vintage Stratocaster and placed it upright onto a skinny black guitar stand. He then promptly stepped up to the microphone, called the party to order, and delivered a well-rehearsed speech about my dad.

"The reason we're here today," he told the crowd, "is to celebrate one of the coolest cats I know… my big brother, Brian." On cue, everyone clapped and whistled in response to Uncle Jeff's deliberation. "It's hard to believe, but Brian is turning the big 'four-zero' today, and there is no place I would rather be than here, with our family, on this beautiful summer evening."

Once again, the partygoers politely applauded, their eyes volleying back and forth between Jeff and the guest of honor, my father.

"Some of you don't know this," Uncle Jeff slyly spoke into the microphone, "but Brian was our first lead singer, way back in the 1960s."

This news was shocking to me. *My dad? In a band? Before I was born? How was that even possible? How had I never heard about this before?*

While I stood there awestruck, Uncle Jeff persisted with his singular mission. "I know he doesn't play much music anymore," he continued, "but I'm hoping we can get him up here and pull him out of rock and roll retirement for one more song."

Everyone at the party clapped and cheered, while Uncle Jeff casually walked over to my dad's table and offered him his hand. I don't remember ever seeing my father blush quite as brightly as he did at that moment in time: his cheeks flushed a vibrant shade of crimson as he chuckled uncomfortably.

"Come on up, Big Kahuna," Uncle Jeff commanded, undeterred by my father's uncharacteristic bashfulness.

Despite my dad's reservations, despite his unusually reticent demeanor, he acquiesced to Uncle Jeff's request. With a resigned shrug of his shoulders and a whispered *"What the hell?"* under his breath, my dad got up from the comfort of his plastic chair and ambled up towards the band.

What transpired next was nothing short of a revelation. My dad, my nerdy English teacher father – mind you, the same guy who wore button-down shirts and ties to work *every single day of his life* – joined the band on its makeshift stage to perform a song.

And, against all odds, he *rocked*.

Appropriately enough, the song that they played was a Beach Boys tune, "Help Me, Rhonda," and my father strummed gracefully along with the band while he simultaneously handled lead vocals. What I heard that day was not the muffled, off-key warble of an amateur; instead, my father sang like the ghost of Dennis Wilson – a chilling echo, considering Dennis's death only three years earlier. Whereas Al Jardine's vocals on the original studio recording of "Rhonda" are a polished triumph and Brian Wilson's live solo rendering is a strained aching, Dennis's live performance (which you can hear on the *Made in California* box set) is a grizzled, emotive rendition.

For three minutes, my dad transformed from sweet to sultry, from lemonade to liquor.

And it was a sight to behold.

Although Dad was normally the reserved, prim-and-proper Carl Wilson type, this was his moment of triumph – his wild, carefree Dennis Wilson side. During the entire performance of "Help Me, Rhonda," my father was a rock star of the first degree, a superhuman figure transcending the mundane ordinariness of his humdrum day job and his static suburban life. Though Uncle Jeff was the one shredding on the guitar solo, all eyes were on my father, the birthday boy who was breaking free from the comfort of the shore and throwing himself to the anarchy of the waves.

Those were the three most inspiring minutes of my childhood.

When the song was finished, the partygoers clapped and hollered and hooted and shouted – and my dad soaked it all up, beaming the widest smile in the world before returning to his flushed red demeanor. He waved at everyone, stepped aside from the microphone, and then shuffled back to his plastic chair by the barbecue where he was greeted by kisses from my grinning mother.

Just like that, my dad's three-minute tenure as a Superman rock star was over – and he abruptly returned to his commonplace Clark Kent life. From my vantage point behind the tiki torches, it appeared as if my father had given up the rock and roll ghost: as he eased himself into the pale plastic patio furniture, I could see his spirit deflating, returning to its resting state of reservation. Even with the flurry of guests giving him high-fives and pats on the back, he seemed humble and unassuming. In that moment, he was a true paradox – a large man with a small presence.

The rest of the evening was uneventful and anticlimactic. Like any ersatz *luau*-themed party, it was a pale imitation of true Hawaiian culture and heritage – something that I would intimately see firsthand many years later when I married the love of my life. At the time, though, I was a little confused by the Polynesian iconography of the evening; the wafting torch flames and dried grass looked rustic and foreign to my childish eyes. To me, the plastic reproductions of tikis and leis evoked distant lands that reminded me more of the mystic setting of *Alice in Wonderland* than an American state where real people actually lived.

Later that night, once the guests had left and we were cleaning up the paper and plastic remnants of the party, I meekly approached my dad and stood diminutively in front of his hefty frame. He looked down at me with a confused expression on his face.

"Yes, Junior?" he asked tentatively, his chin cocked quizzically to the side.

I had so many thoughts racing through my head, but all I could muster was a three-word whisper. "You play guitar."

My dad laughed in billowing waves. "You're an observant little guy, aren't you?"

"I didn't know you played guitar," I whispered. "Or sang."

"Well," he smirked, "there are a *lot* of things you don't know about me, kiddo."

I didn't move from my spot on the grass, though discarded paper napkins blew past us like little white tumbleweeds on the green lawn.

"Is there something else…?" my dad asked.

This was the moment that I had been waiting for all night. I tried to speak, but I stuttered and stopped on my first attempt. Sensing my uneasiness, my dad crouched down close to me and tenderly lifted my chin to face him.

"What is it, son?"

My gaze was glued to the ground, and I traced the smeared footprints on the grass with my eyes as I tried to muster up the courage to speak. When I finally felt confident enough, I looked my father straight in the eyes and muttered the four words that would change my destiny:

"Will you teach me?"

My father's response was perfect. He hugged me tightly and spoke softly into my nervous forehead.

"Of course," he said.

His smile melted away all my worries and concerns, and I knew at that moment in time that everything was going to be all right.

CHAPTER SIXTEEN
"Fun, Fun, Fun"

Apparently, though, I wasn't the only star-struck Smith child that night: both Charles and Marina made comments to their respective parents about learning musical instruments after seeing the elder Smith brothers play together at my dad's birthday party. The following weekend, after we all had a few days to recuperate from the big shindig, we drove to the practice space of the Stuttering Surfers and took our first steps on the long journey towards becoming musicians.

Considering the talent of the band, I expected their practice space to be a generously sized music hall or a lavish recording studio. Instead, it was a modest room in an industrial building on the outskirts of Ojai. As we approached the gray exterior of the structure, I was convinced that we were stopping by an office space for the restaurant that Uncle Jeff owned and operated, the *Surfer's Choice Pizza Parlor*. However, as we made our way through the drab, concrete halls, it felt like we were heading deeper and deeper into an abyss – a dark cavern from which we might never emerge. After what seemed like ten minutes, our trek (which reminded me vaguely of the intro sequence to the television show *Get Smart*) led us to our destination: the practice space of the Stuttering Surfers.

The large wooden door that served as the gateway to this enchanted realm contrasted sharply with the dull concrete theme of the building. When we opened the door, it was like entering a rock and roll Narnia – no lions, witches, or wardrobes required. After maneuvering through the unassuming pathway, we were surrounded by a dozen guitars, a full drum kit, microphone stands, keyboards, and more amplifiers than I could count. The room was cozier and more cluttered than I had anticipated, and it was a tight squeeze to get the five members of the Smith family into the band's practice space. Somehow, we made it through the tangle of microphone cables and found ourselves spots on the faded plush couch in the back of the room. But before we even touched a single piece of equipment, Dad and Uncle Jeff sat us all down in order to give us our first lesson.

"The thing about being in a band," Uncle Jeff started, "is that no one can do it alone. You can't have five lead singers all wailing at the same time, just as you can't have five lead guitarists all shredding simultaneously. What you need to do is listen to your band members, feed off of each other, and work together."

My dad, ever the teacher, chimed in to clarify. "Think of it like baking a cake," he explained. "You need a mixture of different ingredients, textures, and tastes. If you have too much flour, baking soda, or even sugar, the results will be disastrous. The elements that make up the final product need to be combined in the proper proportions. And when you do it right, it's magical."

Marina, Charles, and I silently nodded our heads in understanding. This felt more like being in school than partying like a rock star. But, as a result, I began to understand a vital piece of life's precious puzzle that day: once you get a peek behind the curtains, reality is hardly ever what you imagine it to be.

Uncle Jeff walked away from the couch and started picking up various pieces of equipment. "While we can teach all three of you how to play the guitar," he told us, "you'll be better off if each of you selects a different instrument."

My dad immediately turned to my sister. "Marina, you're the oldest, so you get first pick. What would you like to play?"

Without hesitation, she reached for a brown Fender Telecaster that rested lazily on its stand. As she gripped the neck of the guitar, she rubbed her hand along the sunburst finish of the instrument's body. "I want to play guitar like you, Dad," she squealed to our father.

My father smiled and gave her a hug. "That's wonderful, sweetie," he told her. "The guitar is the only instrument I learned how to play, and it's a great one."

Next, Uncle Jeff turned to Charles. "What about you, Chunk?" he asked his son.

Charles slipped artfully through the spaces between instruments, carefully dodging cables and stands as he made his way across the room. Finally, he settled in front of the Ludwig Blue Vistalite drum set against the wall and tapped his pointer finger gently against the snare. Self-consciously, he turned around to face the rest of us.

"Can I play the drums, Papa?" he asked his dad.

"Of course!" Uncle Jeff exclaimed. "The foundation of any good band is the drummer, and every musician needs someone to guide them through the rhythm."

Two down, one to go.

My father pushed his glasses up to the bridge of his nose and then looked over in my direction. "Last, but not least, is you," he said softly. He stared down at me with his hands perched on his sizable hips. "What do you think, Junior?"

After the night of my dad's party, I had been dead-set on playing guitar like him. However, Marina had already picked the six-string guitar, and I *definitely* didn't want to copy my older sister (especially after Uncle Jeff's speech). Still, I noticed a larger guitar on the side of the room, one with an elongated neck and a dark lacquer that starkly contrasted the instrument's sterling white pick-guard. Strangely enough, this guitar only had four strings... but it just looked *so cool*. I didn't know it at the time, but that beautiful 1982 Fender Precision bass guitar would lead me to a lifetime of obscurity and second-in-command status.

No one notices the bass player. But I didn't understand that as a seven-year-old kid.

I pointed from across the room to the instrument. "What about that one, Daddy?" I asked.

My father walked towards the instrument and picked it up. "This one?" he asked, a little startled by my selection. "The *bass guitar...*?"

Slowly, I nodded my confirmation.

"Huh," he grunted. "I never pictured you as a bass player. What do you think, Jeff? Should Junior go for the bass?"

Uncle Jeff chimed in enthusiastically. "Absolutely! You *did* name your son after Brian Wilson. He might as well play the same instrument as his namesake." My uncle rubbed his bristly chin and a glimmer of a grin crept across his face. "Heck! Maybe we can get him to learn some keyboards, too, so he can be just like the Big Brian."

My dad contemplated that thought for a second. "Hmmm," he finally hummed in affirmation. "I guess his fate is already preordained, huh?"

"*Exaaaaactly,*" said Uncle Jeff, stretching out the word like warm taffy on a summer day.

It always feels awkward when people speak about you as if you're not in their presence. This is compounded even more so when your parents (or other adults, for that matter) seem to be making decisions about your destiny without fully consulting you. While I had requested to play the big guitar (which I was subsequently informed was called a "bass"), I hadn't mentioned anything about piano. Ever. Wasn't the piano just for old people? And little girls? Why would any ordinary seven-year-old boy want to play the *piano*?

Though I felt like a small soldier in the commanding presences of my dad and Uncle Jeff, these two great men who would be our musical generals, I somehow found the courage to speak up. "Dad," I said with a crack in my voice, "I don't want to play piano. I want to play guitar."

"Don't worry, Junior," my dad smirked in reply. "You'll learn to play both."

And, over the next few years, I did. That morning was the first mile of the marathon that became my music career, and I had no idea that selecting instruments in the confines of a cluttered cave would one day lead me to the fringe territory of rock and roll stardom.

CHAPTER SEVENTEEN

"Lonely Sea"

S ome kids spend countless hours of their childhood on the baseball diamond, pitching fastball after fastball. Others spend never-ending evenings in ballet class, learning how to pirouette and arabesque. Many more simply sit idly in front of a television, consuming cartoons like a bowlful of candy.

Marina, Chunk, and I spent our childhoods learning how to play musical instruments. At first, we were terrible: our petite hands were too small to fit around the long necks of guitars, too weak to beat the heads of drums with sticks, and too tender to play for extended stretches of time. However, it didn't take very long at all before our blisters transformed into callouses and our awkward repetitive movements turned into muscle memory. We were still untrained amateurs, mind you, but we were growing into our instruments like children growing into oversized clothes.

Teaching us to play music was one of the greatest gifts that our parents gave us. While it did force us to invest considerable time and energy of our childhood into tedious hours of practice, the dividends we reaped in only a few short years were substantial. By the time that Chunk and I got to junior high school, we were able to jump from "beginning band" to "advanced band" in Maricopa Middle School's music program; and, whereas Chunk and I had always felt like outsiders at school, like lonely ships adrift in a pre-adolescent ocean, the school's band program offered us safe harbor. Though we were surrounded by kids twice our size, most of them had only half our talent – which meant that we earned the respect of some intimidating peers in a very short period of time. This cultural capital carried us beyond the borders of middle school bullying into a sheltered oasis of polite peer interactions during our tween-age years.

Thank God for rock 'n' roll – the holy institution that's been saving kids from social awkwardness since 1954.

Since Marina was three years older than me (and Chunk, obviously), we narrowly missed being in middle school together. While this allowed us to avoid the awkward "little brother at the same school" syndrome, it also meant that Chunk and I were forced outside of our comfort zone in band class. Nevertheless, despite the fact that we didn't ever have the opportunity to play music together at Maricopa Middle School with Marina, she still joined us for our weekly practices and lessons with Uncle Jeff.

While this might seem like a mundane detail, it had a profound impact on us. Chunk and I found ourselves collaborating with a wide assortment of musicians in mixed formations, playing in a variety of styles and genres. At home, we had our main "band" with Marina: we were a three-piece group, fronted by a female singer, tackling mostly classic rock cover songs. In sharp contrast, Chunk and I were the backbone of the school's jazz band program, playing more complex instrumental pieces of music. Because of this, playing music at Maricopa Middle School felt more like a formal academic experience, while jamming with Marina at home felt like an organic, authentic extension of ourselves.

There would soon be one overlapping factor between jazz band and our homegrown rock 'n' roll experiment: Ethan Hidalgo. A fellow student at Maricopa Middle School, Ethan was a guitar prodigy who played in the same Advanced Band class as Chunk and I did. On our first day of school in sixth grade, Ethan was sporting a Beatles *Abbey Road* t-shirt over his ripped-up blue jeans; most of his face was obscured by shaggy black hair and he seemed to be perpetually staring at his Converse, diverting his gaze away from both his classmates and teachers.

Since Chunk and I were both overweight outsiders in a school comprised primarily of pencil-thin preteens, we were finely attuned to the body language of fellow outcasts.

We knew right away that Ethan was one of us.

Eventually, Ethan would become the third musketeer in our small group of Maricopa misfits. We had very inauspicious origins, making small talk outside the soundproofed walls of the band room. I'm pretty sure that our first conversation went something like this:

> **ME:** Hey.
> **ETHAN:** Hey.
> **CHUNK:** Cool shirt.
> **ME:** Yeah.
> **ETHAN:** You like the Beatles?
> **CHUNK:** Mostly their later stuff. Like starting from *Revolver*. The early albums were too happy.
> **ETHAN:** Huh. I like the early stuff.
> **ME:** Me, too. Paul McCartney was a kickass bass player. Even from the beginning.
> **ETHAN:** Yeah.
> **CHUNK:** Yeah.
> *[Awkward shuffling of feet]*
> **ME:** Uh… You guys want to sit together at lunch?
> **CHUNK:** Cool.
> **ETHAN:** Yeah. Cool.
> **ME:** Cool.

Middle school boys are eloquent creatures, are they not?

Just as Chunk and I had always found ourselves clustered together in elementary school, we were pleasantly surprised to see Ethan in many of our middle school classes. I suppose the fact that we were all in the Gifted and Talented Education program (also known in its acronymic incarnation as G.A.T.E.), as well as the same band period, meant we didn't have much choice in the matter. Nevertheless, we found a kinship in our shared awkwardness, a common currency of un-coolness that brought us closer together.

As we learned soon enough, Ethan was facing his own flightless demons that led him to join our fragile fraternity. Our new guitar-slinging friend was a latchkey kid, raised by a single working dad, whose family lived in the not-so-posh Casitas Springs area that flanked the feathered fringes of Ojai. Ethan's father was a quiet, weary man with a lilting Spanish accent; and, though Mr. Hidalgo rarely ever played for us, he was an impressive *guitarrista* with a seemingly inexhaustible repertoire of *corrido* and *mariachi* tunes. I never got to meet Ethan's mom: she was a ghostly presence whose ivory skin and golden hair were not reflected in the dark features of her biracial *mestizo* son.

Whereas Chunk and I had the luxury of family perpetually circling our simple spheres, Ethan frequently found himself alone in the humble, mud-caked dwelling that he called home. So, while Mr. Hidalgo picked up extra shifts at the local *Costa Supermercado* to make ends meet, Ethan had ample time to fine-tune his guitar acrobatics. Between God-given talent, musical genetics, and endless hours of practice, Ethan soon became a formidable force in jazz band. Chunk and I thought that *we* were impressive musicians, but Ethan made us look like amateurs.

Soon enough, our trio of makeshift misfits became inseparable. Beyond bonding over our parents' record collections, we sought solace in old black-and-white horror films and classic science fiction novels. All those old monster movies and battered books shared recurring themes of loneliness and isolation – and we gravitated towards those sad, solitary figures of yesteryear. In our own ways, we all felt a little like Frankenstein's monster and the Wolfman and Meg Murry and Ender Wiggins. For two overweight half-Jewish cousins and their biracial best friend from the opposite side of the railroad tracks, the fantastic freedom of fiction freed us from our mundane lives and provided relief from our adolescent restlessness.

In short time, Ethan became the Johnny to our Ponyboy and Sodapop; however, unlike the Curtis family in S.E. Hinton's *The Outsiders*, we had musical instruments on our side. And that would make us cool enough in just a brief period of time.

Middle school might be the absolute worst part of the human experience. Although you feel incredibly lonely and isolated in those three traumatic years, you fail to recognize that *all kids* feel terrible about themselves in that perpetual state of prepubescent awkwardness. Chunk, Ethan, and I might have thought that it was "us against the world," but we were wrong: it was millions of small clusters like ours, all bonding within shared experiences of seclusion. No one at Maricopa Middle School felt cool or looked cool or acted cool.

With one notable exception: Serena Rios.

Even in the sixth grade, Serena was a gorgeous, vibrant, insightful beauty of a girl. With long honey-blonde hair that cascaded gracefully down her perfectly tanned skin, she was the fantasy of every single boy at school. She dressed immaculately, spoke eloquently, and laughed delicately. She brightened up every room that she entered with a bewitching smile and enticing eyes. And, most tellingly, she didn't seem to suffer from any of the insecurities that are so common to middle school kids.

In short, she was the exact opposite of me. And Chunk. And Ethan. And every other single kid in the entire student body.

Serena wouldn't really become aware of us for a few more years, but we were always aware of *her*. When she spoke, our hearts sighed; when she walked by us, our stomachs contracted. She was the closest thing to a celebrity that our little campus could claim.

And, as you'll soon see, she was only going to get smarter, hotter, and more intricately woven into our lives.

The thing about small towns like Ojai, California, is that the lives of its citizens seem inextricably bound together. Families all know each other, kids grow up together, and the tight-knit community retains an uncompromising stranglehold on everyone within the city limits. We were Ojai kids, born and bred, prone to frigid nights and stiflingly hot days. By the time that we were enrolled in middle school, we had been fully indoctrinated into the cult of Ojai living, complete with the baffling weather and the indescribably bizarre mixture of leftover hippies and upscale hipsters in the town's population.

Despite all the publicly embraced quirkiness of Ojai's citizens, when I think back to middle school, I just remember feeling incredibly unwelcome and alone. Sure, I had the love and support of my family, but my own introverted tendencies and manifesting insecurities left me on the periphery of the middle school experience, watching the world from the sidelines while my classmates all seemed to be living happy, carefree existences. Fortunately, I found another group of allies who seemed to cherish my presence and respect my talents: my teachers.

In the springtime of my sixth-grade year, my otherwise-intimidating English teacher, Mrs. Winters, pulled me aside after school to speak with me about something I had written for her class. As a summative assignment for a unit on Robert C. O'Brien's *Mrs. Frisby and the Rats of NIMH*, we were required to compose a poem inspired by the story; it's been decades now since I've read the book, but I remember feeling strangely moved by the story of the hyper-intelligent rodents struggling to survive in a world that perpetually tries to crush them. Strange as it might sound, I deeply connected to this little science fiction novel and felt a kinship with Mrs. Frisby's story, especially as she attempted to reconcile her current life with the secrets of the past. In any case, something clicked in my brain while I worked on this assignment, and I spent hours crafting a piece that showed how the setting of Mrs. Frisby's home reflected the journey that she took over the course of the novel. Mrs. Winters recognized something in that poem, something that even I couldn't see, and she pulled me aside after class to share her thoughts with me.

"Well, *Mr. Smith*," she said with strange warmth in her otherwise chilling voice, "it looks as if you are aptly named. You have the makings of a *word*-smith, young man. I am very impressed with this poem of yours, and I have no doubt that you will continue to surprise your teachers in the years to come."

To be fair, the poem was probably not the masterpiece that she made it out to be. Though it might seem harsh to say so, most high school poetry is terrible – and most middle school poetry is even more exponentially horrific. By comparison, my rudimentary piece of writing probably seemed like a welcome respite from the tortured rhyme schemes of my classmates. Nevertheless, I was happily stunned by Mrs. Winters's kind comments. I thanked her profusely and shyly crept away to the playground, blushing the whole walk there.

I wish I could find my *Mrs. Frisby* poem, but it's been lost somewhere in the dusty boxes of my attic, sandwiched between the yellowing pages of report cards and the tattered threads of old t-shirts. That was my first experience receiving critical praise – and because kind words from Mrs. Winters were a rare commodity, I treasured them. With a handful of compliments, she bolstered my self-confidence with rolling waves of optimism, tidal movements that could melt even the iciest hearts.

Looking back now, I recognize that the seeds of my future occupation were planted at this precise moment in my life. There are a variety of reasons why people choose to pursue a career in the field of education, but I feel like most teachers fit into one (or more) of the three following categories:

1. People who were *cool* in their formative years – and who desperately want to recapture that fleeting feeling of glory, that impermanent sense of self-satisfaction.

2. People who were *uncool* in their formative years – and who want to prove that they've become much cooler in the years afterwards.

3. People who were *very uncool* in their formative years – and who want to help guide other uncool youths through this awkward (and oftentimes painful) set of experiences.

I would like to believe that I fit into the third archetype. Though most of my decision to become an educator stems from what happened later with my father, I can see now that there were always hints about my ultimate career path – clues that foreshadowed my fate as an English teacher. The long months of feeling like a lonely sea, an isolated force of nature, helped guide me towards a life path in which I could help other solitary rivers unite into larger bodies of water.

This has become my life goal. Through the small waves that I create in my classroom, I hope to help lonely puddles, rivers, and lakes flow to the ocean – to that common, cleansing water in which we can all join together with our shared humanity.

CHAPTER EIGHTEEN

"Little Saint Nick"

The rest of middle school was an unforgiving blend of heartache, hormones, and homework. Though there were some notable highlights (I won a few school writing contests, the Smith family took a weeklong trip to Northern California, and Serena Rios was always in my G.A.T.E. classes), most of the weeks passed by in a blurry buzz of never-ending schooldays. Through it all, though, we maintained our weekly music practices – and, as could be expected, our little family band was becoming pretty polished.

Marina, Chunk, and I even made our world debut at a Fourth of July neighborhood block party in the summer of 1991, playing a set comprised entirely of female-fronted classic rock songs (think Fleetwood Mac, Jefferson Airplane, and Heart). As you can probably guess, we weren't brilliant. Heck, we weren't even *in tune* half the time. Nevertheless, Marina sang her heart out while Chunk and I provided an adequate musical foundation for her talents. Clearly, she was the star of the show, while the boys were merely her backup band. There was no ego involved, though: Chunk and I were just happy to be part of the act. During our performance, we did capture the attention of some mildly enthused and impressed bystanders, all of whom seemed shocked to see a band of kids playing such anachronistic classic rock. Perhaps we were just a novelty act, but (in our developing minds) we were serious rock and roll musicians… who just happened to be kids.

If you define a "show" as a band playing on a stage in front of a semblance of an audience and perhaps coupled with some mood lighting, then this performance was more akin to a rehearsal on our front lawn. We had no elevated surface to raise us above the soil and concrete, nor did we have any electric-powered lights dramatically illuminating our profiles.

However, we did have an audience. Sort of. Apart from the passersby who cocked their heads in amusement at our raw performance, we had a solid group of family members and friends listening attentively from a flock of lawn chairs haphazardly assembled in the middle of the street. Seeing as how Chunk and I weren't the outgoing types, our social circle was more like a social amoeba – single-celled and in its early formative stages. Marina, in sharp contrast, had a small, evolved crowd of girlfriends and acquaintances to cheer her on, primarily comprised of her teammates from the Sespe Creek High School junior varsity soccer team. As such, I found myself frequently distracted from the notes that I was hitting on my bass guitar; I was lost in the golden hair, sun-kissed skin, and captivating eyes of the older girls who watched us casually from the street.

While Marina was clearly the studious type, she also had a passionate, aggressive side – the part of her that was most frequently unleashed on the soccer field. We sometimes saw fleeting glimpses of this during our garage rehearsals, but she unwaveringly channeled her emotions in full force the day of our block party performance. In this context, my sister was not the overbearing sibling from down the hall, but a singer with a strong stage presence – full of fierce fire and fury. Because we were different genders and were born three years apart, Marina and I didn't have many opportunities to bond. From my vantage point on the lawn, though, my sister suddenly seemed like the coolest girl in the world, and I was proud to be her little brother.

Plus, her friends were hot.

In any case, we played for a solid sixty minutes on that golden July afternoon, sunlight streaming through the mottled leaves of the trees that lined our street. It was a beautiful, perfect midsummer daydream. For one glorious hour, I forgot about my insecurities, my social anxiety. And, despite the ever-present burden of my physical weight, I felt lighter than the finches in the sky, freer than the airplanes that streaked white clouds of exhaust across the atmosphere.

After we finished our set, our parents rushed towards us, throwing their arms around us and beaming with pride. My mom kept ruffling up my thick, unruly hair while my dad and Uncle Jeff chuckled in a celebratory fashion.

"Man, this is wonderful!" my dad exclaimed. "You guys are like a real-life version of *The Partridge Family*! That was incredible to watch! Don't you think so, Jeffrey?"

Uncle Jeff nodded his head in agreement, grinning widely.

Before we disassembled our gear, my dad asked each of us to grab our instruments and pose for a photo. We smiled clumsily and inelegantly, but with the earnest sense of victory that accompanies such a prosperous public performance. With the snap and whirl of his Polaroid camera, my dad took picture after picture, handing each of us a snapshot to commemorate our first gig. In my copy of the picture, Marina is glowing radiantly, guitar in hand, while Chunk has his drumsticks raised to the sky in an irreverent pose. Yet, even in this moment of victory, I'm distracted by something out of the frame and my face is angled away from the camera with only a hint of a smile on my lips. It wasn't the most flattering picture, but it was the truest depiction of our personalities. We were goofy kids getting our first taste of conquest. And we loved it.

Though it's been bleached and aged by the intervening years, I still have that picture taped to the inside of my guitar case.

Around this same time, Chunk and I became obsessed with the television show *Twin Peaks*, David Lynch's bizarre murder mystery series that ran from 1990-1991. Though *Twin Peaks* seems a little dated when viewed from today's perspective (especially the ridiculous hairstyles), at the turn of the decade it was the coolest, edgiest piece of entertainment around. Chunk and I were fascinated by the fate of Laura Palmer, bewildered by the Black Lodge, and frustrated by the cliffhanger series finale that left so many questions unanswered. Thanks to the show, I even developed my first celebrity crush: Sherilyn Fenn. To me, she seemed like the raven-haired reincarnation of Marilyn Monroe, right down to the red lipstick and prominent beauty mark. I was in love. At least as much as a twelve-year-old boy can be.

One notable piece of trivia from this era: Chunk, Ethan, and I started calling ourselves "The Bookhouse Boys," taking our name from the secret society of do-gooders on the show. We even started making a home for ourselves in the Maricopa Middle School library, an otherwise sparsely attended location on the school's campus. The librarian, a wild-haired ex-hippie named Mrs. Melville, encouraged our regular presence in the facility, engaging us in conversation about *Twin Peaks*, *Star Wars*, and other nerdy franchises. Of course, she also convinced us to check out books while we were there – usually J.R.R. Tolkien and Ray Bradbury, though we did consume novels by Orson Scott Card, Madeleine L'Engle, Piers Anthony, and (most importantly for our developing literary passions) Stephen King. It's important to note that we even ventured into the foreign territory of "banned books" by checking out the library's battered copies of a slim white book with a rainbow frame on the cover: J.D. Salinger's *Catcher in the Rye*.

Whether it was wizards, spaceships, haunted relics, or mentally unstable high school kids navigating the lonely streets of New York City, we were eager to devour all of Mrs. Melville's recommendations. To us, any fantastical adventure was an escape from the normalcy of our tedious middle school lives.

Why are these trivial details about *Twin Peaks* and library books important? Believe it or not, these seemingly incongruous puzzle pieces will later help illuminate the inspiration behind some of Call Field's quirkier moments – and even the band's various names.

David Lynch would be proud.

Two months after our little block party performance, there was a seismic shift in the world of rock music: Nirvana released its massive *Nevermind* album, and the stale, mechanical formula of pop radio suddenly collapsed in a flurry of distortion and aggressive songwriting. Almost overnight, the grit and integrity of classic rock were relevant to the mainstream media, and electric guitars once again captured the *zeitgeist*. It didn't matter if you wanted to call it grunge, punk, or just rock and roll – whatever it was, it was magical.

After months of endlessly listening to Kurt Cobain and company, I picked up Marina's electric guitar for the first time in the summer of 1992 and started toying around with it every afternoon while she was at soccer practice. Fortunately, with my experience playing bass and piano over the prior five years, I learned the basics of the instrument pretty quickly; after all, if you can learn how to play a power chord, the simple magic of a root note coupled with a fifth (along with a healthy dose of distortion) can make anything sound impressive. Of course, I had to follow our house rule dictating that "homework always comes first," but the rest of my afternoons and evenings were spent obsessively decoding the mysteries of that magical musical instrument.

The autumn months subsided like the crackling leaves falling from the oak trees outside my bedroom. Though our little section of Ojai never saw snow, the evenings turned colder and colder as the fall faded into winter. Temperatures dipped and dropped dozens of degrees lower than the summer months, and we bundled ourselves in layers of flannel (suddenly fashionable, thanks to the Seattle grunge movement) as we navigated through November into December. By the time Christmas rolled around, I found myself utilizing a portable heater in the garage while I thumped away on the various musical instruments that were at my disposal.

Christmas morning arrived on the chilly wings of winter, and our home on Lago de Paz Court suddenly sported frosty windowpanes to match the season. By the time that I woke up, the whole house had been filled with the scent of chocolate-chip pancakes and freshly roasted coffee. To me, that aroma – not cinnamon or mint – will always be the defining characteristic of Christmas. As I scrubbed my blurry eyes with the backs of my hands, I saw that the whole family was clad in the obnoxious kitsch of tartan red- and green-themed pajamas; when I appeared in the kitchen, dazed and sleepy-eyed, my mother handed me a fluffy Santa Claus hat.

"Come on," Mom commanded, shoving a cup of hot chocolate into my hands. "Let's go open some presents!"

With an enormous grin, she led the way into our den, like Rudolph on a foggy night. The rest of us followed her, half-awake and half-asleep, to the giant decorated Douglas fir that occupied the far corner of the room. Underneath the glittering and blinking tree, a few dozen presents sat tidily on display, waiting patiently to be opened by our family members.

Even though my father was raised Jewish – and had never celebrated a single Christmas until he started dating Mom – he embraced the yuletide spirit with admirable aplomb. Maybe it was because his own sizable belly shook like a bowlful of jelly, but Dad had a soft spot for Santa Claus and reindeer and shiny glass ornaments. It wasn't a betrayal of his Judaic roots, mind you, but a way to honor my mother's Catholic customs, too.

"There's enough room in our house for a menorah on the mantel and a fir tree by the fireplace," he would say.

While visitors might have been shocked by the juxtaposition of Jewish iconography with the tinsel trappings of noels and nativity scenes, our family melded the disparate decorations of each into something singularly Smith-ian. In our household, Hanukkah and Christmas coexisted like innocent friends rather than vicious enemies. To us, it didn't feel like a blasphemous paradox to find dreidels stuffed inside Santa Claus stockings. It was just the way my parents celebrated the holidays: as if each religion required equal reverence.

Prominently featured on the mantel next to our shiny brass menorah was another family heirloom: a Smith family *matryoshka* doll that my father's ancestors had brought with them from Russia decades before he was born. In the hazy fog of my early morning Christmas awakening, it struck me that perhaps I was a bit like that diminutive wooden figurine, cradling multiple aspects of myself in layers like the shells in a Russian nesting doll. In that regard, it didn't feel so far-fetched to be a Jew who celebrated Christmas and Hanukkah side-by-side. Those were lofty visions for a recently Bar Mitzvah-ed eighth-grader, but I desperately desired a sense of binding security from those intricately interwoven threads. I felt insecure enough in every other facet of my life.

One unintended side-effect of this dichotomy, however, was that I felt like I had one foot on an immobile dock and one on a moving ship. When my eyes traveled back and forth between the menorah and the Christmas tree, I realized that I didn't necessarily fit in with either side: I didn't feel entirely at-home with my peers in Torah school, nor did I fit in with my classmates at our predominantly Christian public school.

It wouldn't be fair to compare my isolated religious background to Ethan's experiences as a biracial kid in a small town, but growing up in a mixed-religion household helped me understand – in some small, limited capacity – what it might feel like to be torn between two warring worlds. I never felt as comfortable as my father did with this duality, but I just figured that it would come with time.

As he did on every Christmas morning, my dad played his well-worn copy of *The Beach Boys' Christmas Album*, the gentle crackle of the vinyl record complimenting the warmth emanating from our nearby fireplace. It was one of those idyllic, small-town Americana moments that Norman Rockwell captured so elegantly in his stylized paintings, and our family was the veritable picture of a happy household. Even without the dangling carrot of pristinely wrapped presents, we simply enjoyed each other's company and basked in the radiant glow of Christmas morning.

Of course, the inevitable Christmas curiosity crept in and we eventually took turns opening the presents that had been meticulously arranged underneath our twinkling tree. The stock market must have treated my parents well that autumn, because Mom and Dad went all-out with their gift-giving: Marina received an expensive designer purse with a leather exterior, my dad got two huge speakers for his stereo, and my mom ended up with a stunning diamond necklace that shot sparkles across the room as it reflected the glimmering glow of the fireplace.

When it came time to open my *big* present, Mom slid over an inordinately large, oblong box, snugly covered in myrtle green wrapping paper. As I slid my fingers under the sharp creases and unhooked the scotch tape that bound it together, I caught a glimpse of my parents anxiously watching me. My dad gave a huge, toothy grin, while my mom giddily clenched her teeth and raised her eyebrows in anticipation.

Finally done fidgeting with the wrapping, I tore into the green paper, opened the sand-colored cardboard box, and saw the most perfect present a kid could receive: a butterscotch-colored Fender Telecaster. Clearly, my parents must have noticed my ceaseless garage jamming over the preceding months, because there before me was a $500, genuine, American-made electric guitar.

"We figured you should have your very own instrument," Mom explained, "rather than borrow Marina's all the time."

"Do you like it?" Dad asked nervously.

I beamed up at them with a smile bigger than Santa's sleigh. "I *love* it!" I squealed, leaping up from the carpet to tightly squeeze my parents in a bear hug. Marina, too, sprang from the floor and joined our makeshift dog pile embrace, and the Smith family had another picture-perfect Norman Rockwell moment right there in the flickering radiance of the fireplace.

That shiny, new Fender Telecaster under the Christmas tree was a life-changing gift. Needless to say, I was forever indebted to Little Saint Nick – and my parents, of course – for delivering the coolest present a twelve-year-old kid could want:

My very own electric guitar.

More than the expensive gift, though, it was the love of my tight-knit family that moved me. In fact, I got a little teary-eyed in that green and red setting on Christmas morning. If ever there was a perfect family moment for the Smiths, that was it right there – amid the flickering of the fireplace and the warm smell of chocolate chip pancakes, basking in an overwhelming sense of love and security.

It *should* have been one of the most perfect moments of my childhood.

And yet...

And yet...

Despite the perfect glow of firelight and the giddy expressions on the faces of my family members, I felt something cold and dark moving within me – a cancerous emotion spreading stealthily through my chest. As I watched my dad and mom and sister in their almost cartoonish happiness, I recognized that I should have shared those same feelings. However, even in that flawless family moment, I felt light-years away from them. While my face might have produced a façade that symmetrically reflected their happiness, my heart twisted in on itself like a distorted carnival mirror. Somehow, I didn't feel worthy. I didn't feel like I belonged here... or anywhere, for that matter.

How could I possibly feel sad at such a happy time? I wondered to myself. *Life doesn't get more perfect than Christmas morning, right?*

It's hard for most people to grapple with the complexities of depression and mental illness as they begin to manifest in hearts and minds, and that challenge is even more exponential for preteens and teenagers. In many ways, I was walking in two worlds. On the surface, I seemed a happy-go-lucky overachieving middle school kid. But, underneath that, festering below the shallow exterior, I was quietly suffering.

Ironic as it might seem, the bells and whistles and tinsel and trimmings of Christmas morning only exacerbated the underlying darkness growing inside me.

I was a walking paradox: a sad kid on Christmas Day.

In that moment in time, I should have felt loved and safe and secure.

Instead, I felt helpless.

And alone.

CHAPTER NINETEEN

"Make It Good"

Months went by, as winter defrosted into spring and bloomed into summer and finally placated itself back into autumn. As we wrapped up our middle school experience, Chunk and Ethan and I looked boldly forward to high school – and the chance to reinvent ourselves as we crossed this strange, incomprehensible threshold into our teenage years. Little did we know, however, that high school isn't a fresh, unmarked chalkboard; rather, it's a stone tablet that shares your former scars and marks and etchings with a new, larger audience.

The biggest difference between middle school and high school is that high school students smell better. Otherwise, it's pretty much business as usual – although the homework is significantly more demanding. The same rules of attraction apply, with the gorgeous girls making moony eyes at the handsome boys, while the socially awkward kids sit moping on the sidelines. However, Chunk and I had developed a scheme to earn cultural capital at Ojai's Sespe Creek High School. We were going to join the football team.

I know, I know.

You're probably thinking to yourself, *Wait... Brian is the shy, sensitive type. He's not into sports. He isn't the kind of guy who would throw around a pigskin on the gridiron. There's no way Brian would play high school football.*

What can I say? I've been defying expectations my whole life.

Plus, I *really* didn't want to take a P.E. class.

I don't remember exactly what inspired our decision, but I have a feeling that we got the idea from an offhand comment made by one of our middle school PE teachers – something about how Chunk and I were built by God to be linemen. Basically, he was implying that we should use our height and weight for something productive: taller fat kids should do more than just be tall and fat. While the comment might have been a backhanded compliment, once the seed was planted in our minds, it germinated and blossomed into a full-blown mission. Sure enough, Chunk and I had continued our trajectory of physical growth throughout middle school. By the time that freshman year rolled around, we each surpassed the 200-pound mark, with broad shoulders and protruding chests that seemed to *almost* catch up with our enduring guts. We were on track to continue the Smith family legacy of big men with big appetites, but we also felt uncomfortable in our skin. For us, football seemed like a way to utilize our girth for a good cause. So, we signed up for the team immediately.

During the summer of 1993, we attended the first morning of football practice with heads held high, despite our trepidation. As we looked around the damp, glistening field, Chunk and I saw a smattering of incoming ninth-grade students, most of whom were dwarfed by our substantial bodies. The football coach eyed everyone suspiciously, but he contentedly provided an indiscriminate grunt when he reached the two Smith boys. For whatever reason, Coach Montaña decided to read through the names on his roster in reverse alphabetical order; I can't say for certain, but I'm pretty sure that he did this just to mess with our heads. As he made his way through the names on his checklist, he sized up each individual candidate and jotted down notes on his clipboard. When he got to the "S" section of the alphabet, Chunk and I stood a little straighter, shoulder-pads square and helmets stiffly pointed towards the sky.

"Smith, *comma*, Charles," Coach Montaña read aloud.

Chunk raised his hand. "Here, sir," he answered timidly.

As Coach examined Charles, I could tell that Montaña liked what he saw. He scribbled a few extra lines before flipping back to his roster.

Anxiously shuffling in place, I knew that I was next, and I anticipated Coach Montaña calling my name. He took his pencil, pointed at the succeeding student on his list, and began to read.

"Br…" he started to say.

I interjected, nervously spitting out my nickname. *"RICK*, sir," I said, unable to hide the slight quake in my voice.

A look of confusion came over Coach Montaña for a split-second. Clearly, he was not used to being cut off mid-sentence.

"Did you say… *Brick?"* the coach asked, slightly puzzled.

"Uhhh… no, sir," I responded tentatively. "My first name is Brian, but everyone calls me Rick."

Coach Montaña sized me up from behind the shield of his pitch-black sunglasses.

"Son," he said with a lazy drawl, "you're built like a brick wall. As far as I'm concerned, you will be *Brick* from this moment on – at least out here on the football field."

I smiled and nodded in affirmation as Coach Montaña coolly sauntered down the line to the next teammate.

And that, dear reader, is how I got my nickname. Henceforth (for the rest of my high school career, at least) I would be known as *"Brick"* Smith. And, though the name was not entirely flattering, I owned it. I came from a line of big men, and I accepted the fact that I was destined to become a large slab of flesh; however, the opportunity to use my heft as a pragmatic piece of the team's foundation felt like a chance to reinvent myself. I would never be the quarterback or the running back or the wide receiver of the Sespe Creek High School football team… but maybe, just *maybe*, I could be a brick wall, a lineman who played a vital role in the course of each game. Linemen never get any glory, but they are the pillars of a football squad – the ones who defend the quarterback and maintain a sacred wall of protection for the leader of the team.

For that reason, I had no qualms about becoming a *Brick*.

I managed to fly under the radar during the majority of my freshman year in high school, apart from the occasional embarrassing public praise from my teachers. Though music and football ate up a considerable amount of my time, Mom and Dad made sure that my education always came first; fortunately for them, I had dutifully developed into a diligent student by ninth grade, tediously taking copious notes in all my classes and perpetually studying for tests (even with nary a quiz or exam in sight). As exhausting as this regimented routine might have been for fourteen-year-old Brick, my parents wouldn't have had it any other way.

As my dad told me, "School is your job. You do well in school so that you can go to a good college and get your degree and learn the trade secrets for a profession that will be spiritually and financially rewarding. But you can't get from point A to point B in a timely fashion without following the straight line that's been laid out for you."

True to form, I started making my own trenches of paperwork on the dinner table every afternoon when I got home from football practice. We must have been quite the comical sight: Marina, my parents, and I all stationed in sections of the living room and dining room with various assortments of homework to keep us occupied. Of course, it's also hard to find an excuse for a break when you're surrounded by studious family members with stacks of papers even bigger and more intimidating than your own. *That*, my friends, is peer pressure at its finest.

The sole escape route that my parents found acceptable? Practicing music. If I needed a break from geometry proofs or thesis statements or geography worksheets, the only place that I could take a stretch break was the safe haven of our garage. There, amid the amplifiers and microphone stands and guitars, I could find my release.

Overwhelmed with homework? Sit at the piano.

Girl troubles getting you down? Pick up a guitar.

Need to decompress after football practice? Grab the bass and jam along with your favorite albums.

My parents wisely directed us to channel our break time into something productive, an activity that allowed us to develop our passions and skills into worthwhile talents. Mom and Dad were smart, and I repeatedly thanked them years later when Call Field finally started to make it in the musical big leagues.

Never underestimate how the seeds that you water will grow.

CHAPTER TWENTY

"Hold On, Dear Brother"

Though I was slowly (but surely) gaining confidence, I still had a long way to go before my social status would transform from invisible to ubiquitous, from *under the radar* to *in the spotlight*. I played football during fall semester and did track & field during the spring, so there was some visible recognition from my peers when I wore my jersey on game days; however, I still did my best to avoid being noticed by my classmates. While I had clearly grown from my younger days, I still felt self-conscious – about my weight, my appearance, and my social awkwardness. Because of these insecurities, I tried to disappear into crowds at every occasion and avoided public outings at all costs.

The problem, though, is that it becomes increasingly hard to hide in high school when you're over six feet tall and weigh *well* over two hundred pounds. While my mind might have been sharper, a little like George from *Of Mice and Men*, I still felt like the tall, lumbering Lennie. Despite the fact I was growing into myself, physically changing from a boy to a man, I was uncomfortable in my own skin and struggling to fit into my social surroundings.

I might have been content with this sheepish trend of invisibility for an indefinite period of time, but Marina had something else in mind, a plan that would quickly change everything for me and Chunk – and even Ethan. As my first year in high school approached its end, we started seeing notices crop up for the school's annual talent show. I thought nothing of it, but (unbeknownst to me) Marina had signed us up for an audition. As she explained it, she wanted to go out in a blaze of glory: she had already been accepted to UC Berkeley (my dad's alma mater), and she wanted one last grand public performance before she left us for northern California.

What better way to go out in style than to rock the high school talent show?

When she first informed us, Chunk and I were mortified. Sure, we had played the Fourth of July block party a few summers before, but this was something completely different: people we actually *knew* would see us play. Though Marina was popular and well-liked at our high school, Chunk and I were almost invisible; unlike my sister, we chose to lead nondescript lives that would provide us with the anonymity that we so desperately desired. Playing the school's talent show would destroy that comfortable inconspicuousness and thrust us unwillingly into the limelight. I can't speak for Chunk, but I know that I simply didn't feel ready for that at the tender age of fourteen.

Marina was a smart one, though. When we initially balked at her suggestion, she went straight to Dad and Uncle Jeff, explaining how she needed Chunk and me to do this one measly favor for her.

"*Really*," she reasoned, "they owe me for *all* the hours we've spent together practicing in the garage when I could have been hanging out with my friends. I should've been enjoying my youth and living the life of a teenager, not babysitting these boys."

Subsequently, Uncle Jeff and Dad sat us down and explained that we really didn't have any choice in the matter.

"Besides," Uncle Jeff reasoned, "what's the point of developing a talent if you can't share it with the world?"

Though our fears might have gotten the best of us at first, Chunk and I knew that Uncle Jeff and Marina were right. We had spent far too many hours honing our chops to keep our musical prowess tucked away in the garage. It was time for us to share our talent with the world.

Because Marina was the oldest and most assertive of the group, she took the helm of our little ship and started picking out potential cover songs for us to play. With her as our leader, we tackled a wide variety of tunes, struggling to find the perfect soundtrack for our talent show performance. We rammed our way through the Ramones' "I Wanna' Be

Sedated," blasted through Heart's "Barracuda," sweated through Weezer's "Undone (The Sweater Song)," and finessed Fleetwood Mac's "Go Your Own Way." We tried a few more contemporary tunes, notably Sheryl Crow's "Leaving Las Vegas" and The Breeders' "Cannonball," but those songs didn't have the aggressive melodies that Marina needed to show off her vocal chops. Though female singers often get relegated to the Joni Mitchell, soft-rock stereotypes, there are women out there who can really, truly *rock*.

Even as a senior in high school, Marina was one of those women.

Though Chunk and I could decently carry a tune, Marina had a beautiful, confident voice that commanded power and grit beyond her seventeen years of age. I might have been the more proficient musician by that point, but she was – without a doubt – the *singer* of the family. Marina had undeniably inherited the same passionate voice that I witnessed my dad deliver on the day that he performed with the Stuttering Surfers at his fortieth birthday party. She was clearly her father's daughter.

We spent a lot more time toiling away in the garage in the weeks leading up to the audition, and we were a pretty tight trio by the time tryouts rolled around. Still, though, Marina wasn't quite satisfied with what she was hearing. Two days before the auditions, she told us about her concerns.

"Something's missing," Marina sighed, pacing up and down in front of her amp.

Chunk and I were surprised. "What are you talking about?" I asked her defensively. "We sound great! You're killing it with your vocals, and we're totally in the pocket over here."

"No, that's not it," she responded. "You guys are solid. It's just…"

"Well, what is it?" Chunk asked, his eyebrows arched anxiously.

"I think we need a lead guitarist," Marina clarified. "All these songs are turning out decently, but they sound like demos. Like works-in-progress. What we need is someone who can really *shred* to help round out our lineup."

She paused, and then stared sullenly over at us. "I don't have any friends who play instruments, though. Do you guys know anyone who can do the lead guitar thing...?"

Chunk and I looked at each other and shared a smile.

"What about Ethan?" I asked.

"*Ethan...?*" Marina wasn't sold on the idea. "Like your little friend, Ethan? *That* Ethan...?"

"Yeah," Chunk assured her. "Have you ever heard him play before? He's good. *Really* good. We've been playing together in jazz band and orchestra since sixth grade, but he's a big classic rock fan. I think he knows every guitar solo the Beatles ever recorded."

"Seriously?" Marina was doubtful. "Ethan *Hidalgo?*"

Though I didn't know for certain that Ethan would be interested in playing a bunch of cover songs with a rough-around-the-edges garage band, I figured it was worth a shot to invite him.

"Let's give him a call," I suggested. "It can't hurt to try, right?"

It turned out that Ethan wasn't just interested – he was earnestly excited by the prospect of practicing with a full rock band. Thus far, his experiences playing music had been limited to lonely bedroom jam sessions with his dad's record collection or tamely maneuvering jazz numbers with the school orchestra. However, none of these experiences brought him the fulfillment that he desperately wanted. Not fifteen minutes after I called him, Ethan showed up at our door with his Gibson SG, his Marshall amplifier, and a suitcase full of pedals.

"So, where do I plug in?" he asked.

Marina was skeptical. As she looked down at Ethan's rig, his skinny arms assembling the equipment like a seagull building its nest, she didn't seem very impressed.

"Are you sure about this?" she mouthed to me quietly.

"*Trust me,*" I whispered back.

When Ethan finished assembling his gear, he turned to the three Smiths and nodded his head. "What's first?" he asked, his eyes wide and eager.

"How about we tackle Weezer?" Marina suggested. "Do you know the 'Sweater Song' riff, Ethan?"

"Of course," he muttered matter-of-factly.

"Want me to start us off?" Chunk asked.

"Go for it," Marina said.

With four clicks of his drumsticks, Chunk set the tempo for our first attempt. Right on cue, Ethan started the familiar arpeggio on his electric guitar, the notes perfectly locked in tempo and exhibiting the right hint of grit for the song.

Marina looked over at me with a pleased look, and then started singing the first verse of the song. By the time that we hit the chorus, when Ethan stomped on his distortion pedal and the instruments exploded in a furious celebration, we all felt the electricity in the air. Something magical was happening to us, transforming us – and this added musical element made our little family band sound complete in a way that we couldn't have anticipated.

The real test, however, was the guitar solo in the bridge. If Ethan could nail that part, he would seal the deal. True to form, he lunged into the solo, his body lurching back and forth while his shaggy dark hair shrouded his face. Not only did Ethan perfectly recreate Rivers Cuomo's guitar solo, he somehow found a way to *improve* upon Weezer's original recording, inserting a hint of Chuck Berry into the band's indie pop tune. And, when we arrived at the song's final sing-along choruses, Ethan started yelling into the closest available microphone with respectably in-tune vocals. By the time that our impromptu performance crescendoed into its distortion-filled conclusion, we all felt unequivocally elevated and empowered by what had just transpired.

As the sounds of our instruments faded out like waves cresting back to the shore, the only audible noise was the electric hum of our amplifiers permeating the room. Suddenly, Chunk started laughing uncontrollably. I followed suit, guffawing gracelessly, before Ethan and Marina joined in our chorus of cackles.

"Holy crap!" Marina yelled out between a non-stop series of laughs. "Why didn't you guys tell me that we had *Eric Clapton, Jr.*, right in front of us *this whole time?*"

"Dude!" I yelled at Ethan with an immeasurably wide grin. "DUDE!"

"Does this mean I'm in…?" Ethan asked hesitantly through the locks of dark hair obscuring his vision.

Marina looked him straight in the eyes. "Definitely," she said.

And that is how Ethan Hidalgo officially joined our band.

In a band, you'll find that there's a natural, innate chemistry with certain musicians. Because Chunk, Marina, and I had cultivated our camaraderie over the course of several years, we had already worked our way through the awkward mishaps that plague all beginning bands; Ethan, however, just stepped right in and seamlessly completed our lineup. His talent as a guitarist and his shared love of classic rock helped him gel with us in a way that would have been implausible for any other teenage guitar player. It was pretty miraculous, all things considered – especially since Ethan, Chunk, and I were only freshmen in high school.

Nonstop jam sessions filled the next two evenings, with our family trio helping Ethan find his position in our well-established lineup. Mind you, it wasn't difficult, considering Ethan's already prodigious talent, but we also wanted to sound as polished as possible for our big audition. This was, as Marina continuously reminded us, her last chance to fulfill her rock star dreams before she left for college. We exhausted ourselves preparing for the audition, but we also had the luxury of years' worth of practice together; Ethan was simply the last missing piece in our musical puzzle.

It seemed strange, then, that we were actually nervous when we auditioned the following day. Though we would only be playing in front of a small panel of teachers and students, it seemed as if this was the *moment of truth*, our "make-or-break" chance to prove ourselves. While Ethan, Chunk, and I couldn't stop pacing outside the auditorium, Marina seemed completely cool and collected. Perhaps her age had given her confidence and wisdom. Or, perhaps, she just knew that we were going to nail the audition. In any case, she was our undisputed leader, the one who had united us together and who would lead us into battle.

It wasn't a lance or bayonet, however, that she held in her hands when she called us inside. It was a blue gel pen. "Hey, Brian!" she yelled from the darkness of the theater, beckoning me to join her at the front. "It's our turn to sign in!"

Leaving Chunk and Ethan behind in the theater seats, I meekly grabbed my frayed black Patagonia backpack and followed my sister to the front of the stage, where a clipboard perched on the elevated platform. Marina began to write her name, froze, and then sheepishly looked up at me.

"Oh, crap," she muttered, running her hands up to her thick, coiled hair. "What are we going to call ourselves?"

On the clipboard in front of her, she had started to sign her name, *"Marina and..."*

"The Smiths...?" I suggested.

"Too 80s," Marina muttered. "What about *Marina and the Munchkins...?*"

"This isn't the *Wizard of Oz*, dummy," I said, rolling my eyes.

Marina scowled at me. "Well, then, what do *you* suggest, jerk?"

I looked at the paper, looked back at Ethan and Chunk, and then smiled mischievously at her. "Write '*Marina and the Bookhouse Boys*' on the paper," I told her.

"The *Book... House... Boys...?*" she asked, knitting her eyebrows in confusion.

"It's *Bookhouse*," I told her. "One word, not two. Trust me. The guys will get a kick out of it."

Marina shrugged and scribbled our band's new name: *Marina and the Bookhouse Boys*. It had a nice ring to it.

We all took our seats and waited for the auditions to begin.

As most people can attest, high school talent-show acts run the gamut from inspiring prodigies to embarrassingly painful hacks. That afternoon, we sat through audition after audition, ranging from flag troops to singer-songwriters to tap dancers to (I kid you not) a magician wearing a green sequined jumpsuit. Some of my peers were exceptional and some were terrible, but most of the acts fell somewhere in-between. When it came time for us to take the stage for our audition, our confidence was bolstered by the not-so-impressive competition. We plugged in, checked our volume, and gave Marina the all-clear sign.

Our fearless leader approached the microphone and began. "Hey, everyone," she said. "I'm Marina Smith. And these are the Bookhouse Boys. We're going to play a song for you now."

With that, Chunk clicked his drumsticks together to count off the song.

One. Two. Three. Four.

And we proceeded to rock.

I'm not sure if it was the mediocre acts that preceded us, or the fact that we were actually pretty darn good, but the judges were hypnotized from the very first chord. Ultimately, we decided to play Weezer's "Undone (The Sweater Song)," just as we had at our first rehearsal with Ethan a few days earlier; and, like that initial practice, it was a magical moment. Merely by looking at the wide eyes and open mouths of the judges, I knew we had them in the palms of our hands. They smiled, nodded, scribbled notes, and seemed genuinely entranced by our playing. After we finished, they clapped enthusiastically, and we gave an awkward bow.

As we started the process of packing up our equipment, we couldn't contain our excitement. We had just auditioned for the Sespe Creek High School talent show – and the judges seemed to have *loved* us. What more validation could we possibly need in life?

It came as no surprise the following day when we saw that *Marina and the Bookhouse Boys* was the first act listed on the "congratulations" notices posted around campus.

We came, we saw, we passed the audition.

A few short weeks later, in late May of 1994, Marina and the Bookhouse Boys played the annual Sespe Creek High School talent show. We had come a *long* way from the little kids jamming in our garage and putting on a Fourth of July performance on our front lawn. Though I don't remember every small detail of the evening's performance, one thing was for certain: it was nothing short of victorious.

The teachers and students who ran the talent show made the decision to place our band in the final slot of the evening's line-up. At first, we felt slighted; however, after listening distantly to an hour and a half of mostly mediocre student performances, we gradually realized that we had been strategically placed at the end of the show to provide a grand-slam finale for an otherwise forgettable evening. Anxiously, we waited in the adjacent green room, reclining in the creaky theater seats that had been patched up with felt and duct tape. Carnegie Hall, it was not.

But we didn't care. This was going to be our world premiere, and we were ready to show everyone that the Bookhouse Boys were a force to be reckoned with.

Finally, the time arrived for us to take our places backstage. We followed the glow-in-the-dark Painter's Tape that guided our way from the green room to the main stage, and waited in the wings for the penultimate act (an impressive hip-hop dance troupe) to finish their performance. As we shuffled around awkwardly in our designated spots, Marina put her arms around me and Chunk.

"Should we have, like, a team *'hurrah'* or something?" Marina asked us. "You know, like a group huddle? And then we all shout *'team'* or something?"

"This isn't soccer practice," I said to her.

"I know that, dork," she scolded me. "But we should still say something, right?"

"Whatever," Ethan chimed in, waving his hand casually. "Let's just do it. It can't hurt, right?"

"*Exactly*," Marina asserted with an exaggerated gesture, holding her palms up to the rafters above us. "Thank you, Ethan." She scanned the faces of the three boys huddled around her. "What should we chant?" she asked us.

Ethan, Chunk, and I looked at each other with stumped looks on our faces.

And then inspiration hit.

"I've got it," I announced to the band. "On the count of three, we'll all say '*Cooper.*'"

"'*Cooper...?*'" Marina asked quizzically, her eyebrows scrunched tightly together.

"Yes!" I shouted to the group. "Like *Agent Cooper.*"

Marina didn't get it. "Agent Cooper?" she asked.

"YES!" I repeated. "Agent Dale Cooper."

Again, she looked at me with that familiar confused expression. Ethan and Chunk, however, glowed and nodded their heads

"It's from that TV show, *Twin Peaks,*" I clarified.

Still, I was met with the same perplexed look from my sister.

"Because we're the *Bookhouse Boys...*" I explained. "We got our name from *Twin Peaks*. And Cooper was the hero of the show. So, we should all say '*Cooper.*'"

Marina just sighed and shook her head. "You boys are so weird."

The four of us huddled in a ring and put our hands in front of us, our forty fingers nervously hovering over each other in the middle of the circle.

"*COOPER!*" we yelled together, flailing our hands in unison towards the darkened ceiling.

Right on cue, the lights dimmed, and the audience erupted into applause for our predecessors. We hurriedly took our places next to the instruments and amplifiers that had been backset behind the tableaux curtains of the stage. The announcer, a high-profile senior at Sespe Creek High School (whose name I can't for the life of me remember), made some canned jokes before providing a brief introduction for our band.

"Comprised of three freshman boys and one senior girl," he began, "this final act for the evening is here to show that even the oddest of pairings can result in some great music. Ladies and gents, please welcome to the stage... *Marina Smith and the Bookhouse Boys!*"

The curtains sluggishly lifted, and the audience was slowly revealed before us like the unveiling of a game show prize. As soon as the drapes hit the rafters, Ethan started plucking the familiar guitar arpeggio of Weezer's "Sweater Song," and the rest of us followed suit. We skipped the tune's spoken-word intro and plunged right into the first verse, with Marina's smoky voice filling every corner of the theater. Her vocals carried confidently with each succeeding line, as Ethan, Chunk, and I ably created the foundation for her to enchant the crowd. The main spotlight was centered on her tall, glamorous frame; she strummed her electric guitar with authority and stomped the bruised floorboards with her high-heeled shoes. She looked and sounded like a rock star, and we recognized that we were in the presence of greatness.

The first verse progressed fluidly and smoothly, without a hitch or a hang-up. And when we hit the chorus of the song, kicking in the distortion on the electric guitars, the crowd erupted into a frenzy of cheers and whistles and howls. By the time Ethan stepped forward into the spotlight to wail on his guitar solo, his wild hair flurrying around his head like a dark halo, the crowd was *ours*. They were spellbound through the last ringing guitar chord, as the humming electricity of amplifiers cascaded and ultimately faded into nothingness.

For a split-second, a stunned silence fell onto the crowd like a light rainfall. Within moments, though, the audience of our peers, parents, friends, and faculty erupted into the torrential sounds of applause and celebration. We stepped forward, soaking in this magical moment, before taking our bows and leaving the stage. Eventually, the clapping subsided, and the stage was left vacant and empty. The student MC thanked everyone for coming and wished the crowd a good evening.

And it was over.

Backstage, we literally jumped up and down, all semblance of coolness or maturity lost in the thrill of the performance high. We hugged and laughed and screamed and let our bodies shake uncontrollably.

Though we were usually reserved, even-tempered high school students, we might as well have been preschoolers manically dancing along to a Disney film.

Ultimately, it was Marina who broke the spell and ushered us back into reality. "Let's go meet our adoring public," she commanded. So, we followed our fearless leader, leaving our amplifiers and instruments – our suits of armor – on the unattended high school stage and walked out into the crisp May evening. Watching the throngs of bodies filter out of the auditorium exits might normally have made me feel anxious and insignificant, but that night I felt like royalty observing the movements of the peasants below.

A few of Marina's friends saw her and immediately ran over to where we were standing. They all took turns squealing and giving Marina oversized hugs, as if they were trying to squeeze the rock star magic out of her slender limbs. A few of the older students patted the band members on the back and congratulated us on a great performance, but all the eyes were on the glowing Marina. She laughed and held court with her friends and acquaintances, while Chunk, Ethan, and I contentedly stood on the sidelines. We weren't the ones conjuring and charming in the center-stage spotlight, but we were simply happy to have been part of the sorcery.

I learned a vital rock and roll lesson that night: *the lead singer of the band will almost always become the focal point of an audience's love and affection.* It was a lesson that I would see enacted over and over in the next six years, from high school talent shows to college frat parties to small clubs to headlining venues. Though a band is a multilayered unit comprised of various cogs and gears, the lead singer inevitably receives the lion's share of attention. Like the pitcher or quarterback of a sports team, the primary vocalist is the most visible member of the band.

But how successful is a quarterback without his linemen or a pitcher without his infield crew?

The old aphorism says that it "takes a village to raise a child" – but it also takes a full band to showcase a lead singer's talents. Remember that the next time you're fawning over the frontman or frontwoman of your favorite group.

That being said, I was actually *okay* hiding in the shadows, standing twenty feet from stardom. With my introverted disposition, it was enough of a victory to simply perform in front of a colossal crowd. In that regard, I was content being a brick, a pillar, a lineman, a bass player. Though I wouldn't always be this modest and egoless, I was so smitten with the exaltation of performing with a band – especially one in such a celebratory, victorious setting – that nothing else mattered to me.

I wish that I could have stayed that humble forever.

When the chattering crowds eventually dispersed and the hangers-on stopped hanging out, we made the sad, lonely trek back to the empty stage to pack up our gear. In sharp contrast to the suffocating, celebratory mood that immediately followed our performance, the pack-up and load-out felt strangely anticlimactic. This was another eye-opening experience for me: rock stars never talk about loading their own equipment, doing the heavy lifting of amps, and roaming through empty halls after a show. As with everything else in life, illusion and reality held strikingly different expectations. The naïve rock and roll tropes of never-ending love and adoration frequently fail to describe the occupational hazard of lonely isolation that comes with the job.

Fully spent after our performance and the revelry that followed, we unobtrusively wrapped up our cables and packed up our instruments. Throughout it all, Marina and the other guys were strangely quiet. We each broke out in an occasional chuckle as we reflected on the earlier magic of the evening, but these outbursts were followed by a hushed silence that immediately consumed all of us. This strangely isolated and weirdly intimate time contrasted sharply with the lush celebration of just a few minutes before; it felt like an emotional hangover after a heavy night of carousing. Despite the captivity of the quiet, we soldiered on and loaded our equipment into the trusty Econoline van that we had borrowed from Uncle Jeff.

Exhausted and depleted, we all packed into the van and drove home in silence.

When Marina and I arrived back at our house on Lago de Paz after dropping off Chunk and Ethan, we barely made it through the front door before Mom and Dad enveloped us in tight, smothering hugs. They could hardly contain their excitement, and they kept gushing over how proud they were of their two talented children.

"You guys were rock stars up there!" shouted my dad.

"And you sounded so professional," Mom chimed in. "It was like watching a real band on that little stage!"

"It looks like you guys inherited Uncle Jeff's musical genes!" Dad beamed proudly.

Mom and Dad rhapsodized about our performance for at least ten minutes before they relented and the celebratory family congregation in our crowded kitchen dispersed. Our parents let out contented sighs, turned off the florescent kitchen lights, and let us trudge back to our respective bedrooms.

Even with an event as brief as our one-song performance, I was exhausted. The emotional and psychological energy expended on the evening left me feeling spent. While the talent show hadn't been as grueling or violent as the previous season's football practices, I could feel my wearied soul tugging me towards the safe harbor of my twin-sized bed. I didn't even bother brushing my teeth. I slipped off my jeans, wrenched off my sweaty t-shirt, and climbed into the heavenly cushion of my comforter.

That night, I slept the contented sleep of a rock and roll superstar. It didn't matter that my fame was relegated to the small fishbowl of my high school – I felt an emotional high and sense of accomplishment that I've rarely captured in the years since.

This was my redemptive reward for all the years of unending practice and toiling away in my garage.

And it felt magical.

CHAPTER TWENTY-ONE

"Here She Comes"

A ll things considered, the last month of my freshman year was relatively anticlimactic. After our majestic performance at the school's talent show, I walked around campus a little prouder and a lot lighter. Every congratulatory comment from my classmates bolstered my swelling sense of self-confidence. For once, I inhabited my large frame and *owned* it, in the same way that I had seen Dad and Uncle Jeff use their physical presence as a buoy, rather than an anchor. I was growing outward, rather than recoiling inward.

Appropriately enough, as my body started taking a more athletic shape from hours sweating on the football field and the track, I even started sprouting up higher, growing to an impressive 6'3" by mid-June. For the record, I haven't grown an inch since then, but I don't think I'll ever feel taller than I did walking down the Sespe Creek halls in the weeks after our talent show performance.

When the end of the school year rolled around, I got to watch Marina walk across the stage at the Sespe Creek High School commencement ceremony. She was a dominating presence at graduation, giving a top-notch valedictorian speech that blended humor and sentiment expertly in a captivating concoction. Even after all those years playing music together in our garage, I don't know if I've ever been prouder of Marina than I was seeing the spellbound audience hanging on her every word. She might have been a rock star for five minutes at the school's talent show and a stellar athlete for four years on the soccer field, but her true crowning achievement was standing atop the makeshift stage in her maroon gown and enchanting thousands of people from behind the locus of an unadorned brown podium.

Marina inspired me to reach for the same heights that she soared. I promised myself that I would follow in her footsteps in three short years and take center stage at my own high school graduation. I wanted to continue her tradition of excellence while establishing myself as a unique, independent individual – which is not always an easy task when you grow up in the shadow of such a powerful presence. Nevertheless, her victory was *our family's* victory, and we shared in the celebration of her success. I was proud of my big sister.

Best of all, it was the end of the school year and the beginning of summer – a time that promised new beginnings and new adventures. Alas, my celebratory spirit was short-lived. Though summer always conjures the connotation of freedom, frivolity, and unfettered fun, overachieving high school students rarely get to enjoy a full, unencumbered vacation. As much as I counted down the months and weeks and days and hours until the end of the regular school year, I also recognized that I would be facing a new challenge the week after my sister's graduation...

That's when the dreaded evil of summer school would rear its ugly head.

Now, let me state for the record that I did not take summer school classes because I was credit deficient or in need of remediation; rather, I enrolled in summer school so that I could free up more space in my schedule for the coming school year. In recent years, budget cuts have minimized the ability of public schools to offer summer courses for the purpose of acceleration; however, in the more monetarily stable economy of the 1990s, high school students could actually take summer school classes to "get ahead." In my case, I knew that I needed to knock out an extraneous, uninteresting graduation requirement in order to squeeze jazz band into my class schedule for the following school year.

And that's how I ended up taking college-prep Chemistry in the summer of 1994. After a beautiful three-day weekend, in which the promise of summer tantalized me with its golden sunshine and bolstering warmth, I returned to the stuffy and claustrophobic classrooms of Sespe

Creek High School for the beginning of summer school. When I walked onto campus on that depressing Monday morning, I knew that I would be voluntarily giving up my freedom for the sake of academics. So, as I joined the throngs of unenthusiastic high school students in the school's cafeteria, I prepared myself for the six-week doom ahead of me – and waited patiently for a stay of execution.

As luck would have it, I was one of the fortunate few whose name was called from the waiting list. It was like winning the lottery in reverse: instead of receiving a monetary prize, I was burdened with the gift of extra schoolwork. With a strange mixture of defeat and duty, I grabbed my backpack and headed to the classroom where Chemistry would be taught that summer school session. I sulked glumly through the classroom door, where the teacher, Mrs. Marsh, directed traffic and assigned seats.

"And you are Brian Smith, correct?" she asked, her glasses slightly askew on the bridge of her nose.

"Yes, ma'am," I answered. "Though I actually go by 'Rick.' Just so you know."

"Duly noted, *Rick*. You will be sitting in the back-right corner," she directed, pointing to an empty seat on the far side of the room. She squinted her eyes, as she scanned her makeshift seating chart. "You will be right next to… ah… Serena Rios."

I looked across the classroom, where I saw the golden glow of the beautiful girl who had haunted my English classes since middle school. Her flawless, tanned legs stretched out underneath the rugged confines of her desk, and her bare shoulders hinted at the sheer perfection of every inch of her skin.

Maybe I had won the lottery after all.

Though I generally wasn't a fan of science classes – the periodic table held no romance for my adolescent heart – I was pleasantly surprised by how smoothly class went during those first few hours. Mrs. Marsh was a cynical, sardonic woman with a deadpan delivery, and she did her best to make the less-than-thrilling subject matter engaging and accessible. My dad had warned me that her demeanor took some getting used to, but he also assured me she would make the torture of summer school a little less painful. Sometimes, it pays to have your parent on staff at your school: you get the scoop on (and some of the gossip about) your prospective teachers.

My summer school classmates were an odd juxtaposition. Half of the students had failed the previous semester and needed to make up the course for graduation, while the other half was comprised of go-getters (like myself) who wanted to get ahead for the coming year. Because of this, we were a motley crew of individuals, some of us diligently taking notes while others despondently stared off into space. We had slackers, stoners, and surfers – side-by-side nerds, never-do-wells, and nobodies. It was quite an eclectic mixture, but also a pretty accurate representative sampling of Sespe Creek High School's student body.

The most important student body, however, was the one sitting directly to my right: Serena Rios. Though we had never carried on an actual conversation before, I had studied her from afar – almost as if she were the most famous celebrity in the SCHS graduating class of 1997. I knew that she was an Honors student with a challenging schedule packed as tightly as mine; I knew that she was a star on the freshman girls soccer team; I knew that she wore a crucifix that dangled tantalizingly near the valley of her clavicle; and I knew that she frequently wore her long, honey-blonde hair down, letting it cascade gloriously down her bare shoulders.

I also knew that she didn't know I existed.

Or so I thought.

Mrs. Marsh spent the first hour of class examining the course's interminable syllabus. When she finally finished that exhaustive (and exhausting) review, Mrs. Marsh passed out an introductory worksheet listing a wide variety of environmental issues that she expected us to match up with chemical antecedents. She instructed us to work with a partner sitting next to us, then set a timer for five minutes; as the class erupted into a small storm of conversation (some of it chemistry-related, some of it decidedly *not*), Serena turned to her left and set her eyes on my sizable frame.

Oh, my god, I thought to myself in a moment of panic. *She's looking at me.*

"Hey, Rick," she called to me nonchalantly.

Oh, my god, I thought to myself. *She knows my name.*

Serena cocked her head to the side and squinted her hazel eyes. "You're Marina Smith's little brother, right?"

This wasn't the first time that I had been recognized by my familial relationship with my big sister, nor would it be the last. It was, however, the first time that I would carry on a conversation with the gorgeous Serena Rios. In this circumstance, I had no problem capitalizing on the fame of my older sibling.

"Uh... yes," I answered succinctly (and not entirely confidently).

"I played with her on the soccer team last year," Serena explained. "Well, technically, I only *practiced* with her. She was on varsity and I was stuck on the frosh-soph team. But she was always really nice to the younger girls. Some of the upperclassmen were pretty condescending to the freshmen, but Marina always treated us with respect. I appreciated that."

Astoundingly, Serena was even prettier up close than she was from across the classroom (which had been my only vantage point and frame of reference for the last few years). Her blonde hair seemed more honey-colored, with dark hints of hazelnut streaking underneath the surface layers, and her golden skin seemed perfectly shaded to match her sun-kissed hair. It was hard not to stare at her perfectly defined features, the smooth slope of her nose and the soft curves of her cheeks. However, I also knew that staring at her face too long was like staring at the sun – destined to end with a blinding awkwardness. So, though I was tempted to simply gaze adoringly at her, I turned my attention back to the dull black-and-white terms on the Xeroxed handout before me.

Serena, however, was not quite done making small talk.

"Did you play with her at the talent show thing last month?" she asked, gently tapping her pencil on the cold, unflinching desktop.

I responded affirmatively and we continued to chitchat about the thrill of live performances. As it turned out, Serena had been taking voice lessons since elementary school, and had been performing at recitals (mostly musical theater kind of stuff) for the last few years.

"I've never done any singing with a live band, though," she added. "I definitely need to add that to my bucket list."

Note to self, I thought, *find a way to play music with the hot girl sitting next to you.*

Our conversation flowed more naturally than I would have anticipated. For all my years as an awkward, overweight, socially anxious kid, I had always felt insecure about my ability to communicate with my peers. Apart from the Bookhouse Boys, I didn't really have many friends, nor did I have an easy time talking with strangers… especially attractive ones of the opposite gender. There was something about Serena, though, that set me at ease, that simultaneously made me feel comfortable and confident – despite the obvious discrepancy in our popularity at Sespe Creek High School.

Much to my surprise, Serena was the popular girl who didn't act like a popular girl, the hot girl who didn't constantly remind everyone how much more attractive she was than her peers. In that regard, Serena was an anomaly in the world of high school students: she could navigate multiple worlds flawlessly, making herself equally at home with jocks, popular kids, and (apparently) socially awkward nerds like me.

Despite every early indication that summer school would be a treacherous, painful experience, it was looking like Chemistry might not be so bad after all.

We soldiered on through summer school, deciphering moles and mass and molecules. As we worked our way through the Chemistry curriculum, Serena and I found ourselves building our own bonds – though they were emotional more than molecular. Our lab partner chitchat easily segued into non-school-related discussions, and I found myself comfortably conversing with her on a regular basis. Still, though, I didn't see any reciprocity of my massive crush: while she might have laughed at my jokes and listened to my didactic explanations, there was no gleam in her eyes that even faintly resembled adoration.

That changed, however, with one snide comment from a classmate.

Marcus Huskey was an obnoxious bruiser of a kid, perpetually smirking and squinting and making malicious remarks at the right volume for all his classmates to hear. He was simultaneously bulky and squat, like God had smashed together the clay from which Marcus was molded until the kid ended up like a cross between Napoleon and a WWE wrestler. Marcus's build came from his time as a lineman on the Sespe Creek football team. Despite his membership on the squad, he was more tolerated than respected – someone whose misogynistic and racist rants tended to isolate, rather than unite, the folks around him. Of course, Marcus wasn't sharp enough to catch the fact that his comments were consistently met with an uncomfortable silence; as a result, he developed a false sense of regard and an arrogant sense of entitlement. Throughout most of summer school, he had kept his insults aimed at the teacher or his lab partner or his fellow football players. However, it wasn't long before he got too comfortable and started making easy targets out of his other classmates.

Between units on covalent bonds and stoichiometry, Mrs. Marsh took a little detour and led us through a mini-unit on her favorite topic: dominant and recessive genes. I don't know how the heck our teacher managed to integrate Gregor Mendel and heredity into a *Chemistry* class, but Mrs. Marsh took every opportunity to weave her passion – genetics – into the seemingly unrelated field of chemistry. Maybe it was because she had a petite framed poster of Mendel on her classroom wall next to the periodic table; or, maybe it was because she was lazy and wanted to recycle curriculum from her biology course. Who knows? In any case, I've learned over the years that high school teachers can pretty much manipulate the mandatory adopted course syllabus to include all kinds of curricular diversions. As long as teachers cover what they *need* to cover, everything else is fair game. Go figure.

Anyway, though technically a subject covered in *Biology* class, genetics somehow ended up temporarily invading Mrs. Marsh's summer school Chemistry course. During an off-the-cuff lecture on the Principles of Inheritance, she discussed how certain traits like earlobes and tongue rolling and whistling – and even depression – could be passed down from parents to children.

"Some of you," Mrs. Marsh explained, "might find yourselves looking at your own skin tones. Ask yourself: does my skin look my mother's? Or does it look like my father's?"

"As long as your skin is white, it doesn't matter who you got it from," Marcus smarmily spat out.

Mrs. Marsh soldiered on, either unaware of Marcus's comment, or unwilling to address it in front of the class. "Sometimes," she explained, "you might find that your skin tone is a blend of your two parents. If a mother has lighter skin and a father has darker skin, then you might inherit traits of each and find yourself with a shade somewhere in the middle."

Marcus, who sat a few rows ahead of us on the right-hand side of the room, turned around to face Serena with his usual malicious smirk.

"Hey, Rios," he snarled at her with smug self-satisfaction. "She's talking about mutts like you. You're half-*beaner* and half-white, but you only *look* half-*beaner*."

The class went dead silent. I glanced over at Serena and saw her face turn bright red. Her eyes started to tear up and she tilted her head down.

I don't know what possessed me, but I suddenly found myself yelling back at him. "Better than being half-jackass and half-asshole like you, Marcus. Shut your *jack-hole* mouth and turn around."

The class erupted in a chorus of laughter, and Marcus shrank in his seat, as if he was trying to disappear into the plastic and corrugated steel of his desk. This time, it was Marcus whose face turned scarlet amidst the stares and stifled laughs of his classmates.

"*Mr. Smith and Mr. Huskey!*" our teacher scolded. "That is quite enough! I will see the both of you after class!"

With a furrowed brow and frenetic pace, Mrs. Marsh jabbed at the chalkboard, attempting to recover our attention from the momentary disruption. She continued her lecture, describing other hereditary traits, but my heart was beating too fast to concentrate on the lesson at hand.

"Thank you," a muted voice whispered closely.

I looked to my right, and saw Serena staring in my direction – with a grateful smile forming on her perfect lips. Once again, she mouthed the words "thank you" before turning her attention back to the teacher.

Though I had spent countless hours staring at Serena over the course of the preceding years, I saw something in her eyes at that moment that I hadn't witnessed before, an expression that looked like deep appreciation – or maybe even adoration.

For the rest of that day, I thought about that ambiguous expression in her eyes for those sweet (albeit brief) moments. Even after school, when Marcus and I sheepishly stood side-by-side in front of Mrs. Marsh's desk, I couldn't stifle the smile that crept across my lips every time I thought of how Serena had looked at me.

I had never felt so proud in my life.

CHAPTER TWENTY-TWO

"Then I Kissed Her"

In the aftermath of the "mutt" comment, Serena and I became something more than cold, clinical lab partners. Instead, we developed a natural, friendly rapport – like nerdy partners-in-crime, unified against the forces of boring lectures and tedious homework (and Marcus Huskey).

Summer school makes strange bedfellows, indeed.

Over the course of that sweltering season, we settled into a comfortable routine: working studiously during class, passing notes during the redundant lectures, walking home to her house after school, and working together on the seemingly endless hours of homework that awaited us each afternoon. While the first few study sessions were focused exclusively on catalysts and covalent bonds and chemical reactions, we eventually started exchanging small talk in-between the worksheets and homework assignments. There was never any flirting – or, if there was, I was too dense to catch on. Rather, our conversations mostly tended towards a shared love of 1980s John Hughes movies and pop-punk bands like Green Day and the Ramones.

Occasionally, though, our talks drifted into more personal territories. Serena opened up about her family life: her parents had divorced when we were in middle school, her mom and dad had started over with new spouses, and she found herself shuttling back and forth between different houses on alternating weeks. Though I had previously pegged Serena as a perfect girl with a perfect life, I was mistaken; she was complex and conflicted, like so many other troubled teenagers forced to grow up prematurely. There was also an unmistakable air of sadness that seemed to surround her like kicked-up dust on a dirt road. While her makeup and hair and skin and smile might have seemed flawless to me, she was clearly hurting on the inside – and in need of someone who could listen to her without judgment.

Believe it or not, beautiful girls are actually just normal human beings in disguise.

I didn't realize it at the time, but we had established a sturdy friendship during the six weeks of summer school. While a month and a half might not seem like enough time to build an enduring relationship between two young adolescents, the six and a half hours each day that we spent side-by-side forged our bond in a way that neither of us could have predicted. It didn't seem likely that a socially awkward, slightly overweight nerd like yours truly could thrive in the company of a breathtaking girl like Serena, but there we were – a dynamic duo battling against the evil forces of college-prep Chemistry.

On that final Friday of summer school, Serena and I triumphantly marched to her house, reveling in the fact that we had conquered our final exam – and defeated Chemistry in the process. Though we no longer had any homework to haunt our afternoons, she asked if I could walk her home. At the time, I didn't think anything of it; after all, walking to Serena's everyday was now part of our daily routine.

As I dropped my weathered black Patagonia backpack by the front door, I reached into the bag and pulled out a water bottle. All the while, Serena watched me closely, studying my movements while her right foot tapped rhythmically on the wood-paneled floor of her dining room.

"*Sooooo...*" she began hesitantly, drawing out the vowels like strings of bubblegum, "since we don't have any homework, do you want to stick around and watch a movie or something?"

I was taken off-guard by her proposal. As far as I could tell, we were "work friends" – the kind who only spent time together when there was schoolwork to tackle. The idea that we might be hanging out beyond the confines of Chemistry class seemed like a luxurious novelty.

Was I really worthy of this girl's leisure time? I wondered.

"Yes!" I replied – a little too eagerly, like a puppy dog watching its owner from the window. "What did you have in mind?"

"Let's look," she suggested, jumping up from her upholstered oak chair. She slithered over to the bookshelves that lined the walls of the room and tilted her head sidewise to read the vertical titles. Delicately, methodically she traced her fingers along the spines of VHS tapes that occupied each row, finally stopping in front of a purple box with a pink-and-blue title.

"How about *The Breakfast Club*?" she suggested.

"Excellent choice," I said.

Serena walked over to her television, popped the cassette into her VHS player, then made her way back to the leather sofa that faced the TV. She plopped down on the middle cushion of the couch, her frayed jean shorts gliding up her tanned legs, and then beckoned me with a deft movement of her arm.

"Come on over," she commanded, patting the cushion next to her.

As I cautiously stepped towards Serena, I studied the couch like a chessboard. The fact that she had placed herself in the middle square left little room for physical space between our two bodies, so I hesitantly made my way to the unoccupied corner closest to where I stood. No sooner had I landed on the thick leather of the cushion then Serena kicked her bare legs on top of my lap. Though I was frozen, I desperately wanted to squirm in my place. I was trapped between a rock and a hard place – or, more accurately, a couch and a hot girl – with nowhere to run.

"Just making myself comfortable," Serena explained, nuzzling her head into a pillow.

The black screen faded to an image of constellations and a rotating Earth, drums pounding from the speakers as the Universal logo appeared. Shortly thereafter, the definitive John Hughes soundtrack tune, "Don't You Forget About Me," kicked in with the familiar *"Hey, hey, hey, hey..."* incantation. Try as I might to get lost in the film, I couldn't escape the fact that I was comfortably/uncomfortably close to the gorgeous girl that I had worshipped from afar since the early days of middle school. It seemed improbable, if not impossible, that I could end up here in this situation, with her legs sprawled across my lap and our bodies stationed so close together.

As the movie unfolded with exterior and interior shots of Shermer High School ("zip code 60062"), I found myself concentrating less on the television screen and focusing more on the John Hughes-like drama unfolding in Serena's living room. The moment was simultaneously beautiful and terrifying, and I was desperately afraid that I would do something stupid to ruin it. Fortunately, Serena broke the movie-theater-like silence with her sweet voice.

"You know," she chimed in, "there's this theory that every single high school kid can be grouped into a category. My Drama teacher, Mr. Lee, used a word I'd never heard before, something about a perfect example…"

I thought for a second. "Was it *'archetype'*…?" I asked.

"That's it!" Serena exclaimed, popping her legs up (and away from me) into a triangle-shaped bridge on the couch. Though I instantly felt relieved by the physical space between us, I became acutely aware that I also missed the simple contact of her body against mine.

"Anyway," she explained, "we watched *The Breakfast Club* in Drama class around Christmas and Mr. Lee explained how everyone that you know fits a certain… *arch-e-type*."

She stretched out the last word, massaging the pronunciation. I thought to myself how lucky that simple Greek-Latin hybrid word was, for it to elicit the intense response that required finessing from Serena's enticing lips. In that moment, I would have given anything to be that archaic word exhaled from her mouth.

"So, basically," Serena continued, "you fit into one archetype from this movie. You're either *the Brain*, *the Athlete*, *the Basket Case*, *the Princess*, or *the Criminal*. Unless you're some weird combination of a few characters."

Having seen the movie several times over the years, I had no doubt that I fit the *"Brain"* mold. I had always identified with Brian – and not just because of our shared given name. Like me, Anthony Michael Hall's character was a socially awkward nerd who never quite fit in with any particular social clique. Though I had never considered suicide by flare gun (as Brian's character does before the opening credits of the film), I understood his quiet despair and his unceasing desperation to feel accepted.

"So, I'm obviously '*the Brain*,' right?" I proposed with a quick glance away from the screen towards Serena.

She didn't respond right away. Instead, she kicked her legs out onto the ottoman in front of the couch and tapped her left pointer finger against her scrunched-up chin.

"I always took you for '*the Athlete*,'" she finally said. "I mean, you play football. Track and field, too. Right?" She paused, contemplating my categorization. "But you *are* Mr. Super-Student, so I guess you could be a *Brain-Athlete* combination."

That's strange, I thought to myself. I had never really considered myself a jock, and I never expected any of my peers to identify me as anything other than a social outcast with good grades. Clearly, there was more to my public perception than I had realized.

"I don't feel much like Emilio Estevez," I told her with a frown.

"Really?" She seemed surprised. "You have his self-confidence. The way you conduct yourself... like with that idiot, Marcus Huskey. Maybe you're not as arrogant as Emilio Estevez's character, but you've got the *intensity*..."

I screwed up my face in disbelief, not sure what to make of her estimation.

"I can see some similarities," Serena finally concluded, "whether you do or not."

As much as Serena and I had gotten to know each other over the previous six weeks of summer school, it was clear that she was utterly clueless about who I *really* was. Maybe, though, that was a blessing. She didn't know about my insecurities or my loneliness or my longing to be accepted. To her, I was just another football player – albeit one who could help her with Chemistry homework.

Turning to face her again, I posed the same question to Serena. "So, which archetype do you think *you* identify with?"

Once more, she tapped her finger placidly as she pontificated. This time, however, she maintained a steady gaze on the television screen.

"I'm sure that people think I'm *'the Athlete*,'" Serena answered in a fragile, earnest voice. She hesitated for a second. "But... I think, deep down inside, I'm actually *'the Basket Case'* on most days."

For the first time that I could remember, Serena looked uncertain – even vulnerable. It was hard for me to imagine that a girl who seemed so utterly flawless could harbor insecurities like me.

"I mean, with my parents and their divorce and being shuttled back and forth between houses." She sighed before she continued. "And like what Marcus said about me. I *am* a 'mutt.' I know he was just being a white-power jerk, but it still stung."

"How come?" I asked.

Serena suddenly seemed agitated – even angry. "Do you know what it's like to be caught between two worlds? To be 'too Mexican' for your white family and 'too white' for your Mexican family? I don't fit in anywhere. With anyone. Even with my own family members. It's enough to drive *anyone* crazy."

Serena exhaled loudly, closed her eyes, and then took a deep breath as she tried to regain her composure. Ultimately, she ended up staring at her lap, examining her hands and scraping at her cuticles. I just sat there on the couch listening.

"And that's why I'm a *'Basket Case*,'" she concluded, her voice as soft and delicate as lavender petals.

I could feel my heart thumping in my chest as I tried to think of something to say to her. I wanted to tell her that she was crazy for thinking she was crazy. But, even in my head, I knew how crazy that sounded.

Finally, I just mumbled my response to her. "I think you're beautiful," I told her, hardly more than a whisper. I closed my eyes and scrunched up my nose uncertainly. "If you're a 'mutt'... well, then, you're the most beautiful mutt in the world."

Perhaps calling the girl that you worship a "mutt" isn't the wisest move. Just saying. In retrospect, I obviously recognize that it wasn't the smoothest (or most racially sensitive) pickup line; but, at the time, I was a floundering teenage boy who was professing his crush on the wounded girl he adored. I hope that you can forgive his ignorance more than I have.

After my words died in the din of the *Breakfast Club*'s dialogue, I couldn't bear to look at her. With that kind of confession, I felt starkly naked and vulnerable, like I had emotionally stripped down to my boxer shorts in front of a supermodel.

But she didn't laugh. She didn't cry. She didn't say anything at all.

"And that's why you're a '*Claire*,'" I explained, gradually opening my eyes. "You're the perfect girl. You're beautiful and smart and kind and… Having divorced parents is nothing to be ashamed of. Neither is being a 'mutt.' You're just unique. You're *you*."

When I finally worked up the nerve to glance over at her, I could see her eyes slowly reaching up at me. She seemed surprised, but her expression registered something else that I couldn't quite pinpoint. Did she feel hurt? Betrayed? Flattered? My simple soon-to-be-sophomore senses failed me at that critical juncture.

"You really think I'm perfect…?" she asked. She didn't seem to be fishing for compliments, but rather asking me in earnest.

"Of course, you're perfect!" I spluttered (again, perhaps a little too enthusiastically). "You're like royalty at Sespe Creek High School. And you've always been that way – more perfect than everyone else around you."

Serena responded with a broad, silent smile. The afternoon sun that filtered through the windows of the living room seemed to create a halo around her glowing skin.

"I bet nobody ever called Molly Ringwald a *mutt* in Chemistry class," she countered with a half-hearted smile. Despite the well of hurt that I had inadvertently tapped into, she seemed to have regained her composure.

"If you're concerned about being a '*Basket Case*'… I think you're crazy for not seeing how perfect you are," I told her.

She smiled wanly with that same half-hearted expression.

"Anyway," I added casually, "you're a lot prettier than Molly Ringwald."

Serena examined me, her eyes locked on my own, as if she was looking at me for the very first time.

"You're too sweet," she whispered, her words barely audible over the sounds emanating from the television screen.

Though there were obviously more pressing matters at hand, all I could think about was that she had called me *sweet*. My stomach was doing backflips.

"And while I respectfully disagree with you," she added with a snort, "that's very kind of you to say. Thank you, Rick."

Without any further comment, Serena tilted her face back towards the screen and leaned her head against my shoulder. We sat there in silence for half an hour, watching the social experiment of *The Breakfast Club* unfold before us on her television screen. Huddled together there on the leather couch in her living room, we were *athletes* and *brains* and *princesses* and *basket cases* – all wrapped up in the adolescent bodies of two teenage kids.

Finally, right around the time in the film that Brian sheepishly admits that he's a virgin, Serena broke the silence.

"Have you ever slept with anyone before?" she asked nonchalantly. She still hadn't moved from her position resting against the top of my shoulder.

I laughed out loud – perhaps a little too loudly and uncomfortably, I might add – before I was able to say anything in response. I had never even *kissed* a girl before, and sex was as far off my radar as voting or going to college or drinking alcohol. It surprised me that Serena would even have to ask that question.

"Not even close," I finally mustered the courage to say.

"*Really...?*" she asked. She seemed honestly surprised by my response. "I thought all big, tough football players were supposed to be these experienced predators or something."

"You'd be surprised," I told her. "We're not all like that. There are actually a few decent gentlemen on the team."

I hesitated before asking the question that lingered like smoke in the air.

"What about you…?" I uttered, my voice faltering ever-so-slightly.

Serena looked up at me with her captivating hazel eyes and smiled. "Not even close," she whispered, her lips twisting gracefully into a grin.

Rather than divert her attention back to the television screen, she kept her luminous eyes focused on me. She seemed impossibly close to me, like a ghost that had inversely materialized into a solid, corporeal form.

"I know I haven't said it enough," she began with a gentle tenor in her voice, "but thank you for your help with all this summer school stuff."

"Any time," I told her, my own voice softening. "I got to see you every day, and that made it a lot easier to sit through lectures and labs and endless piles of homework."

Serena slid her hand onto my chest, her palm resting on my sternum and her manicured fingers stretching over the spot where my heart thudded beneath my ribcage. Though I tried with every fiber of my being to play it cool, the rapid thumping beneath Serena's fingers undoubtedly gave me away.

Literally and figuratively, my heart was a traitor.

When I tilted my head down to look at her, I was startled to see that Serena's eyes were already fixed on me. I moved my chin forward slightly, almost imperceptibly, towards her face; rather than pull away, however, Serena arched her body forward and inched closer to me. We continued this dance of millimeters, taking turns bringing our lips closer together. I could smell the cool peppermint of her chewing gum and I could feel the warm breath that cycled in and out of her mouth.

Finally, after what seemed like an eternity of yearning, our lips touched.

And we kissed.

She tasted like the most exquisite dish imaginable, even as the waxy texture of her cherry Chap Stick distracted me from the perfection of the moment. Abruptly, without warning, Serena pulled back from me and giggled.

"You've never done this before, have you?" she asked, her eyes narrowing mischievously.

"What do you mean?"

"I *mean*," she clarified, "you've never kissed a girl before."

I exhaled, feeling my chest deflate from the pressure of holding my breath captive.

"Is it that obvious?" I asked nervously.

She grinned slyly at me. "I think it's sweet," she said.

"Like I told you," I reminded her, "*not even close.*"

"In that case," she directed, leaning forward and tracing her fingers under my chin, "just follow my lead."

I don't know how long we sat there on her living room couch, but Serena turned my first kiss into a crash course on making out. Who knew how confusing and complex it could be for lips and tongues to interact? It was like a game of mimicry, with Serena making a move and me doing my best to imitate her subtle gestures. For some reason, though, the strange sensation of saliva and lingering lips felt natural to me; it was as if the bonds that Serena and I had developed in our summer school science class (a completely different kind of chemistry) had transferred over to the decidedly un-classroom-like environment of her living room couch. We were like two natural elements, kickstarted by the catalyst of our hearts, learning to move in rhythm and synchronicity.

Looking back now, after more than two decades, the whole thing seems very sweet and innocent. True, our hormones were raging, and our hearts were palpitating. However, the act itself was pure and honest – like the mutual caressing of scars and imperfections from two barely teenaged kids. It was gentle and tender and thrilling and perfect.

It was exactly what a first kiss was supposed to be.

Until her parents showed up.

Just as I was getting brave enough to slide my hand down from the soft texture of her bare arms down to the sliver of exposed skin at her waistline, I felt Serena's body tense up.

"*Shhh!*" she hissed, panic-stricken.

From our spot on the couch, we could faintly hear rattling keys and the click of a lock just outside her front door.

Serena's hazel eyes flew open in a moment of terror, and she whispered a terrified warning. "My parents!"

Within a split second, Serena had jumped off the couch and jolted upright, smoothing the creases of her clothing as the front door swung open.

"Hey, Mom! Hi, Oscar!" she shouted as she ran to greet them at the door.

I awkwardly made my way to Serena's mom and stepdad, trailing behind her and extending my hand as I approached.

"I, uh… I'm Brian," I stuttered, before realizing that I had inadvertently used my given name – not the name everyone actually called me. "I mean… Rick."

Serena's mom took my hand evenly, studying my nervous face for any sign of illicit activity. **NOTE TO SELF:** when meeting the parents of a potential girlfriend, always remember to introduce yourself with *only one name.*

"Well… which one is it?" she asked coolly with a raised eyebrow. "Brian or Rick?"

The stoic expression she shot me spooked me to the core.

"Sorry, ma'am," I apologized. "My name is Brian Richard Smith. I usually go by Rick, because my dad's name is Brian."

"Or *Brick*," Serena chimed in, her voice faltering slightly.

"That's my nickname on the football team," I clarified.

Serena's stepdad, Oscar, instantly brightened. "Ah! A football player!" he interjected. "What position do you play, Rick?"

"I'm only a lineman, sir," I responded stiffly. "Nothing too glamorous or exciting. I just take lots of hits and try to prevent the QB from getting sacked."

I could tell from Oscar's expression that his enthusiasm had waned. "Well," he responded with a condescending sigh, "it takes all kinds to make up a team, right?"

Still unsure if I could salvage the dreaded "first meeting" with Serena's mom and stepdad, I nodded hesitantly and waited for their cues to speak.

"I was a quarterback myself, back in the day," Oscar explained. "I played all through high school and even in college. We'll have to swap pigskin stories sometime."

"For now, though," Serena's mother interjected, turning her attention to her daughter, "we need to have a talk with Serena about having boys over to the house when we're not home."

"Y-yes, ma'am," I stammered, clutching my arms tightly to my chest. I quickly gathered up my water bottle, shoving it unceremoniously into my battered backpack. As I hurriedly pulled the zipper, concealing my scribbled notes and tattered papers from summer school, I offered up one final comment.

"It was very nice to meet you both," I mumbled.

"And the same to you," Serena's mother answered with a polite – but frosty – reply.

As I stumbled out the door, I turned back to see Serena's mother and stepfather shifting their attention to their daughter, like sharks lurching towards wounded meat. From her vantage point, only Serena could see me, so I silently mouthed *"I'm sorry"* across the hall. In her horrified state, she didn't respond with any gesture. She just stared coldly, eyes open wide with a sense of panic or terror... or perhaps even regret.

CHAPTER TWENTY-THREE

"Friends"

T he next day, I called Serena's house. No one picked up. I left a rambling, circuitous message on her answering machine before hanging up the phone, and I assumed that Serena would get back to me sometime soon (if not immediately). Subsequently, I spent the rest of the day waiting by the telephone, anxiously jumping up every single time I heard the familiar ringing sound that permeated our house.

But she never called.

That entire weekend, I was a bundle of nervous energy, hoping optimistically that my golden afternoon with Serena was the beginning of something epic and life-defining: a promise that she would extinguish the interminable loneliness that I had felt for years and years. Yet I also knew, deep in the caverns of my heart, that her lack of communication was a foreboding sign. If she had felt as passionately about our first kiss(es) as I had, why hadn't she called?

My suspicions were confirmed when Serena showed up – unannounced – at my doorstep on Monday afternoon. When I swung the door open, I smiled brightly and reached out to give her a hug; rather than respond with a tight squeeze, however, she limply patted my back and waited for me to release her. Still, though, the thrill of her bare skin touching mine felt electric: as she pulled away from me, I could feel her sun-kissed arms graze my naked shoulders, and I shuddered unexpectedly. I had never in my life been so grateful that I was wearing a tank top, the full length of my shoulders and arms exposed and ready to brush against her perfect skin.

"Can we go somewhere… to talk?" she asked.

"Uh… sure," I mumbled, stumbling over my own tongue.

Right about then, I had a feeling that this conversation was not going to end well.

"Okay," she whispered back. "Do you mind if we go somewhere quiet and secluded? Maybe the beach?"

"As long as I don't have to wear a swimsuit," I joked.

She responded with an awkward, pained smile, her flawless lips drawn back tightly and trembling ever-so-slightly.

This was *definitely* not going to end well.

After informing my parents that I was going to the beach, Serena and I hopped into her sister's wine-dark Acura Integra and drove through the short stretch of Highway 33 that terminates in the twisting embrace of US 101. Although she was not yet 16 years old, Serena had a learner's permit and a copy of her older sister's driver's license; while neither of us should have been on the road with the seasoned truck drivers and soccer moms that sped down the claustrophobic corridor of Highway 33, we risked dabbling in this adult world, confident that we would be invincible to any of the pitfalls that children face when reaching beyond their means.

So much of navigating adolescence is like learning how to drive. In theory, it should be easy to switch lanes, maneuver through traffic, and arrive home safely… but, in reality, it's never that simple. We weather scratches and crashes and dings and dents. It's a miracle that anyone survives their teenage years without significant bodily damage.

The whole drive from Ojai was painfully uncomfortable. Each of us tried to initiate small talk, but we also knew exactly where this road was going to lead. Every twitch of Serena's hand and every flutter of her eyelids was simultaneously intoxicating and horrifying. While I had spent a few brief hours believing that I actually had a chance with *the* Serena Rios, it was quickly dawning on me that I was in over my head. In the world of high school romances, I was a minor league Casanova and Serena was a World Series Helen of Troy.

Finally, after what seemed like an eternity to my adolescent mind, we pulled into the scuffed-up parking lot of the Ventura Harbor. There, just beyond the concrete rim of the sidewalk, the sandy dunes known as Surfer's Knoll awaited us, patiently waving from the edge of the horizon.

Serena looked straight ahead, placidly staring out the dirtied frame of her windshield. Without averting her gaze, she asked, "Do you mind if we take a walk?"

"Sure," I muttered, half to myself, half to the stale air that enveloped us. I unbuckled my seatbelt and pulled the car's door handle, opening up into the foggy afternoon. Though I had envisioned the beach as sunny and light, we were greeted instead by a cold, thick murkiness that wrapped itself around our underdressed frames. I distinctly remember regretting that I hadn't grabbed a jacket to throw over the thin fabric of my tank top.

We weren't prepared for the weather any more than we were prepared to make decisions about our future. Nevertheless, we had no choice but to step out into the cold, unforgiving afternoon.

No matter the speed of my pace, Serena was always a few steps ahead of me, leading the way, determining where our path would end. Without much hope, I slowly trailed her slender body, matching my footprints in the sand where her flip-flops made gentle demarcations.

Right foot. Left foot.

Right foot. Left foot.

Repeat until you reach the shoreline.

Finally, after descending a crumbling dune and wading through countless piles of debris on the shore, Serena sat down on a moist clump of sand a hundred yards from the tide.

She still wouldn't look at me.

"So… what did you want to talk about?" I asked her tentatively.

She sighed and languidly stretched out her arms in front of her like a bored feline. "You know," she began, "I was really lucky that I got seated next to you in Chemistry." She glanced over in my direction discreetly before continuing on. "Because, I mean, I could have been placed next to Andrew McIntyre or Marcus Huskey… and then I would have spent the whole day inhaling secondhand fumes or fending off racist insults. And you were really fun to study with. And a great lab partner and all that…"

"So, let me get this straight," I cut her off, "you dragged me all the way out here to chitchat about our summer school class?"

Serena took a deep breath and sighed again, then plunged into a perfunctory delivery that sounded more like rote memorization than an earnest conversation.

"I want to thank you," she explained mechanically, "for all of your help this summer with Chemistry. I really would have struggled with everything in that class if it hadn't been for you. And I'm glad we got to be such close friends."

I was dreading where this conversation was headed.

Serena delivered her soliloquy facing the tide, as if she were speaking to the weeping waves – not to me.

"Your *friendship*," she stressed that last word, "has really meant a lot to me."

Silence permeated the air between us, and all that remained was the steady, rhythmic crash of waves breaking against the shore.

It took me a good minute or two before I could muster the strength to say anything. When I finally did speak, my voice cracked like an egg, my desperation thinly seeping out like shattered yolk.

"Can we talk about this?" I pleaded.

Serena sighed again. "There's really nothing to talk about," she told me.

I know it's not very macho to admit it, but my eyes watered up like a puddle, quivering shyly in the cold air. The Cure said it best: "boys don't cry" – except when they do, of course. We spend our youth wearing a mask of masculinity, crafting an illusory mirage of strength, but the truth is that teenage boys are just as vulnerable and sensitive as anyone else.

Though I don't remember much of what we spoke about afterwards, I know that Serena and I tried to craft some kind of casual conversation in the aftermath of her decision. She offered the usual consolatory compliments – the *"you're a great guy"* speech – but she made it abundantly clear that we had no future together.

"Look, Rick," she sighed, "You're sweet and kind and smart, but…"

"But… *what*?" I asked.

Serena's jaw clenched tightly. "But that's not enough," she told me coolly.

"Oh," I mumbled, my blurry eyes fixated on the moist sand in front of me.

"I know it sounds weird," she explained, "but while you're the kind of guy that I want to marry one day… you're just not the kind of guy that I want to date *right now*."

Serena's comment shattered my concentration on the ground in front of me. It seemed like a double-edged sword, a backhanded compliment. She obviously liked me enough to equate me with marriage material, but there was something about me that made me undesirable in her enchanting hazel eyes.

"How does that work?" I asked.

Her face scrunched up into a distorted grimace. "You know in chemistry… how dissimilar elements react to each other differently? You and me, we're like hydrogen and oxygen. We complement each other. We work well together and even fuse together when necessary. We're like water – fluid and natural." She turned to me with a grin. "I learned that from you, by the way," she said with a strained smirk.

"So, what's wrong with hydrogen and oxygen?" I countered, ignoring her last comment. "Isn't that what you want? Someone to complement you?"

"I want something more than just a *complement*," she said, turning back to me with fire in her eyes. "I want something dynamic, something *explosive*. If I'm hydrogen, then I want... I don't know... chlorine or hydrogen chloride or something. Some kind of romantic catalyst that *transforms* me."

"Okay, then," I tried to negotiate, "you realize that when hydrogen and chlorine interact, they consume each other? They don't just catalyze – they *destroy* each other. Is that really what you want?"

"I want something powerful and dramatic," she shot back. "I don't want easy and comfortable. Comfort led my mom and dad to boredom. Boredom led them to contempt. And contempt ended with my parents getting divorced and finding new spouses and shredding my life to pieces."

Serena was getting more and more worked up throughout her diatribe, and her words seemed almost volcanic, building towards a dangerous eruption. She looked like she was ready to spew lava, but she caught herself just before exploding; she took a stilted breath through her nostrils and angled her body rigidly in my direction. "And I don't want that, Rick. I don't want comfort and complacency. I want something that possesses every fiber of my being."

Though I wanted to divert my attention to anywhere but her incendiary eyes, I couldn't shake her stare. I leaned in and tried one last Hail Mary effort.

"I want to be that for you," I told her, my voice quivering.

Without missing a beat, her glowering eyes bored into mine. "But you're not," she said with a maddening sense of composure. "You will *never* be my catalyst."

I'm pretty sure that a small piece of my adolescent soul died in that single heartbreaking moment.

I felt like a boxer on the losing end of a fight, mustering the strength to stand up but consistently taking blow after blow. Each word I uttered, every desperate phrase must have seemed like a floundering jab; I was flailing about, but not yet ready to give up. All the while, Serena was effortlessly dodging my every move.

I was defeated, emotionally battered, and ready to throw in the towel.

Just as the outlook appeared dire and disastrous, she looked me in the eyes with a wan smile and asked me the question that ultimately floored my adolescent heart.

"We can still be *friends*, though… right?"

With that one simple rhetorical question, my heart crumpled.

Total. Knock. Out.

I swear I had a physical reaction to those seven words, like I'd been punched in the gut and the wind had been sucked from my lungs. I could feel my heart collapsing on the ropes of the ring. My little teenage soul felt like a collection of black eyes and bloody lips.

And then Serena fell silent, the volcano of her tongue finally dormant.

The boxing match was over.

I distinctly remember the frigid feeling of the air that day. There was no warmth, no comfort from the coastal California weather – just a cold, bitter melancholy that permeated the afternoon mist. As Serena and I sat side-by-side on the crumbling dunes of sand, we dug our hands inside the small shelter of our pockets, seeking warmth from the seaside chill. We didn't huddle together or use each other's bodies to stave off the cold; instead, we sat in isolated spots at a safe and uncomfortable distance.

Throughout the defeated silence, I could hear my teeth rattling at irregular intervals, punctuating the stillness that eventually settled between us. Like a soft, inconsistent metronome, the waves crashed in syncopated rhythm against the beach, caressing the shoreline with stark white breakers. Serena and I stared ahead of us for what seemed like an hour, just watching the repetitive movement of the water.

Finally, Serena nudged me in the ribs with her elbow. "Ready to go?" she asked.

I couldn't look at her. I kept my line of sight down, away from her frustratingly beautiful face, and mumbled a somber reply.

"Sure."

We sat up from our sandy seats, stretching out the limbs that had been stationed, stiff and unmoving, for the duration of our conversation and its uncomfortable aftermath. As we trudged back to Serena's car, I avoided her gaze; instead, I focused on our footfalls as they stained and scarred the sand dunes. Slowly, we traipsed across the cracked sidewalk and into the weathered parking lot. Once we arrived back at the wine-dark Acura, Serena nimbly twisted her keys into the driver's side door and slithered into the vehicle. As I stood there on the passenger side, waiting beside the weather-beaten door, Serena took her sweet time alone in the car: it wasn't until after she settled into the beige upholstery of her seat, buckled herself in, and cranked the heater that she *finally* leaned across the front seat and unlocked the door for me.

When I pulled the door open, Serena's eyes caught my own and she gave me an innocent, pitying smile. Just as quickly, I diverted my attention to the seaside, shifting my weight into the passenger seat before slamming the door.

The car ride home felt like an eternity. Serena repeatedly tried to initiate small talk, but I refused to engage her. I kept my answers short and succinct, providing very little fuel for her to ignite the campfire of conversation that she wanted. Eventually, she got tired of trying and simply turned up the volume on her car stereo. Through the tinny speakers, I could hear Green Day's "When I Come Around" – that boisterous anthem of bitterness and hope that would saturate the airwaves in the next few months.

I stared out the window, my eyes grazing the lush green mountainside that flanked either side of Highway 33, as Billie Joe Armstrong's voice reverberated throughout our borrowed car. It was an imperfect comfort, a small salve in the face of my mounting heartbreak. Still, I let the song course through me, wondering if I would ever have better days ahead of me.

Despite Green Day's radio reassurance, I didn't know if Serena would *ever* come around. I wondered if she could ever become like Molly Ringwald's character in *The Breakfast Club*, capable of seeing beyond social conventions and physical appearances; regardless, I had a gut feeling that – like the film's Brian the Brain – I would be left alone and suffering while she found someone else better-suited to ignite the flame that she so desperately craved. But when would the Judd Nelson character show up in our narrative (much to my dismay), sweeping her up in a maelstrom of fire?

Sooner than I anticipated, it turns out.

When we finally pulled up to my house on Lago de Paz Court, I was doing my best James Dean impression, trying to maintain a stoic demeanor – despite the crumbling feeling in my cavernous chest and the bitter chill that stung my bare shoulders. Wordlessly, I unstrapped my seatbelt and popped open the car door.

As I stepped out onto the street, I started my sullen stroll up the walkway to my front door, stopping only when I heard Serena's voice call me from behind.

"Hey!" she shouted.

I sighed, turned around slowly, and forced myself to look up into her eyes from across the concrete median of the sidewalk. Though I did my best to hide my hurt, she must have seen the wavering strength in my trembling face.

"Are we… okay?" she asked gingerly.

"Yes," I mumbled. "We're okay."

"Good," she grinned back at me. "Because you really have become one of my best friends, Rick. I would hate to lose you over this."

"Right," I agreed halfheartedly. "Then I guess I'll see you around…?"

"Right," she echoed back, a relieved smile spreading across her perfect lips.

With a rumble of her engine, Serena sped away down Lago de Paz and waved ardently with her left hand out the window.

Literally and figuratively, she was leaving me behind.

I locked myself in my bedroom for the remainder of the afternoon, pulling the covers of my comforter over my head and choking back the sobs that seemed to reach up from my chest like emotional vomit. Anyone with an ear pressed to my bedroom door would have heard muffled moans escaping through the blankets and pillows. When my mom rapped on my door later in the evening, I told her that I had the flu and that I wasn't coming out. She graciously acquiesced and gently reminded me that I should call for her if I needed anything. Maybe she knew that Dayquil and Tylenol weren't the cures that I needed, but she consoled me through the charade and let me remain sequestered in my room.

It's true: high school boys cry. In a world of machismo posturing and caricatures of masculinity, it's frowned upon for men to feel anything – we're supposed to be pillars of strength, souls of brick and mortar.

I'm here to tell you, though: Bricks cry, too.

By the time I finally arose from the cave of my bedroom hours later, I could feel an awkward tingling on my face, arms, and (most painfully) my bare shoulders. Staring skeptically in the mirror, I saw that my usually pallid face had become flushed and rosy, a shade that was mirrored on my exposed epidermis.

"*How can you get a sunburn without any sun...?*" I remember asking myself in disbelief as I examined my tender, pink skin in the unforgiving light of the bathroom mirror.

California can be cruel in the summer.

Despite the deceptively unprotective afternoon fog at Surfer's Knoll, I was left with a stinging reminder of my painful conversation with Serena: a nasty sunburn that would eventually take a full week to heal. Though it pained me to think of her, I couldn't help but imagine that her dandelion skin would emerge unscathed from our afternoon on the beach. The reassuring smile and wave that she had given me when she drove away seemed proof positive that she was immune to the pain and suffering that I felt that evening.

They might not intend to do so, but girls will give you sunburns with a grin.

CHAPTER TWENTY-FOUR
"The Warmth of the Sun"

Puppy love is a strange, strange thing. I didn't understand it back in the mid-1990s and I barely understand it now. Basically, it boils down to this:

Being a teenager in love is like being romantically bipolar.

Now, before you rush to judgment and prematurely condemn me for my insensitivity to mental illness, please let me explain. As someone who has struggled with depression and anxiety and bipolar tendencies for four decades now, I am acutely aware of the earthquaking effects of psychological complications. I know that comparing mental health to romantic entanglements is not a perfect parallel, and I might come across as callous or inconsiderate, but I'd like to make the claim that there's an uncanny similarity between teenage romance and bipolar disorder. I'm not minimizing the profound complexities of mental illness, mind you, but rather trying to illustrate the marathon distances between the highs and lows of both bipolar disorder *and* teen heartache. And, having lived through both, I can honestly attest that the overlapping circles in this Venn diagram are more tightly intertwined than one might suspect. Bear with me as I try to explain my reasoning in my own feeble way, and please forgive me if you feel that I'm being thoughtless or unsympathetic.

As anyone can attest, the highs of young love are achingly stratospheric, and the lows... well, they're lower than the deepest pits of hell. Ironically, though this experience is so staggeringly disarming, it's also almost universally felt by young adults. Basically, we all get our hearts broken and we all find ourselves reeling in the aftermath.

For many people, the closest that they'll ever come to the darkened despair of depression is in the wake of a breakup. Likewise, the acrobatic elation of blossoming love (and the brain's accompanying chemical effects of dopamine and norepinephrine) is the extent of their experience with the razor's-edge bliss of euphoria.

That's just the way life goes when you're a teenager.

And it's even more overwhelming when you just so happen to be clinically depressed.

The night after my conversation with Serena at the beach, once the tears had temporarily subsided into raw and itchy eyes, I snuck into the living room and raided my dad's CD collection. As my fingers tapped the spines of hundreds of jewel cases, I searched desperately for something – *anything* – that could give me reprieve from the pain that flooded every fiber of my being. My usual freshman soundtrack, Pearl Jam and Nirvana and Weezer, seemed too aggressive and abrasive. I needed something calmer, more soothing, to satiate my saddened soul.

It was then that I stumbled upon my dad's Beach Boys box set, *Good Vibrations: Thirty Years of the Beach Boys*. Though I'd been stretching away from the soundtrack of my youth in my early adolescent years, the Beach Boys seemed comforting to me that evening – like musical chicken soup, if you will. I snatched up the CDs and rushed back to my cave.

I tried listening to the whole album, but I found myself skipping past the upbeat songs (for obvious reasons) and dwelling upon the ballads scattered throughout the first disc: "Their Hearts Were Full of Spring," Surfer Girl," "In My Room," "The Surfer Moon," "Don't Worry Baby" – and, ultimately, "The Warmth of the Sun."

Have you ever had that serendipitous moment when you stumble upon a song that seems ripped from the headlines of your life? The kind of song that captures the complex cauldron of emotions that are haunting you at that precise juncture of your existence? It's a rare convergence, but it has the power to conjure makeshift memories – even a lifetime later.

For the fifteen-year-old Brian Richard Smith, the precocious young man struggling with that first dizzying experience of heartbreak, "The

Warmth of the Sun" felt like an aching valentine from a musical ancestor. Underneath the refrain's heavenly strain of wordless vocals, the song captures heartache in its purest, unadulterated form. Just as I was encountering the torturous rite of passage known as unrequited love, I found music that echoed this age-old sentiment – in the digital grooves of my father's CDs, nonetheless. Hearing Brian Wilson's soaring falsetto in that recording, lighter than air and heavier than heartbreak, allowed me to feel temporarily liberated from the cage of my aborted relationship.

Years later, when I started teaching *Romeo & Juliet* to my freshman English classes, it dawned on me that there's something primordial – archetypal, if you will – about the kind of unrequited love described in "Warmth of the Sun." The line from William Shakespeare to the Beach Boys is not as dramatic (no pun intended) as one might imagine: when it comes to tortured romance, the Italian city of Verona and the California suburb of Hawthorne are closer than the 6,300 miles that separate the two towns. In fact, every time that I read the scene in which Lord Montague describes Romeo creating an "artificial night" in his bedroom (after Rosaline breaks his heart), I find myself inadvertently humming a few bars of the song.

"*Black and portentous,*" indeed.

From the removed, somewhat-objective perspective of an adult, I can vouch for the fact that things get better – that there *is* a Juliet who will erase the scars that Rosaline leaves behind (preferably without the double-suicide in the final act). You can hear that hope resonating in "The Warmth of the Sun," when the tense uncertainty of the verse lifts off into the soaring vocals of the song's chorus, optimism and clarity arising from the aching ashes.

Even in the deepest despair of endless embers, there is hope.

I just hadn't found it yet.

As I lay in my bed, contrite and contracted, listening to "The Warmth of the Sun" on repeat, I felt enveloped in the dark clouds of my own "artificial night." Serena and I had just encountered that same kind of one-sided romantic relationship – we had brushed up against a classic case of unrequited love. However, while she had emerged unscathed like Rosaline, I had been transformed like Romeo into a state of puppy dog scrutiny and insecurity. It's rather embarrassing now to think back with the hindsight of several decades and recognize just how paralyzed I was at the time. I don't know what it was about her, but Serena managed to get under my skin, like an infectious disease that wreaked havoc on my heart. Realistically, I should have shrugged this off like a simple scratch; instead, I let her blonde hair and golden skin pierce me through every layer of skin and bone.

Fun fact: Brian Wilson and Mike Love finished writing "Warmth of the Sun" on the day that John F. Kennedy was assassinated. In the song, that subconscious sense of longing tends to transcend the typical teenage relationship and resonates on a larger national scale. In the wake of Kennedy's assassination, a teenage boy mourning the loss of his girlfriend must have seemed insignificant... and yet, that sense of grief is timelessly universal, transcending genders, races, creeds, colors, orientations, and the many other distinctions of individuals.

Grief is grief and loss is loss.

As I learned later in my life, loss and grief are paralyzing forces, capable of dismantling hearts and souls with unhurried hands.

As a fifteen-year-old boy, though, I thought that being dumped by Serena was the end of my world. Little did I know, I would have much bigger trials ahead of me – losses that would transform me from a child into someone older and sadder... but also wiser.

But I'm getting ahead of myself.

Alas, the solace of the sun wasn't enough to ease my tormented soul that afternoon. I couldn't find comfort by heading to the beach and enjoying the warmth of the summer weather; in my circumstance, the beach was actually the scene of the crime. The coastal California weather was cruel that day: there was no sun to warm my skin while I fought through the heartbreak and mourning of my brief summer fling.

The rest of that day seems like a blur, as if the afternoon haze crumpled the script of my memory and tossed it nonchalantly in the trash bin of time. Obviously, there was some sort of dénouement to the scene: I'm sure I crawled out of bed and ate dinner and showered and carefully applied that gelatinous green aloe vera lotion to my painfully pink skin. Like everything else from that time in my life, however, nostalgia has tempered the painful transaction with a sort of halo, a fuzzy filter that resonates more with flashes of still frames than with the lucidity of a short film.

I've always wondered, though: what happens when the warmth of the sun fades? How do you find comfort when there is no solace in the sun? For Brian Wilson, the passing of the sun's warmth meant coldness and isolation and loneliness and despair. The early success he found as a member of the Beach Boys didn't prepare him for the frustration he felt when the band's touring and recording schedules expanded in unprecedented ways. Just as the boys in the band were riding wave after wave of success, Brian snapped and quit touring. For him, it was a matter of self-preservation: he couldn't continue to churn out hits on the radio *and* play to packed audiences *and* travel to venues *and* produce legendary recording sessions...

But at that precise moment in time, making music was the farthest thing from my mind. With Serena, I felt like I had clutched a winning lottery ticket in my fragile fingertips – only to have it cruelly ripped from my grasp and torn to shreds before my eyes. And yet, my hands were tied. Serena was in the driver's seat of our relationship, and I had no more power to steer her heart than I did to steer her car from the passenger's seat.

That being said, all you really need to know is that I was sad and broken.

And incomplete.

CHAPTER TWENTY-FIVE

"You Need a Mess of Help to Stand Alone"

I spent the next week watching my sunburned skin peel off in small, tender strips, while I nursed a broken heart and faked a brave façade. I might have been devastated that Serena was solely interested in being friends, but a teenager's anguish only warrants so much sympathy from the outside world. I hid my heartache from my family – which was surprisingly easy, considering how much time and attention everyone spent on Marina, helping her prepare for her upcoming departure to UC Berkeley. While they fretted over packing boxes and shopping for the bare necessities of a dorm room, I was quietly combating the symptoms of a broken heart.

It was no different on the football field, where I became an aching automaton, blocking hits from my peers on the offensive team of Sespe Creek's newly adjusted junior varsity squad. During practice, my vision remained focused on the potential attackers on the defensive line, the uniformed teammates who tried to rush past me during scrimmages in order to tackle the quarterback; my mind, however, was on the soft, bronze skin of Serena Rios – and the steely resolve that I needed in order to salvage any semblance of a relationship with her. To my teammates, this distraction probably came across as something more akin to stoicism or aloofness, but I didn't care. As far as I was concerned, the fewer people who knew about my melodramatic misery, the better off I would be.

A few weeks later, when Coach Montaña called us together for an important pre-practice team meeting to introduce our newest teammate, a kid named Steve Öken, I couldn't concentrate. I was still too distracted by Serena to pay any attention to the coach's announcement. According to

Montaña, the new guy with the funny-sounding last name was a star player transferring from Malibu Cove High School, and Steve (the aforementioned transfer student) would be taking over as starting quarterback for the JV team.

Big deal.

From my vantage point in the back of the crowd, his lean frame seemed diminutive – he couldn't have been more than 5'8" or 5'9", nor could he have weighed more than 165 pounds. His weathered football helmet obscured the features of his face, so he seemed more like a shadow than a quarterback. As I stood on the periphery of the huddle, my vision blocked by dozens of bulky teammates, I realized that I would have to wait for another occasion to meet our new comrade-in-arms. That was fine with me.

During the previous season, my teammates and I on the freshman football team had been moderately successful, earning a respectable 6-4 record. That being said, we clearly had serious weaknesses in some of our key roles – most notably the quarterback and receiver positions. I couldn't help but wonder if this new QB might strengthen our little squad enough to finally defeat our crosstown rivals at Nordhoff High School. If nothing else, I figured injecting new leadership into the lineup might help boost the team's morale.

As he wound down his introduction, Coach Montaña clapped his meaty hands together and ordered us to break, dispersing the team into various shapes and formations on the football field. As usual, I took my place on the edge of the offensive line. Though I rarely got much acclaim, I took pride in playing offensive tackle, and I did all that I could to keep the QB safe from any intruding forces. Just as Coach Montaña had nicknamed me, I was a "Brick": a solid part of our team's foundation, a piece of the structure that kept our most valuable asset – the quarterback – safe and sound.

You know that distracted, dazed feeling you get when you're sleep-deprived or overmedicated? I must have felt the same way in my lovesick state, because my mind was definitely *not* in the game that afternoon. When the Center snapped the ball back to our new QB during a routine play, I was too busy staring off at the mountainsides to notice; the next thing I knew, Marcus Huskey in his scuffed-up practice jersey was knocking past me and heading straight for the quarterback. By the time I flipped around to catch sight of the action, all I could make out was the lithe frame of the QB flipped horizontally with Marcus's imposing physique sprawled out on top of him.

"WHAT THE HELL!" the QB yelled out across the field as he dusted himself off. He ripped off his helmet and spat in my direction, his strong cleft chin jutting forth from his face. "Thanks for doing your job, ogre!"

I wished that I could have produced some sort of searing comeback on the spot or had the guts to deck him for his insult. Instead, I just stood there as mute as a brick wall. I might have been a wordsmith in front of my teachers, but I was wordless before my peers in the heat of the moment.

From my vantage point a few yards away, I could just see the outline of a chiseled face and specks of freckles splattered across the QB's cheeks. He grumbled something under his breath, put his helmet back on, and turned back to face the coach.

The rest of the afternoon at practice, the new kid seemed simultaneously cocky and superhuman. He threw impressive distances and moved with the grace and agility of a pro. Slowly, I could see the reactions of my teammates shifting from skeptical optimism to wide-eyed awe.

The new kid was good.

We all knew it.

And he knew it, too.

The next few hours whizzed by in a flash of soiled shoulder pads, scratched facemasks, and scuffed helmets. Somehow, despite my inner turmoil, I banished Serena from my thoughts – for a few hours at least – and did my best to stay focused on the field in front of me.

Finally, as my teammates and I sizzled with sweat in the summer sun, Coach called an end to practice and directed us back to the locker room. I turned to follow the crowd – but froze when I heard my name echo across the stadium like an unexpected gunshot.

"*BRICK!*" Coach Montaña commanded with his gruff voice, "I need you to stick around."

Crap.

Collecting my helmet, I walked back to face the mountain of a man who dictated our fates on the field. I could tell from his upturned lips and tense jowls that this was not going to be a fun conversation.

At first, he didn't say anything. He just stared at me in that omniscient x-ray manner championship coaches utilize to intimidate their athletes.

"You need to get your head back in the game, son," he began patiently. "I don't know what's going on inside that helmet of yours, but you need to be *present* on the field. Every time that someone slips by you, you're letting *someone else* get hurt. If you get bruised and battered, then that's on you. But if another player gets hurt on your watch, that's a guilt that *you* will have to live with."

"Yes, sir," I responded meekly, my voice quivering with each little word.

"You're a lineman, the thickest that we've got," he continued. "I need you to protect Steve *at all times*. As far as I'm concerned, he's a big pile of cash and I need you to be the bank vault that guards him. From now on, you'll be the one that elevates him, shields him, and enables him to lead you to victory. Without Steve, you're not going anywhere."

Coach paused, studying my face. He waited two... three... four seconds, his eyes burning right through me like ultraviolet rays through pale, vulnerable skin.

"Do you understand me, Brick?"

"Yes, sir," I answered, a little more confidently this time.

"Good," he said. "Then we're done here. Get yourself changed and go home."

Coach Montaña flipped up the pages of his clipboard, gave me a foreboding nod, and walked away towards the end-zone.

So, not only was I failure romantically – I was now a liability on the football field, too. As I meandered back to the locker room, my mind wandered to the other self-defeating aspects of my life in which I was a disappointment...

I was depressed.

I was overweight.

I was an ugly, acne-scarred nobody.

I was lonely, and about to become even lonelier once my big sister moved away to college.

That's another problem, I thought to myself, picking at that mental scab of self-doubt. *What's going to happen to the Bookhouse Boys now that Marina is leaving us behind?*

With Marina's departure looming on the horizon, I had scheduled a few practices with our newly revised trio: me, Chunk, and Ethan. However, as much as I desperately wanted to swing behind the microphone for that lead vocalist slot, it just wasn't the same without Marina. Sure, I was a serviceable vocalist, capable of hitting the notes... most of the time, at least. But, no matter how hard I tried, I lacked the bravado and vibrato to fill that vital vocal role.

I knew that there wasn't much I could do about most of the shortcomings in my life. *I can't change my genetics, I can't shake myself out of the funk in my heart, and I can't just magically make myself popular*, I told myself. *But at least I can still play music...*

I just needed to find a lead singer, someone who had a mesmerizing voice and the innate ability to captivate a crowd. But where the heck was I supposed to look?

In the end, the voice we needed the most came from the place that we least expected.

The football field.

I kicked loose dirt along the path back from the stadium, surveying the mountains that staggered along the horizon line. Growing up, the mountains always seemed like an imposing part of the landscape. But, over the years, they had become meaningless, motionless monoliths, standing rigidly unnoticed, like the drawn curtains on a stage.

Ojai was a valley, a safe enclave that provided shelter from the waves a few miles southwest and the heat that inevitably rises the farther you drift inland. And yet, for all the cover of those mountains that enclosed us, it felt strangely claustrophobic. The dirt-brown half-moons that rose drudgingly from the ground, dotted and speckled with green from shrubbery and trees, seemed insurmountable. No matter where you stand in Ojai, those mountains surround you, providing safety and security – but also a sense of stagnation.

Trapped, I thought to myself. *I am trapped.*

I remember thinking back to *The Odyssey*, that classic mythological travelogue that we had read in my freshman English class. When Odysseus and the remnants of his crew are trapped on Calypso's island, they have no idea how much time has elapsed in their lives; they're content and fooled into believing that they're happy. It isn't until the gods intervene that Odysseus realizes that he's wasted away years of his life in this secluded oasis.

Ojai felt very much like Calypso's island to me. Though only a short drive away from the beach and ocean waves, my hometown was simultaneously safe and suffocating. Walking back to the locker room, the heat further wearing down my haggard spirit, I looked about my surroundings, surveying the misshapen lumps of the hillsides and aching for the tantalizing hint of a cool breeze from the distant ocean. But Ojai was a desert landscape, complete with cactus and parched earth. Though my fading sunburn reminded me that I wouldn't last too long in the exposed sun, I couldn't shake the feeling that my life would be forever stifled if I spent the next few decades confined in this little town.

I knew one thing: I needed to find a way out of the valley, as far away from the stifling heat and desiccated desert landscape as I could travel.

I needed to escape the mountains.

By the time that I got back to the locker room, the place was deserted. Gone were the clanging of locker doors and the shuffling of exhausted bodies. Usually, the facility was a cacophony of busy sounds, capped off with the voices of teenage boys posturing in pathetic attempts to prove their misbegotten masculinity.

And yet, breaking through the silence, some sort of siren's song reverberated between the ceramic tiles and rusting metal lockers.

Is that the radio? I wondered. *Or someone singing in the locker room?*

It was quiet at first, distant and dim. As I strolled through the rows of empty lockers, the voice grew louder and more confident, eventually swelling into a full-fledged melodic roar.

I knew the song, too. It was one of my favorite Social Distortion tunes, "Ball & Chain." What I didn't know was the identity of the singer.

A few years before, my dad had taken me to see Neil Young & Crazy Horse in Los Angeles on their *Ragged Glory* tour, and one of the show's opening acts had been Social Distortion. The minute that Mike Ness and company started their first song, I was captivated. Like Neil Young, Social D. bridged the gap between ancient, archetypal Americana and fresher, crunchier punk rock. When the band played their definitive hit, "Ball & Chain," at the show, the crowd erupted into pure, unadulterated adoration. From that moment on, I had been a convert to the *SxDx* crowd, preaching and singing their praises with religious fervor. In the intervening years, I had memorized every lyric and melody and guitar riff on their self-titled record – with my favorite remaining the blisteringly beautiful "Ball & Chain."

Now, suddenly, I was hearing the same song in a serendipitous moment in the steel and ceramic corners of my high school locker room. It was uncanny, to say the least.

As I walked closer, the mystery voice surged and soared from the verse to the chorus. Like Social Distortion's singer, Mike Ness, this Phantom of the Locker Room had a grizzled, weathered tone – a depth and maturity that was well beyond anything I could muster during band practice with Ethan and Chunk. And yet, there was also a sense of earnestness in his singing, a tender empathy that couldn't be faked by a rank amateur.

This guy has great taste in music, I thought to myself. *And his singing is good. Really good.*

I stood there silently, awestruck by the disembodied voice floating through the rafters. It felt a little creepy and voyeuristic, listening in on a stranger singing aloud in what he *thought* was an empty room – while, unbeknownst to him, someone else was standing in the shadows of those rusty steel lockers. But this mystery voice was so captivating, I didn't care. Decorum be damned.

In a way, it was akin to hearing Marina sing: he had the same kind of unrestrained power and emotion in his voice, the unwavering confidence of someone who knew how to harness musical magic from the depths of his heart and soul.

Though a part of me undoubtedly felt jealous of the mystery voice, my own insecurities were overshadowed by the unbridled potential of what I heard. I needed to know what teenager could capably conjure such palpable power from his vocal cords. When I finally reached the back row and gained the confidence to confront this Phantom of the Locker Room, I turned the corner…

And there he was. The new guy.

Steve Öken sat there on the wooden bench, bare-chested and bravely singing at the top of his lungs while he unlaced the filthy cleats that adorned his feet. As I casually approached, I couldn't help but notice that he was perfectly sculpted – like an Adonis with the kind of *G.I. Joe* physique that makes every normal guy feel jealously inadequate.

Bastard.

"It's Steve, right?" I asked.

Caught off guard, he jumped and turned to face me.

"Yeah," he said, eyeing me skeptically. "That's me. Who are you?"

I held out my right hand. "I'm Rick Smith," I said. "But everyone calls me *Brick.*"

Steve extended his arm and shook my hand. "Steve Öken," he said, introducing himself.

"Oaken…?" I asked. "Like an oak tree…?"

Steve gave me a noncommittal shrug, sizing me up while I spoke.

"That's an interesting name," I said.

"It means 'desert' in Swedish," he explained.

He studied me for a second before saying anything else, his sharp blue eyes obscured by squinting eyelids. From this proximity, I could see that his sandy blonde hair hid subtle traces of auburn and the freckles that adorned his cheeks speckled a rugged, symmetrical face. The guy looked like a model, like the kind of teenager who would grow up to be the star of an action film.

Bastard.

Finally, the realization hit him, and he smirked condescendingly at me. "You're the lineman who got me sacked," he grunted.

"About that…" I mumbled. "I totally screwed up. I'm sorry."

"Eh," he shrugged. "It happens, I guess. Just don't let it happen during a game, or else we'll have some real problems."

"Of course," I promised sheepishly. "It won't happen again."

We stood there awkwardly for a few seconds before I broke the silence.

"So… Social Distortion?" I asked tentatively, raising an eyebrow.

Steve's eyes lit up. "You know Social D.?" he shot back, surprised.

"I saw them a few years ago with my dad," I gloated. "They opened for Neil Young and Crazy Horse, along with Sonic Youth."

Steve's eyes widened in awe. "You saw them *and* Neil Young?"

"You like Neil Young, too?" I asked. "No one else here knows who he is."

"My parents are big fans of all that classic rock stuff," he told me.

For half an hour, Steve and I sat and talked about Social Distortion. We debated the merits of their self-titled major label debut versus the *Somewhere Between Heaven and Hell* album (Steve favored the first, while I preferred the latter); we marveled at their seamless blend of genres (I was a bigger fan of their forays into country music, and Steve merely tolerated those tunes); and we discussed what it meant to *really* be "punk" (Steve thought it had more to do with image, but I argued it was ideology).

Even though we had just met, it felt like talking with Ethan or Chunk. Our lively discussion flowed easily and fluidly without the tension that typically accompanies first-time conversations with strangers. There's an unspoken rule between music-obsessed hipsters: when you bond over a common fandom, the social strata between you is overshadowed by the gravity of your shared passion. Though Steve and I were in different worlds – he was the genetically-gifted athletic superstar heartthrob, and I was clearly *not* – none of that mattered during our conversation.

Finally, I glanced at the clock and realized that I was long overdue at home. As I packed up the rest of my things, I turned towards Steve and cocked my head, debating whether or not I should go with my gut feeling.

Screw it, I thought. *What's the harm in asking?*

"So, Steve..." I began cautiously. "Have you ever... you know... played in a band or anything?"

His eyes lit up feverishly. He didn't need to say a word.

"Never," he told me. "But I would *love* to do that one day. How cool would it be to just stand up on stage in front of those giant lights and roaring crowds? Can you imagine what that would feel like?"

"Actually," I smirked, "I *do* know. I have a band."

"You do?" he asked skeptically, a bit surprised by this revelation.

"Yup," I answered. "And we might be looking for a new singer."

Steve's face went electric and his chapped lips curled up into a bold smile. "Where do I sign up?"

CHAPTER TWENTY-SIX
"I Should Have Known Better"

So, there we were, a bunch of soon-to-be sophomores surreptitiously starting (or restarting, as it were) a rock band. My predictions were right: Steve fit seamlessly into our little ensemble and he brought something miraculous back to the table, something we thought we had lost with Marina's departure. Our first few practices were like a cursory overview of punk history, as we played everything from the Ramones to the Clash to Bad Religion to Social Distortion to Green Day. It was like punk rock karaoke with a live band, and we reveled in every single magical minute of it.

During that first practice with Steve, I remember the nervous energy that crackled through the room like the buzzing of a Fender amplifier, the anticipation that *this could be something*. Ethan started things off with the chainsaw distortion of his electric guitar as we plunged into "Blitzkrieg Bop," Chunk and I following his lead as we lurched back and forth in tandem. By the time that Steve started chanting, "*Hey, ho, let's go!*" it felt like a call to action, a conjuring, a commencement.

From that moment, it was clear to us that something special was starting here in this humble garage. Chunk, Ethan, and I had developed our own chemistry, but something had been missing – until now. I had been a serviceable singer in Marina's absence, but I didn't have the sheer intensity or unencumbered emotion that Steve naturally possessed. I neither looked nor acted anything like a lead singer; I lacked the swagger and the stage presence that a punk band demanded from its captain.

With his chiseled face and proud stature, however, Steve was a perfect fit for the frontman slot. I still sang lead on some songs interspersed throughout the set, but it was clear from the "*hey, ho*" get-go that Steve was going to be our lead singer. There was a sense of gravity, gravel, and gravitas in the way that he sang those songs, a depth that I couldn't begin to approach. As I discovered, a lot of people can sing – but very few are truly *singers*.

Steve Öken wasn't just a singer, however.

He was a *lead* singer.

And I was not.

Something else notable happened right around this same time: I got braces. My poor misaligned teeth, filled with awkward gaps and uncouth spaces, required some orthodontic reorganization. Thus, my parents shelled out their hard-earned cash and put a down payment on my dental reconstruction.

My father, with his own crooked smile and jagged teeth, was determined that I wouldn't face the same maxillofacial fate. His parents (my grandparents) couldn't afford braces for him, he explained, which resulted in a lifetime of asymmetrical smiles and misshapen teeth. Consequently, my father was adamant that Marina and I would have perfect smiles – cost be damned.

Interestingly enough, my dad was determined to get braces of his own a few years down the line, once Marina and I had finished up college and no longer drained Mom and Dad's financial resources.

"After I retire," Dad told me at the time, "there are a million things I'm going to do. And getting braces is at the top of the list."

"Won't you be a little too old for braces?" I asked with typical teenage skepticism.

"You're never too old for *anything*," he reassured me. "Just you wait. When I retire, I'm going to get a mouth full of braces, hop on an airplane to Hawaii, and record an album of my own songs." His eyes glazed over dreamily, envisioning this mythical landscape of retirement. "Who knows? Maybe I'll even write a book. The future is wide open with endless possibilities."

"Sure, Dad," I told him as I rolled my eyes. I couldn't visualize him doing any of those things – especially getting on an airplane. The thought of him as an older, balder, fatter version of himself, sipping a piña colada on a beach seemed comical enough – even without a barbed fence of braces covering his crooked smile. I snickered to myself at the thought.

"You'll see," he reassured me with a grin. "I'll surprise you."

To make a long story short, I ended up with a mouthful of wired brackets that summer.

Here's the thing about braces: although they obviously serve a very profound purpose, straightening and salvaging your smile, they make you feel hideous. Your gum-line is overtaken by the overbearing presence of metal, and your speech becomes significantly stilted. Though the ultimate goal is to make you feel confident and attractive, braces tend to have a crippling effect on self-conscious teenagers. Basically, they silence you. If you're a quiet wallflower, then it's no big deal. If, however, you're trying to sing in a rock and roll band... well, then, the results are absolutely disastrous.

All the while, I couldn't help but give in to my own daydreams – not about Hawaii or writing a book, mind you, but about Serena Rios. To my tortured adolescent heart, she was more tempting than any tropical destination, more beautiful than any bucket-list fantasy. So, despite the "brace-face" self-consciousness I felt, I had the brilliant idea of inviting Serena to one of our band practices.

Maybe... just maybe, I told myself, *this might help win her over.*

Perhaps, if she saw me in this setting, on my home turf, she might reevaluate her feelings for me.

After all, what girl isn't smitten with a guy in a rock band?

That is, of course, if you're the *right* guy.

After our disastrously brief (or briefly disastrous?) romantic entanglement, Serena and I had walked an awkward tightrope of a relationship. We spent more than a few hours just talking on the phone, yours truly providing emotional support as she rattled off the frustrations that she faced in the wake of summer school. During those intimate conversations, she talked openly about splitting time between her divorced parents, trying to maneuver the channels of mixed racial heritage, even combatting social hierarchies on the soccer field. I listened attentively, just grateful to be hovering in her atmosphere.

Even though Serena claimed she had no interest in me as a boyfriend, she still maintained that we should stay *good friends*. Obviously, to a heartbroken teenage boy, this kind of paradoxical predicament can be sheer torture. Nevertheless, somewhere in the deep recesses of my heart, I held onto a flicker of hope that things would change. If only I could convince her that I was the spark, the fire that she needed in her life. But how could I show her that I was the catalyst she craved?

As I kept pondering these questions, I had a life-changing epiphany – the inspiration striking me like a bolt of lightning, while I sat with a chiming guitar in my hands and a throbbing pain in my heart.

If you want a girl to like you, I realized, *write her a song*.

It was a foolproof plan. Or so I thought.

With all this drama fluttering around me like embers in a hearth, I was determined to impress Serena with my rock and roll romanticism. Of course, writing a song sounds a lot easier than it actually is. In reality, the construction of a three-and-a-half-minute pop song might take days or weeks – or even months. I knew, though, that my window of opportunity was limited.

I had written a handful of songs before, mind you, but they had all seemed trite and formulaic – simple songs written by a simple boy at a simple time in his life. This song, however, needed to be something powerful, moving – capable of winning over the heart of a preternaturally sophisticated teenage girl.

I remember sitting at the edge of my bed with my dad's acoustic guitar in my hands and a pad of lined paper nuzzled into the snaking sheets. My dad was fond of extrapolating his amateur theory that any song worth its salt needed to sound complete with just an acoustic guitar and a voice; otherwise, he explained, it's all just smoke and mirrors. So, with his advice at the forefront of my mind, I clutched that old, wooden instrument to my chest and wrapped my fingers around the strings on the guitar's neck. As I sat and strummed and sighed and sang, I kept coming back to something that Serena had said during our conversation on the beach.

"*I want something dynamic, something explosive,*" she had told me. "*Some kind of romantic catalyst that just transforms me...*"

"Well," I said aloud to myself, "if she wants something explosive, then I'm going to give her fireworks."

I stopped cold in my tracks.

Explosive... I thought to myself. *I should write about something* explosive *in my song.*

I tapped my trembling ballpoint pen and scrawled out every single word even remotely connected to that conceit: *fire, flame, lights, matches, sparks, consuming, grenades, detonate, bomb, time bomb...*

I hastily scribbled word after word onto that yellow legal pad, my chicken-scratch handwriting barely even legible to myself.

While I jotted down every synonym from the synapses simmering in my brain, I knew that I wanted to be the explosive power that Serena craved so badly. I wanted to be her *time bomb*, her *fireworks*, her *all-consuming flame*.

I should state for the record (no pun intended) that I had been listening to a lot of my dad's old vinyl Ramones albums that summer, dousing myself in the aggressive simplicity of their songs. "I Wanna' Be

Sedated," in particular, kept weaving itself through my thoughts with its catchy chord progression and hummable melody. As I sat on the edge of my bed, staring at the half-empty notepad in front of me, I found myself singing, "I wanna' be…"

And then the line popped into my head:

I wanna' be your time bomb.

That was my opening salvo. Inspired by the Ramones, Serena, and that godforsaken summer school chemistry class, I could feel the embryo of a song gestating in my brain. I prayed that this little kernel of an idea might work, might help guide my shameless paean to Serena Rios.

I quickly scanned through the other words on the list, and I immediately latched onto *detonate*. My fingers dashed back to the frets of the guitar as words spilled forth on the page.

I wanna' detonate…

Where would a lover detonate, though? On a page? On the radio? Would that be consuming enough?

I wanna' detonate… in your arms.

I smiled to myself as I wrote down the rest of the line.

This is exactly *the song that Serena needs to hear*, I thought. I wanted her to know that I could be compulsive and dangerous. If she wanted a lover who would transform her and consume her, then I would *be* that for her.

At least, you know, in song form.

I scribbled away all afternoon, alternating between pen marks on a page and strums on my dad's Martin D-28 guitar. I structured the song's chords in the general vicinity of *A*, moving from *A* to *D* to *C#m* and back to *D*, followed by *A* to *D* to *E* and then resolving back to *D* once again. Slowly and steadily, I wove more and more words from my notes into the melody until I had the first verse and first chorus completed.

> *I wanna' be your time bomb*
> *I wanna' detonate in your arms*
> *Yeah, I'm the match you're looking for*
> *I can be the flame you adore*

I'll be the light in your sky
Fireworks like Fourth of July
This blaze, high above the sea
Will consume you and me

In my fifteen-year-old mind, I foolishly assumed that this was a foolproof way to win Serena's heart. I knew that she had some sort of fondness or attachment to me – our time together outside of class seemed to validate that. And my time studying the history of rock and roll had convinced me that chicks can't resist guys who write them great songs.

This has *to be a sure-fire bet*, I told myself. No pun intended, of course.

Within a few days, I had a pretty solid draft of the song ready to bring to the band. Our Tuesday/Thursday jam sessions were quickly becoming the highlights of my week, and I couldn't wait to share my words and melodies with the guys. I scratched out four handwritten copies of the lyrics and chords on lined paper, threw them in my guitar case, and brought them to our next practice.

"I have something I want us to play," I announced proudly to the group when we reconvened in my garage.

"What's that?" Ethan asked. "Another Social Distortion song? A Weezer cover?"

"Even better," I smiled proudly. "It's our first *original* song."

The guys straightened up as their eyes stretched open. Writing original songs was a whole new realm for us, a way to expand our horizons into uncharted territories. And I could see from their reactions that their curiosity had been piqued.

"Well, play it," Chunk demanded. "Let's hear it."

I passed out the handwritten copies of the lyrics and chords, popped open my bass guitar case, and propped myself up on a wooden chair. With reckless abandon, I started thumping away on the bass, hitting that droning D note over and over, before I started singing in my shaky voice.

"I wanna' be your time bomb..." I spouted off as the boys in the band listened with rapt attention.

For the next three minutes, I couldn't bring myself to make eye contact with the guys. However, as I hit the last ringing note of the final chorus, I looked up and saw them all staring at me intently. No one said a word, though – not at first, anyway.

"That song..." Steve began before trailing off. "That song is good. Like *really* good." He seemed skeptical for a second. "And *you* wrote that?"

I nodded.

"All by *yourself*...?" Steve's eyes scrunched up in disbelief. "No one helped you?"

I laughed and nodded again. "All by myself," I beamed proudly.

Steve looked around the room and saw his reaction mirrored in the eyes of our bandmates. His fervor felt infectious as he turned to the guys.

"Well," he said, "what are we waiting for?"

We picked up our instruments and rammed our way through the song together for the very first time. I didn't know it then, but "Time Bomb" would be the song that we played at the start of every single practice and every single show for the next few years. It was also the first of countless times that we would thrash and bash and strum and sing something that *I* wrote.

A week later, we felt like we were ready to take over the world.

Once we had "Time Bomb" down, I mustered the courage necessary for the second part of my plan. After practice one day, I called a band meeting.

"So, guys," I began. "What do you think about maybe having someone..." I paused. "Some *people* come and watch us play?"

"Like here? In the garage?" Steve asked.

"Yeah," I casually answered. "You know, just to have an audience or... *something*."

Chunk shot me a side-eyed grin. "You just want to invite Serena," he guessed.

I turned scarlet at the mention of her name.

"Who's Serena?" Steve asked innocently enough.

"She's the hottest girl in our grade," Ethan said with a smirk. "At least Brick thinks so."

"Shut up, Ethan," I spat back. I didn't think it was gentlemanly to *kiss and tell*, so I hadn't told the boys about my prematurely interrupted make-out session with Serena. That memory was something personal and precious. I didn't want to tarnish it with cheap talk and the objectification of women.

"She's just a good friend," I explained nonchalantly, shrugging my shoulders to downplay the high-stakes nature of my gambit. "She and I have spent a lot of time together this summer and we've gotten... close."

"Not close *enough*..." Chunk chimed in.

"Shut up, Chunk," I whined.

"Well, maybe I'll have to meet this mystery vixen," Steve yawned as he stretched out his arms. "I'm always game for hot girls. You could say that they're my forte."

Steve, on the other hand, had *no problem* objectifying women.

In any case, it was agreed: we would invite Serena and some of her friends over to practice, wow them with our musical prowess, and steal their hearts forever. There was no way my plan could go wrong.

Or so I thought.

As I imagined it, my five-part blueprint for winning over Serena Rios looked something like this:

- ❏ **Step One:** Write Serena a killer song.
- ❏ **Step Two:** Invite her to band practice.
- ❏ **Step Three:** Wow her with my musical skills.
- ❏ **Step Four:** Serena falls madly in love with me and passionately proclaims her feelings from the mountaintops.
- ❏ **Step Five:** We live happily ever after.

It seemed like a totally fool-proof plan. What kind of girl can resist a guy who writes her a great song and then serenades her with his rock band? What could possibly go wrong?

I had already finished step one, so I started working on step two. I was tempted to pick up the telephone and casually call her (just as I had done dozens of times throughout that summer), but my nerves got the best of me: my hand shook violently every time I even *thought* about reaching for the receiver. Coupled with the fact that I was still maneuvering the phonemic intricacies of speaking with my recently acquired braces, I was basically a nervous wreck. So, in the true fashion of a hopeless romantic, I actually composed a handwritten invitation for Serena. Yes, a handwritten invitation. Ugh.

Serena Rios, it read. *You are formally invited to a practice of the Bookhouse Boys, to be held August 1 at 1997 Lago de Paz Court. It'll be explosive. Feel free to bring friends. – Brick*

Later that afternoon, I stealthily dropped off the letter on her front porch, hightailing it out of sight before anyone could catch me. As much as I desperately wanted to see Serena laugh, to hear her say my name, I also felt utterly petrified. So many doubts ran rampantly through my mind: *What if it backfires? What if she wants even* more *space because she thinks I'm some weird stalker? What if she completely misses my metaphor and thinks I'm a crazy arsonist?*

At the time, I thought I was being clever with my note. *It'll be explosive*, I had written brashly. Serena had wanted a catalyst in her life, and I hoped that this might inexorably ignite something in her frozen heart.

True, I was playing with fire…

But *I* was the one who was going to get burned.

Ultimately, the day ended up providing a *different* kind of spark, one that would light a long line of fuses and eventually change the entire course of my life.

Pretty dramatic stuff for a simple band practice.

In the days leading up to that ill-fated practice, I stressed over every little detail. You know all those teen movies when the protagonist freaks out before a big date? They're not too off-the-mark, really. Even punk-rock high school boys fall prey to such silly shenanigans: I fretted about what to wear, how I should do my hair, what kind of position I should stand in. I cut my nails. And then cut my nails again, a few days later. I cleaned up my room. I repositioned the trophies on my desk and reordered the books on my shelves.

In short, I was a wreck.

Finally, the big day arrived. I wasn't even sure if Serena was going to make it: I hadn't heard from her since I dropped off my invitation, and we no longer faced the forced collaboration of Chemistry class that forged our fates together. As the guys filtered into the garage for practice one by one, I must have emanated electric energy.

"What're you all jazzed up for?" Ethan asked.

"Today's the day that Serena's supposed to show up," I reminded him.

"Ah," he responded mutely.

I watched the clock from the corner of my eye as we tuned up our instruments and flipped on our amps. The minutes seemed never-ending, the second hands of the clock's face moving at a glacial pace.

When is she going to show up? I kept asking myself.

The boys and I talked and joked and tuned as we waited for our special guest, the junior royalty of Sespe Creek High School.

When the door finally creaked opened – after what seemed like an eternity of waiting – it was my mom whose head appeared through the cracks.

"You have some *vis-i-tors*, Rick," she said with a singsong voice. "Should I tell them to come back another time?"

"*NO!*" I shot back (perhaps a little too excitedly) before catching myself. I smoothed my sweaty palms against my cotton t-shirt. "Um, please send them in."

"*O-o-o-kay*," my mom sang back, winking indiscreetly.

Moments later, three gorgeous, tanned girls emerged through the doorway like petite sun-glossed angels. The leader of the pack was instantly recognizable as Serena, though her skin had darkened from a butterscotch shade to a hazelnut hue.

"Hi," she meagerly mewed.

"Hey," I said.

"Is it okay that we're here…?" she asked hesitantly. "I got your note, but I wasn't sure."

"Yes, of course," I reassured her, a brief surge of confidence bolstering my spirits. "Come on in."

The three girls navigated their way through the cables and cords on the ground, maneuvering over to the unadorned couch propped against the south wall of the garage.

Turning to her left, Serena touched the shoulder of the tallest girl, a blonde with honey-colored skin and high cheekbones. "This is Amy," Serena said, as the tall girl stuck out her hand.

"Nice to meet you," I said as my hand met hers.

"And this," Serena intoned as she turned to her right, "is Megan."

A shorter girl, raven-haired with chestnut skin, stretched out her hand and met my gaze with her crystalline azure eyes.

"Hi," she said quietly.

Serena looked at me quizzically, cocking her head at a forty-five-degree angle. "You got braces," she noted.

"You're observant," I slurred back at her with my mumbling mouth. Except it sounded something more like "you're *ob-zh-ervant*."

As if it wasn't already hard enough to speak in front of hot girls.

I turned around to the guys and introduced them.

"This is Ethan and Charles," I said, gesturing behind me.

There was a flurry of handshakes and waves, Ethan and Chunk looking as nervous as I did in front of these exotic and exquisite creatures.

"And this," I said finally, "is the new guy, Steve."

Steve took Megan's fingers into his own, quickly shaking her hand before moving on to Amy. When he got to Serena, however, their eyes locked. Time seemed to stop. Her tan fingers lingered in his palm as they studied each other's faces, taking just a little too long for the trance to break.

"Charmed," Steve whispered as he held her gaze.

"And likewise," Serena blushed.

The moment left me reeling, deflating like a punctured balloon. "Should we get started?" I asked to no one in particular.

Without lifting his eyes from Serena, Steve responded affirmatively. "Let's rock and roll," he murmured.

We picked up our instruments, listened to Chunk count off a tempo, and then plunged into "Blitzkrieg Bop." The air felt electric, as if our guitars and amps fed into the sizzling spirit of the room's atmosphere. I looked up at the girls, and they were glowing, wide-eyed with mouths agape.

Maybe this would work out after all.

One song after another, we locked in a tight rhythm and ambled our way through the discordant dynamics of a punk rock quartet. Steve's voice was an edgy interloper, looping its way through the curves and grooves of the soundscape that Chunk, Ethan, and I created for him.

When I looked up at the girls, however, I noticed that their eyes were trained almost exclusively on Steve. Though Ethan, Chunk, and I were thoroughly rocking away on our respective instruments, all the attention in the room was focused on our new lead singer. Occasionally, I would catch the shorter girl, Megan, looking in my direction and smiling enthusiastically. Serena, on the other hand, never *once* looked over at me. Instead, her rapt attention was focused on the microphone of the lead singer – and the chiseled face immediately behind it.

Between each song, the three girls would clap enthusiastically, sometimes stretching and repositioning on the uneven padding of the couch. Before they could say anything, however, I would start thumping the bass guitar strings to signal the start of a new tune. There would be no between-song banter today, I decided. If the other guys in the band objected, they kept their reservations to themselves.

After a searing half-hour of non-stop punk rock cover songs, the band decided to take a short break. I rushed over to Serena and her cohort a little too eagerly, like a puppy dog greeting its owners at the door.

"So, what do you think?" I asked, wiping a stream of sweat from my brow.

"You guys are *amazing*," Megan said, looking up at me with wide blue eyes.

Serena, still not looking in my direction, agreed. "Yeah," she agreed emphatically, "unlike anything I've ever seen."

I followed the line of her eyesight... straight to the corner of the room where Steve casually leaned against the doorjamb with a half-consumed water bottle in his hand.

Amy was making small talk with Ethan, complimenting him on his guitar playing and reaching out to stroke her perfectly manicured fingers against the frets. The two smiled at each other in the meek, reserved manner of a blossoming flirtation.

Serena reached out and placed her hand on the outside of my bicep. Her touch was electric, but I did my best to suppress any outward display of emotion. "So, um... I was thinking," she began, finally looking me in the eyes after avoiding my gaze all afternoon, "maybe you guys might be interested in playing at a party?"

"What party might that be?" Steve asked from his solitary corner.

Serena looked away from me again, speaking directly to Steve. "I'm having this birthday party thing, a *quinceañera*, next week," she explained to him, as if no one else was in the room. "And, um, it would be really cool if you guys could play." She paused for a second, seemingly unsure of herself. "You know, if you're interested."

I looked around the room, first at Chunk, then Ethan, and finally at Steve. All three guys nodded their heads in varying degrees of excitement and anxiety.

"Count us in," Steve smiled at her.

"Cool," Serena muttered with a spellbound expression on her face.

"Cool," Steve echoed back.

The fuse had been lit.

CHAPTER TWENTY-SEVEN

"All Dressed Up for School"

I don't remember much about the week between that ill-fated band practice and the actual day of Serena's birthday party, though I assume the band must have rehearsed every single day with a renewed passion and vigor. And I can't say for certain, but I must have also perseverated over how I should dress for the big event. However, while many memories of that week rely on speculation, I do have a perfectly clear recollection of one pivotal, life-changing event: learning how to tie a necktie.

My dad, as always, was a source of encouragement and wisdom.

"If you're going to attend a fancy party," he explained, "then you better learn how to knot a necktie correctly. After all, you want to look dashing for the ladies in the audience, right?" He winked at me with crinkled eyes, his crow's feet folding into the creases of his temples.

Unexpectedly, my father threw me a balled-up necktie, a sapphire stretch of silk fabric with patterned elephants marching in rows across the backdrop. I studied the necktie, letting it uncoil in my hands like a baby snake and watching it unravel towards the floor.

"Follow me," he instructed as he marched off to the nearest bathroom. I threw the sapphire tie over my shoulder and trotted off behind him.

My father positioned us directly in front of the long horizontal mirror that devoured half of the bathroom wall. We looked like a strange split-screen "before and after" picture: despite my full head of hair that starkly contrasted his balding crown (not to mention the extra hundred pounds of weight he carried that distinguished us), we were nearly doppelgängers. It was eerie – an unexpected premonition of my future through the looking glass.

Immediately transforming back into a classroom teacher, my father cleared his throat, signaling his intent to start our lesson. "Every morning," he began, "when I put on a necktie, I think of it as a game. Sometimes I nail it on the first try, and sometimes I have to do it over and over again until I get it right."

At this point, he quickly demonstrated for me the procedure, wrapping the maroon fabric of his necktie gracefully in loops until it coiled perfectly around his thick neck.

"However, not all neckties are created equal," he dryly noted to me. "Some are longer. Some are shorter. Some are thicker and some are skinnier. Ultimately, though, what you want to do is maneuver the tie so that the very bottom of the fabric touches the middle of your belt buckle." Once again, he flawlessly wrapped and knotted the long stretch of fabric into a perfectly measured length.

I stared at him blankly, dumbfounded and unsure of where to begin. "Soooo…" I hemmed and hawed, twisting the silk series of elephants between my stubby fingers, "What do I do first?"

My dad, without missing a beat, unraveled his tie and turned his body to face mine. "First," he began, "you balance the lengths of the ends asymmetrically, so that you have more of the big diamond side hanging down." He demonstrated as he spoke, tugging on the thicker side of his maroon fabric until it hung disproportionately lower than the thinner end.

"Okay," I mumbled, clumsily mimicking his movements to the best of my abilities. "What's next?"

My father took in a deep breath, as if preparing to admit a dark secret to a cruel jury. "Bear with me," he continued, "because I know this next part sounds silly."

"It can't be any sillier than I feel right now," I muttered.

"Do you know what a *mnemonic device* is?" he asked me curiously, the corners of his eyes drawn in mild skepticism.

"Sure," I told him. "It's a way to help you remember something. Like that thing with the solar system. '*My very energetic mother just sent us nine pizzas.*'"

My father looked at me as if I had lost my mind.

"It's to remember the order of the planets," I explained, rolling my eyes at his ignorance. "You know. Mercury, Venus, Earth, Mars, Jupiter, Saturn, Uranus, Neptune, Pluto. *My very energetic mother...*" I counted off the planets on my fingers as I spoke, tapping my thumb with each new word.

My dad chuckled, bobbing his head with his toothy smile. "Yes, just like that."

I shuffled uncomfortably on the tile floor, once again tracing shapes on the rows of silk elephants that adorned the fabric draped around my neck.

"So, what's your mnemonic device for neckties?" I asked.

"It's like this," he explained, "*the wave washes over the beach once, then washes over it again, and then the wave creeps back into the ocean.*"

"I don't see how a tie is anything even remotely like a wave," I told him with typical adolescent snarkiness.

My dad just smiled and nodded his head. "Follow my lead," he instructed, grabbing the thicker end of his tie. "*The wave washes over the beach once.*" As he spoke, he looped the thicker end of his necktie over the thinner end. He turned away from the mirror to face me. "Got it so far, Junior?"

"Sure," I said, imitating his movements. "That's simple enough."

"Next," he continued, "*the wave washes over the beach again.*" He looped the tie over a second time, so that the fabric now had two loops cascading over each other.

"Okay…" I responded uncertainly, doing my best to replicate his fluid movements. "I think I got it."

My dad straightened his back, studying himself in the mirror with serious concentration. "And now, *the wave creeps back into the ocean.*" As he succinctly enunciated each word, he pulled the thicker end of the necktie through the fold that had been created by his clavicle. Finally, he pulled down on the largest expanse of fabric and tightened up the fluidly formed knot that gracefully slid towards his neck.

I copied his movements to the best of my abilities, sliding the large diamond through the folds of the fabric and squeezing the knot tight at the top. When I looked in the mirror at the end result, however, I could see that my tie didn't make it down to my belt. In fact, there was an embarrassing amount of t-shirt showing underneath the bottom of the tie. Slowly and methodically, I undid the knot and tried to string it together again. This time, however, it was too long, draping past the bottom of my belt and stretching out halfway to my knees. I grumbled under my breath as I fumbled with the fabric. Just like the real ocean, with its unpredictable shifting tides, the waves of silk refused my attempts to tame them.

Looking on, my father gently reassured me. "Don't worry, Junior. Just like everything else in life, this gets easier the more that you do it.

Keep practicing and it will all flow together smoothly. Eventually." Just to hammer home his point, he undid his tie, restrung it, and tightened it up in a series of fluid, unassuming movements.

I was simultaneously awestruck and withering in frustration over my inability to properly complete such a simple task. "But it only takes you *ten seconds* to get your tie right," I yelped in exasperation.

A gleam appeared in my dad's eye as he looked at me. "Have you ever heard the old folktale about the emperor's portrait?" he asked.

"It's not ringing a bell."

"Well," he began, plunging into his dramatic English teacher voice, "many years ago, there was an emperor who wanted the perfect portrait to adorn the walls of his palace. According to the story, he hires the best painter in the kingdom to depict his likeness. Months go by, then *years*, but the painter never delivers his expected masterpiece. Finally, one day, the Emperor huffs off to the painter's modest home and demands that the artist produce a final painting… right there on the spot."

I eyed him cynically. "What does this have to do with *tying a tie?*" I interjected.

"Just wait," he assured me, "it'll all make sense in a minute."

I'm sure I must have rolled my eyes or done something similarly obnoxious, but my dad just continued his story unperturbed.

"So, under intense pressure, the artist sits there at the easel, dips his brush into the paint, and proceeds to create the most beautiful, remarkable portrait that the emperor has ever seen. An hour later, the portrait has been completed and the emperor is simultaneously thrilled and frustrated. The emperor turns to the painter and angrily asks him, 'Why did you make me wait for *years* when it only took you a few minutes to complete my portrait?'"

Despite the adolescent temptation to mock everything that adults say or do, I remember being amused by my dad's storytelling at this point. Even if I had no idea where this folktale was heading, something about it resonated in my teenage heart.

My father, sensing just how invested in the story I had become, continued the tale in a softer, more deliberate voice. "When he hears this complaint," my father continued, "the painter just smiles at the Emperor, as if he's been expecting this exact reaction. 'Let me show you something,' the artist says, before leading the ruler to an adjacent art studio. Once they enter the studio, the Emperor sees dozens and dozens – perhaps *hundreds* – of portraits scattered around on easels and walls and even on the floor. 'You see,' the painter tells the Emperor, 'it didn't just take me *one hour* to craft your portrait. It took me *years* of painting in order to create your perfect portrait in one hour.'"

My father casually flipped the bottom of his silk tie as I leaned against the wall, pondering the meaning of the myth. "It didn't take me just ten seconds to tie this necktie," my father explained. "It took me *decades of practice* to be able to tie this piece of fabric in only ten seconds."

That lesson has stuck with me over the years. Every time that I hear about a band that becomes an "overnight sensation" or a first-time filmmaker who creates a genius debut motion picture, I wonder about the amount of time, effort, and training that went into that piece of art. When you encounter the flawless final product, what you *don't* see is the hours and hours of preparation and frustration that went into the creation of the work. *Pet Sounds* – arguably the greatest album of all time – didn't emerge fully formed from the brain of Brian Wilson in one single night. By 1966, the Beach Boys had already released ten albums of material, and *Pet Sounds* was Brian Wilson's crowning achievement – after a decade spent learning and practicing and fine-tuning his craft.

Twenty-eight years after the release of *Pet Sounds*, when I began writing my own songs, I started small. I wrote "Time Bomb." But then I wrote another song. And then another song. And another song after that…

Hit records don't appear out of nowhere: a songwriter usually produces many precursors and prequels as he gradually masters his craft. Writing "Time Bomb" for Serena was one small step for me, but one giant leap for my band.

It was also the catalyst for an entire decade of fire and ashes – musical and otherwise.

CHAPTER TWENTY-EIGHT
"Hang On to Your Ego"

The day of Serena's *quinceañera*, I was a bundle of nerves. Here I was, Mr. Heartbroken Bass Player, getting ready to woo the most gorgeous girl I knew – on the day of her birthday party, no less. Needless to say, I was about as calm as a motion-sickness-prone kid on a rollercoaster.

The afternoon flew by in a fuzz of shaky hands, misshapen neckties, and ill-fitting suits. Though Ethan, Chunk, and I only looked *mildly* uncomfortable and out of place, it was small consolation. We were entering uncharted territory – and the great unknown is capable of tormenting even the bravest teenager. We were no exception.

At least we came prepared. We had worked out our setlist days in advance, giving us the tiniest crumb of confidence on that intimidating afternoon. After much deliberation, we decided to play three carefully selected cover songs (with the microphone primarily in possession of our new lead singer) before concluding with our band's first original tune, "Time Bomb" – which we would dedicate to Serena on the momentous occasion of her fifteenth birthday. If nothing else, at least we would look like consummate professionals to the partygoers. Or so we hoped.

The party itself was a swarm of paper streamers and pink taffeta and enticing Mexican cuisine. Serena's family (both her mom's *and* dad's sides) had rented out the reception hall of the Libbey Park golf course in Ojai, and the entire facility looked like it was decorated for a wedding. I had never been to a *quinceañera* before, but it looked a lot like a fancy "sweet 16" party or a Bar Mitzvah reception, with lots of pristine white fabric and precious lace.

For this shindig, Serena was clearly the star of the afternoon, with professionally photographed portraits of her printed in poster-size reproductions. Everywhere in the hall, family photos were adorning the walls, standing on easels, and even hanging from the ceiling. Despite Serena's fears of being the "Basket Case," the party was well-attended; in fact, I think the entire Sespe Creek High School girls' soccer team was there – including some of Marina's friends from the varsity squad. A few of the young ladies who recognized me as Marina's brother gave me an approving nod and a smile... though none actually engaged me in conversation. So much for nepotism.

From across the room, I could see that Serena looked absolutely stunning, elegantly clothed in a luscious white silk dress that draped from her sun-kissed shoulders down to her sparkling silver high-heeled shoes. She was a vision, and my poor heart skipped a beat (or two) when she started walking in my direction.

Though Serena seemed graceful strolling down the sidewalk in sneakers – and running across a lumpy soccer field wearing cleats, for that matter – she teetered and tottered uncomfortably in her silver stilettos. As she made her way through the banners and streamers, she looked as if she might topple at any second. Like a little girl playing dress up, she had not yet mastered the adult world of heels.

When she finally arrived at the stage area, where the guys and I were dutifully setting up our equipment, she scanned the room in all directions before leaning into me and whispering discreetly. "Do I look okay?" she asked. "I feel like a walking doily."

"You look amazing," I told her.

She smiled politely and then continued looking around, tapping her perfectly manicured purple nails against the sides of her white silk dress. "Are all the guys in the band here? I don't see Steve..."

That's a weird thing to ask, I thought to myself. *Why would she care about Steve when she just met him a few days ago at band practice?*

"Ah, he's around here somewhere," I answered.

"Okay, good," she said. "I just wanted to make sure." Though I stood only a foot in front of her, she kept turning her head away from me, her eyes intently scanning the room.

"Are you okay?" I asked her.

"Yeah, yeah," she assured me. "I've got to go visit with my grandparents, but I'll see you in a little bit."

I expected her to lean in for a hug, but she simply walked away, tottering off in her high heels through bustling bunches of partygoers.

The party went as parties do: a flurry of guests sought the hostess's attentions and affections, the DJ played obnoxiously loud pop music, and the cooler high school kids in attendance awkwardly flirted with members of the opposite sex. Chunk, Ethan, and I stooped uncomfortably at a table in the far corner of the room, seemingly light-years away from the rest of our Sespe Creek classmates.

Steve, on the other hand, was a social butterfly. Whether joking with the jocks or cheering up the cheerleaders, he was the center of attention – a beacon of light in a darkened room. Just as he had done at band practices in the weeks leading up the party, he captivated the crowds around him, commanding attention equally from friends and strangers alike. I envied that magnetism, that ability to effortlessly glide from social group to social group without succumbing to shyness or anxiety. It was clear to me then that Steve was everything that I was not: a character foil to my protagonist, a burning flame to my flickering match.

His light would only shine brighter in the hours to come.

At long last, the time arrived for us to hit the stage for our performance. The DJ gave us a five-minute warning, and I could feel the tension rising from my stomach through my chest and into my throat. Like a tidal wave, anxiety covered every inch of my body, effortlessly soaking my soul through layers of skin and bone.

This is it, I told myself. *It's now or never.*

Just as we'd done at our talent show debut with Marina, we huddled together in a circle like a mismatched football team and placed our hands together, one atop another. "On the count of three," I told the boys, "we say *Cooper*."

"*Cooper*...?" Steve asked, eyes skeptically askew. He glanced around the circle, looking for some sort of confirmation, while his hands hovered hesitantly above ours.

"From *Twin Peaks*," I said, sweat forming above my brow. "You know. Agent Dale Cooper."

"It's a tradition..." Chunk explained sheepishly.

"All right," Steve grumbled, insouciantly admitting defeat. He shrugged and threw his hands on the top of the pile. "Whatever."

Together, we formed a hydra of hands – a many-headed musical beast ready to take on any challenger. "*COOPER!*" we chanted in unison, lifting our hands apart and raising them towards the ceiling.

Chunk, Ethan, Steve, and I found our places onstage and began to tune our instruments. Based solely on facial expressions, I could tell that Chunk and Ethan felt just as nervous and anxious as I did; Steve, on the other hand, glowed with an uncanny confidence. Somehow, this newcomer to our band looked ready to hurdle any obstacle that might cross his path, and he exuded a cocky energy that made him appear significantly older than the rest of us. Though this was Steve's first gig as our singer, he looked like *he* was the pro, like *he* was the one who owned the stage – while the rest of us were simply cardboard props.

The celebratory pop music dimmed like movie theater lights and the static crackle of the DJ's microphone interrupted the gentle murmur of conversation at the taffeta tables. As the voices at the party faded into white noise, the DJ called attention to the front of the room.

"Ladies and gentlemen, *hombres y mujeres*," he announced. "We have some very special guests here tonight to help us celebrate. The birthday girl has invited some of her friends – *una banda* – to play *la música rock*, so we're going to let them entertain us for a few songs. *Por favor*, please welcome to the stage... *The Bookhouse Boys!*"

The partygoers clapped politely but unenthusiastically, unimpressed with our introduction. This was not a punk-rock crowd quivering with anticipation or hanging on our every word; this was a multigenerational gathering of grandkids, grandparents, and everything in-between. I scanned the audience and saw faces of all shades and shapes, wrinkles and creases.

Only then, looking down from the stage, did that deferential doubt pop into my head. *What have we done?* I asked myself.

I didn't have much time to ponder that rhetorical question. Right on cue, Chunk clicked a four-count on his drumsticks and the band plunged into the opening hailstorm of "Blitzkrieg Bop." Ethan's buzz-saw electric guitar launched into the power chord progression of the song, while Chunk and I thumped along on our respective instruments.

The crowd was caught off-guard at first. Undoubtedly, they must have asked themselves, *"What is this loud, anarchic music doing at such a classy event?"* However, despite the skeptical demeanor of some elderly attendees, I saw some disbelieving smiles on the faces of our peers – and even on the lips of parents in the crowd (many of whom must have remembered the 1970s heyday of the Ramones). For a few seconds, the crowd seemed evenly split between the elders and the youth…

And then Steve started singing.

His opening shouts of *"Hey, ho, let's go!"* instantly caught the attention of the audience. While I mean no disrespect to Joey Ramone (one of my musical heroes, mind you), I have to admit that Steve sounded even better belting out the song than the tune's original singer. The prodigious gut feeling that tingled through me the first time I heard Steve singing in the locker room resurfaced while we were on that compact stage. Even as I walloped the strings of my bass guitar, I found myself entranced by our lead singer. This guy was good. *Really* good.

When I looked down at the crowd, I discovered that I wasn't alone. Every single set of eyes in the venue seemed glued to Steve. Young, old, in-between – it didn't matter. As I scanned the audience, I saw Serena's mom, her arm draped around Oscar, nodding her head in approval as she watched Steve's every move. Oscar seemed equally enthralled with the music, swaying his shoulders side-to-side as his gaze paralleled that of his wife. I recognized Megan and Amy in the crowd, both of them decked out in figure-hugging sequined dresses – and both staring at Steve.

And then I saw Serena.

Her mouth slightly agape, her perfect lips parted just enough for a stilted breath to escape, she looked spellbound as she stared at the stage...

At Steve.

My stomach dropped and I lost my place in the song, awkwardly fumbling through a few notes before I regained my footing. Instantly recognizing my uncharacteristic error, Chunk and Ethan shot me confused glances. While I tried to find my place again, I assured them with a few non-verbal gestures that I was okay. If Steve noticed, he didn't care; he was too busy strutting around the stage like Mick Jagger to be distracted by any imperfections from the band playing behind him.

A little over two minutes after we started, we hit the last ringing chord of "Blitzkrieg Bop" and waited for the audience's response. Without any hesitation, the tables in front of us cheered, whooped, and clapped. The enchanted high school girls sighed while eagerly slapping their hands together; the tough teenage boys nodded their heads in approval, jaws jutting out in a show of silent respect.

We had them. Or, at least, *Steve* had them.

Before the applause had a chance to wane, Chunk counted off our next tune: Social Distortion's "Story of My Life." Ethan dialed down the distortion on his guitar for the opening chords, but when Chunk and I came in on the second measure, the song swelled with our entrance; shortly after, Ethan punched his Gibson's distortion and slid through the lead guitar riff. By the time that we all chimed in on the "*la-la-la-la-la*" group vocals, the tacit approbation in the room seemed amplified into outright admiration. The partygoers knew that they were witnessing something special: the birth of a band with limitless potential.

Once again, when Steve leaned into the microphone, the crowd was in the palm of his hand. Like Social Distortion's singer, Mike Ness, Steve had a grizzled swagger in his voice – a confidence unmatched by his peers (then and now). Despite his muscled physique, Steve moved lithely across the stage, gliding and sliding and generally captivating the room. We all benefitted from his stage presence, obviously, but it was hard not to feel the pangs of jealousy creep in with each crescendo of applause. There was no doubt about it: Steve was the focal point of the group. The boys, the girls, the parents, *and* the grandparents all stared at him unflinchingly.

Even Serena.

Especially Serena.

Her gaze was rigidly focused on Steve as he strutted across the stage and gesticulated wildly in the way that only a true showman can pull off. All the while, Serena was like the moon orbiting the sun, bound by gravity to the celestial body in front of her. And all I could do was bear witness to the attraction.

As we finished up "Story of My Life," the crowd clapped and cheered with unadulterated enthusiasm. It felt good, hearing that kind of affirmation. Chunk and I had put in countless hours together over the years, and the additions of Ethan and Steve to the band bolstered our lineup. When you're tediously laboring away in your bedroom or your garage, you don't know if you're making any progress – or if you've developed into something more than a commonplace, amateurish talent. Hearing the crowd at Serena's party was a vindication, a reminder that we had cultivated some impressive musicianship that we could finally share.

We made it through "Blitzkrieg Bop" and "Story of My Life," which meant that it was *my* turn to sing lead. Though we agreed Steve would handle the majority of the vocals that day, I had convinced the band to let me sing lead on a cover of Green Day's "When I Come Around" – the same song that had been playing in Serena's car during our long drive back from Surfer's Knoll. Despite the stasis of our stalled romance, I hoped that this would spark a nostalgic memory for Serena, a reminder of the time that we had spent together during Chemistry class and that fateful summer day when we kissed. The guys reluctantly agreed, though it was obvious how hesitant they felt. I didn't really care, though, about their reservations. I just wanted to impress Serena. I would have done anything in my power to show her how dynamic and "explosive" I could be. This, I figured, would be the perfect opportunity.

It's now or never, I thought as I nervously walked up to the mic. This go-round, rather than Chunk tapping out the tempo on drums, Ethan started off the song with palm-muted guitar chords; after the first measure,

Chunk and I thundered in and joined the fray. Keep in mind that this was months before *Dookie* became a national phenomenon, so we looked like ultra-cool hipsters playing a cover of a relatively obscure punk band from the Bay Area. It didn't bother me, though. This song was meant for Serena. I was going to woo the girl that I cherished in front of this captive audience. We were off to a solid start, and though few folks in the audience had even heard of Green Day at that time, the crowd initially seemed engaged. And then I started singing.

To be fair, I did hit *most* of the notes that day… just not all of them. I faltered here and there as I meandered through the verses, but that's to be expected of an amateur singer in a high school rock band. The problem, however, is that I immediately followed Steve – a preternaturally talented young man with golden vocal cords. It didn't help that I struggled to sing through my newly wired braces, the slurred sibilance creating stark static in the microphone. As I soldiered on through my one moment of glory as a lead singer, I could sense the dynamic of the room changing, shifting away from the band to other, more captivating aspects of the party. It was like the air had been let out of our tires, as if the vibrant locomotive engine that had powered us down the tracks had simply stalled.

And I was the one responsible.

When I looked over at Serena, I could see that even *she* wasn't paying attention to the band anymore. Rather, she was engulfed in conversation with Megan and Amy, their voices twinkling with the secretive glint of private gossip. Occasionally, the girls would glance over at the stage, but never in my direction. Even when the song was over, and the crowd politely offered a smattering of unenthusiastic applause, Serena didn't bother looking up at me. There was no heartfelt "thank you" reserved for me this time.

In fact, she didn't even clap for me.

After three of the longest minutes of my life, I moved away from the microphone and let Steve strut back towards center stage. Almost immediately, the room's attention swirled back to the gravitational pull of his charisma. We were all planets orbiting Steve's frame, never daring to stray too far from his commanding presence.

"We have one more song," Steve told the crowd. His lips curled into a charming, roguish smile, and you could almost hear the sound of a hundred hearts simultaneously melting. "This next tune is something the band wrote for the birthday girl. This one's for you, Serena."

Wait a minute, I thought to myself. *The "band" didn't write this song. I did.*

I didn't have an opportunity to raise objections, however, as Chunk immediately counted out the intro to "Time Bomb" – and the rest of us followed suit.

"*I wanna' be your time bomb*," Steve belted out to the crowd – in a voice substantially stronger than I could ever muster. "*I wanna' detonate in your arms...*"

Things obviously weren't going according to plan, I realized. When Steve once again placed his lips behind the microphone, I was banking on him delivering my message to the world – specifically, to one very special girl in the room. The fact that he neglected to mention anything about *me* writing this song for *her* only reinforced my frustration.

This was supposed to be my moment to win her over.

Instead, it was becoming something else.

Serena's eyes betrayed her. She wasn't looking in my direction, wasn't gushing over the fact that I had scripted lyrics and conjured chord progressions for her. Instead, she was focused solely on the body behind the microphone – the one singing *my* words and *my* melodies. Though *I* was the one who had written the message, it became crystal clear then.

She was falling for the messenger.

It's a strange thing to watch someone else sing your songs on-stage. At first, it can be empowering, even flattering. After a short while, though, a sense of jealousy arises from deep within the caverns of your chest, a fear that no one will recognize that the song – the original construction of lyrics and music – was written by someone else.

Does the architect feel jealous while someone else cuts the ribbon in front of the structure she has designed? Does the gourmet chef ever feel slighted when the waiter delivers his culinary creation?

To put it in Beach Boys terms: did Brian Wilson ever worry that he wouldn't get credit for the melodies he crafted? Did he fret that another singer (whether it be Mike Love, Al Jardine, or Carl Wilson), would receive all the credit, while the composer stood alone in obscurity?

Because that is *exactly* how I felt the afternoon of Serena's party.

Throughout the three-minute performance of "Time Bomb," not a single person looked my way. Not a single set of eyes strayed in my direction. Not a single glance settled on the bassist who played on the side of the stage with a breaking heart. And when the riotous applause erupted after the song's conclusion, not a single person knew that *I* was the one who had written the song.

When I scanned the room, I saw the partygoers trading shouts and hollers as their hands slapped together with unrestrained excitement. This was a special moment for Serena, for the band onstage, and for the audience. It was a special moment for everyone…

Except me.

Because when I looked over at Serena and I saw the tears of joy welling up in her eyes, it wasn't me that she was thinking about.

It was Steve.

Hours later, after the lights of the party had dimmed and the guests had gone their separate ways, the Bookhouse Boys lingered behind to disassemble our equipment. As we unplugged our amps, wrapped up our cables, and tenderly placed our instruments in their respective cases, we felt an uneven mixture of exhilaration and anguish – with the anguish coming exclusively from me, obviously. Standing amid a floor of discarded streamers and deflated balloons, I felt my spirit sagging with the weight of defeat. I remember handling my hefty bass guitar, lifeless without the requisite electricity flowing through it, and thinking how empty it all seemed – the music, the party, the friendships. Sullenly, I placed my soundless instrument into the muffled plush of its guitar case and snapped the lid shut.

"Hey, guys," I called out to Ethan and Chunk as they packed up their equipment. "I'm going to catch some air before our ride gets here."

The pair nodded silently, perhaps recognizing how distant and defeated I looked.

Leaving my bass behind, I walked out through the wood-paneled doors of the hall into the cool embrace of the twilight. Keeping my eyes to the ground, I kicked an empty Pepsi can, the sound of the hollow aluminum ricocheting across the unattended sidewalk. Though no one was in sight, I could hear a faint murmur of conversation emanating from across the courtyard of the venue. The voices sounded familiar, and I instantly recognized one of them as Steve's. A part of me felt so angry that I wanted to slap the hell out of his perfectly chiseled face. Once I regained a modicum of self-control, I stormed off towards the silhouetted figures in the distance.

As I got closer, I could see two bodies huddled close together: a petite girl whose left leg was planted nervously against the edge of a wall, her silver heels seemingly cemented into the gray brick, and a muscular shadow of a young man leaning towards her. His arm was propped rigidly against the same wall, as if he were a superhero chivalrously preventing the structure from crashing down upon the girl's diminutive frame. I immediately recognized that the boy was Steve, undoubtedly flirting with some pretty young thing from the party... Of course, as he himself had noted, "hot girls" were his forte. This was, apparently, a master at work.

From my vantage point, I could only make out Steve's figure. I was beyond the peripheral vision of the young lady, whose white silk dress snaked sensually around the corner of the wall, flowing gently in the slight wind that breezed through the corridor. I couldn't see her face, but I noticed her perfectly manicured purple fingernails sneaking in brief brushes against Steve's arms – a pat here, a tap there, followed by a giggling slap against his forearm. I hid beneath the shade of a low-hanging palm tree and watched the couple flirt, waiting for an opportunity to confront Steve. As I saw it, he was a predator and she was his willing prey. The teenage incarnation of myself hiding in the shadows, on the other hand, couldn't imagine in a million years what that must have felt like for either party – the hunter *or* the target.

"Well, I've got to go," Steve said. I could just barely make out his words from my position a few yards away.

"Do you *have* to leave?" the girl asked, disappointed.

"Yeah," he sighed. "I need to get back and help the guys pack up."

"But you haven't given me my present," the girl whined coyly.

"Oh, really?" Steve asked, his rapacious voice inviting the girl closer. "And what might that present be?"

The girl's arms extended forward, and her face became visible from behind the brick wall. As she leaned toward Steve, she grabbed ahold of his collar with her purple fingernails and pulled him closer – his shoulders leaning in towards her, her face reaching up to meet his.

And their lips touched.

She kissed him.

Serena kissed him.

If you want a girl to like you, write her a song.

Just make sure she knows that *you* were the one who wrote it.

Not the lead singer.

Suddenly, a violent nausea swept over my body, as if my stomach was conspiring against me in this moment of crisis. I could feel the sickness ripple through my limbs until I couldn't stand or breathe or speak or cry; my legs suddenly felt heavier than tree trunks and my chest felt like it had been wrapped tightly in chains. For a split second, I lost my balance, my feet stumbling as I lurched away from my voyeuristic viewing.

Making my way back through the winding sidewalk pathway to the abandoned parking lot, I could feel the sting of betrayal tugging at my eyelids. I sat down on the edge of an excoriated curb, my fingers searching through the holes in the worn concrete for anything that could numb the sensations coursing through my fifteen-year-old frame. The ends of my fingernails scraped the jagged border of a broken concrete slab, lacerating the distal edges. Rather than pull away, however, I continued scratching and scratching until my fingernails were covered in a dusty white residue.

By the time that Steve surreptitiously sat down beside me on the curb, I was so wrapped up in my self-pity that I didn't hear or see him approaching. The lights of the party had dimmed, and the twilight seemed to fade like recessing waves on a shoreline. We sat there for a few minutes before Steve said anything. When he finally did speak, though, he commanded the conversation and steered us towards a destination only he could have planned. Strangely enough, it felt like being onstage again – just as I had seen earlier that evening, the world revolved around my new lead singer. Like everyone else, I was merely a satellite orbiting his life.

"I want to talk with you about a few things," Steve began calmly, his composed tone sharply contrasting the tempest in my heart. "We have something here, Brick. You, me, the band... We've got a future together."

While I realized that Steve's words held a lot of truth, I refused to nod or shake my head or even acknowledge his presence.

"Did you see the way they looked at us tonight?" he asked. "I've never experienced anything like it in my life. We were rock stars up there, Brick. *Rock. Stars.*"

Begrudgingly, I nodded in agreement, though I still refused to utter a single word. I wouldn't give him that satisfaction.

Steve shifted his position on the curb, kicking his legs out in front of him. "We were amazing tonight," he continued. "But we need to make some changes."

Despite my anger and frustration and agony, I couldn't stop myself from answering. I turned to face him, my eyelids flittering and convulsing as I tried to hold back the welling waters behind my eyes.

"What do you mean by '*changes*,'" I asked, my voice quaking.

"Here's the thing," Steve began. "You're clearly a *really* talented musician and you have a lot of potential as a songwriter. Did you see how the audience responded to 'Time Bomb' tonight?"

I saw everything, I thought to myself. *Before* and *after the show.*

Even though I didn't offer him any audible response, Steve persisted with his sales pitch, undeterred. "I think you have a real shot at making a career out of this, playing bass and maybe even writing songs..." He hesitated briefly. "But you'll never make it as a singer."

His comment took me by surprise. I didn't fancy myself Robert
Plant or Roger Daltrey or anything, but I also didn't think of myself as a
hopelessly untalented vocalist.

"What's that supposed to mean, exactly?" I shot back, trembling.

Steve drew his frame upright, his posture defensive and deliberate.
He continued to tread lightly as he proceeded. "Don't get me wrong, you
can hit the notes," he admitted, "*most of the time*. But let's be honest: you
have a really *thin* voice. You simply don't have the vocal cords to sing for
a rock band."

"And you do," I mumbled.

"You're right, Brick," he echoed back. "I do."

Steve let his statement hang in the air momentarily, like smoke
wafting upward from a pipe. "You can sing, Brick, but you're not a *singer*.
You just don't have the fire or the charisma that this band needs… that this
band *deserves*."

His words stung, but I also knew that he was right. *He* was the
singer, and I was just someone who could hit the notes. Most of the time.

"Frankly," he admitted, "it's kind of embarrassing to see you up
there singing like that. We had the audience for those first few songs, and
then when you took over… Well, your singing was more like a
commercial interruption. The audience completely lost attention. I mean,
we *had them* until you started singing. And then we lost them. Right until
you handed back the microphone to me." He took a cool breath and
blurted out his summary. "You're just not *lead singer* material."

"That's a really shitty thing to tell someone," I gasped.

"I'm just being honest with you," Steve said, his voice returning to
a softer, maddeningly calm tone. "Like I said, I think you can make it as a
musician. Maybe even as a songwriter, if you can keep writing songs as
good as 'Time Bomb.' But you're *never* going to be a singer. It might be a
shitty thing to say, but it's the cold, hard truth."

I was at a crossroads. I wanted to hate him, to pummel his perfect
face, but I also felt myself unwillingly sucked into his scheme like another
victim of his gravitational pull. I could go with the easy path, full of

yelling and screaming and cursing. I could tell Steve that I was done with him and the band and that he could go to hell. Or I could bite the bullet.

Let me tell you, it wasn't an easy decision.

"So, what do you propose?" I finally muttered.

Steve smirked at me, his eyes lighting up. "I'm glad that you asked," he said. "Here's what I'm proposing. We team up. Let's be honest, Brick. No one really cares about the songwriter."

Serena sure didn't, I thought to myself.

"Unless…" Steve suggested vaguely, letting his words trail off.

"Unless *what?*" I asked, taking the bait.

"Unless you have an attractive salesman to peddle your product, Brick." He patted me condescendingly on the back and left his arm draped over my shoulders. "Musically speaking, you're the brains. I'm the brawn. Independently, we can only go so far. But *together…*"

Once again, he let his words float into the ether of the suddenly absent summer breeze. Even the earth seemed to hang on his every word.

"*Together*," he continued, "we can go farther than either of us would ever make it on our own. You need me. And I need you."

As much as I hated to admit it, he was right.

Steve continued outlining his master plan. By joining forces, he contended, we could conquer the world. With my musical skills and his singing, we could turn this band into something magical, something that could lead us to fame and fortune. This band had *potential*, he claimed, but it would only work if he and I *worked together*.

Though my ego was beyond bruised, I felt myself drawn further into his web. Steve was (and still is) a fantastic salesman. Coupled with his unique, powerful voice, he had exactly what we needed to fill our band's frontman slot. I did not.

"One more thing," he added. "We've got to change the name of the band. The *Bookhouse Boys…?*" He scoffed. "Really? What are we? A bunch of nerds in a library? Or are we a punk band?"

For the first time all evening, I laughed. Steve probably thought I was chuckling at the ridiculous nature of our band's name; the truth, however, is that I suddenly saw the gap between the two of us. I was a

Bookhouse Boy, quiet and reserved. Steve, on the other hand, was a punk-rock singer. Could those two irreconcilable characters ever find harmony as they played side-by-side?

"So, we're in agreement?" he asked. "We change the name of our band?"

This is our *band now?* I thought to myself.

"Fine," I whispered.

Steve straightened his back, perched upright on the curb, and tucked his legs beneath his muscular arms.

"And one last thing," he sighed, a hint of uncertainty in his voice.

"Yeah?" I asked.

"About Serena…"

I didn't even flinch.

"She's yours," I told him, resignation spreading across my face like black clouds across a gray sky.

He nodded solemnly, with the knowing expression of a victor after his opponent has conceded defeat.

The deal had been made.

Serena and the band were now his.

Once again, I felt trapped. For a few glorious days, it seemed as if all the stars in my life had aligned: the band was thriving without Marina, we had a promising new addition with Steve taking over the frontman's microphone, summer school had subsided into summer vacation, and I had my first kiss (with my dream girl, nonetheless).

Just as quickly, however, it was all stolen out from under me – like a clichéd magic trick in which the cloth is jerked free of the table and all the fragile china remains unmoved.

The Bookhouse Boys were no more.

My heart had been broken by Serena.

And the icing on the cake: our new lead singer had stolen my band *and* my dream girl…

I was no longer treading water.

I was drowning.

CHAPTER TWENTY-NINE

"Wind Chimes"

I spent a protracted, isolated weekend moping in my bedroom. I wasn't just devastated: I was immobilized, unable to muster the determination to simply get out of my bed that morning, that afternoon, that evening, through the night, and even into the next day. Periodically, one of my parents would knock on the door, asking if I was okay and offering me food or drink. I would mumble something about not feeling well, tell them to go away, and then crawl back under the covers. God only knows how long I could've lasted in my ceaseless state of self-pity and self-loathing, had it not been for my parents.

Depression is a funny thing. It cripples you, destroys you. It leaves you feeling hollow and empty and useless. Early-onset depression, which tends to manifest itself at different times in children and teens, sometimes gets overlooked by adults – especially in high-achieving students, like myself. The fact that I was so overwhelmingly crushed by the events described in the previous pages should have been a red flag to everyone around me. My parents, my sister, my friends, and/or my teachers should have known that something was awry with your humble narrator from a very early age. Someone should have noticed something.

Alas, such was not the case.

Though the summer of 2000 was undoubtedly the worst time of my life, a season in which I *completely* fell apart, there were hints of that impending breakdown threaded throughout every stage of my life. Whether it was my childhood anxiety or my inability to cope with Serena breaking my heart or my withdrawal after the *quinceañera*, I had a tendency to shut down and drop out at the first sign of a seemingly insurmountable roadblock.

As we crawl ahead from the summer of 1994 through the next few years of my life, keep in mind that the darkness of depression had already cast a heavy shadow over my mind. While things would get better in just a matter of years, the 1990s were a hard time for me, a decade that I would prefer not to revisit – or even think about, for that matter.

A lot of people struggle to understand Brian Wilson's emotional breakdown in 1967 and his subsequent decade spent in limbo, as he failed to cope with his fragile faults and simply disappeared into the safe security of his bedroom. Not me. Though I was just a fifteen-year-old high school kid, I understood it better than I should have.

While I hadn't experienced the drugs or the schizoaffective disorder or the scars from child abuse that temporarily destroyed the Beach Boys' resident genius, I felt so emotionally crippled in the aftermath of Serena's *quinceañera* that I couldn't bear to face anyone. Instead, I kept my bedroom door locked, playing the second half of *The Beach Boys Today!* album on endless repeat until my father finally took it upon himself to rouse me from the self-indulgently gloomy cave of my room. Being the Beach Boys fanatic that he was, I'm sure he could tell from hearing "Please Let Me Wonder" and "Kiss Me, Baby" over and over that something was amiss. He knocked on my door, cracked it open a few inches, and entered my room before I could even gather the strength to say a single word.

"We should talk," he said firmly, his eyes fixed upon my dormant frame. "Why don't you hop in the shower and throw on some clean clothes? We'll go get something to eat."

When I didn't move from my prostrate position, my dad grew a little more assertive.

"You have thirty minutes," he directed in his stern teacher voice. "Get moving."

Though I *really* didn't want to get out of bed, I knew better than to fight against my dad's orders. Defiance was not tolerated in my family, and my parents had made it very clear from my childhood on that we did *not* disobey their requests. Plus, my stomach was churning with hunger.

"Yes, sir," I mumbled.

And like a smelly, pimply, unshaven Lazarus, I arose.

I lurched to the restroom and took my first shower in days. I can't imagine how repulsive I must have smelled. Emerging from the sizzling steam of the bathroom, I threw on clean clothes, tied up the shoelaces on my ink-black Converse, and exited my musty man-cave. It felt like a monumental task just to walk through the narrow hallway into our kitchen, but I begrudgingly limped forward.

"Well, look who it is," Marina snarked at me. She was still a few days away from her departure for college, and she seemed to find great joy in harassing her little brother at every opportunity.

"Shut up, Marina," I grumbled.

My dad, sitting at the kitchen table with a copy of James Joyce's *Portrait of the Artist as a Young Man,* tossed me a set of keys. Though they chimed through the air as they sailed towards me, I gracelessly fumbled as I tried to catch them.

"It's a good thing you're a lineman and not a wide receiver," Marina muttered under her breath.

My dad forced a grin and nodded his head in my direction. "It's time for a driving lesson," he informed me. "You're going to learn how to steer today. And then we'll get something to eat."

You would assume that the prospect of learning how to drive would motivate even the most heartbroken teenager, but I just grunted bitterly and followed my dad out the front door to his old, beaten-up Buick Regal.

As much as I tried to muster the strength for a simple smile, I couldn't do it. In fact, when I stepped into the driver's seat, I just stared off into the distance at the claustrophobic hills of Ojai's colossal Sulphur Mountain. I knew that somewhere out there, miles and miles from my stifling suburban street, thousands of rivers and creeks would make their way to the wide berth of the Pacific Ocean. From my vantage point on Lago de Paz Court, however, the mountains seemed confining and suffocating. I wasn't sure that I would ever be able to breathe easily as long as I was trapped in this sweltering desert of a town.

Lost in my daydream, I completely forgot to unlock the passenger-side door. My father, God bless him, just patiently tapped on the glass window and gave me a pouting smile. I leaned over the center console, unlocked the door, and pulled the handle.

Wrestling his large frame into the passenger seat, my father grimaced as he contorted his substantial belly into the seatbelt. "You know someone really loves you when they unlock your car door for you," he told me sarcastically, attempting to catch his breath as he buckled himself in. "Does Serena do that for you?"

I muffled a moan. "I really don't want to talk about Serena right now, Dad."

"Fair enough," he murmured back, his tempered voice barely more substantial than a whisper.

I released a weary sigh from my lungs. "To answer your question, though… No. She doesn't. She lets herself into the car first."

My dad pondered that thought for a second. "A girl who unlocks your car door for you first – *before* she lets herself in – is considerate and thoughtful," he told me. "She's the kind of girl that you don't let go."

"What about the girl who doesn't?" I asked, my fingers wrapped around the wheel.

"She's *not* the kind of girl you want to keep around," he answered. "Trust me."

My father… always full of sage advice. Even if I didn't want to hear it.

Over the next hour or two, we slowly rolled through our neighborhood streets at something akin to a sloth's pace. I wasn't exactly a quick learner at this kind of stuff, and I became increasingly frustrated as I grappled with even the basic mechanics of the gas pedal and the brakes. If you gave me a book, I was golden; put me in charge of my own destiny, however, and I struggled to steer.

My dad, meanwhile, never lost his patience with me. There was no barking of commands or sneering at my limited skills or anger at my inability to apply gentle pressure to the brake pedal. After one particularly jarring application of the brakes, though, I shifted the car into neutral, closed my eyes, and placed my forehead on the steering wheel. For a minute, I remained frozen in that position, unable – or unwilling – to lift my head from the worn leather casing.

"Are you okay?" my father asked cautiously.

I clenched my eyelids tight. "I don't know where I'm going, Dad." Tears threatened to spill forth from my stinging eyes, and I bit my lip hard.

He paused, waiting for some kind of cue. When none came, he gently placed the palm of his left hand on the edge of my shoulder.

"We're not just talking about cars now, are we?" he asked.

I opened my mouth, ready to tell him about Steve and Serena and the band and everything else that seemed to be crashing down around me. I wanted to tell him about how crippled and isolated and broken I felt, about how something dark and debilitating had a perpetually steady grip on the space between my ribcage and my lungs.

But no words came out.

Instead, as my lips quivered uncontrollably, my body began to convulse. Sobs and tears streamed effortlessly from the firm creases of my eyelids onto the cold, uncaring casing of the steering wheel. The saline streaks silently trickled down the serrated bumps of the circular shape pressed to my forehead.

"Can you steer us for a little while?" I finally asked, somehow making words form between the sharp pain of my eyelids and the dense tension in my chest.

"Of course," he said. "I could use some coffee, anyway. Let's go find someplace quiet."

Slowly, warily, I pulled myself free from the seatbelt, my posture rutted like a crumpled envelope. I opened the door, emerging from the driver's side, and felt the wave of the inland summer heat jolt my limbs. We rounded the back of the car's frame and switched seats, my dad stolidly situating his large frame behind the steering wheel. After I painstakingly buckled my seatbelt in place, Dad hit the gas and we proceeded up Creek Road towards the imposing expanse of Highway 33.

We spent most of our drive making small talk, my dad doing everything he could to elicit some kind of response from me in my emotionally emaciated state. I wasn't intentionally standoffish, but I'm sure I must have come across that way. God bless him, my father never lost his calm and sensitive demeanor. Through most of the drive, I kept my eyes diverted to the mountains to our North, studying the browns and greens that dusted the peaks of the summer hills.

After switching from the 33 to the 101 and veering off to the tranquil Main Street freeway exit in Ventura, I felt a vague sense of déjà vu: this was only a few sand dunes away from that long, heartbreaking conversation with Serena, the beach-born backdrop where she made it clear that we would never be anything more than friends. Instead of careening towards the Pacific Ocean, however, we drove up Main Street past the San Buenaventura Mission. Finally, we turned onto Palm Street, up a steep ramp of gray charcoal pavement, and parked right outside my dad's favorite coffee shop, Café Voltaire.

In the mid- to late-1990s, Café Voltaire was an ultra-hip café/restaurant in downtown Ventura. This little locally run establishment served up the best coffee in town, and the unconventional urban décor made it feel like an edgy bohemian library. Plus, it was named after a French philosopher. As could be expected, my English teacher father was smitten with the place.

It might sound strange, but this little coffee shop served as a pivotal setting during my adolescence. Growing up in the Ojai Valley area, I felt trapped by the towering mountains and the curving arroyos. Just a few miles west, however, was Ventura – our sister city, situated on the edge of the ocean. Whereas Ojai seemed insufferable in its oppressive heat, Ventura always benefitted from the coastal airflow that could tame even the most sweltering days. So, when the Smith family wanted to escape from the smothering arms of our hometown, we would hop on the 33 and head for downtown Ventura; there, among the beautiful breezes and the scenic sunsets, we would breathe easier and reboot ourselves. Of course, since it was *my* family, our journey always had a destination dependent on food and drink: after an afternoon relaxing at Surfer's Knoll or roaming the sidewalks of the Harbor Village, we would inevitably wind up at Café Voltaire, where my dad would always order a hefty serving of coffee with his meal.

As a child, I was completely and utterly disgusted by coffee. The thought of drinking that bitter, pungent liquid seemed absolutely revolting. My father, on the other hand, pretty much considered it a sacrament.

"The Greek gods had their ambrosia," he would explain, "but mere mortals have the gift of coffee. It's just too bad that java doesn't provide immortality."

"You can keep your coffee, Dad," I would tell him. "I'll stick with Coca-Cola."

"To each his own," he would reply with a wink.

That afternoon, however, as we emerged from my dad's car, the sunlight seemed particularly oppressive, blinding me and forcing me to shade my eyes with an awkwardly cupped hand. My dad gently placed his palm on my back, urging me forward from our parking spot to the smooth surface of the concrete. We moved silently, side-by-side in the summer heat, until we approached the café. As we walked past a set of rusty, ornate wind chimes that had been tied to the tree by the entrance, I watched the metal pieces sway in time with the breeze.

How terrible to be a set of wind chimes, I thought to myself, *floating on the simplest wind, but bound for eternity to the rigid, unmoving limbs of a tree.*

We continued walking towards the café, the subtle strains of the wind chimes twinkling behind us. When we reached the entrance, my dad swept his arm forward, opening the door for me and holding it in place until I entered. As always, my father placed me first – in every aspect of life.

We politely studied the menu, scanning the black slates adorned with little white block letters that described entrees and prices. Realistically, though, neither of us needed any time to examine our culinary options. We were going to order the same things that we always ordered: coffee and Coca-Cola. We were creatures of habit.

After we paid the cashier, we looked around the packed café for a place to sit. My dad took the lead, directing us toward an isolated booth tucked away in the back corner of the venue. We quietly settled into our seats, and I fiddled clumsily with a razor-thin napkin on the table.

Finally, my dad broke the silence.

"I know the past few weeks have been hard for you," he said gently. "But you can't hide in your room forever. You need to talk about the things that are bothering you. If you hold everything bottled up inside your heart, you're bound to feel lost and overwhelmed."

I nodded silently.

"So, this is what's going to happen today," he told me. "We're going to sit here with our drinks. We're going to make some small talk. And, when I finish my first cup of coffee, you're going to tell me what's *really* going on with you." He paused and looked down at his thick hands. "When you talk, I'm just going to listen. I'm not going to judge. I'm not going to give you fake sentiments and lies about life being wonderful. But what I *will* do is give you some real man-to-man suggestions. Ultimately, though, you're going to be the one who determines your own fate. No one else can do that for you. Especially not your old, bald, fat father."

He gave me his puckish grin, stepping up from his seat.

"Right now, though," he said, "I'm going to pick up our drinks from the counter."

I took a deep breath, letting the air fill my aching lungs and clenching my hands into wobbly fists. I didn't want to tell anyone what I was going through, but I also knew that it was pointless to resist my father's directives. Whether I liked it or not, I couldn't circumvent this conversation.

My dad returned moments later, cautiously clutching an oversized mug of coffee and a glass filled with Coke. He handed me the soda and then plopped himself down in his chair across the table. Tenderly, he wrapped his fingers around the coffee cup, as if he held the world in that simple porcelain mug.

"So, small talk..." my father said, his voice trailing off. "I've heard *The Beach Boys Today!* escaping from your bedroom these last few days. On repeat, I might add."

"Yeah," I admitted tentatively, swirling my straw counterclockwise in my cold glass of Coke.

"That's a great album," he said, taking a small sip of his coffee. Steam issued forth from the top, wafting into oblivion, but my dad paid it no heed. "What's your favorite song on the record?"

I took a drink from my soda, nervously chewing the plastic straw while I thought about his question. "It would have to be either 'Please Let Me Wonder' or 'I'm So Young,'" I said. "And the original version of 'Help Me Ronda' with the funky name spelling is kind of interesting, though it's not as good as the rerecorded one everyone knows from the radio."

My dad dumped a packet of pure cane sugar into his coffee, mixing it in with his spoon. "Those are all good choices," he agreed. "But, for me, the song that always hits hardest is 'Kiss Me Baby.' I love that overlapping set of voices at the end of the song. It's so beautifully constructed and angelic."

Despite the fact that I hadn't eaten much in the last few days, I still felt nauseous; the unrestrained hunger that I should've felt manifested itself as queasiness instead of craving. Even the super-sweet, saccharine soda in front of me tasted vaguely sour.

My father, in sharp contrast, kept dousing his coffee with sugar and cream. The almost-black liquid slowly became a caramel color as he added another splash of cream and another packet of sugar.

In fact, as my dad continued swirling the cauldron of coffee in front of him, I could feel the disgust spreading to my face. "Would you like a little *coffee* with your creamer?" I asked, my voice saturated with sarcasm.

My dad wouldn't take my bitter bait, though. He just chortled with his usual deep-bellied laugh, wiping down his spoon with a napkin. "If there's one thing I've learned in my four and a half decades on this planet, it's this: life is too short to drink your coffee black."

"What's that supposed to mean?"

"It means that life is already bitter enough without depriving yourself of the simple pleasures," he explained. "Just because you're drinking from a bitter cup doesn't mean that it will always stay that way. Sometimes, all it takes is a little sweetness – a little cream and sugar, if you will – to make the world more comfortable and complete. Enjoyable, even."

I eyed him suspiciously. "I'll stick with my soda, thank you very much."

"Your loss," my dad said with a smirk.

Once again, we returned our eyes to the drinks before us. We sat in silence for a few minutes, each of us focusing our time and attention on the placid tabletop that divided us.

"I know you probably don't want to talk about it," my dad said, breaking the silence. "But it's clear that something's going on with you. I've been teaching high school long enough to recognize an unhappy teenager from a mile away. You, son, seem like you've driven beyond the neighborhood of *unhappy* onto the open highway of *misery*."

My eyes welled with tears and I choked back a thick clot of muscle that formed in my throat. "You could say that," I admitted sheepishly.

He looked at me with a tender, patently paternal expression. "So, what's going on...?"

"It's a long story," I muttered, a single, solitary tear tracing its way down my cheek. I grabbed a coarse napkin from the tabletop and used it to wipe my eyes.

"Lucky for you," he grinned, "it's summer vacation. I've got all the time in the world."

Over the next two hours, I told him everything. I explained about Serena and the band and the *quinceañera* and Steve and football. I told him about my depression and my anxiety. The whole time, he kept his eyes trained on me and his hands perched upon the table, never interrupting with his reactions or his opinions. A few times, I found myself wiping away streaks of saline from my cheeks, my lips trembling as I unloaded all of my thoughts and feelings in that little bohemian café.

All the while, my father just sat and listened.

Finally, after what seemed like an eternity of my emotional vomiting, my dad softly interjected. "Remember when I asked you earlier about your drive with Serena?"

"Sure," I grumbled.

"You told me that she gets into the car herself before she lets you in, right?"

"Yup," I grumbled.

"I know it's a bizarre question," my father prefaced, "but does she *ever* open the door for you first?" He studied me somberly, awaiting my reaction.

That *was* a bizarre question. Or so I thought.

"No, she doesn't," I said. I eyed him skeptically. "Why do you ask?"

He pursed his lips into a jumbled crease of flesh. "So, she *always* gets in the car before you?"

"Yes," I answered, albeit more emphatically this time. "Does that matter?"

"It *does* matter, Junior," he told me, shifting in his seat and leaning forward. "Like I told you before, a girl who unlocks your car door for you is considerate and thoughtful. That's the kind of girl that you keep around."

I reflected on his words like a convoluted math problem that needed to be solved with multistep proofs. "Why's that?" I asked.

"Because you want to be with someone who respects you enough to think of you as an equal partner, not a burden to carry," he explained. "A strong, healthy relationship requires two companions who look out for each other. Just as you should put *her* needs before your own, she should be willing to put *your* needs in front of *hers*. If Serena treats you as an afterthought, she doesn't deserve you. I know you might disregard what I'm telling you, because every parent is supposed to say this... but you deserve better than that, Junior." He stared at me intently, as if his gaze could burrow through the intangible air and into the thick cage of my cranium.

I snickered sullenly to myself. *Of course,* a parent would say that to his child. I tried to change the subject. "What does that have to do with opening car doors?" I asked.

My father smirked at me in his frustratingly wizened way. "The driver who doesn't open the door for her passenger first is – consciously *or* unconsciously – more concerned about herself than others." He lifted his right hand above the table and extended his pointer finger towards my chest. "And when *you're* driving, Junior, you *sure as hell* better open the door for your passenger first. If someone fails to reciprocate that kind of simple act for you, it's a potential sign that she's selfish and self-absorbed." He leaned back, folding his hands down across his sizable belly. "Call me old-fashioned, but I think chivalry is a vital part of any successful relationship. And it's not about traditional gender roles. It's about loving each other enough to *take care* of each other... Even with something as simple as unlocking the car door for the person you love."

"That's easy for you to say," I spat back bitterly. "You've got the perfect life."

He took a deep breath, his fingers draped over a crumpled napkin, and he hesitated – as if he was unsure about how he wanted to proceed. When he finally spoke, it was with the tender, patient tone of a wounded kindergarten teacher.

"You know, I see a lot of myself in you," he told me. "The good *and* the bad."

My face scrunched up into a defensive scowl. "What's that supposed to mean?" I asked.

My dad took another deep breath before continuing. He seemed to be measuring his words carefully, like an apothecary in front of an ancient brass scale. "When I look at you," he explained, "I see a bright young man with *so much* potential. I see a hard worker, a great student, an exceptional mind, and a talented musician." He paused, letting his fingers wander along the chipped edges of the tabletop. "But I also see a very sensitive human being. You don't shake things off like Marina does, and you've always been troubled by events more than is healthy for you. You, son, are what we call an *'old soul.'* You are mature beyond your years, but you also seem to prematurely bear the weight of the world on your humble shoulders."

I thoughtlessly pinched and folded the plastic straw that jutted from the top of my glass. "Not all of us can be as carefree as you, Dad," I grumbled.

The corners of my father's eyelids wrinkled like sheets on an unmade bed. Slowly, his expression softened into something smoother – more forgiving – and his pupils wavered with the distortion of water in his own hazel eyes.

"It hasn't always been easy for me, Junior," he said softly. "Have I told you much about my own childhood?"

For the first time in my life, my father seemed less like an immovable mast and more like a wavering sail. He had never really opened up to me like this.

"No," I said briskly. "You haven't told me much at all."

His eyes averted mine, glaring down at the knotted wood of the tabletop in front of him. He picked up his spoon and promptly placed it back down on his wrinkled napkin.

"What do you remember about Murry Wilson?" he asked.

I scoured my brain for facts, a flicker of recollection illuminating the darkness of memory. "Murry Wilson... Was he Brian Wilson's father?"

"Yes," my father nodded. "And Carl and Dennis."

"Right. What about him?"

My dad crumpled his lips into a contorted grimace. "Do you remember how he treated his sons?"

My forehead creased as I tried to recall the musical history lessons that my father had provided over the years. "He was kind of a jerk, right? Didn't he hit his kids and verbally abuse them and do other nasty things?"

"That's right," my dad affirmed. "And look how his sons turned out. All three had issues with addiction, and all three have suffered through a variety of doubts and insecurities."

"Okay," I said uncertainly, pausing to figure out where this story was leading. "What does all of this have to do with you?"

"My father – your grandfather – was a mean old bastard. He was an angry, angry man and he took it out on his children. I have a feeling that he and Murry Wilson must have read the same parenting manuals. Yelling and belittling were his preferred methods of communication. And when he got *really* angry, which happened more than it should have, he used to beat me and your uncle Jeff."

My jaw dropped. This was truly shocking information to me. *My father – a survivor of childhood trauma? The happy-go-lucky parent who rarely raised his voice and who never even spanked me? How had I never heard any of this before?*

"I used to go to school covered with bruises," my dad explained, his voice wavering, "but no one ever said or did anything. There was always an excuse. 'I fell off my bicycle' or 'I ran into a door.' At home, I cowered every time I heard his voice. It was like waiting for a bomb to go off and knowing that there was nothing I could do to defuse the explosion."

His voice caught a little as he spoke, but he never looked away from me. This was a confession of the highest magnitude, but my father refused to hide from the absolving illumination of the truth.

"I spent a lot of time trying to cover up these invisible scars that run up and down my spine and my soul," he told me. "As a result, I've been battling a crippling depression my whole life. As a teenager, I felt like the world was blackened and not even a pinprick of light could leak through. I thought I was hopeless, destined to live in misery forever. This went on for years and years..." He squinted harshly until crow's feet formed in the creased folds of his eyelids.

"What changed?" I asked him.

"There were two things. The first, and most obvious, was the love of a good woman. I was an absolute mess when I met your mother, but she never gave up on me. Even in my blackest days, when it seemed like I would never shake the darkness that trailed me like a stubborn shadow, she stuck by my side. Her parents – your grandma and grandpa – took me in and basically adopted me. And, for the first time in my life, I felt loved. *Really* loved. If it wasn't for your mom and her family, I wouldn't have made it through college. I wouldn't have even made it through my teenage years."

He took a deep breath, pulling in the tension as he inhaled and releasing it as he exhaled. It was so strange to see my father, someone who always seemed calm and put-together, walking a tightrope of emotion as he tried to maintain a delicate balance of heartache and hope.

"What was the second thing?" I asked him.

"You're going to laugh," he warned me, chuckling somberly to himself. "It was *teaching*."

"Teaching? Seriously?" I puckered my lips skeptically.

"*Seriously*," he said. "All of my self-pity, my self-absorbed emotions... everything seemed so trivial when I started my career as an English teacher. Suddenly, I wasn't a pathetic, solitary figure, wallowing in the darkness of my own sadness. When I stepped in front of that classroom, in front of those students, I knew that I was part of something bigger than myself – something important, significant. I was a humble gear in the altruistic machine of social change. And, for the first time in my life, I had a sense of purpose. It sounds strange, but it reminds me of playing guitar and developing callouses on my fingers."

"Callouses…?" I asked.

"Yup," he said. "Callouses. You know how your fingertips ache and throb when you first start playing guitar and those strings seem to bite into your flesh? When you literally form blisters until your skin hardens and you start to form callouses?"

I nodded. Like every other budding young guitarist, I'd been there.

"Well, it's a little like that," he explained. "After so many years of feeling like a festering, infected blister, I started to develop *emotional* callouses. My heart hardened. And I grew stronger. And, after a while, things didn't hurt so much anymore."

My father paused in his soliloquy. As silence settled like dust in the twilight of early evening, I let it all sink in. It was hard for the teenage version of myself to imagine that something as seemingly trivial as *teaching* could have saved a man's life. It wasn't like he was a rock star or a master painter or anything like that – something that provided ample fame and fortune for a mere mortal. And yet my father seemed like a man on a mission, someone who had a reason to get up every morning and navigate through the tempestuous complications of his life.

"Have you read *The Catcher in the Rye* yet?" he asked.

"Yeah," I told him. "A couple of times."

"Teaching has always reminded me of Holden's relationship with Phoebe," he explained. "Holden only finds a sense of purpose when he's watching over her, trying to protect her and other children. He's an emotional wreck throughout the book, but he *almost* pulls it together at the end when he's watching Phoebe on the carousel. He so desperately wants to find a solution to his pain and suffering, but he can't find a way to extinguish his own misery."

"Yeah," I agreed. "And he also makes that whole speech about wanting to be 'the catcher in the rye,' right? He wants to be someone who catches little kids before they fall off a cliff. Like the title of the book."

My father nodded solemnly. "Salvation is a strange thing. Sometimes, it's only through catching others that we can catch ourselves."

His statement hung in the air like a stark white gull sailing over the windswept ocean. There was a weight and gravity to his words, something almost tangible in their dignity and humility.

My father gazed through the café's window at the wind chimes dangling precipitously in the patio. "The sense of purpose I got from teaching saved me from the depression of my youth," he said. "But now I see you trying to navigate those same stormy seas, and I don't know how to help you."

I glanced up at him, my eyes welling and stinging. The man I saw in front of me was like a mirror image, separated only by three decades of life and experience. In that moment, it felt like we were kindred souls – stewards of the same tempest-tossed vessel. Yet, despite the threat of a capsizing ship, my father seemed firmly poised at the helm, bravely battling the wind-battered elements.

"Maybe this darkness is hereditary," he told me, "and maybe it's circumstantial. Maybe it's nature and maybe it's nurture. The truth, though, is that it doesn't really matter. What *does* matter is that you find a way out of your own darkness and into the light."

My hands trembled on the table, shaking the barely stable fixture between us. Coarse tears had begun to drift down my cheeks, and I lifted a napkin to dab them away. "How do I do that, Dad?" I asked. "How do I make it out of the darkness?"

He shook his head gravely. "Do you want my *advice*?" he asked. "Or do you want me to make you *feel better*? Because I can't do both."

There was a ripple of a breeze that swept through the café's doors, and I could feel goosebumps forming on my naked arms.

"I need someone to guide me," I admitted, wrapping my arms around myself like a bony cocoon. "Because I don't know what to do."

My father let out a weary sigh. "In my experience," he explained, "people don't want advice. They just want corroboration. Do you want me to tell you how I *think* you should proceed…?"

I nodded somberly.

He took another deep breath, sucking in the suffering of the air and exhaling calmly. "You need to ask yourself what's more important," he told me. "Do you want to leave everything behind? Do you need to distance yourself from the people in your life who are causing you pain?"

He looked into my forlorn eyes, searing past the sadness.

"Or can you weather all of this?" he asked. "The business with Steve and Serena… Can you stick around for the sake of the band that you care about so deeply?"

I turned away from him, diverting my attention to the fragile wind chimes that danced nervously in the breeze. "What would you do?" I asked him.

My father looked down at his nearly empty coffee cup. "People spend their whole lives looking for priceless pearls." He folded his hands before me on the tabletop, forming a makeshift oyster shell with his fingers. "They wait and they wait for something round and symmetrical and perfectly shaped. But life doesn't work like that." He opened his fingers and revealed a hollow space between his hands. "Life isn't comprised of pearls to be gathered and collected on a string of thread. Instead, it's full of *oysters* – temporary moments to relish that will disappear all too soon." He placed his hands flatly on the tabletop, palms up like a penitent parishioner in church.

"Do you always speak in metaphors?" I asked him, rolling my tear-stained eyes.

"Anything can be made into a metaphor, if you try hard enough," he explained. "A good enough poet or songwriter or novelist can take even the most mundane moments in life – like pouring sugar and cream into a coffee cup – and turn it all into something meaningful." He paused, reaching down and slipping his fingers around the circumference of his mug. "And a good enough reader will catch those clues and recognize what the author is trying to say. You just have to pay attention to the words on the page."

"Alright. So, what *oysters* and *pearls* can you offer me, wise father?" I asked my dad wearily and (I admit with regret) somewhat sarcastically.

He gently placed his coffee cup on top of a crumpled napkin and leaned his arms onto the table. He stared deeply into me, his eyes piercing through my skin. "Put your heart and soul into your passion. Even if you feel like a walking blister, you'll soon form emotional callouses – hardened skin that will protect you from the sting and ache of teenage heartbreak."

I shook my head desperately. "I don't know if I can do that," I told him.

He gently grabbed ahold of my arm. "If your passion is this band and your music, don't let *anything* get in the way of that. Don't let your broken heart interfere with those dreams, and don't let your ego get in the way of working with other talented partners who can help you to realize that vision."

"But the lead singer of my band stole the girl I love," I pleaded, exasperated by the burden of the conversation.

Despite my emotional outburst, my father refused to waiver in his Zen-like tranquility. "One day, you'll look back on all of this objectively," he told me. "You'll be able to recognize that broken hearts can be mended, and that friendships – even among bitterly bickering bandmates – can be repaired."

My tongue forcefully pressed against the insides of my teeth, my jaw tensing and clenching as I breathed. "It doesn't feel that way right now," I grumbled.

"You're right," he agreed, "and it won't feel that way for a few years. But your passion as a songwriter and musician should outweigh the pain inflicted upon you by the careless whims of a teenage girl and the betrayal you feel from your friend, Steve." He balled up a soiled napkin in his hands. "And if you feel threatened by all of this, you have two choices: give up your band and your friends or soldier on and pursue your passion."

I nodded absently, my chest echoing like an empty canyon.

"Above all else," he told me, "you need to *take care of yourself.* Some things are more important than rock and roll."

My eyes flittered up at my father, like the battered feathers of a hawk ricocheting against the wind. I looked at him with a new understanding, a new respect.

Some things are more important than rock and roll.

I let the words sink in, saturating my weary heart.

Some things are more important than rock and roll.

Outside the window, those delicate wind chimes seemed to be tempting the fates – testing the limits of the rope that tied them to the bough, forsaking the bonds that kept them chained to the tree.

"But remember this," my dad continued. "Even the Beach Boys needed to put aside their rivalries to create beautiful, lasting music. They had to learn to work with each other, even with stolen girlfriends and artistic disagreements. Brian Wilson might have been the heart and soul of the Beach Boys, but he needed Mike Love to sing those songs they wrote. To put it bluntly, Mike did what Brian couldn't do. Sometimes, you need a messenger to carry your message to the world. If you can't sing the songs yourself, find someone who can."

Though I wanted nothing more than to tear myself free from the tree limbs that tethered me to the world – wanted to fly away into the emancipated distance, chasing the horizon and abandoning my shores – I knew that my father was right. I needed Steve and Ethan and Chunk. And, despite my broken heart, I needed Serena. Even if I faltered and twisted like the wind chimes dangling outside the windows of Café Voltaire, I needed to stay bound to my roots.

"I guess it's settled then," I sighed. "I won't be going anywhere."

"*This, too, shall pass*," he reassured me. "And, one day, these fresh wounds will fade and feel more like cursory scratches than permanent scars."

My father was full of wise words.

I only wish it was as easy to enact them as it was to believe them.

CHAPTER THIRTY

"It's OK"

I had to let a few days pass before I could bring myself to call Steve. Though I knew in the recesses of my heart that my father was right, the wounds of betrayal stung too intensely for me to casually brush them aside. Of course, in many ways, it felt inevitable that Steve and Serena would end up together. It was like some twisted form of Darwinian dating: *survival of the hottest*. While I couldn't help but feel an overwhelming desire and longing for Serena, she was clearly out of my league. Steve, on the other hand, was her perfect match.

And there was nothing I could do about that. I just had to cope with the way that the cards were dealt – and be ready to shuffle the deck for the next hand.

Finally, I relented and invited Steve over to my house so that we could discuss the future of the band. I kept replaying my father's advice in my head: *don't let your ego get in the way*. Despite my reservations and the sick feeling in my stomach, I was determined to make things work.

When Steve strutted through my front door later in the week, he entered with the confidence and swagger of someone who owned the place. I simultaneously envied him and resented him for it, and I had to muster every ounce of self-control not to punch him in his perfectly sculpted face.

After suppressing a scowl, I led Steve back to the Smith family den, where we could thumb through my dad's old record collection and brainstorm ideas for a band name. For a nerdy English teacher, my dad had a surprisingly diverse assortment of music: in addition to the predictable Beach Boys and Brian Wilson albums, he had curated everything from Leadbelly and Led Zeppelin to the Ramones and the Replacements.

Steve and I flipped through dozens of albums, searching for some flash of inspiration. The two of us took turns placing vinyl records on my parents' turntable, talking with a rapid-fire ease about the music that we loved. We dissected the finer nuances of bands like Social Distortion and Bad Religion, discussed whether "solo" acts like Elvis Costello and Neil Young sacrificed integrity when they ditched their long-term backing bands, and argued about whether Morrissey was better with the Smiths or as a solo artist.

Surprisingly, despite the drastic differences in our personal appearances and our social strata, Steve and I had quite a bit in common. Just like that summer day in the locker room, when we talked at length for the first time, we once again bonded over music and its almost mythical, magical powers.

And yet, for all our musical communion and conversation, we still couldn't find a band name that fit our needs. We tossed around a variety of makeshift monikers (*Disillusion* and *Common Thread* and *The Quiet War* are just a few that I remember), but nothing stuck. It seemed to be a hopeless endeavor.

"I can't think of *anything* that would make a decent band name," Steve grumbled, clenching his eyes shut with frustration.

We had just about given up hope, sitting there in the darkening confines of the den, when we stumbled across the exact spark we needed. We were sprawled out, our massive shapes occupying opposite ends of the room, while the ceiling fan above us spiraled towards infinity. I lay down on my back and stared at the opposing wall, my eyes searching for inspiration, desperately fumbling for the perfect name. I glanced over at my dad's vintage rock posters, our old weathered upright piano, the steadily humming ceiling fan, and a dusty old bookshelf.

I remember gazing up at those faded wooden shelves, my mind scattered in a million directions, when I saw it: my dad's beaten-up copy of *Catcher in the Rye*. It had only been a few days since my father and I had discussed the book at Café Voltaire. Now, by some cosmic coincidence, it seemed to be serendipitously placed right in front of me. I ran up to the bookshelf, grabbed Salinger's novel, and tossed it into Steve's lap.

"Have you read this?" I asked Steve as he flipped through the yellowing pages of the battered book.

"Dude, that is the best book ever written," he answered. "I read it in eighth grade, and it changed my life. Phonies and crumby stuff... It's all so true."

I could see him squinting as he turned page after musty page. He formed a lopsided grin out of the right side of his mouth and snickered aloud as he breezed through a couple of passages.

"What about *Caulfield*...?" I suggested.

Steve looked up at me slowly, his eyes expanding like azure balloons, and I swear I could see the lightbulb turning on above his head. "That is *brilliant!*" he shouted, punctuating the air with a swift, deft movement of his hands. "It's perfect!" Steve slapped me on the back and stomped his flip-flopped feet on the fading gray carpet.

For all our posturing, we were still just overgrown kids, prone to the same childish outbursts of joy and celebration.

"I *knew* that you would think of something, Brick," Steve told me. "You and me, we make a killer team. You're the brains. I'm the brawn. And, together, we're going places. *Caulfield* is going places."

So, it was settled: like any other assemblage of self-respecting, hipster teenagers, we named ourselves after the patron saint of angst-ridden high school kids.

The Bookhouse Boys were no more.

Our band was officially renamed *Caulfield*.

CHAPTER THIRTY-ONE

"In the Back of My Mind"

You know those montage scenes in the *Rocky* movies, where they fast-forward through the long weeks of Rocky Balboa training for the big fight and squeeze endless hours of routines into a thirty-second medley of activities? That's what I'd like to do here – not out of sheer laziness, mind you, but because I tend to be a little longwinded. You've already trudged through several hundred pages of my embarrassing personal history, and there's still a lot more left to say.

So, let's do some time traveling.

If they ever make a movie out of my life, this is where they'll insert the montage scene. They'll show swooping shots of the band vigorously practicing, interspersed with glimpses into my daily life. The camera will glide through the back of a tenth-grade English classroom, where I'll sit dutifully with blue pen and yellow notepad, my eyes focused intently on the graying teacher behind her oversized podium. There will be a few frames of me learning how to drive in an old, beat-up Buick Regal, first with my dad in the front seat and then later with me navigating the city streets solo. There will inevitably be a shot of the brightly lit football field, with Steve throwing impossibly long passes and rushing through the end zone as he dodges opposing lineman. They'll show Coach Montaña holding up a trophy above his head, as Steve victoriously gets hoisted onto the shoulders of his varsity teammates. There will be shots of our eleventh-grade AP United States History class, focusing first on Serena's golden cascading hair – and then pulling back to reveal my shoulders at the edge of the frame, as I stare yearningly at her from a distance.

There will also be shots of me with my dad, the two of us sitting on folded chairs in a darkened garage and cradling acoustic guitars in our hands. The camera will show us laughing earnestly, as my dad and I take turns soloing and strumming. The rotating frame will swirl around us in the garage, eventually including my mom in the shot as she brings us cups of steaming hot chocolate and watches us proudly from the doorjamb. Despite the weight of the heartache that I carry on my shoulders, you'll see me smile broadly in the company of my parents. Everything will seem okay – on the surface at least.

Once again, the screen will bleed back into shots of the band practicing, this time with Steve awkwardly strumming an electric guitar while Ethan, Chunk, and I exchange skeptical looks. In the foreground of the shot, you'll see the members of the newly rechristened Caulfield band tightly gripping their instruments; slowly, the camera lens will refocus to the girls seated on the couches of the garage – Serena, Amy, and Megan. All three will be staring lustfully at Steve... while I turn and longingly hold my gaze on Serena.

Eventually, after a brisk sixty-second segment of various cinematographic tricks and tactics, the film will settle down into our AP English Literature & Composition class during senior year. The teacher, a balding man with a large frame and broad stomach, gesticulates enthusiastically while the class listens intently to whatever it is that he's saying. On the whiteboard behind him, you'll see the name EMILY DICKINSON scrawled in green marker with a barely legible script. The background music will slowly fade away as the camera settles in on the face of the instructor.

My father.

It's a strange thing to be the child of a teacher. It's even stranger when you wind up enrolled in your father's AP English class, surrounded by your peers and friends – and even the beautiful girl who broke your heart the summer before sophomore year. Here's the thing, though: it's a little less awkward when your dad isn't just a regular teacher...

He's a *fantastic* teacher.

All those years growing up, I had no idea just how incredible my father was at his job. Sure, I would hear occasional rumblings from upperclassmen in the locker room as they talked about the uniquely cool activity they did that day in Mr. Smith's class. Likewise, I remember Marina and her friends speaking with feverish voices about the ways their eyes had been opened in AP English during their senior year. But hearing is one thing; witnessing firsthand is an entirely different experience.

On the day in question, my dad was covering one of his favorite poets – the aforementioned Belle of Amherst, Emily Dickinson – and one of his favorite pieces, "There's a certain Slant of light." The desks in his classroom that morning were crudely arranged in a circle, with the students inhabiting the seats all facing each other. My father, rather than the hub of the group, was on the outskirts of the room, propped up against the whiteboard that bore his scribbled notes. All of us sat with photocopied prints of Dickinson's poem in front of us, ready for analysis and dissection.

"So, ladies and gentlemen, what do you make of this piece?" Mr. Smith (a.k.a. Dad) asked us.

When my father offered these kinds of discussion-baiting questions, his words were usually met with a brief, tentative silence; my classmates and I typically hesitated momentarily before the floodgates of discussion would inevitably open. Three-fourths of the band (Steve, Ethan, and yours truly) were all in the same class, as was our resident heartbreaking beauty, Serena. Fortunately, my father had enough common sense to keep Steve and Serena seated on opposite sides of the room – as much for his own benefit as for mine.

With this lesson, Serena was the first one to speak. "Mr. Smith," she said, turning to my dad with a flustered face, "was Emily Dickinson clinically depressed?"

As was his tendency with such questionable queries, my father simply offered a good-natured laugh. "Well, Miss Rios," he responded, "that's certainly open for debate." I should note that one of my dad's many idiosyncrasies was calling all his pupils by their last names – something that I, in turn, have utilized with my own students. "Dickinson did lead a solitary existence in Amherst in the 1800s," he explained. "She never married, never ventured too far from home for more than a few brief periods of her life, and she kept a very limited circle of friends."

"She sounds pretty lonely to me," Serena replied, her forehead creased intently.

"I agree," my father said, nodding his balding head. "But you can only garner so much interpretation from an author's personal life. *Perhaps* her work is biographical. *Perhaps* it is purely imaginative." My dad, recognizing his own English teacher proselytizing, encouraged us to return to the text. "Let's turn back to her poem, shall we?"

Automatically, without further prompting, all the students in the room shifted their eyes back to the photocopies in front of them. My father had trained the class to clinically annotate literature, to dissect poetry and prose with surgical precision; instinctively, my classmates highlighted passages from the poem, circled key words on the page, and jotted down notes in the margins.

"So, Miss Rios," he called out. "What gives you the impression that this poem discusses depression?"

Serena's green pen tracked its way across her note-filled page. "There are a few trigger phrases here, Mr. Smith," she observed. "Dickinson uses words like *oppresses* and *Despair* and *hurt*. That's some pretty loaded diction."

A few seats to my right, Ethan nervously raised his hand.

My dad's eyes darted in that direction and my father shifted his attention to Caulfield's lead guitarist. "Yes, Mr. Hidalgo?"

"I just wanted to piggyback on something Serena mentioned," Ethan said. He shuffled in his seat, pivoting to face the object of my (unrequited) affection. "You're right, Serena. Dickinson does use some dark words, but there's also some hope, too. She uses the word *heavenly*, right? And she says, '*Heavenly Hurt, it gives us – We can find no scar.*' So, this light that she's talking about doesn't leave scars. There must be something else going on, besides just a normal, everyday kind of sadness, right?"

I raised my hand, my fingers arching skyward, and my dad pointed in my direction. Even after months in his class, it was still so strange that Dad — my own father — needed to call on me as if I was just another nameless student. I mean, I never had to raise my hand at the *dinner table*, so it was surreal that I needed to follow such formal protocol with my own flesh and blood. I guess that's to be expected when you're enrolled in your father's AP English class.

"Yes, young Mr. Smith?" the elder Mr. Smith cued, waving his portly pointer finger like a magic wand.

"Both Serena and Ethan are right," I said. "Dickinson does imply darkness with the word *hurt*, but she also pairs it with a strange adverb: *heavenly*. That combination of words, *Heavenly Hurt*, is a pretty powerful oxymoron."

"And what do you make of that?" my father asked.

I stammered for a split-second before responding. "Well, *heavenly* invokes something beyond simple human understanding. And that goes along with the reference to churches and music at the end of the first stanza, '*That oppresses, like the Heft / Of Cathedral Tunes…*' And then she says, '*Heavenly Hurt, it gives us – / We can find no scar, / But internal difference, / Where the Meanings are…*' in the second stanza. It's like…" I trailed off.

"Like what?" my father prompted me.

"Like there's something spiritual there," I answered. "Something transcendental. Like she has a deeper understanding of existence because of that darkness in her life. It's counterintuitive, but it kind of makes sense."

My dad nodded in approval, his chest subtly swelling with a sense of pride. I'm pretty sure that a public-school educator sharing this kind of rewarding father-son moment might have been one of the highlights of his teaching career.

Of course, Steve had to chime in and ruin it.

I should note that Steve and I had countless classes together from tenth grade through twelfth grade; during those three years, it never ceased to amaze me how frequently he would disrupt our classes with his anti-authoritarian attitude. Of course, just because Steve was in Honors classes did *not* mean that he was the overly studious type: the drive and dedication that he maintained on the football field didn't transfer over as flawlessly into the classroom. Steve's tendency to buck the system (off the field, at least) knew no boundaries.

I guess that just comes with the territory when you're the lead singer in a punk band.

After slowly lifting his head up from his desk and lazily twirling a pencil in his fingers, Steve cocked his chin to the side and interrupted my father's precious moment. "So, how do you know that's what the poem *really* meant?" he asked. "How do you know she wasn't just stringing a bunch of fancy words together and hoping that they made sense?"

As an English teacher myself, I would venture to say that I encounter this kind of student skepticism on an annual basis. There's *always* a cynical kid who questions the value and validity of the texts read in class; however, a good enough teacher will know how to defuse the situation before chaos ensues. Fortunately, my dad was *exactly* that type of effective educator.

Without missing a beat, my dad flipped the script on Steve. "Those are excellent questions, Mr. Öken. And you're not the first to ask. I will say, however, that writing is an art form. And, just like every other form of self-expression, some art is more powerful than others." My father paused before changing tactics, fluttering his vaguely psychedelic Jerry Garcia necktie between his thumb and pointer finger.

"Now, Mr. Öken," he continued, "if I remember correctly, you're in a band." My dad winked at Steve with that familiar quality of a parent lecturing his precocious child. "When you're singing a song, do you do it carelessly? Or do you follow the unique melodies that have been written by the composer?"

"Well, that's different..." Steve began to say.

"Actually, Mr. Öken," my dad said, cutting Steve short, "it's *not*. A musical composer creates a series of notes in a specific order, utilizing tempo and meter and a variety of other tools. He doesn't just bang random chords on an instrument and then say he's finished. Rather, he *composes*...

he creates something from nothing with the purpose of moving an audience, even if that audience is just himself."

Steve sat there fidgeting, his hands folded tersely on his desk. "So how does that relate to depressing poetry?" he shot back.

"Think of it this way, Mr. Öken," my father said, adopting a gentler tone. "A writer is just like a musical composer. Instead of chords and notes, however, she must use *words*. Each word is carefully selected, much like the succession of notes in a stirring song. A strong enough writer, like Emily Dickinson, can create masterful melodies with the words that she selects. And I, like many other teachers of English, recognize the power and beauty of her compositions."

Never one to back down from a challenge, Steve refused to wave a white flag. "But this Emily Dickinson chick is so obsessed with depression and darkness and death. If she were alive today, she would totally be a Goth kid listening to The Cure all day."

Steve's irreverent comment elicited a few laughs from our classmates and even a chuckle from my father, who leaned his heavy frame against the side of his podium.

Feeling emboldened, Steve soldiered on with his commentary. "I can see why English teachers love this stuff," he continued. "In every single book we read in high school, someone dies. *Of Mice & Men*, *The Outsiders*, *The Great Gatsby*, *The Grapes of Wrath*. Heck, *Lord of the Flies* is a complete bloodbath. Why do you guys always torture us with books about people who kick the bucket? Why does someone always have to *die* in these books?"

My father persisted in his patience, undeterred by Steve's irreverent remarks. "Well, Mr. Öken, once again you've raised some very good points. While there's no easy answer to your questions, I would suggest that maybe your teachers are trying to prepare you for the ugly truths in life. You might feel invincible right now, at the peak of your health and happiness, but I can guarantee that *'depression and darkness and death'* will reach their talons into you soon enough. Perhaps even sooner than you anticipate. It won't always come in the dramatic form of sword fights or gunshots or car accidents or starvation, but death has a funny way of creeping up on you... usually when you least expect it."

My father turned to the rest of the class with a sweeping gesture of his arms. Every single student sat in rapt attention at the exchange in front of us. Dad rarely gave lectures in class, so hearing a soliloquy like this carried an unusual weight and urgency.

With a sense of gravity I had not seen from him all year, my father removed his glasses and rubbed the back of his right hand against his forehead. "Mark my words, everyone," he somberly stated. "You will find yourself in the midst of death and darkness soon enough. And when it comes, you might find yourself facing the same kind of *'imperial afflictions'* that Dickinson describes in her poem."

An eerie stillness pervaded the room, as if a shadow had crept across the sullen student desks. You remember all those novels you read in your high school English classes, when the writer starts foreshadowing some sinister future? It felt like that, as if my father's off-the-cuff classroom commentary was conjuring an imposing darkness just beyond the horizon. Death was just a shadow's fall away, and the world was about to lose some of its glowing effervescent sheen.

My dad sensed the attention of these high-achieving AP students shifting away from his meticulously organized agenda.

"And on that note," he continued, "let's redirect ourselves to the task at hand: Emily Dickinson's poem..."

After class that day, our usual coterie of college-bound students filtered through the wooden portal that separated us from the rest of the heat-addled campus. As usual, Steve had his thick, muscular arm draped around Serena's delicate neck; Ethan and I, in sharp contrast, flanked the couple on either side of their intertwined frames. Ethan trailed behind Steve just slightly, like a puppy following its master, while I kept a respectable distance from Serena's adjacent body.

"Hey, Brick," Steve called to me, his line of sight tracing across Serena's slender frame in my direction. "Your dad is pretty cool. For an old guy."

Ethan and Serena nodded subtly in agreement.

"That makes sense," Serena added, "considering how perfect you turned out."

There was an awkward lull in the conversation as an unspoken understanding passed between the four of us. Serena and I might not have shared the intense romantic relationship that bound her to Steve, but her complimentary words bordered on flirtatious – at least in some sensitive eyes.

Steve squeezed her a little more tightly, drawing her closer to him with a simple movement of his bulky arms.

"I guess I'm just lucky," I said, trying to soothe the seething situation. "Some of us are simply blessed with good parents." I thought carefully for a second, the quiet stillness punctuated only by our tame footfalls in the concrete halls. "I just hope that no one *we* know dies," I added, almost as an afterthought. "At least not for a long time."

CHAPTER THIRTY-TWO
"Forever"

The rest of my senior year passed by in a flurry of essays and assignments and college applications and scholarship submissions. I always warn my AP English students that their last few months of high school will fly by, and they never seem to believe me – and yet, year after year, they find themselves reiterating the same kind of shock and surprise at the sheer brevity and weightlessness of time. When you lose track of the day-to-day with football games and winter holidays and spring track meets and weekly band practices, a lot of time will evaporate – like drops of dew on the morning grass as it burns away under the glare of the springtime sunshine.

Now, I don't mean to "*retcon*" this story too much, but I do want to add an important set of memories from that time of my life: the weekly jam sessions with my father. Though our humble garage had been densely populated by musical instruments for a few years by that point, it had always been the scene of young punks playing loud and fast music. In all those sweaty hours, the aluminum garage door and the tangerine-carpeted floors had been beaten and battered by buzz-saw guitars. Soon enough, though, the garage would also become home to quieter songs – the sounds of settling down.

I'm not entirely sure how it all started. At some point or another, my dad must have volunteered to show me an old folk song or two; soon enough, though, that one-time event evolved into weekly jam sessions in which my dad and I would transform into acoustic jukeboxes, playing the best folk rock songs from the 1960s and 1970s. My dad was never much of an acrobatic guitarist: he would humbly joke that he could only strum as well as the next ex-hippie. In reality, though, he was actually a pretty decent picker on his Martin D-21.

Throughout our time together in that weathered old garage, we played a variety of his favorite music – with lots of old tunes from Bob Dylan, Neil Young, the Grateful Dead, and Crosby, Stills & Nash. It was always just the two of us, strumming our way through song after song, our voices uniting as one in familiar family harmony. Despite my anticlimactic debut performance at Serena's *quinceañera* a few years earlier, I had been diligently working on my vocals; God bless my father, he sat through endless hours in which I struggled to learn harmonies. It was a slow, tedious process, but my dad tended to invoke his teacherly demeanor each week, patiently working with me as I attempted to master the complex task of singing something more challenging than a simple melody – while I simultaneously strummed away on the hand-me-down Fender acoustic guitar that Uncle Jeff had loaned me. Though I was primarily playing bass guitar those days in our Caulfield band practices, there was something natural and organic about taking that wooden acoustic instrument in my hands each week, free from the static and hum of the electric amps buzzing behind the bass.

One of my dad's favorites, the song that I remember playing most frequently during that time, was CSNY's "Teach Your Children." Graham Nash's sweet, earnest tune might have been a plaintive plea for peace when it was written in the middle of the Vietnam War, but it meant something else for me and my dad: it was a song about fathers and sons and the legacies of family. It was *our* song.

Nevertheless, I did understand and appreciate the irony of being an electric punk rock kid playing old folk music on wooden, acoustic instruments. As I would encounter many times in the future, I found myself walking a line between two worlds: I was neither bound to the antiquated realm of aged folk songs, nor the new sphere of youthful, angry punk. I was musically amphibious – between old music and new, quiet and loud, acoustic and electric, folk and punk.

Though it wasn't as dramatic as the battles that Serena faced, reconciling her mixed heritage and the drama of her divorced parents, I

121121111111111111

could feel a sort of kinship with her. During those months we spent together in summer school Chemistry, she shared some profound feelings of isolation, revealing the depths of frustration that come when you're caught between two worlds. She was like a stranded mermaid, navigating water and dry land simultaneously – and feeling caught in a tug-of-war between each.

I couldn't help but wonder, though, as I strummed through those folk songs with my father in the garage, if anyone ever *really* fits in anywhere. We are all eternally facing battles between the disparate aspects of our lives – whether cultural, musical, professional, ethical, or romantic. I was simply caught between two overlapping circles, my identity forged in the Venn diagram of youth and age.

"You're an old soul," my father would tell me. "Not many kids your age would care about folk songs like this."

He was right. I *did* feel like an old soul. I was too tame and boring for Serena, lacking the incendiary qualities that she dreamt about. I was too static and stationary to be the frontman that Caulfield deserved. I possessed a geriatric spirit, trapped in a teenager's body.

Amusingly enough, when it came time to compose my college admissions essay, I embraced this disparity in myself: I wrote about being trapped between youth and aging, between acoustic and electric.

I'm an old soul, I wrote, *living in a young man's world…*

They were the tender words of a self-conscious young man, someone who had experienced a relatively sheltered life and who had no conception of the heartbreak to come. When I wrote my personal statement for grad school just four short years later, I would have a very different story to tell…

But I'm getting ahead of myself.

Apart from those conflicted feelings of self-doubt and frustration, however, I could sense a subtle change in myself. Music was giving me a sense of confidence I had never felt in all my tempestuous years of childhood and adolescence. Of course, flourishing academically in school didn't hurt either. I was ranked number one in my graduating class, well on the way to valedictorian status – although Serena didn't trail too far behind me. For all these qualities, though, it was the time spent with my father that seemed to have the biggest impact on my formative teenage years.

When I look back on my pre-college days, I remember those garage jam sessions as some of my happiest memories – times when I could escape the insecurities and anxieties that had plagued me my entire life. Those moments with my father were pure and golden and constructive.

I only wish those days could have lasted forever.

CHAPTER THIRTY-THREE

"Graduation Day"

Though approaching high school graduation is like seeing the finish line of a four-year marathon, the last few meters before snapping through ribbons and stumbling across the final mile marker feel interminable. For one, you've got ridiculous high-stakes assessments like final exams and AP tests; you also have all the added pressure of college hovering over you like threatening gray clouds in a cobalt sky. Amidst all this darkness, though, there is the wistful promise of your high school commencement ceremony, a rite of passage that will usher your way into adulthood… if you can survive the ceremony's speakers and singers.

Here's the thing about most graduation speeches and songs: by and large, they're terrible. No matter how intelligent, insightful, and interesting the performers might be, they are hindered by the monolithic weight of the monumental task in front of them. As a result, they craft "thoughtful" reflections on the high school experience and the uncertainty of the future in the most general, vacuous terms possible.

Most of the time, it's pretty painful.

To paraphrase The Smiths' "Panic," commencement speeches and songs say nothing to you about *your* life. Sure, everyone can deliver a monologue rhapsodizing philosophically about milestones and new beginnings, but the words are often two-dimensional generic caricatures. To be fair, there have been some excellent commencement speeches over the years (check out Steve Jobs and Steven Colbert for two of the best), but most diatribes are tortuous to sit through. Add in the fact that most high school kids have limited experience performing publicly, and it's a recipe for disaster.

The only things worse than graduation speeches are graduation *songs*. I've seen more than my fair share of high school commencement ceremonies in the last twenty years, and most of the musical selections make my skin crawl. With some notable exceptions (a la Green Day's "Good Riddance," Fleetwood Mac's "Landslide," and The Beatles' "In My Life"), the songs that kids sing at graduation are either schmaltzy ballads, amateurish originals, or pop songs that only relate thinly – *very* thinly – to the ceremony itself. Though I can respect students who write original material, I have a hard time with pop songs: too often, it feels like the singers are trying to squeeze square pegs into circular openings, leading to performances that feel unnaturally forced. For music snobs like me, this is quite the conundrum – a musical Catch-22 that leaves your ears aching and your soul cringing.

Such were the thoughts going through my head in May of 1997, a month before our commencement ceremony at Sespe Creek High School. For three long years, I had fantasized about following in Marina's footsteps and serving as my graduating class's commencement speaker, soliloquizing grandly in front of the masses like my older sister had done. But a funny thing happened following that formative experience at the end of my freshman year: music had overtaken my life and become my singular obsession, overpowering all other daydreams and desires.

I no longer wanted to deliver a graduation speech.

I wanted to *sing*.

As tryouts for graduation speakers and singers loomed before me, I felt the irresistible force of fate beckoning me towards the stage. Grandiose visions occupied my mind's eye, and I knew that I wanted to contribute something... but I wasn't prepared to perform anything remotely appropriate for the occasion. I told the band as much, admitting that I might not have a song ready for us in time for tryouts.

"Besides," I explained, "I don't know if Sespe Creek's administration would embrace a punk band for a graduation ceremony."

The guys in Caulfield all seemed to understand. In fact, I suspected that Ethan and Chunk were secretly relieved: it's a lot of pressure to play before thousands of people at a stiflingly formal event (especially when the audience hasn't come specifically to see you perform), and neither of the boys seemed particularly thrilled about the prospect.

Steve, on the other hand, was determined to sing at graduation.

This did present some problems, however. Though our lead singer undeniably had a singular voice, he was a mediocre guitar player. Basically, Caulfield served as Steve's crutch. Without us, he was irregular and amateurish, not much better than an open mic hack – albeit one with a killer set of vocal cords.

To make matters worse, Steve picked a truly strange selection for his audition: "Today" by The Smashing Pumpkins. Don't get me wrong, I think Billy Corgan is an absolute genius and I adored his band when I was an angst-ridden teenager. That being said, the lyrical link to graduation is tenuous at best; the traditional tropes of growing up, reflecting upon the past, and starting a new chapter of life are conspicuously absent from the song. While "Today" is an undeniably catchy and well-written tune, it isn't even the best graduation song in the Smashing Pumpkins' oeuvre: "Tonight, Tonight," "Disarm," and "1979" all would have been much better selections. Coupled with the prominent sexual overtones of the lyrics, I wasn't so sure that a panel of conservatively minded high school faculty members would approve. I tried to insinuate as much during my conversations with Steve, but he wouldn't listen. No surprise there.

To put it bluntly, I knew that Steve's first solo foray was doomed from the start. Despite my misgivings, though, I did the only sensible thing that a friend and bandmate could do. I wholeheartedly supported Steve's misbegotten audition.

That's what friends are for, right…?

But I had a backup plan.

Unbeknownst to anyone (especially Steve), I was writing something. Since good graduation songs are few and far between, I figured that an original composition might give me an edge for the audition. The competition was fierce: not only did I have to compete with Steve, but Sespe Creek High School was packed to the gills with band students and teenage thespians and choir kids with strong voices. Plus,

Serena hinted that *she* was going to try out, too. At least she had the common sense to pick a more appropriate selection: the *Wizard of Oz*'s torch song, "Over the Rainbow."

As the days before the audition collapsed and folded into each other, I struggled to find the right words, the perfect melody – heck, even a suitable chord progression evaded me. Bizarrely enough, inspiration arrived from the strangest of sources...

Stephen King.

I can't recall what led me to walk through the dusty stacks of books in the Sespe Creek High School library that spring afternoon, but as I drew my fingertips across the shelves of novels, I was desperately searching for a spark to stoke the embers of epiphany. I traipsed up and down the aisles, passing Mark Twain and John Steinbeck and Toni Morrison and Harper Lee and countless other authors whose timeless works lined the walls. Just as I was about to admit defeat, however, I reached the library's rows of Stephen King novels...

And that's where inspiration hit me: in the Fiction section of a public school library.

Back in middle school, *Stand by Me* was one of my favorite films. With a stellar cast of young actors and a killer soundtrack, the movie captures a complicated coming-of-age narrative – and even throws in (or *throws up*, if you remember that pie-eating scene) some comedy for good measure. Somewhere along the line (sophomore year of high school, perhaps?), I decided to read the original source material: a short story by Stephen King, entitled "The Body," which appeared in an idiosyncratic collection of the author's novellas.

Different Seasons.

With its nondescript cover, depicting four vaguely threatening personifications of the seasons, it didn't exactly look like appropriate source material for a graduation song. And yet, the combination of those two words lit a match in my brain.

Life is full of different seasons.

Kneeling down on the musty carpet like a penitent churchgoer, I thought about Pete Seeger's "Turn, Turn, Turn" and the book of

Ecclesiastes from which the verses were taken. My brain cycled through a litany of images as I crouched next to the Stephen King books, my mind's eye envisioning the four seasons representing different stages in life. Robert Frost had nailed it with "Nothing Gold Can Stay," but maybe there was room for another piece of writing with the same themes – lyrics that could describe what it feels like to be an outsider in a world of happy-go-lucky teenagers, words that give voice to those of us who dream of better lives beyond the hollow halls of our hallowed high school.

When the time comes for different seasons, I thought to myself.

And there it was.

I literally threw my backpack to the ground, frantically ripping it open to grab a pencil and paper. The words came so quickly that I felt like a lyrical clairvoyant, channeling the voices of forgotten high school ghosts. Like Frost, I started with a biblical allusion, a quick reference to "the fall" that equated growth with the loss of innocence; I continued to draw inspiration from "Nothing Gold Can Stay," weaving in some nature imagery to illustrate the stormy moods of adolescence. Finally, I made sure to incorporate contrasting feelings of bitterness and hope – the yin and yang of teenage existence.

After half an hour of eliciting frantic chicken scratch from my ink-stained fingers, crossing out and rephrasing lines on page after page, I stepped back and looked at my creation.

"Different Seasons"

Days have passed and so have dreams
We are children grown
Fallen from the bliss of innocence
Now we've seen and now we know
Now we've seen and now we know

And when the time comes for different seasons
A change of weather for the heart
You'll stand tall knowing that you've come this far

Stormy days seem so far away
Though they're just on the horizon
But if we look to the stars for inspiration
We'll survive, we'll carry on
We'll survive, we'll carry on

And when the time comes for different seasons
A change of weather for the heart
You'll stand tall knowing that you've come this far

I've swallowed enough lies to know what's true and not
All my years taken with a grain of salt
And after leaving a bitter taste in my mouth
I just want to spit it out

And when the time comes for different seasons
A change of weather for the heart
We'll stand tall knowing that we've come this far

Looking back now, there are several things that embarrass me about the song; at the time, though, it felt like a monumental victory for me. It's amazing how a fist-pumping triumph of your youth looks so amateurish from an objective adult perspective. When I examine "Different Seasons" these days, I can't help but cringe when I see an innocuous word like "dreams" or a cliché like "grain of salt." The allusions in the song (to Stephen King, Robert Frost, and the bible) all seem forced and underdeveloped; I wish I had done something – *anything* – to incorporate more references to at least one of those pieces of literature.

The complete lack of punctuation also irks me to no end: there are no commas, periods, colons, semicolons, or dashes anywhere in the lyrics. I realize it's just an English teacher pet peeve, but I feel like song lyrics should follow the same rules of punctuation as prose and verse; otherwise, you're just feeding the misconception that song lyrics aren't "works of literary merit" or "real poetry."

What was I thinking?

I wish the forty-year-old English teacher incarnation of me had been around to give the seventeen-year-old student version of me some constructive feedback back then. Of course, being as stubborn as I was, as immobile as a brick wall, I might not have taken that kind of sage advice – even from myself.

Like looking at naked baby photos, there's something horrifyingly embarrassing about examining your own youthful writing. All of the bad habits, immature choices, and careless errors feel tender and shameful. But, like I mentioned earlier, I was incredibly proud of the song at the time – and I even considered it to be the finest set of lyrics I had ever composed (up to that point in my life, at least).

I spent the entire drive home humming fragments in my head and constructing makeshift melodies for the lyrics. Like a ship emerging from the fog, I could slowly start to make out how the verses and choruses would sound when intertwined. I just had to figure out how to match up the right chords.

By the time that I got back to our house on Lago de Paz Court and picked up my guitar, I had already pieced together most of the song's sections. Heck, I was even beginning to envision what it would sound like with a full-band arrangement. I took the sheet of haphazardly scrawled lyrics, grabbed a pen, and slowly transcribed the chords, one section at a time. The song ended up in the key of *E*, relying upon the humming sound of ringing open chords for the chorus, and utilizing muted power chords for the verses.

When my dad popped his head into the garage later that afternoon, he gave me a confused look. "Is that Green Day?" he asked. "Or Weezer?"

I smiled back at him.

"Even better," I said. "It's me."

A week after I finished writing the song, I found myself standing in the cavernous auditorium at Sespe Creek High School, listening to pedantic instructions about the audition process. We were each given a five-minute window of time ("Different Seasons" was *exactly* 4:00 minutes long), and we were warned that the panel of staff members might ask us questions about our material – especially if they detected any questionable content.

I had a momentary feeling of déjà vu, a recollection of standing in this exact same venue three years before when *Marina and the Bookhouse Boys* auditioned for the school talent show. It seemed like a lifetime ago. So much had changed since then – most notably the convoluted conundrum with Steve and Serena, but also the rotating cast of lead singers in our band. There was also the fact that I was writing original songs, not just covering someone else's material.

Different seasons, indeed.

Before the festivities began, I scanned the room to see whom I would be facing in this competition. There were maybe a dozen students altogether, a motley crew of folks from a broad spectrum of social circles; apart from Steve, however, each of my opponents came armed only with a CD for his or her instrumental backing track.

It's going to be karaoke at its finest, I figured.

If nothing else, I imagined that Steve and I would have an edge over the competition with our live instrumentation. You never knew with teachers in the 1990s, though, because so many of them had terrible taste in music – with the obvious exception of my father, of course.

The school's principal, Dr. Gardner, sternly reminded us about the rules of this audition. "All acts," he informed us, "will need to wait outside the auditorium until immediately before their audition times. You will not be allowed any false starts or 'do-overs,' so make sure that you get it right the first time."

As he marched in front of us like a maddeningly calm caged animal, I found myself biting my fingernails anxiously. Suddenly, he stopped and stared right at me. "There will be no favoritism or nepotism," he added. Subsequently, he glanced around the room to make sure that everyone understood. "All applicants," he said, "will be judged solely on the quality of their work and performance. No other considerations will be given." Principal Gardner then proceeded to place a schedule on the auditorium door and directed us to wait our turn outside.

As we headed for the grass beyond the foyer, the applicants fidgeted nervously. We took turns examining the schedule of performers, analyzing the song choices and assessing our competition the same way that Coach Montaña had sized me up the first day of football practice almost four years before. This time, though, no one could hide behind the shelter of tinted sunglasses.

I skimmed through the list, hunting for my name like a bulky predator stalking its diminutive prey. Serena's name hovered angelically at the very top of the paper next to her selection, "Over the Rainbow." Below her were a who's-who of Sespe Creek musical royalty, ranging from Tyler Jamison performing "Brown-Eyed Girl" to Stephanie Green singing "Wind Beneath My Wings" and Jennifer Martinez covering "On My Own." Steve's name was buried somewhere in the middle of the list, sandwiched between a few other classmates whose names I've since forgotten. It wasn't until I got to the very bottom of the page that I finally saw my own name.

Rick Smith: "Different Seasons"

I had been placed last. Dead last. Whether this was an intentional maneuver or not, it terrified me that the committee would see every single performer before yours truly. After closely scrutinizing the list, I saw that my competition ran the gamut from sentimental show tunes to saccharine weepers to unabashedly raucous rock songs – with nary an original composition in sight. No one had tried to write something of their own.

No one, of course, but me.

They called for Serena first, and she nervously kissed Steve before turning for the entrance. As she walked away, Steve slapped her on the butt, barked "Go get 'em, baby," and winked lasciviously at her.

Time passed slowly, with just a hint of muffled melody escaping from the thick doors of the auditorium. After five minutes, Serena emerged from the theater. She looked a little shaken, but she gave a relieved smile when she saw Steve. As she exhaled uneasily, Dr. Gardner called from the darkened entrance to the auditorium and Tyler made his way to the stage. As soon as he crossed the entrance, the door closed ominously behind him.

One by one, my classmates were called up to the unimpeachable darkness of the cavernous auditorium. Some emerged from the womb of the theater red-faced and trembling; others seemed to jump jubilantly from the exit as if they'd just slain invisible dragons. When it came time for Steve's turn, I walked over to him and wished him luck.

"I don't need luck," he grunted, looping his burly arm around Serena's shoulders. "I've got this one in the bag."

Shortly thereafter, the auditorium door swung open and Stephanie Green rushed past us, tears welling in her soft blue eyes. Most of us turned away in deference to her emotional outburst, but Steve just scoffed and trailed her with his icy gaze.

"Another one bites the dust," he said with a smirk.

From the darkness of the theater, Dr. Gardner called Steve's name. Steve grabbed his guitar case in his right hand, pecked Serena on the lips, and ambled over to start his audition. Though Steve's confidence usually worked in his favor, I couldn't help but wonder if the judges would interpret his nonchalant nature as careless cockiness.

Would the panel disregard Caulfield's lead singer because of his arrogance? I silently speculated to myself. *Or would they drink the punk-rock Kool-Aid and join the cult of Steve?*

While Steve was inside playing his Smashing Pumpkins cover, Serena and I made small talk. It was mostly inane, pedestrian conversation, and I tried my best to maintain some semblance of decorum. Though my heart throbbed with jealousy, I desperately wanted to present myself as indifferent and unaffected by her relationship with Steve – even if nothing could be further from the truth. The afternoon sun reflected off her honeyed hair, and she looked radiant. It seemed to me, at the time, a cosmic tragedy that she would choose Steve over me. Like all teenage boys in the lonely, unaccompanied corner of a love triangle, I felt trapped and paralyzed by my relationship with this captivating girl. If she didn't have the foresight to pick a guy who would treat her right, however, that was her problem – not mine.

Within a matter of minutes, Steve flung the door open triumphantly and insouciantly strolled to where Serena and I stood. She threw her golden arms around him and kissed him on the lips. As Serena and Steve stood locked in an embrace, I shuffled uncomfortably in my spot.

From the recesses of the theater, Dr. Gardner called Jennifer Martinez's name. She took a deep breath, puckered her lips firmly, and then walked forward to meet her fate.

I turned to face Steve and cleared my throat. "How did it go?" I asked.

He grinned wolfishly. "I nailed it."

"Did they ask you anything?"

He stifled a brief breath, like he was inhaling from an invisible cigarette. "They wanted to know about the lyrics. They asked me how the song relates to graduation. I told them that graduation day would be the greatest day ever, so the song should be pretty self-explanatory."

"Anything else?" I prodded.

"They asked me how long I had been playing guitar. Weird question."

The plot thickens, I thought to myself.

Though he didn't see them as flaws, Steve had a couple of potential strikes against him – just as I had predicted. Still, I figured that the power of his singular voice might be enough to compensate for his instrumental deficits. Before I could ask any further questions, though, Dr. Gardner called my name from the threshold of the theater.

It was my turn.

Steve turned to me with his hand outstretched. "Good luck, buddy," he said. "May the best man win."

In my eyes, Steve had already won. He had won Serena's heart. He had won the lead singer slot in my band. Heck, with his unblemished good looks and gritty voice, he had won the genetic lottery the day he was born. In the face of all that overwhelming evidence, I was nothing but a second-place loser.

"Thanks, Steve," I said with an air of resignation as we shook hands.

Serena gave me a knowing nod and a smile – her best wishes, expressed mutely and illicitly.

Hands quaking, I grabbed my guitar case and headed towards the yawning auditorium.

When I passed through the door, I was enveloped in a stifling darkness. I felt like Odysseus entering the underworld or Alice slipping through the rabbit hole. From the center of the auditorium, a small group of teachers sat together, hunched over their clipboards and illuminated only by the sliver of light from a desk lamp.

From my vantage point, I could make out the faces of Principal Gardner, Mrs. Ciénaga, Mr. Vallejo, Miss Wassermann… and my dad.

I was surprised to see my father there, part of the judging panel and ready to watch me perform. I understood then why Dr. Gardner had mentioned *nepotism* and *favoritism* in his introduction: he wanted to make it clear that I would be judged by my merits, not by the fact that my father was on the selection committee.

"Good afternoon, Rick," Dr. Gardner said in his rigid, poised voice. "It's my understanding that you will be playing an original song for us today."

"Yes, sir." I said quietly, away from the microphone.

"You need to speak up, young man," Dr. Gardner said. "We need to hear your voice."

I stepped up to the microphone and heard the subtle buzzing of the room's amplification system. It was just like our P.A. back home, but magnified exponentially to fill the shadowy corners of the theater.

"Before we start," my dad interjected, "may I speak with my son for a moment?"

Principal Gardner leaned back in his seat and spoke soothingly – more softly than I had ever heard his usually stern and disciplined voice. "Of course," he said.

My dad placed his clipboard on an empty auditorium seat and awkwardly jogged up to the stage. My father was many things – a brain, a musician, a writer – but he was decidedly *not* an athlete of any caliber. Nevertheless, as he made his way to where I was standing, there was a sense of urgency to his wobbling gait.

By the time that he reached me, he was breathing heavily, winded from the quick burst of exercise. He leaned in closely, breath dense with fatigue, and whispered into my ear.

"Sing the hell out of it," he said. "Sing your song like you mean every word. Because you do." My father smiled at me, gave me a quick hug, and then returned to his seat.

There I was, alone at the microphone, standing solo underneath a lonely spotlight. It wasn't the first time I was on a stage, nor would it be the last time; however, the fact that I was taking centerstage here, playing without the support of a band, meant that this was a uniquely virginal experience.

I won't lie. I was scared to death.

Despite my trepidation, I stepped right up to the microphone stand, took a quick test strum of my acoustic guitar, and coughed into the mic.

And then I started playing.

It began comfortably enough, as I thumped minimalistic power chords on the guitar – first an *E* chord then a *B* before sliding higher into the *C#m* and ending on the *A* that rounded out the chord progression for the intro of the song. When I croaked out the first line of the first verse, I had a brief moment of panic as I realized the gravity of the moment.

"Days have passed and so have dreams," I sang, struggling to hit the right notes. I was terrified, and that unleashed anxiety echoed in my shaky voice.

But then I thought of my father and his words of guidance: *sing the hell out of it.*

I closed my eyes, channeling air and strength from my diaphragm, and launched into the long notes of the second line. *"We are chillllll-drennnn grooooooown,"* I belted out, my voice growing bolder with every second I stretched out the melody.

With that line, I could feel something transform – within the air, within the audience, and within myself. As the judges shifted in their seats and leaned forward, I could sense that their initial vague attentiveness had been replaced by a more intense interest. I suddenly felt empowered. This was my song, and I was going to *own* it. As my dad had advised, I was going to *sing the hell out of it* and give this audition everything that I had.

"Different Seasons" is a song about coming of age and having the strength to thrive in the face of adversity. It would have been hypocritical to deny myself the courage that the song's lyrics demanded. While my voice maintained its usual thin quality – more Rivers Cuomo than, say, Eddie Vedder – it was charged with electricity and full of the emotion that I usually kept walled up behind layers of modesty and humility. This time, though, I was smashing through the bricks and mortar, announcing my presence to this small, important audience of judges.

After four minutes of the boldest performance I had ever given in my entire life, I hit an open *E* chord and let the ringing strings echo through the empty cavern of the auditorium. I felt like Pete Townshend delivering a windmill blow on his guitar or a strongman throwing his barbell weights to the ground. As the sound of the chord slowly faded and gently atrophied in the theater, I became acutely aware of the staff members on the panel and their muted responses. While they were smiling and nodding and jotting down notes on their clipboards, there was something missing.

They weren't clapping.

A wave of insecurity instantly washed over me, and I began studying their faces for any sign of a reaction – good *or* bad.

Did they like it? Did they hate it? What were they writing? Why weren't they clapping?

My heart started beating rapidly in my chest and I felt a familiar sense of panic rushing out from the center of my ribcage. Just when I thought I might have an anxiety attack right there on the stage, Principal Gardner looked up from his clipboard and spoke.

"Thank you, Rick," he said gently. "We will post the results tomorrow."

I didn't move. I felt glued to my fragile spot on the creaking stage.

Dr. Gardner unflinchingly returned my stare. "You are excused, young man," he said, commanding me to leave.

I stared blankly at the judges for a split-second. "Thank you," I muttered softly into the microphone. It was all I could muster.

I packed my guitar into its case, snapped the lid shut, grabbed the handle, and turned towards the door. As I pressed my way out of the darkness into the bright light of the afternoon sun, I took one last glance back at the judges.

My father was smiling wider than the Cheshire Cat. He seemed proud – perhaps prouder than I had ever seen him.

And his look was mirrored on the faces of all the staff members around him.

That night at the dinner table, I felt queasy and defeated. No one else seemed to notice, as my mom and dad continued on with their small talk between bites of barbecue chicken and mashed potatoes. Eventually, my mom turned to me with a concerned expression on her face.

"Are you all right, Junior?" she asked. "You haven't said a single word all night."

I stopped moving around the hills of mashed potatoes on my plate and placed my silverware down. It took a great deal of strength, but I looked up at her and spoke softly.

"I'm just thinking about the audition today," I mumbled, blushing a shade of crimson darker than the barbecue sauce that was slathered on my dinner plate.

My mother and father exchanged a knowing look and smiled at each other.

"How do you think it went?" my mom asked cautiously.

"Well, I *thought* it went okay. I mean, it felt good while I was playing the song. But after it was over, I just... I don't know. I don't know if they liked it."

My father turned his wizened eyes towards me. "Why do you think that?" he asked.

"Well," I mumbled, "no one clapped."

My father just laughed. It came out boldly, like an earthquake, and startled everyone else at the table. I think the silverware even leapt up from our dinner plates.

"*Of course,* they didn't clap!" he bellowed. "How can you keep a poker face if you're applauding?"

I hadn't thought of it in those terms. "So... they didn't hate the song?" I asked nervously.

My father, still chuckling to himself, took another bite of chicken. "Well," he said, "what kind of a poker face would I have if I ruined the surprise?"

"Wait... You know who they're going to pick?" I asked frantically, my eyes jolting open and growing wider with every passing millisecond.

"I know who *I* recommended," my father said casually. "But the ballots are all top secret. Ultimately, Dr. Gardner will be the one who tallies up the votes, makes the final decision, and shares the results. No one – myself included – will know until tomorrow morning."

"How do *you* think I did?" I asked him.

"I think you need to wait, like everyone else," he told me mischievously, his eyes twinkling like stubborn crystals.

I got my answer the next morning before school. At 7:45 sharp, Principal Gardner stepped outside the entrance to the main office with a tape dispenser and a sheet of freshly printed paper. As he proceeded to post the results, a small crowd of students rushed to the window.

I could feel my chest thumping, louder than the telltale heart in Poe's story, and I thought that every student at Sespe Creek must have been able to hear the nervous beating emanating from my ribcage. I anxiously made my way to the window, straining to look above the heads of the students in front of me. There, printed in stark black letters on a snow-white canvas, were the results that I had been waiting for:

> *Congratulations to this year's commencement ceremony performers:*
>
> **Speaker #1:** *Alan Perez*
> **Speaker #2:** *Michelle Wright*
>
> **Singer #1:** *Serena Rios, "Over the Rainbow"*
> **Singer #2:** *Rick Smith, "Different Seasons"*

I got the spot.

Well... *one* of the spots, anyway.

I couldn't believe it. Somehow, against the odds, I had been selected. I would be singing at my high school graduation – and, more importantly, I would be performing an original song that *I* wrote. After the shock had dulled slightly, I felt the rush of victory stream through my limbs. Here was an example of the underdog with a guitar and a shaky voice edging out the seasoned singing veterans tackling musical cornerstones of popular culture. I beat out the gal singing *Les Misérables*, the guy tackling Van Morrison...

And Steve.

"Oh, crap," I muttered under my breath, the realization suddenly sinking in.

As each of the performers skirted around me to read Dr. Gardner's list, I could see the defeat drawing over their faces. A few of my classmates were instantaneously overcome by emotion, turning away to hide their tear-stained faces from the crowd; more, however, were kind enough to pat me on the back and congratulate me. When Serena finally made her way to the window, she let out a stifled scream of joy and hugged me, a hint of happy tears filling the corners of her blazing eyes. The two of us were wrapped in a moment of shared triumph. And it felt amazing.

Those three perfect seconds were exactly what I had wanted.

For years.

Serena pulled back slightly, but she kept her body pressed against mine. Instinctively, she pecked me on the cheek. "I am so proud of you," she told me, an expression of awe flourishing on her flawless face like streaming sunlight slanting through window shades. She reached up and placed her hands on my chest, her fingers gently caressing the creases in my shirt as she kept her eyes locked on mine. "I think that maybe... maybe I..." She seemed ready to share an important secret with me, to unburden herself of some earth-shattering revelation.

"What...?" I asked her softly.

But I never got to hear what she wanted to tell me.

It was an almost-perfect moment, on the precipice of a profound paradigm shift – until I glanced behind me and saw Steve.

His eyes were half-closed, hiding his emotions behind the thin shield of his eyelids. He clenched his jaw shut, biting down on the inevitable feeling of defeat that might have been rising from deep in his throat. He took one nasty glance at me – and then another at Serena – before turning around and storming away from the office.

After seeing her boyfriend's reaction, Serena's face blanched. She immediately pulled away from me and rushed over to Steve's side, trying in vain to slide her fingers into his fisted hand. He ignored her, continuing to storm off down the scuffed-up sidewalk as she followed him, her mouth bunched up in what seemed to be pleas of reconciliation. From my line of sight, I could see that a storm was brewing. All of this was going to end badly.

Some people are graceful losers.

Steve Öken was not.

Even though I should have been floating on cloud nine, I couldn't shake the feeling that this graduation audition had further complicated the byzantine love triangle between Steve, Serena, and me. Though Ethan and Chunk hadn't weighed in with their opinions yet, I knew that my oldest friends would feel conflicted, too.

This could very well mean the end of the band, I realized. For all their bravado and swagger, lead singers are often delicate creatures with fragile egos. And I had just thrown down a gauntlet at Steve's feet.

I had rightfully earned my spot as graduation singer, and the "best man" *did* win this time – fair and square, I might add. However, a lingering doubt in the crevices of my mind kept me wedged tightly in the sandbar, anchored on soil when I should have been gliding out into the untamed ocean.

I had won... but at what cost?

Obviously, the judges had seen something in me, had determined that I was a strong enough performer to warrant a slot at the school's commencement ceremony. And yet, despite their endorsement, I kept hearing Steve's words from that fateful day at Serena's *quinceañera*...

"You'll never make it as a singer," he had told me.

Even after all the time that had lapsed since then, his words haunted me, rattled around in my brain like pennies in a tin can. That ancient August evening was the moment when my confidence had been destroyed, when Steve Öken had solidified his spot as the lead singer of *my* band, and the nascent Bookhouse Boys were transformed into something new – Caulfield.

But shouldn't this be my *moment to shine?* I wondered. *Shouldn't I finally have a second to stand in the spotlight? Shouldn't I be allowed to emerge from the darkness after being relegated to the shadows for so many years?*

And yet...

And yet...

Something tugged at the corners of my brain, refusing the tempting sensation of vindication. I could feel the ripples and creases in my mind, the doubts and uncertainties knotting themselves in deliberation. As much as I wanted to rejoice in this moment of triumph, I couldn't shake the feeling that I only clutched a shallow victory in the palms of my hands.

I sat there equivocating back and forth with myself for a long time. It was just as easy to justify going solo as it was to deny myself that distinguished opportunity. For all my desire to bask in the glory of this moment, I was stuck at a very cruel crossroads without a clear path to the horizon.

As I tortured myself with these infernal internal debates, I thought back to a phrase from the last story in Stephen King's *Different Seasons*, "The Breathing Method." To paraphrase King's golden line: "It's the *story* that's important, not the *storyteller*."

What's more important? I asked myself. *That my song be shared with the world or that I sing it myself?*

And I knew the answer to that question.

I might compose the message, but I needed someone else to deliver it for me.

It reminded me of something I had read in one of my dad's books about the Beach Boys. Dennis Wilson, Brian's brother, once claimed that "Brian Wilson is the Beach Boys. We're his messengers." Even Brian Wilson knew when to give away a precious song to someone else – whether it was Carl singing "God Only Knows" or Al crooning "Help Me, Rhonda," Brian understood that his voice wasn't always the best suited to deliver a song to the world.

It's the song, I realized, *not the person who sings it.*

I knew what I had to do.

As the morning lurched into afternoon, I felt my stomach rioting against me. I needed to act, and I needed to do it quickly. After lunch, I asked my creative writing teacher, Mrs. Arenas, if I could leave class and speak with the principal. She dutifully wrote me a pass and I made my way through the halls, building up the confidence to speak with Dr. Gardner and reviewing talking points in my head.

By the time that I reached the administration building, I had it all figured out. I knocked on the principal's door and waited for him to look up from his meticulously organized desk. When our eyes met, I gave him a staged smile and began to speak.

"Dr. Gardner, I have a proposition for you," I announced.

Principal Gardner leaned back in his leather chair and beckoned me to continue with a regal wave of his wrinkled hand.

I mustered all the courage I could cultivate from the caverns of my chest cavity, and I launched into my sales pitch. "Our commencement ceremony deserves nothing but the best musical performances," I explained. "And while I'm *incredibly* honored that you selected me to sing at graduation, I'm not a strong enough singer to pull this off by myself."

Dr. Gardner listened dutifully to every word. Though he initially seemed surprised by my request, Sespe Creek's principal maintained his usual stoic composure, methodically folding his hands in front of him like he was constructing a steeple out of his fingers. "What do you propose, Rick?" he asked.

It felt strange trying to convince Sespe Creek's stern leader to make a substantial change to a school event. However, my seventeen-year-old boldness overshadowed any inherent trepidation I might have had. I suppose that my dad's position on campus helped bolster my confidence, but looking back now, I'm surprised at how audacious I was with my demands.

I took a deep breath. "Before you rush to any conclusions," I warned him, "please hear me out."

"I'm listening," he assured me. He nodded, mutely urging me to continue.

"I've been thinking about it since you posted the notice this morning," I said. "And I've come to the conclusion that I need my band up there onstage with me…"

"Your *band*…?" he asked skeptically.

"Yes, sir. I'm really proud of the song that I wrote, but I also know… I mean, I'm *confident* that Steve Öken can sing it better than I ever could."

"Didn't Steve Öken try out with that Pumpkin Smashers song?" Dr. Gardner asked, his lips pursed quizzically. He shifted in his leather chair, crossing his legs and leaning back slightly.

"That is correct, sir," I said. I neglected to correct Gardner's butchering of the Smashing Pumpkins moniker. It didn't seem like the right time. "I've worked closely with Steve for three years now, and he… well, he has a better voice than I do. Of course, I'll still be up there, strumming my acoustic guitar. But he'll be the one in front of the microphone." I looked down at my fidgeting hands, feeling more like I was in group therapy than the principal's office. "Our band, Caulfield –"

"Like *Holden Caulfield...*?" Dr. Gardner interrupted, nodding his head and looking impressed. "*Catcher in the Rye* is one of my favorite novels. I used to teach it to my own students, when I was still in the classroom." His eyes glazed over with the look of tender nostalgia – perhaps recalling simpler times in his career, when the weight of an entire school wasn't resting on his weary shoulders.

"I *love* that book," I told him, quickly latching onto this literary Achilles' heel. "In our band, Caulfield, Steve is the lead singer. My cousin, Chunk – I mean, *Charles* – is the drummer, and Ethan Hidalgo plays lead guitar. I think that if Caulfield played my song acoustically, without any amps or electric guitars, it could be something *really* powerful. It would definitely make our graduation ceremony a memorable one."

Principal Gardner paused and narrowed his eyes into razor-sharp slits, as if he was studying the wall chart in an optometrist's office. "I believe that can be arranged, Rick."

I wanted to bolt out of my seat and hug the man. He didn't strike me as the warm and fuzzy type, though. "That's wonderful!" I told him, exhaling with relief. "Thank you, sir!"

"Is there anything else...?" he asked, shifting his glasses on his nose.

I chewed the inside of my cheek as I geared up for my next request. "Since setting up a band to play for one song is something of a commitment, would it be possible for us to serve as the backing band for Serena Rios as well? I mean, rather than a dull, karaoke sing-along version of 'Over the Rainbow,' wouldn't it be more memorable with a live band onstage?"

"You do have a point," Dr. Gardner agreed. "As long as Serena doesn't object, I would support having your band as her accompaniment."

I imagined Serena and Steve locking lips in front of a microphone, and I chuckled to myself. "I'm *positive* that Serena will agree," I told him.

"In fact, during one of the first conversations that I ever had with her, she told me that 'singing with a live band' was on her bucket list."

I thought back to that fateful first day of summer school, when I had been serendipitously seated next to my dream girl. As it turns out, I *had* found a way to play music with the hot girl who sat next to me in Chemistry class. It just didn't turn out exactly like my fifteen-year-old mind had envisioned.

Before I let myself get swept up in my own sea of nostalgia, I turned my attention back to the task at hand. "And there's one more thing, sir…"

"There's *more…*?" he asked, a brief exhalation of exasperated amusement escaping his lips.

"Just one last addendum," I assured him. "For the benefit of all parties involved, can you find a way – if at all possible – to avoid crediting me with this idea? There are some…"

I paused, racking my brain for the right word.

"There are some *complications* with the players in this scenario," I explained, "and I think it might be in our best interest – for *all* of us – if we can find a way to make this look like an administrative suggestion. Does that make sense, sir?"

Principal Gardner once again shifted his glasses to the bridge of his nose and leaned forward in his leather chair. "This is a very unconventional proposition," he told me. "But, you've made a convincing case. While I am not in the habit of taking requests from high school students – especially *this number* of requests – I also understand your concerns. Obviously, I can't promise you anything. That being said, I'll see what I can do."

"Thank you, sir," I said, respiring my relief with a large sigh. My shoulders relaxed and my chest felt infinitely lighter.

As we wrapped up our conversation, Dr. Gardner asked his secretary to send out call-slips to Serena and Steve, and he assured me that he would speak with the two of them later that day. Just as I was preparing to head out his door, he stopped me to share one last observation.

"You know, Rick," he said with his firm, impassive voice, "in all my decades in this profession – first as a teacher, then as an administrator – I can't recall many high school students who would have the foresight or maturity or even *sophistication* to make this kind of request."

"Thank you again, sir," I mumbled meekly, my cheeks flushing crimson. I hurried out of his office, feeling like I had just converted a fumble into a touchdown.

It all worked out much more easily than I anticipated. True to form, Principal Gardner used his administrative magic and executed my plan without a hitch. The guy might not have been a teddy bear, but he took care of business *quickly*. Maybe he *was* that impressed with my sales pitch. Maybe he owed my dad a favor. Maybe he just had a soft spot for *Catcher in the Rye*. Who knows?

I found out later that Dr. Gardner didn't even mention my name in his meeting with Serena and Steve. In fact, the two lovebirds assumed that my dad must have been the party responsible for rearranging our graduation roles. Ultimately, Steve and Serena consented, and Dr. Gardner agreed to let Caulfield (with special guest singer Serena Rios) perform at Sespe Creek's 1997 commencement ceremony.

Some might call it cowardice. Some might call it obedience. After all, my idea to have Steve and the band perform at graduation clearly took the pressure off my trembling shoulders. Truthfully, while it would have been easy for me to just strum my guitar and sing to the best of my limited capabilities (as I had done at the audition), I knew that stepping back from the spotlight was the *right* thing to do. Yes, it might have been more emotionally fulfilling to finally stake my claim as a solo artist, but the fallout from that decision had the potential to rip apart my band – to destroy the potential of this prodigious young project that we called Caulfield.

In the weeks after the announcement, Caulfield got together with Serena to work out an arrangement for "Over the Rainbow" that didn't sound like bad elevator music karaoke. As I watched Serena's lips linger close to the microphone during rehearsal, I envied the mic's metallic mesh for its proximity to my dream girl's breath. When I started high school as a freshman, I never could have predicted that I would be performing at graduation with *the* Serena Rios, or that she and I would develop such an intense friendship over a few short years. The world had seemed so drab back then, so black-and-white and clouded over with grim grayscale grief.

Serena had brought color to my life in unexpected ways, but I still found myself wishing upon a rainbow for a pair of ruby red slippers – or, in my case, ruby red *Converse* – to take me far away from this humdrum life, to a land of lullabies where dreams really did come true.

It hurt to know that Serena wouldn't be a part of that dream, but I didn't really have a say in the matter. She saw me more as Toto than the Tin Man. Nothing I could do would change that perception.

Or so I thought.

Ultimately, our rendition of Judy Garland's show-stopping *Wizard of Oz* theme song wasn't quite as goosebump-inducing as Israel Kamakawiwo'ole's ubiquitous ukulele version, but the band's acoustic instrumentation helped strip back some of the song's show-tune melodrama and make it more palatable for a 1990s audience.

In contrast to this more mundane and understated interpretation of "Over the Rainbow," our full-band acoustic version of "Different Seasons" felt electrified and engaging. I had been in the habit of writing loud, punk-leaning rock songs for a while by then, but "Different Seasons" was one of those rare compositions that seemed to work equally well in an acoustic or electric setting. And my prediction was correct: Steve sang the song much more emotively and powerfully than I ever could have done. His voice was truly a once-in-a-lifetime gift. My thin, high-pitched vocals simply paled in comparison.

Fortunately for me, there was already a precedent for this kind of rock and roll bait-and-switch. There's a reason that Pete Townshend had Roger Daltrey sing lead on the vast majority of songs by The Who, or why Robbie Robertson employed Levon Helm's singular singing in The Band: Townshend knew that Daltrey's voice had the raw power that his own voice lacked, just as Robbie understood that Levon's singing was far more memorable than his own.

The best parallel that I can think of comes from – you guessed it – the Beach Boys. Like Pete Townshend and Robbie Robertson, Brian Wilson recognized that he could utilize other singers to compensate for his own vocal limitations; unlike The Who or The Band, however, Brian had a small army of singers in the Beach Boys lineup at his disposal. In Peter Ames Carlin's *Catch a Wave: The Rise, Fall, and Redemption of The Beach Boys' Brian Wilson*, the author recounts a story about how Brian was initially embarrassed by his singing: as a teenager, he felt that his voice sounded too feminine. However, to counterbalance his own weaknesses, Brian learned how to use the combined voices of the other Beach Boys as instruments in his own mini-choir – each of them possessing characteristics, ranges, and styles that matched nicely with different compositions.

The sad truth is that someone else can often sing your own song better than you can. Like it or not, I was inextricably bound to Steve Öken the same way that Pete Townshend was tied to Roger Daltrey, as Robbie Robertson was entangled with Levon Helm, like Brian Wilson was linked to Mike Love.

It's the song that's important, I reminded myself, *not the singer*.

Learning how to maintain equilibrium in teamwork's tug-of-war can feel overwhelming at times. It was an ocean of experience that I would spend the next three years of my life navigating, with wildly successful – but eventually disastrous – results. Our high school graduation ceremony was simply a harbinger of things to come.

The final month of high school can be an awkward time of transition, filled with mixed messages and bittersweet emotions. The typical terms used for the end of high school, "graduation" and "commencement," reflect this bipolar split. However, like every other milestone in life, this time is simultaneously a beginning *and* an end. The Romans were clever enough to create a god to signify this transitional period: Janus, the two-faced deity who stares endlessly in both directions at the same time. Janus represents beginnings and endings, doors and passageways – and he should be identified as the patron saint of high school gradu-mencement.

If "Different Seasons" had a face, it would be that of Janus, staring back at the years of Sespe Creek High School and forward to the future of UCLA. In only a matter of months, I would be heading to Los Angeles, leaving the comforts of rustic Ojai for the academia of posh Westwood. I didn't know what would happen with Caulfield or with my friends or with my family, but the sheer promise of beginning again, of starting over, was thrilling enough to propel me forward through the final weeks of high school.

The day of Sespe Creek's graduation, I was a small wave in a larger river. My fellow students and I wore matching ceremonial tassels and quadrilateral caps and oversized gowns, each of us struggling to look dignified in the ridiculous robes that have come to define high school commencement ceremonies. As I made my way through the throngs of students, each with a unique identity hidden behind the camouflaging conformity of our two-toned gowns, I couldn't help but feel lost. I was a simple grain of sand in this complicated hourglass of young men and women, and we were all spilling through the halls like particles filtering from one end of a glass canister to another.

The campus looked like an ocean of maroon and black, as students in ill-fitting graduation gowns made their way from classrooms to hallways to their reserved plastic chairs in the stadium. Once seated, they would wait anxiously through a tedious, protracted ceremony until that one glorious moment when each of them crossed the stage with a diploma frame in hand.

It was a surreal experience. We were teenagers on the verge of adulthood, but we reverted back to kids in those moments of anticipation. It was like Christmas morning for the cynical adolescents who had forgotten the sweet, innocent thrills of childhood.

Before the ceremony, students cloistered together in classrooms based on meticulously organized rosters that placed us alphabetically amongst our peers. The classrooms, which once seemed so large and intimidating, felt strangely small and impotent. They had been stripped of their mystically menacing powers, and the rooms now simply looked quaint and feeble. My classmates, some of whom I had known since elementary school, were occupying their time by posing for photographs, applying makeup, or simply gabbing with friends.

Rather than mingle with our fellow soon-to-be grads, Ethan, Chunk, and I sat in desks at the far corner of the classroom. We were older and wiser, but – for a moment – we were still the antisocial Bookhouse Boys of Maricopa Middle School, sitting by ourselves in the midst of a hundred small celebrations. Like children wading in the shallow depths of the ocean, balancing on the sand while cascading waves rocked their bodies, the Bookhouse Boys once again maintained a stoic distance from our surroundings.

For once, though, it didn't feel like we were ostracized outcasts. Rather, we were self-assured young men, weathered by our years of outsider status, but finally comfortable and confident in our seclusion.

We were pillars.

We were monuments.

We were bricks.

And we were ready to leave our old world behind.

Though everyone imagines that graduation will be an enchanted day with flawless summer weather, such is rarely the case. In all my years of teaching, I've seen just as many foreboding firmaments on that last day of school as I have casually sunny skies. Some years, I've been witness to a hazy sun leisurely sinking and setting in the distance; other years, I've desperately prayed for reprieve from the rain as wisps of water flowed freely from the sky.

The day of my commencement ceremony at Sespe Creek was gray and gloomy, promising only the unanticipated: not a brighter sunrise, but a darkened twilight.

As I sat nervously in my white plastic chair, I watched the waving palm trees taunting the ominous sky, battered as they were by an imposing wind. Back and forth, back and forth, the palm trees rocked and swayed as they struggled to stand tall. The decorative flowers, staged like baroque chess pieces on the provisional stage, seemed ready to tilt and tip over at any moment; stray balloons, purchased at supermarkets and flower shops, ripped free from the hands of their owners and floated to the heavens like the unfortunate characters in *Logan's Run*. Our tassels fluttered about gracelessly, batting our faces with each careless gust of wind. Even the dueling California and United States flags, those twin imposing figures of authority, whipped loudly and awkwardly with each shift in the air.

Despite the foreboding warnings of the weather, we refused to let our smiles sag. This was *our* moment – graduation day. It was our time and our place and our rite of passage. We could see our own emotions echoed in the faces and forms of our peers. Much like the booming amplification of the speakers, which provided a massive slap-back delay that would put Sun Records to shame, the resonance of the experience transcended our divisive differences. We were all *one* in that moment. We all adorned the school's maroon and black colors, our individual shades fading casually into the frames of our neighbors and friends.

Like the dormant stadium lights that towered over our heads, we felt full of potential. The possibilities for our futures seemed limitless, even in the face of the overwhelming darkness in front of us. As we sat and listened to the rushed voices of staff representatives and carefully selected student speakers, we eagerly stretched out in our seats, reaching our legs and fingers away from us and towards the unbending skyline. The square black mortarboards that adorned our heads promised structure and security – a perfect symmetry for the life that would follow graduation. In reality, though, our lives would be much more like those tassels dangling before our eyes, floating unrestrained without any secure place to land.

For a split second, I was reminded of the wind chimes that dangled precipitously outside Café Voltaire – those fragile, delicate wisps of metal that threatened to come loose from the flimsy suspension of their ropes. I only hoped that, as we tempted the tenuous fates of the future, we wouldn't forsake the bonds that had tethered us to our roots.

Finally, after an endless supply of awkward public speakers (all of whom pandered to the audience with canned, sterile quotes from old movies and ancient poets), it was time for Caulfield to rouse the crowds from their somnambulant states. Principal Gardner gave us an underwhelming introduction, inviting "a selection of student musicians" to the stage, but even his resigned stoicism couldn't detract from the monumental moment at hand.

Ethan and I began strumming the first few chords of "Over the Rainbow," approximating the gentle strains of Israel Kamakawiwo'ole's ukulele rendition from *Facing Future*. All of our punk rock tendencies, our aspirations to push the limits and harness distortion, became secondhand desires. Instead, we were a quiet quartet backing up the soaring voice of Serena Rios. From my vantage point on the side of the stage, I could only see half of her frame: podiums and floral displays blocked the rest of her body from my view. She was only a few feet away, mind you, but it felt to me like a million miles. The distance between us had grown from that summer of Chemistry and kisses. Now, we were each on the cusp of new paths, new journeys that would lead us further and further away from our brief point of convergence.

As she sang with that unexpectedly fluid, fine-tuned voice of hers, the crowd was captivated. Like her lead-singer boyfriend, Serena had the superhuman ability to hypnotize with her looks, her charm, and her voice; and yet, Serena's small frame never demanded the arrogant penance that Steve did when he sang. With each lilting note and turn of phrase, Serena's voice promised sweet nostalgia and open arms. Even her song, "Over the Rainbow," hinted at the grand life just beyond the horizon, just out of reach. Happy little bluebirds and lullabies and troubles melting away – all of this was just a short distance from where we lived and breathed and sighed. In the middle of that gusty evening wind, which threatened to knock down the tender trees and delicate flowers onstage, her song was a salving reprieve.

Would the future transport us to a brilliantly colorful Oz? Or would it take us someplace darker, a dire location draped in drab black-and-white hues? Only time would tell.

As expected, Serena's performance was met with enthusiastic applause, closely trailed by hoots and hollers (and even catcalls) from the crowd. She was bright and beautiful and swelling with pride, the darling of Sespe Creek High School's graduating class of 1997, even in her final hours as its unassuming queen.

How could Caulfield follow that?

Principal Gardner, clapping with an enthusiasm I didn't think possible for him, stomped his way to the stage. "Next," he announced into the static of his microphone, "we have an original composition by one of our own students, Mr. Brian Richard Smith."

Unexpectedly, the crowd of classmates below the stage started bellowing something. It started with a small cluster of bulky football players, my compatriots on the field for the last four years. As they chanted, it sounded indistinguishable – almost guttural, in fact – and it took me a second to realize what they were shouting…

"Brick! Brick! Brick!"

They were chanting my name.

Little old me. The nerdy, socially awkward valedictorian who couldn't get elected prom king in a million years… They were shouting my name.

Or my nickname, at least.

Brick. Brick. Brick.

I could've milked that momentum for another minute or two, but I took it instead as my cue to begin "Different Seasons." I hit that opening *E* chord hard, strumming with all the punk-rock energy I could muster on the acoustic guitar I nervously clutched in my trembling hands. My father had kindly leant me his old Martin D-21 for this performance, and I was surprised at how vibrant the guitar sounded as I held it tightly to my chest. The strings resonated with an ancient power, something indescribably beautiful and delicate and precious. This was my father's guitar, a small wooden instrument that stretched its immortal sound from its birth in 1961 to this exact second in 1997. It was a performance thirty-six years in the making.

This was my moment.

Or, at least, it *should* have been.

Despite the fact that it was *my* name being cheered, *my* song about to be performed, I could see Steve anxiously gearing up to conquer the crowd. Ever the showman, Steve marched to the forefront of the stage, all swagger and self-confidence. Every pair of eyes in that stadium followed him, just as I witnessed during Caulfield's inaugural performance at Serena's *quinceañera* three short years before.

"Class of 1997," Steve bellowed from the base of the stage. "This one's for you!"

And – yet again – the crowd was *his*.

In that instant, it seemed to me that I would never experience the "moment of glory" that all performers treasure. Instead, I would always be overshadowed and overwhelmed by Steve Öken's unyielding silhouette.

As the band maneuvered through the initial lines of my song, I could sense a tide swelling, a primal force like a resilient wave starting to crest. Ethan's slithering lead guitar riff heralded a sea change for the performance, and the audience became even more attuned to our playing. Chunk's drums, although muted by the brushes he used in lieu of drumsticks, propelled us forward and demanded the audience's attention. By the time that we hit the end of the first verse and Steve belted out the eponymous lyrics of the chorus, *"And when the time comes for different seasons,"* the climactic chords captivated the crowd – even eliciting a surprising howl that swelled louder than the threatening wind.

It was beautiful. It was majestic. It was everything I had hoped for when I composed the song.

For a brief second, I didn't care about Steve's reckless desire for attention. Instead, I felt the power and pride that comes with the act of creation – and I didn't need public recognition for my work. I was filled with joy by the fact that I had composed something consequential; the fact that it was being performed live at such a monumental occasion meant everything in the world to me. Despite all the drama, despite all the rivalry and jealousy, I felt at peace. For once in my short life, I felt content.

When we finished playing, the last chord ringing out through the sullen summer air, I swear the wind actually stopped. It was almost as if we had harnessed the metaphysical power of youth and defeated nature with a knockout punch. No mere breeze could stop us. We were Caulfield – and we were seizing the day. *Carpe diem* and all that jazz. Accordingly, with that final note fading, the crowd lunged into a riotous applause. They clapped for me, for the band, and for the shared communal experience of graduating from high school. In that monolithic stadium, we were unified and fused by the power of the moment – and the power of song.

The rest of the graduation ceremony continued on like graduation ceremonies always do. There was the endless percussion of bodies and handshakes thumping on the raised platform of the makeshift stage; the ceaseless snap of photography capturing the earnest, beaming smiles of graduates; the intermittent screams, shouts, and cheers of a group gone mad with joy. There were no naked bodies streaking across the stage – just streaking mascara and eyeliner, as students felt overcome with the joy and excitement of this formal validation.

Each day should be like this, I thought to myself, scanning the familiar faces around me. *Every single day should be a commencement.*

Every morning should begin with a new chapter and all the hope that it implies, building and building on the pages that preceded it while forging ahead with the story that you've written and continue to compose.

And, as you make your way through the trials, tribulations, and celebrations of the day, you can take solace in the fact that each subsequent morning will provide you with the opportunity to begin again. As Scarlett O'Hara says in *Gone with the Wind*, "Tomorrow is another day" – and the same holds true for the next week, the next month, the next year. The greatest gift that humanity has is the capacity for reinvention; whether we choose to rise from the ashes like an army of phoenixes or sullenly lie defeated in the cinders is our own decision.

Every single day should be a commencement.

The burden should be lifted from your shoulders daily, and you should revel in the lightness of living.

As I walked out of the stadium that evening, each step carrying me farther and farther away from campus, I made my decision: this day was going to be the beginning of my new life. I would no longer be bound by the bricks and mortar of my past, by the names and faces that had defined me. I would claim my own identity and start anew.

This was my graduation day.

And yet...

And yet...

There was something missing.

For all the beauty and majesty and glory of graduation, I couldn't escape the nagging feeling that something inside of me was still *incomplete*. Despite the irrepressible victory of the evening, there was still a vague, echoing emptiness that rattled me to my core.

I had no hands to hold or lips to kiss when I walked off that stage. I had no arms to embrace me, console me, or congratulate me. Unlike Steve and Serena, who seemed perpetually locked together at the torso like intertwining vines, I had no companion to share this moment. Even with family and friends surrounding me, I felt like I was living half a life, aching for that sense of completion that I assumed a romantic engagement could provide.

In other words, I was a typical teenage boy: lovesick and anxious and grieving for a life that was just beyond my grasp.

That night at dinner, after the school celebrations had fizzled to a frozen tedium, I couldn't shake the feelings of loneliness that had been swelling inside me like a river after the rainfall. As both sides of the Smith family – mine and Chunk's – situated themselves into the plush booths of a local Chinese restaurant, the Hǎiyáng House, I felt something akin to the anticlimactic strain of a quiet theater after the symphonies have faded.

Was this all there was to a victory? I didn't feel all that different. Though undeniably relieved of the burden of high school, I still felt weighed down by forces beyond my control. Even after a few hours in a graduation gown and the ceremonial moving of tassels, I was still just me.

Brian Richard Smith, Junior.

Rick.

Brick.

Whatever.

Victory didn't taste as sweet as I had anticipated.

I was clearly distracted, swathed in my own thoughts rather than the festivities around me. My mother and father, both of whom flanked me on either side of our booth, would occasionally reach out a gentle hand and squeeze my arm; when they did, I would smile at them, feigning joy despite the shadows of covetous clouds that I couldn't shake from my brain.

After dinner, as we sat around a table of disassembled dishes and leftover libations, my father raised his water glass and tapped the side with a silver fork. "Attention, everyone," he called out to the two dozen or so family members seated in the restaurant. "We are here tonight to celebrate the achievements of two fine young men, Rick and Charles."

My family clapped politely as Chunk and I sheepishly stared down at the empty plates in front of us. The other passive patrons in the restaurant never would have guessed that the two unassuming young men being celebrated were the backbone of a local punk band. For all intents and purposes, we were just two teenagers with normal clothes and boring hair and uncomfortable shoes.

"Rick and Charles are both pillars of strength," my dad continued. "They have built themselves incredible foundations for the future, and I have no doubt that there will be many bright days ahead of them." He raised his glass unnaturally high above his head and clanged the side once again with his fork. "Cheers!"

As I scanned the room, I saw dozens of beaming eyes focused on Chunk and me. Some were seemingly lost in nostalgia for their own fleeting youth, others simply in awe of the fact that the two little boys who used to play *Star Wars* in the backyard had grown into full-fledged adults. Even Marina, who had come back home from Berkeley for our graduation, seemed wistfully emotional, dabbing her eyes with the ends of her napkin.

I guess it's true what they say. You're only young once. And even then, it's not for very long at all.

An hour later, when we quietly pulled into our driveway amidst the somber sparkle of the dew-dipped evening, my father pulled me aside. Mom and Marina both rushed out to the garage, presumably to find valuable storage space for our leftovers in the outside fridge. My dad, however, held me back.

"Come into the living room and sit down," he instructed. His tone seemed strangely formal, as if he were about to lecture a class full of students, rather than share a private word with his son.

I shot him a look of confusion, but I nevertheless followed him into the adjacent room. As my dad settled into a recliner, he leaned forward and folded his hands together.

"I'm really proud of you, Junior," he told me. "I know you've had to make some tough calls recently, but I feel like you're the bigger man for having done so. You're an old soul, son. And while that can be isolating and frustrating, it'll serve you well in the long run."

I blushed and kicked my legs up behind me on the living room couch. We talked for a few minutes, reflecting on the bizarre events of that red-letter day.

"You might not miss Sespe Creek High School," he told me, "but Sespe Creek is going to miss you. All of you. Chunk, Serena, Ethan – even Steve. They'll be your friends forever, but they only inhabited the halls of my school for a few short years."

In a fashion, my father was grieving the loss of students that he'd embraced and taught. In just a few short years, I would also understand the bittersweet port of graduation, that tenuous transition between worlds.

My father checked his watch and started to rise from his seat, his massive frame looming large above me like a miniature god. "I think that's been enough time," he said, tapping the glass surface of his timepiece.

"Enough time for what?" I asked, rising to meet him eye-to-eye.

"We've got something for you," he said, his voice hushed with a conspiratorial tone. "Follow me."

Dad led me back to the garage, the site of so many late-night jam sessions and casual conversations. Though the room looked the same as it always did, I saw one oddly shaped oblong present in the middle of the room. The 3½-foot item, covered in celebratory cap-and-gown-themed wrapping paper, was propped awkwardly on its thin side. I turned to my dad with a confused look on my face.

"Go ahead," he prompted me. "Open it up."

I knelt down on the floor, propped up by one shaky knee, and tore into the wrapping. Under the crinkles and crunches of the paper was a slightly frayed, graying guitar case. I flipped the latches and opened up the lid. Inside was a very familiar sight.

It was my father's vintage Martin D-21 acoustic guitar.

It was the same guitar that I had used at the graduation ceremony earlier in the evening, but here it was now, adorned with a big red bow.

I'm not sure what kind of temporal-defying, time-traveling tricks Marina and my mom must have performed to wrap it up in the small window of time while my father and I talked in the living room, but they pulled it off. I looked back at my father with yet another confused look.

"It's your guitar," I muttered quietly.

"Correction," my father answered with a crooked, clandestine smile. "It's *your* guitar."

As my dad explained it, I wouldn't be able to take a piano, an amplifier, or a bunch of effects pedals with me to my dorm room.

However, an acoustic guitar would be the perfect instrument for me to store in my cozy new residence at UCLA.

"You'll still be able to write songs," he enthusiastically expounded, "but you won't piss off your neighbors in the process."

I couldn't think of anything to say. My father took advantage of the silence and filled it with further explanation.

"Selfishly," he continued, "I'd like to see you get in touch with your acoustic side and write some quieter songs. What I saw tonight, with the band's performance of 'Different Seasons' – it showed me how much depth and potential you have as a songwriter."

I nodded silently as my eyes started to glaze over.

"There is something in you, Junior," he said, "that needs to be shared with the world. You have a heart and a soul and a voice. You have words and melodies trapped inside you. The worst thing you can do is to keep it all caged up."

I remained mute, hands prostrate at my side.

"Besides," he added, almost as an addendum, "it's better than me keeping it and just letting it collect dust in the garage."

I didn't know how to respond. My father's guitar was his prized possession, the most expensive and valuable thing he owned. Though I had established myself as a wordsmith over the last few years, I was literally without words. I grabbed my old man in a big bear hug, choked up as I was, and held him tighter than I ever had before.

After a good thirty seconds, my father and I released each other from our embrace. Nevertheless, he still held me at arm's length, his hands pressed firmly to my shoulders.

"You just have to promise me one thing," he grinned widely.

"What's that?" I asked, swiping a rogue tear from the corner of my right eye.

"That you buy me a new guitar when you get to be a big rock star."

I smiled back and shook his hand.

"Deal."

CHAPTER THIRTY-FOUR

"All Summer Long"

The summer after graduation was a magical one. Though the first few mornings after I donned that cap and gown felt like a long, hazy weekend, the hours turned into days that turned into weeks that eventually became months. This is the beauty and majesty of the summer after you finish high school: at first, the days take on the charmed quality of an extended weekend, but as time effortlessly passes by, it begins to feel more akin to spring break, with afternoons that bleed together and nights that don't require a premature curfew to squelch the interminable spirit of youth. I'm pretty sure that I slept at least twelve hours a day for that first week, as I recuperated from the bold, sleepless nights that had preceded graduation. As the days rolled on and on, though, my body adjusted to the surplus of unscheduled hours and I began to feel like a normal human being once again.

For the first time in my life, I felt liberated and unencumbered by my past. There were no summer school classes to contend with, no research paper deadlines to dread, no unrelenting responsibilities to preoccupy my mind. Of course, the three months that spanned mid-June to mid-September were not completely free and easy: I did get a summer job and do my fair share of chores around the house. My parents, ever the diligent middle-class workers that they were, insisted that I find a part-time place of employment to help pay for gas, car insurance, and the like.

"Just because you're going away to a big, fancy school," they told me, "it doesn't mean that you get a free ride."

True to form, they suggested something appropriately nerdy and close to home: the Ojai public library.

That's right. This Bookhouse Boy had once again returned to a house of books.

For four hours a day, five days a week, I shelved novels and helped confused patrons navigate the Dewey Decimal System. And, during my hours traversing through the aisles and organizing the library's dusty tomes, I found myself lost in thought – composing melodies in my mind while I worked. Writing "Different Seasons" had sparked something in me, lit a fire of inspiration that I didn't dare extinguish. Every shift, I carried a small paper notepad around in my back pocket, and I utilized every available opportunity to scribble down lyric ideas and chord progressions. I must have looked strange to the clientele and to my supervisors, crouched over dusty bookcases while I frantically scratched my pen on a small notepad. Those moments of inspiration served me well, though, as I composed the basic skeletons for dozens of songs during my time at the library that summer.

It's amazing what you can do when your brain is left to its own devices.

As a result, Caulfield's repertoire of original material expanded exponentially in a very brief period of time. Mind you, most of the songs lacked the resonance of "Time Bomb" (which would ultimately became our de facto opening number for the next few years), but this burst of quality songs was an early stroke of good luck – like finding golden nuggets of melody while panning in the first stream of inspiration.

The band spent countless hours during those months working up new material and refining the handful of songs that we had mastered over three years of rehearsal. Thanks in large part to our high-profile performance at Sespe Creek's graduation, we played a bunch of small- to medium-sized gigs (mostly coffee shops and house parties). The majority of our shows were uneventful and sparsely attended – nothing like our final, farewell performance at Sespe Creek. We didn't mind, though, because every opportunity to play music felt like a gift to us. We simply rejoiced in the fact that we could crank up our amps and play our songs for the world.

As with so many of my summers before, the garage became my safe haven, my port of deliverance. Whether it was my dad and I casually strumming acoustic guitars or the band bashing away with full-fledged rehearsals, the garage was where I spent my precious summer days. Looking back now, it feels like a golden time: we were just dumb kids reveling in the sheer joy of creating music. The summer felt very much like that of the narrator in Wilco's "Heavy Metal Drummer" – we weren't stoned (nor were we playing Kiss covers, for that matter), but the world felt beautiful and pure and golden. Those months in my parents' garage, sweaty and loud as they were, captured an Eden-like innocence that I have never been able to replicate... especially considering the fallout that loomed just beyond the horizon.

Everything since then has been like "chasing the dragon," trying to reclaim something that can never be recaptured. When I think back to the best times of my youth, the first thing that flashes before my eyes is the summer of 1997, when Caulfield simply played together for the sheer joy of making music in that sweaty, tangerine-carpeted garage. I rarely get nostalgic about the band, but when I do, it's for that brief period of time when we were young and carefree – all summer long.

Unfortunately, though, every summer must end. It's inevitable that Eden must fall, and the fleeting golden weeks whisper away to the recesses of autumn. Though we had enough sand to fill a substantial hourglass that summer, we knew that September would eventually roll around and scatter us into various corners of Southern California.

With the impending college-catalyzed diaspora hovering at the edge of our peripheral vision, we felt uncertain about the future of Caulfield. However, we promised ourselves that we would reconvene during winter vacation and revisit our little musical project. We didn't know what would happen in the interim, but we all felt okay with the temporary hiatus.

As they say, if you love something, you should set it free; if it returns to the amplifier-filled garage, then it's meant to be.

It's true for lovers.

And it's just as true for rock bands.

CHAPTER THIRTY-FIVE

"Surfer Girl"

When mid-September finally rolled around, the members of Caulfield all went their separate ways: Chunk headed to UCSB, Steve commuted to Cal State Northridge, Ethan escaped to Cal Poly San Luis Obispo, and I ventured off to UCLA. As we became Gauchos, Matadors, Mustangs, and Bruins (respectively), we knew we would be radically transforming ourselves from immature high school kids... into immature college kids. We packed our clothing, computers, and guitars into our parents' cars, and headed off to not-so-faraway locales, where we would immerse ourselves in the culture of a new world: the realm of higher education.

By the time that I boxed up all of my belongings, my room looked empty and desolate. Most of my posters had been stripped from the walls, my bookshelf was half-emptied, and (most importantly) my dad's Martin guitar was no longer on its stand by my bedside. My bedroom looked like a miniature ghost town, haunted by the memories of an ordinary childhood and a less-than-extraordinary adolescence. The veins of this mine had been emptied and the gold had been transported elsewhere. All that remained was the shell of the cave.

As with so many other aspects of my youth, UCLA's move-in day was a family affair. Because Los Angeles was only a stone's throw away from our little hometown of Ojai, Chunk and his parents volunteered to help with move-in day. So, we piled up in two minivans (one of which was packed to the gills with personal belongings) and caravanned to Westwood. The drive to Los Angeles was uneventful, with only minor traffic on the 101 and 405, but the Sunset Boulevard off-ramp was backed up with car after car of would-be Bruins. And, after what seemed like an interminable amount of time staring at the red taillights of the cars in front of us, we eventually managed to inch our way onto the UCLA campus.

Finally, we had arrived.

Approaching the campus from Sunset and Bellagio was an exhilarating, overwhelming experience. It still seemed surreal that I would be a real UCLA student in a matter of days (a genuine, authentic Bruin!), and the fact that I was transporting my entire life in a series of cardboard boxes didn't help ease the typical tension in my mind. Like every other kid in my dorm hallway, I would display the doe-eyed gaze of wonder common to incoming freshmen.

Of course, I did have a secret weapon in my corner: my guitar. Whereas many of the other poor souls in my residence hall would be playing the roommate edition of Russian roulette, I was banking on the fact that my musical background would help me score instant *coolness points* with my future floor-mates. Little did I know just how important some of those faceless future companions would be.

The grand, austere Bellagio entrance to the UCLA residential area is framed by columns and arches meant to emulate classic Roman architecture. Though the campus is relatively young, just about a century old, this kind of antediluvian design invokes the classic learning of ancient times – as well as the accompanying wisdom that such education provides. Seeing these anachronistic columns was simultaneously inspiring and intimidating to a young eighteen-year-old suburban punk.

In awe of the architecture, I had to ask myself: *Do I belong here, in this classy institution of higher learning? Am I worthy of stepping foot on this hallowed campus?*

As we cautiously drove over a series of monotonous speed bumps and approached the residence halls, I saw the same looks of astonishment and nervous excitement reflected on other young faces. Suddenly, I realized that this initiation was part of the college induction process. Self-doubt precedes self-actualization. None of us really belonged here… yet. But we would soon enough.

And I was thrilled to see what would happen next.

As opposed to the wondrous, awe-inspiring feeling of setting foot on campus, the process of transporting box after box of belongings from our minivans to the residence halls left us exhausted. It was a sweltering mid-September day, compounded by the heavy lifting of cardboard containers, and our crew of robust Smiths must have left a small river of sweat trailing from the cars to the dorms. The white blanket of concrete was blinding in the afternoon sun, with a shimmering haze reflecting off the sidewalk. Through it all, though, we kept our spirits high as we made our way back and forth into my new home: Hedrick Hall.

Like most dorms, Hedrick Hall had the static, disconsolate feel of temporary housing. It was simultaneously industrial (with its white hallways and gray carpets) and domestic (with homemade, hand-painted butcher-paper posters adorning the walls). Every dorm had its own theme, and our Resident Advisor had selected an ocean motif: paper cutouts of seaweed trailed down the halls, while mermaids and mermen (mer-*Bruins*, technically) were plastered on each blue door. As my relatives and I huffed and puffed down the hall, stopping periodically to shuffle the heavy boxes in our shaking hands, we all felt the nervous buzz of excitement that permeated the air. Move-in day was clearly a rite of passage – a demarcation of the limitless lives that we were about to build.

For me, the future was waiting just around the corner. Literally.

After our awkward adventure of shuffling, lifting, and staggering through the halls, we began to unpack. Though the walls were bare and bland, I saw potential for reinvention, revolution, and revelation: these empty walls (like my life) were ready to be redecorated with memorabilia from my past, present, and future. Sure enough, the desolate-looking dorm room was soon adorned with rock posters and bedding; immediately afterwards, I filled up the skeletal bookshelves with my dog-eared novels from home. Priorities, you know. The tiny, tidy shelves still looked vacant compared to the overflowing stacks at the Ojai public library, but the books on songwriting and music biographies helped make the room look a little more familiar. A little more like home.

This precise moment in time, though I couldn't have realized the extent of it, was the hinge that would swing my entire life in new directions and propel it into uncharted territories. While I don't remember what I ate for breakfast that morning or what t-shirt I wore or even what classes I had just signed up for, I remember one key detail from that first day at UCLA...

Meeting the girl across the hall.

I'm not sure how we managed to avoid crossing paths for the entire morning move-in, but somehow the neighbors across the hall were still a mystery to me in the afternoon hours. By that time, I had already unpacked my clothing, set up my computer, and rearranged the furniture. Just as I was about to unlock my guitar case, I heard loud voices immediately outside my dorm room door speaking in an unrecognizable accent. I remember trying to determine what dialect it was – it sounded almost like Portuguese, but primarily with English vocabulary.

College was definitely going to be an adjustment for this small-town Ojai boy.

As my father and I meticulously organized my CD collection and my bookshelf (using the Dewey Decimal System for inspiration, I might add), we talked about what college might be like. My mother, aunt, uncle, and cousin had gone venturing out to Westwood in search of a pizza parlor, so Dad and I were left alone in the newly populated dorm room. Dad reminisced about his own college experience, recalling what it was like to pack up all of his Southern California identity into cardboard boxes and relocate to Berkeley.

"At least you won't have to worry about Vietnam and the 1960s counter-culture revolution," he laughed. "With any luck, your college experience will be totally drama-free."

If only that were true.

It was right around this time that a muscular, meticulously dressed Asian-American teenager knocked on the door. He casually strolled in, messenger bag slung across his protruding pectoral muscles, and extended his right hand.

"Hi," he said with a beaming smile, "I'm Victor. It looks like we're going to be roommates this year."

We shook hands, and I'm pretty sure his sturdy grip left my poor fingers feeling crushed.

As his eyes scanned back in the direction of the hallway, he crinkled his cheeks in frustration. "My boyfriend is around here somewhere…" he began.

"Did you say… *boyfriend*?" I asked.

"Yes. Yes, I did," he shot back defensively, his eyes darting back and forth between me and my father. "Is that going to be a problem?"

"No, not at all," I quickly answered.

Victor studied us for a brief – but tense – moment, as if determining whether fight or flight would be a better option in the caged confines of a dorm room. Finally, he relented with an approving nod of his head, his strained posture relaxing. "Good," he said with a relieved sigh. "Sorry if I came across as standoffish. You can never be too careful with strangers, you know?"

Dad gave him a sympathetic, knowing look, and stretched out his hand. "Don't worry," my father assured Victor, giving him a buoyant handshake, "we're about as liberal and open-minded as they come. You won't have any problems here."

As it turned out, Victor was a pretty remarkable guy. His family was from Santa Maria (just about 100 miles north of Ojai), he ranked #3 in his graduating class, he was an accomplished cartoonist (anthropomorphic dinosaurs were his specialty), and he planned on majoring in Computer Science. As soon as he saw my guitar case tucked away in the corner of the room, he started talking rapidly about his own musical background.

"Do you mind if I play?" he asked.

"Of course not," I told him. As soon as the words were out of my mouth, Victor rushed for the instrument and opened the clasps on the side of the case. As he strummed and picked, I was astonished: his hands moved so rapidly, it was like watching a roadrunner fly between the frets. After sixty seconds of speedy soaring across the strings, he handed the guitar back to me.

My father and I just stared at him in disbelief.

"Wow," my father muttered.

"Wow," I echoed.

Victor smiled proudly. "I think you and I are going to be a good match," he laughed. "I'll have to bring my bass guitar from home. Maybe we can squeeze in some late-night dorm room jam sessions."

"As long as you guys let me sit in," my father joked.

I could already tell that this was going to be a good year.

After Victor departed to track down his parents and his boyfriend, Dad and I returned to the dull decorum of decorating my dorm room. As we unpacked box after tedious box, we could hear the gentle lull of exotic music from across the hall. The door to my dorm stood slightly ajar, leaving the lilting strains of ukulele and steel guitar wafting towards us like a tropical breeze. It was strangely soothing, but also a bit of a jarring juxtaposition with the industrial space of the residence hall.

"Do you hear that?" my father asked with a grin. "You're going to be neighbors with a surfer dude."

I heard voices from the room across the hall and the muted sounds of bare feet inching closer to my door. In my head, I pictured a big, buff, bronzed beachgoer with sandy-blonde hair and a dazed look in his eyes.

Just what I need, I thought to myself. *Another Adonis like Steve to make me feel bad about myself.*

Imagine my surprise then, when the figure that emerged from the room was not some brawny blonde surfer... but a petite young woman with dark, striking features. Even two decades later, I can recall the image clearly: her chestnut-brown irises were partially hidden behind the reflection of rectangular glasses, and her flat-ironed raven hair fell straight to her bronze shoulders. She had a small, nearly imperceptible arrowhead-shaped scar hovering to the side of her right eyelid, but it stood out more like a birthmark full of character than a hideous imperfection. As I took in the scene, I couldn't help but sneak a look at her gorgeous, tanned legs, which emerged from light-blue cut-off shorts and trailed down to the black flip-flops on her delicate feet. A dark purple baby-doll t-shirt (adorned with an adhesive name tag) clung tightly to her curvaceous frame. And right there, in the center of her shirt, was the printed image of a surfboard.

She was, I thought to myself, the most beautiful girl that I had ever seen.

And she smelled like tangerines.

"Hi! I'm your neighbor across the hall," she said, introducing herself. "Is the music too loud for you?"

"Uh, no," I stumbled. "I actually kind of like it."

I stood awkwardly for a second, temporarily stunned into silence by the gorgeous girl in front of me. And then I remembered my manners.

"I'm…"

I paused. Normally, I would have introduced myself as "Brick" or "Rick" or even "Junior." But I realized in that moment that this was my chance for a fresh start – an opportunity to leave my multitudinous nicknames behind, buried back in the towering mountains of Ojai.

"I'm Brian," I said finally, reaching out my right hand and gesturing to my father. "And this is my dad… also named Brian."

The heretofore unnamed, gorgeous girl shook my hand and my father's hand in quick succession.

"Nice to meet you both… Brians." She winked at us, and my heart melted into a muddy puddle.

My father smiled broadly and nudged me indiscreetly in the ribs.

Once again, I had forgotten my manners.

"And you must be…" I stared at the rectangular name tag on her shirt, which read N-O-E-L-A-N-I, and took my best guess: "Noel-Annie?"

The cute girl from across the hall laughed lightly before correcting me. "It's actually pronounced *No-eh-lah-nee*, but you can just call me *Lani*. It's Hawaiian."

I felt like an idiot. Two minutes after meeting the most beautiful girl EVER and I had already made a fool of myself.

But the best was yet to come.

"*No-eh-lah-nee*…" I repeated, carefully massaging the syllables, meticulously enunciating each phoneme, and gently caressing the sounds on my eager tongue. "Is that a family name? Or does it have an English translation?"

She squinted her gorgeous eyes and chewed her bottom lip. "I was actually named after my *tūtū*," she said, pausing after the last word. "That's Hawaiian for *grandma*. But the name translates roughly to '*Beautiful Girl from Heaven*.'"

Without thinking, I blurted out the first thing that popped in my head. "You must be the most accurately named person in human history," I promptly muttered.

Immediately after I said it, I regretted it. And I blushed.

Lani blushed, too. And laughed uncomfortably. "Thank you," she said, her bronze cheeks flushing a light shade of crimson. "That's very sweet of you."

We both stood there awkwardly for a moment – me paralyzed with fear over what I had said, while Lani shifted her weight from one flip-flop-adorned foot to another.

"Anyway," she continued, breaking the silence, "I have to get back to unpacking. But it was nice to meet you both."

With a quick wave goodbye, she twirled around and headed back to her room across the hall.

As soon as she was gone, my father turned to me with a wide grin. "I think you found your little surfer girl," he said with an oversized smile. "Just watch. That's probably the woman you'll end up marrying one day."

"I should be so lucky," I scoffed in self-defeat.

"You never know," he told me with a smirk. "Just wait and see."

My outstretched arm was halfway to placing a copy of Stephen King's *It* on my bookshelf when I stopped cold in my tracks.

"Dad," I mumbled. "Did I really just say that she was '*the most accurately named person in human history?*'"

"Yes, son," he replied. "Yes, you did."

I sighed and smacked myself in the forehead. So much for starting fresh with a suave blank slate. I was still the same awkward nerd from Ojai, California. But across the hall lived a *Beautiful Girl from Heaven*.

I couldn't have imagined it then, but that chance encounter was the beginning of the rest of my life.

CHAPTER THIRTY-SIX
"Shut Down"

T he first few days at UCLA were simply amazing. As I saw it, college was the ultimate reward for my countless hours of studying and homework and stress: the environment was enchanting, my professors were profoundly inspiring, and my roommate was a perfect musical partner-in-crime. It was an absolute revelation being on my own in a sunny new city that had so much to offer to optimistic, eager young students.

And, best of all, I had two classes with Lani.

That's right: TWO classes with the *Beautiful Girl from Heaven.*

In my first class on the first day of my first year at UCLA, I walked into a freshman seminar on "Literature of the Beat Movement" with Professor Zatoczka, expecting to awkwardly face a dozen other eighteen-year-old hipsters. Instead, I was greeted with a bright smile from Lani, who immediately called out my name. She grinned widely and patted the empty seat next to her, inviting me to join her. Without hesitation, I planted myself in the creaky wooden chair that was mere inches away from the hot girl from across the hall.

It's hard to explain the impact of this small gesture to the insecure eighteen-year-old version of myself. In a sense, it felt like going to a high school prom without a date, only to have the most beautiful girl in the ballroom ask you to dance. It was like an inverted Cinderella tale... only I had no glass slippers to commemorate the event – just a pair of old, scuffed-up Converse.

Professor Zatoczka was a pretty fascinating guy. With his shock of white hair and jutting chin, he seemed more like a photograph from a history book than a real, live classroom teacher. Surprisingly animated and endlessly engaging, Zatoczka had been on the periphery of the Beat Movement in San Francisco in the 1950s – those glory days of Allen Ginsberg's howling and Jack Kerouac's road-tripping. After a few years of living the beatnik life of a poet in the Bay Area, Zatoczka went the traditional route of academia, publishing poetry and teaching freshmen about his famous poetic peers. However, unlike other old white men in their 60s, Zatoczka kept himself relevant and hip, alluding to *The Simpsons* and *Moby-Dick* in the same breath. Needless to say, I was hooked from the first lecture.

Yet, with all due respect to Professor Zatoczka, I had trouble focusing on class discussions while in such close proximity to the gorgeous girl from across the hall. During the first pause in Zatoczka's oration that day, I leaned close to her and whispered, "I'm really sorry about what I said the other day."

"What do you mean?" she asked, her forehead softly scrunching up with concern.

"You know," I said sheepishly, "the thing about your name."

"Oh," she chuckled nonchalantly. "That whole thing."

"Yeah," I echoed back, "that whole thing."

"Don't worry about it," she reassured me with a knowing wink. "There are worse ways to hit on a girl."

Then she smiled that picture-perfect smile of hers, and I just melted. Again.

If she was still talking to me, inviting me to sit beside her, and casually brushing off my awkwardness, maybe I hadn't totally screwed things up.

Maybe I have a chance, I told myself.

Then she whispered back those fatal words that every boy dreads. "Just don't tell my boyfriend," she said. "William might not be quite as thrilled."

And she winked again, immediately placing a nail in the coffin of my heart.

Two days later, when I stumbled into the first day of my Astronomy GE class, I once again ran into Lani – this time, she was a small ray of hope in a dark, cavernous lecture hall. From the bottom of the stairs, I could see her waving and beckoning me toward her row. I looked around, just to make sure that she wasn't gesturing for someone else, but her invitation was (once again) for me. Though I was crestfallen to hear that she had a boyfriend – this lucky guy named "William" (who, I assumed, was some tall, muscle-bound super-jock like Steve) – I didn't ask any questions. I just couldn't pass up the opportunity to spend time with this bright, beautiful girl.

For the record: *yes, I realize how cheesy that sounds from the perspective of a grown man.* However, try explaining that to a gawky, lovelorn teenage boy. Eighteen-year-old me had a very different perspective on the matter. And, to be fair, this is *his* story just as much as it is mine.

It was serendipitous that divine intervention had gifted me these opportunities to spend endless hours in class with Lani. There are tens of thousands of students on the UCLA campus at any given time, and the odds of being matched up in multiple classes with the same person are pretty slim; the fact that Lani was simply a breathtaking beauty made the cosmic coincidence seem even more stellar. If I believed in fate or Calvinistic predetermination, it would have felt like a pretty clear message: *this girl is your destiny.*

There was just one devastatingly inconvenient problem.

She had a boyfriend.

Though Lani and I were both diligent students, which made it easier for us to bond over study sessions in the weeks to come, she had this delightfully distracting tendency to pass notes during class. Usually, it started the same way: she would pass me a blank sheet of lined paper with a question at the top (frequently some casual interrogation about my personal history), on which I subsequently scribbled answers in my illegible penmanship. We filled sheets and sheets of paper over the course of those first few months, sharing thoughts, secrets, humiliations, and accomplishments within the mathematically measured blue margins of those lines.

Twenty questions, she scrawled on one of those first notes, her words leaving perfectly looping purple marks across the page. *What do you want to know?*

Honestly? I wrote, via messy pen-scratch marks in smear-prone blue ink. *Everything.*

She choked out that sweet little giggle of hers, covering her mouth as she snorted out loud. It *was* a pretty adorable snort, though.

That's a tall order, she wrote back. *Where should we start?*

I tapped my pen against my chin, then returned to the paper that served as a flimsy border between us. *Favorite flavor of ice cream?* I asked.

Rocky road, she wrote. *Because it's sweet and nutty and swirling with surprises. Just like me.*

Swirling with surprises, indeed.

Favorite song? I asked.

"Can't Help Falling in Love with You" by Elvis Presley. Next question.

Favorite movie?

Casablanca. I know it's an old black-and-white film, but it's so romantic.

Of all the gin joints in all the dorms in all the world, she had to move across the hall from mine... This girl *was* swirling with surprises.

A sucker for old romantic movies, eh? Interesting...

I hesitated for a second, stealing a glance up at her flawless face. The arc of her lips smoothly curved into perfect cheekbones and fluttering eyelashes. As I found myself hypnotized by her irises, I was reminded of the tiny arrowhead-shaped scar adjacent to her eyelid.

Is it impolite to ask how you got that scar next to your right eye?

She scowled at me. *I was hoping you wouldn't notice,* she wrote, squinting as she furiously scribed out her response. *Car crash. I was six and my mom got sideswiped by some tourist who wasn't paying attention to the road. It's made me self-conscious since elementary school. Next question.*

I grimaced with embarrassment. Was I going to screw this up, too?

Sorry for bringing it up, I wrote, hastily sketching an apologetic-looking sad face in the margins. *Okay. Change of subject. What's your full name?*

Lani grabbed the paper, tilted it so that she could write with her left hand, and scribbled away for what seemed like minutes. Finally, she sat upright and straightened her t-shirt before tilting the paper back towards me. *My birth certificate lists my full name as Noelani Mele'kauwela Aukake'ho'opae.*

You know the old saying, "It's all Greek to me?" That's how I felt staring at that long line of consonants and vowels and swooping apostrophes.

Ummmm... I wrote. *Sooooo... What does that mean? Like, in English?*

It translates roughly to "Beautiful, Heavenly Girl from a Summer Song who Comes Ashore at Summer's End."

And here I thought that "Brick" was an epic name. Yikes.

I wasn't going to make the same mistake that I did that fateful first day in the dorms, when I completely embarrassed myself with capricious commentary about her first name. I decided to change the subject.

Where did you grow up? I asked.

I was born and raised in Maui, she wrote. *The town of Paia, to be exact. My 'ohana's home is situated on a lush, rural property, nestled against a soft, jade hillside.*

In addition to being incredibly hot, she was also incredibly eloquent. I simultaneously felt threatened and intrigued.

I've lived on The Rock my entire life, she continued. *So, it's a bit of an adjustment being on the mainland.*

As much as it's trite to say that two people can come from "different worlds," that's how it felt with Lani. She was from the mythical planet of hot Hawaiian girls, and I was from the quaint, boring Ojai Valley.

She was even using words and phrases that sounded exotically alien to my suburban Californian ears.

At the risk of embarrassing myself... I wrote, hesitating with my pen above the page. *What's "The Rock?"*

It's Hawaiian slang for "the island." Keep up, Brian. Don't be such a lolo.

What's a "lolo," dare I ask? I queried nervously. *And what's "ohana" mean...?*

She shot me a funny, inquisitive look. "Seriously?" she asked me, in a piercing whisper. "Have you never met a Hawaiian before?"

"You're the first," I admitted sheepishly. "So, I'm totally clueless. Sorry."

She reached over and patted my hand. It was the first time that our bare skin had ever touched – and it was electric. A spectral chill raced up my spine.

"Lolo" *means idiot or fool,* she wrote. *"'Ohana" means family. As in "Don't be such a* lolo *or I'll never take you home to meet my* 'ohana."

I stopped for a second, wondering if she was *really* talking about taking me home to meet her family or if she was merely speaking hypothetically. It was hard to decipher her tone from the purple marks on the page.

Next question, Lani wrote. *Something more academic, please. Hopefully, you won't feel as confused talking about school.* Next to that line, she drew a little smiley face with the tongue sticking out.

At least she had a good sense of humor.

What do you want to major in? I asked.

Her neck craned up and she lifted a finger to her sweet, shapely lips. *Right now,* she wrote, *I'm thinking I'll end up an English major (hence the Beat Generation seminar), but I'm also toying with the idea of minoring in sociology. Or journalism. I was editor-in-chief of my high school paper and I published a few editorial articles in the local newspaper, too. I even wrote part of my college essay about writing. Very meta.*

Journalism and sociology. Lani was getting more fascinating by the minute.

What do your parents do for a living? I asked.

My mom is an elementary school teacher, she wrote. Quickly, I snatched the paper from her hands.

Mine, too! I excitedly scrawled.

How funny! she answered. *My dad owns and manages a 1950s-themed restaurant in Paia. Very popular with the tourists, but it also attracts a decent crowd of* Kamaʻāina *(locals). It's all tiki decorations and vintage-looking artwork from the post-war era. He christened it the "Hulabilly Diner."*

Clever name! I wrote.

He named it after his band, she explained. *The Hulabilly Hounds. They play old rockabilly songs mixed with traditional Hawaiian music. They're not famous or anything, but it helps supplement our income. That's been a blessing since my mom got sick.*

I put down my pen and looked over at her. "Sick…?" I asked quietly, so as not to disturb the conscientious students around us (who were clearly paying much better attention to the professor's lecture).

Lani opened her mouth to speak, but stopped herself short. Instead, she picked up her purple pen and scrawled away.

Breast cancer, she wrote. *She's in remission now, but it was pretty scary for a while. It forced me to grow up REALLY quickly. While the rest of my friends were gossiping about boys and cars and surfing, I was just praying that my mother wouldn't die.* She paused, briefly lifting her pen from the page before placing the purple tip down to paper. *It really puts things in perspective when you encounter mortality like that.*

Yikes. Some pretty heavy stuff for *anyone* to deal with – let alone a teenage girl in a tropical paradise.

I can only imagine, I wrote. *Is that what you wrote about for your published newspaper articles?*

Lani's head rocked gently back and forth as she shuffled in her seat. *That was the subject of a few pieces. I actually wrote a lot more about my experiences as a* hapa *girl.*

There she went again with those exotic, foreign words. I felt like I needed a translator sitting next to us. Hapa? *What's that mean?*

Hapa *is short for* hapa haole, she explained. Haole *means "foreigner" or "not a native Hawaiian." Usually, though, it's synonymous with "white." Since my dad is a native Hawaiian and my mom is Caucasian, I'm technically* hapa haole – *or "half-white."*

Is that problematic back home? I asked.

Kind of. Maybe it's just my own personal experience, but having mixed heritage sometimes made me feel like an outsider growing up. Like, I was "too Hawaiian" for the Caucasian side of my family and "too white" for the Hawaiian side. In some ways, it's kind of a lose-lose scenario. No matter how many hours I spent playing ukulele or dancing hula, I was never "Hawaiian enough" for some of the people I grew up with. In the social hierarchy of Hawaii, I was always lingering at the bottom.

After spending so much time with Serena and thinking about how sensitive she felt about being called a "mutt," Lani's revelation struck a chord with me. Like Serena, Lani felt caught between two worlds – pulled in opposite directions by conflicting aspects of her identity.

So, is that how you identify yourself? I asked. *As "hapa haole?"*

Actually, she explained, *I kind of made up my own term.*

What's that?

Promise you won't laugh? She made a nervous grimace in the seat next to me.

Scout's honor, I wrote. *Even though I'm not a boy scout. But please continue.*

She pursed her lips together and hesitated before writing anything. Eventually, she pressed her pen firmly to the paper and quickly composed a response. *I've coined the term "Hawai'Irish" to describe myself,* she explained. *You know, like half-Hawaiian and half-Irish. My dad is native (with deep roots), but my mom's family traces its ancestry back to Ireland. I'm basically a "double-island girl" fated to stand out from the oceans around me.*

That's pretty poetic.

Thank you, she wrote. Lani tilted her head and smiled at me. It was adorable.

You know, this whole "hapa" *thing actually reminds me of a girl back home,* I wrote.

A girl back home? she asked. *Was she as beautiful as me?* Lani added a little winking smile after the question. Was it to defuse the situation? Or was she flirting with me?

I took a deep breath and quickly scribed out a bold sentence. *I've never met anyone as beautiful as you,* I wrote, quickly adding, *Have you always been gorgeous?*

"Gorgeous?" she scoffed, loud enough that the students flanking us on either side looked over in disapproval. Lani leaned in close to me, her lips reaching towards my right ear. "Yeah, right!" she whispered. "I didn't even get boobs until I was a sophomore in high school. Up until then, I looked like a ten-year-old boy."

"Well, you sure don't look like a ten-year-old boy now," I whispered back.

"Thank God for that..." Lani sighed.

Thank God, indeed.

Obviously, I also wrote back my own answers to the multitude of questions we asked each other, but I won't bore you by repeating things that you already know. It was exhilarating, learning all these facts and surprises about the *Beautiful Girl from Heaven.* All the while, we bantered back and forth like old friends, each of us gleaning secrets from the other like lovesick detectives.

I still have those notes, lovingly tucked away in a shoebox in my office. It's been over twenty years now, so the ink has faded a little bit, but the words themselves seem so vibrant and irrepressible. We were just kids, so innocent and green, and we had no idea what life would throw our way in the years to come. It's clear from rereading our scribbled words, though, that we had an undeniable chemistry... even if we had the roadblock of her boyfriend, the mysteriously absent William, preventing any kind of catalytic explosion.

At some point during those illicit note-passing sessions (which were conducted under the pretense of attending Astronomy class, of course), I asked her to teach me how to play the ukulele. I had told her a *little* bit about Caulfield by then, but with the band on hiatus, things seemed tenuous at the time – untethered from the binding ropes of the past. Plus, I was nervous about appearing too arrogant or conceited. After all, Lani came from a household filled with music: her father had his own band, and she'd been playing ukulele intermittently since she was a kid. Still, I desperately wanted her to understand that Caulfield wasn't just a frivolous high school hobby – and that I wasn't a talentless schemer with unrealistic pipe dreams.

So, I took the plunge and requested a ukulele lesson.

Can you show me how to strum a little? I asked.

Sure, she responded. *Though I'd rather teach you how to hula.*

I must warn you, I scribbled. *I am a terrible, terrible dancer. Other girls have died from laughter after seeing me in action.*

I'll take my chances, she wrote, adding a smile to the end of the line.

It's a deal, I told her, *as long as you promise not to disown me afterwards.*

We'll just have to see how bad at dancing you truly are, she wrote.

A few afternoons later, on a crisp October weekend, I was lounging in my dorm room reading the novel *Naked Lunch* for Professor Zatoczka's class. Unexpectedly, I heard a gentle – but urgent – rapping on my chamber door. When I propped it open, I found Lani leaning against the doorframe of her room across the hall. She was wearing denim shorts that were wonderfully short and a soft pink t-shirt that hugged her frame in all the right places.

And she had a ukulele in her hand.

"Is this a bad time?" she asked hesitantly.

"Uh, not at all," I told her, bumbling around for something eloquent to say as I shuffled the ragged pages of *Naked Lunch* back and forth in my hands. "Let me just… um… put this down real quick."

After briefly glancing around the room for an empty bookshelf, I tossed the book haphazardly onto my bed and grabbed my keys. Though we had spent countless afternoon hours together in class and the dining commons (and even a few evenings studying for Astronomy and English), this seemed – in my mind, at least – dangerously close to a date. And I was completely unprepared for such an amorous ambush.

My heart started to beat so intensely that I feared it would erupt from my chest cavity like the Xenomorph from the *Aliens* movies. Perhaps, just perhaps, an extraterrestrial would explode from my ribcage and I would be saved from the potential embarrassment of whatever might happen next.

Taking a deep breath, I followed Lani into her dorm room and immediately noticed that her roommate was nowhere to be found.

"Where's Emily?" I asked.

"She went home for the weekend, so I'm here *all by my lonesome*," she sighed mock-dramatically, her lips protruding with a pout. She plopped down on her immaculately made bed and swung her ukulele over her lap. "Since I'm here all by myself, I figured a little music lesson might help stave off the loneliness. Plus, I *really* don't feel like doing homework right now, so I need a valid excuse to procrastinate."

"Should I… uh… should I get my guitar?" I stuttered. My guitar always felt like makeshift armor, creating a wooden boundary between my body and everyone else around me. Strangely enough, all I could think about in that moment was maintaining a physical border between the two of us – lest I do something stupid.

"Do you think we'll need it?" she asked.

Unable to think of a clever response, I admitted defeat. "I guess not," I muttered sheepishly. I suddenly felt vulnerable and defenseless. Without my guitar, I was a mere mortal with a massive Achilles heel for pretty girls.

And right here before me was the prettiest girl in the world.

I followed Lani into her room, pulled up a pre-furnished wooden chair (standard-issue UCLA dorm-room furniture), and sat down.

Clapping my hands and rubbing them together in the manner of a silent film villain, I pondered aloud. "So, how do we begin?"

"Let's start from the beginning," she answered with a wink and a slight nod of her chin. "It's usually the best place to start. How long have you been playing guitar?"

"About eleven years."

"Okay," she said, "so you know all your basic chords, right?"

"Right."

"Playing the ukulele isn't a drastic departure from playing the guitar," she assured me. "At least that's what my dad says. As long as you know how to strum, you should be able to pick up the chords pretty quickly."

She shifted the weight of the ukulele on her lap and grabbed the neck of the diminutive instrument with her left hand. With her right hand, she plucked the individual strings, from top to bottom.

"The ukulele is usually tuned *G, C, E, A*," she began. "The mnemonic device they teach all the *keiki* is 'Good Cows Eat Apples.'"

"*Keiki*...?" I asked, raising an eyebrow.

Lani rolled her eyes at me. "*Keiki* means 'child' in Hawaiian. Keep up, Brian."

"Yes, ma'am," I muttered back.

"*Anywaaaaaayyy*..." she continued, "you can get all creative with weird tunings if you want, but this is usually the default standard tuning for beginning players. When you strum all the open strings, it's some kind of *C* chord."

"I think it's a..." I squinted my eyes, trying to calculate the chord. "I believe it's a *C6*, if I'm transposing the notes correctly."

"Sure," she said dismissively. "So, to make a proper *C major* chord, you just take your pointer finger and place it on the third fret of the *A* string. Like this."

Lani demonstrated, her elegant fingers brushing the nylon strings as gently as a summer breeze. Her movements were easy and graceful as she casually strummed the instrument in her hands. I stared at her naked fingernails; they were unpainted, un-manicured, but still perfect in their unassuming modesty.

"Now, you give it a shot," she commanded, placing the ukulele in my shaking hands.

Try as I might to play it cool, I couldn't stop my fingers from trembling. I imitated the chord positioning that she showed me and gave the instrument a single subtle strum.

"That's good!" she said, before squinting and grinning. "Maybe it would be easier if you sat next to me, though." She delicately patted the bed on the empty spot beside her, beckoning me to join her.

My heart beat faster than a battered snare in a psychobilly song, and I gulped down the anxiety that threatened to consume me. Obediently, I stood up from the uncomfortable dorm room chair and sat next to her on the stiff twin bed. I purposely sat two feet away from her, leaving a respectable distance between our bodies.

Undeterred, Lani crept closer to me, leaving only inches between our two frames. "Now, let's try something else." She removed the ukulele from my hands and made a pyramid shape on the first few frets of the higher strings. "This," she explained, "is a *G* chord. Let's see if you can do that, Mr. Guitar Player." She smirked and handed the minuscule musical instrument back to me.

I casually took the ukulele back, made a quick *G* chord and strummed. I kept a simple 4/4 rhythm and alternated back and forth between the *C* and *G* chords. "How's this?" I asked.

"You're a quick learner," she said, leaning backwards and bracing herself with her extended arms. "Now let's try something else."

She grabbed my hand and gently pulled me behind her. I sat there awkwardly and gracelessly on her bed, like an unsteady flamingo, with my body facing her back.

"I'll make the chords," she directed, "and you strum." She grabbed my right arm and cradled it around her small frame. Her neck was so close, I could smell the tangerine fragrance of her hair and see the goosebumps that formed on her hyacinth-scented skin.

I draped my fingers across the strings of the ukulele and started strumming. At first, it felt incredibly clumsy; my body was almost convulsing with nervous energy, while she maintained a maddeningly cool composure. Her left hand formed foreign shapes on the frets of the ukulele, and I watched her fingers move gracefully up and down the neck of the instrument. For a few minutes we sat there, our hands working softly, mechanically in tune with each other. The song we played was gentle, sweet, and delicate – suspended like an orchid in the autumn breeze.

"And one last strum," Lani commanded, my hands responding faithfully. She turned her cheek towards me and I could feel the warmth of her breath escaping from her mouth. Our lips were inches apart, so dangerously close that I could almost taste her.

"I... I..." The most I could muster was a monosyllabic mutter.

"Yes?" she whispered back to me, her eyelids fluttering delicately.

I gently leaned my forehead into hers, nuzzling myself into the soft nest of her raven hair. "I have to go, Lani," I told her, panic permeating every inch of my anxious body. "I have to go now."

Without looking back, I stood up, walked to her door, and left the room.

Around noon the next day, I heard an urgent – but strangely subdued – knock on my dorm room door. When I opened the door this time, Lani stood there with her arms wrapped tightly across her chest, as if she was trying to squeeze herself into a state of submission. Her ukulele dangled down from her heart to her waist, the instrument clenched tightly between her fingers.

"I want you to have this," she blurted out, reaching towards me with an outstretched arm and handing me her ukulele.

Silently, I took the instrument from her. As I looked down, it seemed so small and fragile – so easily breakable in my callused hands. I pressed it gently to my chest. "Are you... are you *giving* this to me?" I asked, surprised and confused.

"Consider it a loan," she told me. "A piece of me that you can hold onto until... until you're ready to give it back."

I softly stroked the stiff sunburst surface of the ukulele, that wooden gradient of dark to light, before placing it delicately on my bed. When I turned back, Lani was standing motionless in the doorframe, seemingly immobilized within the wooden portal that separated my room from the hallway. I took a step towards her and stopped.

"Soooo..." I said, rocking back and forth on my heels indecisively.

"*Soooo...*" she echoed back.

I started to say something, just as she began to speak. We both stopped and blushed.

"I'm sorry," I said. "Go ahead."

She took a slow, deep breath, her nostrils quivering. "I feel like getting some ice cream," she said quickly. "Can we go get some ice cream? Maybe that Diddy Riese cookie place south of campus?"

Deep in my heart, I knew (or at least *thought* I knew) where this conversation was heading. I had been relegated to "just friends" status before – most notably with Serena – so I sensed that the familiar, uncomfortable routine of having my heart broken by a beautiful girl was just about to start up again.

And yet...

And yet...

I had been the one to storm out of Lani's room the day before. Had I misread her intentions?

"Sure," I replied coolly. I grabbed my jacket from a nearby chair, where it lounged lazily across the seat, and walked out into the foreboding hallway. "Craving some rocky road?"

"You remembered," she said, slightly surprised and impressed. "What a good student you are."

If only she knew how much I had studied the curvature of her face and the arcs of her purple ink on those pages of notes. I've never paid more attention to anything else in my life. But all the studying in the world couldn't help me to pass the test that she was about to give me.

We strolled side-by-side for five minutes without uttering a single word. The sound of our shoes plodding along the sidewalk became a static pattern, an uncomfortable rhythm in 4/4 time, as we trudged through the winding sidewalks of the school's consecrated campus.

Right foot. Left foot.

Right foot. Left foot.

Repeat indefinitely.

Lani was the first to break the silence. "Do you want to talk about yesterday?" she asked softly, delicately – perhaps even nervously.

"No," I snapped abruptly. "Not really." I anticipated where the finish line for this conversation would end, and I wanted to cut it off at the pass.

My answer caught her off guard, and her gait broke with the perfect symmetry of our footsteps. "Why not?" she probed, her voice equal parts shock and anger.

I had to weigh my words carefully, I realized. If I laid all my cards on the table, told her how I thought she was the most beautiful, incredible, captivating girl I had ever met, she would unequivocally have the upper hand. As I knew from my experience with Serena, relationships are a delicate power-play; something as simple as the wrong word or phrase could sabotage everything that Lani and I had built together during our first few months at UCLA. Whether she knew it or not, I was completely at her mercy. On the other hand, if I came across as callous and cold, then she might write me off as just another worthless boy with a one-track mind. I clearly wanted more out of our relationship, but I didn't want to damage whatever it was that we had – platonic or romantic.

"Look," I began, "I really like you a lot. I think you're fun and brilliant and pretty and just about perfect."

"That's the kind of list I like to hear," she smirked.

"But…" I interjected.

Her grin faded to a sallow scowl. "But *what*…?"

I refused to look at her, though I desperately wanted nothing more than to lose myself in her chestnut eyes and her shimmering smile. With my gaze fixed straight ahead, and my hands thrust firmly into my pockets,

I maintained my distance. I refused to let my heart be broken, as I suspected it inevitably would.

"But you've got a boyfriend," I said. "And I just… I just don't want to be *that guy*, you know?"

My words caught her by surprise, literally stopping her in her tracks. I stopped walking, too, and angled my body to face her.

"And I don't want to be *that girl*," she echoed back coldly.

"Well, then," I said, "it's settled. And there's nothing more to say about the subject."

Actually, there was a lot more to say about the subject.

Several years' worth of things to say, in fact.

We just didn't know it yet.

As we silently marched on towards the ice cream parlor, just past the outskirts of the UCLA campus, the crackling leaves that crumbled underneath our shoes seemed immeasurably loud and grating. Every breath seemed to hold extra significance as we walked side-by-side, dodging bicyclists and Frisbees from the uncaring world around us.

Right foot. Left foot.

Right foot. Left foot.

Repeat for as long as it takes.

When I finally gained the nerve to look up at Lani, there was something about the expression on her face that I couldn't quite identify.

Something that vaguely resembled disappointment, I thought to myself. If I didn't know any better, I might have assumed that she wanted a different outcome from our conversation.

However, this was the way things ended that day – not with a bang, but with an ice cream sandwich on a chilly autumn afternoon.

CHAPTER THIRTY-SEVEN
"Why Do Fools Fall in Love?"

You know what's almost as bad as being dumped by your girlfriend? Being dumped by someone who *should* be your girlfriend... but isn't.

As much as I wanted something more from Lani, I knew in my heart that nothing was going to happen. She had a boyfriend and I needed to give up the ghost in my heart.

Despite some initial awkwardness in the aftermath of our kind-of-breakup conversation and the strained dynamics of our almost-blossoming romance, things returned to a state of equilibrium surprisingly quickly. Even with the acknowledgement that our relationship had reached an impasse, we found it astonishingly easy to slip back into our old patterns. Our hybrid flirting/working (*"flirking,"* as it were) ensured that we spent more time studying together than we *really* needed to spend, all in the name of academics. Unfortunately, this meant that our "moving forward" oftentimes felt more like standing still. Though we could pretend that the chemistry between us would forcibly fizzle, we were powerless to immobilize the elements at play.

Once you light the match, it's hard to contain the fire.

It was right around this time that I became obsessed with Johnny Cash. How's that for a non-sequitur? I mean, I'd always been *familiar* with the "Man in Black" – after all, he's something of a hometown hero, since he lived in Ojai (technically Casitas Springs) for most of the 1960s. Thirty years later, in the 1990s, ol' Johnny was on something of a winning streak: his Rick Rubin-produced *American Recordings* albums saw him reinventing himself as an elder statesman of the Americana scene, further cementing his reputation as a daring, dangerous icon of country music.

Like many young SoCal punk-rock kids, I got my first introduction to Johnny Cash through Social Distortion. The cover of "Ring of Fire" on Social D's self-titled 1990 album was the first time that I ever really connected with country music, and the band's revved-up version made him relevant to a whole new generation of young hipsters. Then, of course, there's the romantic punk-rock aesthetic of Cash's early work. Johnny Cash and The Tennessee Two were rudimentary players with attitude and ingenuity; like the Ramones and the Sex Pistols (who obviously etched their own names into rock's history books), Cash and his cohort made up for a lack of musical aptitude by overcompensating with emotional performances and edgy storytelling. Can you imagine any punk band or hip-hop group of today relating a tale of shooting a man *"just to watch him die*," like Cash did in "Folsom Prison Blues?"

Acoustic guitars be damned. THAT is dangerous punk rock music.

It also blew my mind to know that someone from Ojai – our quaint little touristy town – had made it big in the music industry.

A rock star from Ojai? I thought to myself. *The world is a strange place, indeed.*

Anyway, as I was saying, I became obsessed with the Man in Black during my freshman year of college. I completely, unabashedly bought into the archetypal legend of Johnny Cash – the dangerous, hard-living elder statesman of roots-rock who was experiencing a well-deserved career revival. I plowed through *Cash: The Autobiography*, I purchased every *American Recordings* album on CD, and I even bought a large movie-poster-size reprint of the iconic 1969 San Quentin picture of Cash flipping off the camera (which I placed proudly on my side of the dorm room).

My roommate, Victor, didn't seem to mind – though he wasn't spending much time in our shared room anymore, anyway. After a few months of acting like a recluse in the cocoon of our dorm, endlessly sketching cartoon dinosaurs in BoHo-chic clothing, Victor had suddenly turned into a social butterfly, frequenting the gym daily and hanging out with a boisterous batch of new friends. I was too busy with schoolwork and my not-quite-platonic relationship with Lani to pay much attention, though.

When Lani popped into my room the day after I put up the Cash poster, she literally did a double take. As could be expected, she seemed disconcerted by the image of an angry man adorning my wall.

"What's up with the guy flipping off the camera?" she asked with a skeptical raised eyebrow.

"That's vintage Johnny Cash," I said proudly.

Lani shot me a quizzical look. "Who is Johnny Cash?" she asked.

"You don't know about *Johnny Cash…*?" I was shocked.

"Ask me about Elvis or Don Ho and I'll talk for days. I can't say I know much about this Cash guy."

I then took it upon myself to extemporaneously explain all about the *Man in Black* to the *Beautiful Girl from Heaven*. I even played her an old Greatest Hits CD so that she could hear the choruses of "I Walk the Line" and "Ring of Fire." She didn't seem very impressed, though.

"Trust me," I explained to her, "the minute he passes away, he's going to be idolized and consecrated. He'll be bigger than Elvis Presley. Mark my words."

Though I did overestimate Cash's stature in relationship to The King, my prediction was sadly prophetic. In the years since Cash's death, he's become an industry, a marketable commodity that reaps dividends from imagery and songs that promote a rough 'n' tumble lifestyle that didn't accurately reflect his life. He wasn't *really* like Merle Haggard or

Sid Vicious, no matter how much he espoused those myths in his music. Still, though, Cash seems to be one of those rare cultural icons that unites punkers, pinup dolls, honky-tonk-ers, and rockabilly boys into one calamitous concoction of a crowd.

The reason I bring up all this Johnny Cash stuff is that my relationship with Lani seemed to mirror some of the things I read about in *Cash: The Autobiography*. Like me, Cash spent a long time in love with someone who was just beyond his grasp: his touring partner and muse, June Carter. As I saw it, I was like Cash, pining away for a lover who seemed tantalizingly close but painfully out of reach.

No matter how much I tried to avoid it, I kept perseverating on this tortured love triangle in my life: Lani, her phantom boyfriend, and little old me. I couldn't help but identify with the yearning protagonist of "Ring of Fire" – I felt trapped, anxious to consummate the love that I felt for someone I couldn't have. All the while, I felt burned and consumed by a relationship that was struggling to be born amidst a painful pyre. Of course, it's a bit ironic that *June* – not Johnny – actually wrote the song (with Merle Kilgore, of course) as she was encountering her heart's own conflagration. Perhaps that should have been a reminder to me that unrequited love works both ways… even if it doesn't always look that way on the surface.

I was in love with Lani, but she was in love with someone else.

Or so I assumed.

The fact that Lani kept me so close, that she shared such intimate thoughts and feelings with me despite her romantic involvement with another man, kept my hope alive and stoked the embers in my heart. Lani wasn't just a mythical, idealized dream girl: she was a real, flawed, imperfect human being. For all the perfect curves of her face and her body, she had scars, too – and not just the arrowhead-shaped one hovering near her right eye.

Yet, as we grew closer and closer, all those flaws became endearing: the way she scowled disapprovingly when she felt angry, the way she bit her lower-right lip with her top teeth when she contemplated astronomy, the way she chewed on her pen-cap when she got writer's block. Or the way her smile so often seemed like a stifled grin, as if her lips were an unfinished painting. As if her smile was incomplete.

But I didn't love her *in spite* of those idiosyncrasies; I loved her *because* of those quirks. She was perfect in all her imperfection, flawless in all her flaws.

And that's why I burned.

In the midst of this fiery love triangle and my Johnny Cash obsession, I wrote one of my favorite Caulfield songs, "(Won't You Be My) June." As I found myself falling harder and harder for a girl who was romantically unavailable, the tempestuous nature of Johnny and June's relationship resonated deeply for me. Lani was my *June*, the subject of my unrequited affection. To make it even tougher, she kept ushering me closer and closer to her inner circle, even though she was playing with fire by doing so. I didn't know if she felt the same sense of longing, the kind that consumes you with its aching flames, but I do know that I was becoming increasingly devoured by the boisterous blaze that bounced back and forth between us.

So, after successfully conquering an essay on Allen Ginsberg's "America" late one December evening, I picked up my acoustic guitar and started writing. At first, I just shuffled around with Cash's singular "boom-chicka-boom" sound from his early Sun Records era – soon enough, though, chords started falling into place and a melody began to emerge from the ether. And, just as I emulated Cash's musical style, so, too, did I invoke his tortured relationship with June as an archetype for my own sad, suburban struggles.

Lani was my June. And I burned for her.

"(Won't You Be My) June"

There's nothing quiet about unrequited love:
It resonates like the records at Sun.
While your touch is cotton on the line,
You've been tangled in these thorns of mine...

My heart is swinging like the Tennessee Two
Every time that I get close to you.
How much more can this ring of fire consume?
Oh, my darling, won't you be my June?

My throat is dry from amphetamines,
But I'm sweating every time we meet.
I don't walk the line, but I'd try for you,
Though I'll keep stumbling 'til you say "I do."

My heart is swinging like the Tennessee Two
Every time that I get close to you.
How much more can this ring of fire consume?
Oh, my darling, won't you be my June?

For you, my love, I'd fill a million pages
And kick in every light on the Ryman stage.
But for now, I'll write you a song
'Cuz the right thing's never felt so wrong...

My heart is swinging like the Tennessee Two
Every time that I get close to you.
How much more can this ring of fire consume?
Oh, my darling, won't you be my...

My heart is swinging like the Tennessee Three
Every time you get close to me.
How much more can this ring of fire consume?
Oh, my darling, won't you be my June?

Though I'd written in a variety of musical styles over the years, this was my first foray into the wild, untamed frontier of country music. I was entering uncharted territory with this song, utilizing rhythms and chord changes that deviated dramatically from the pop-punk music I had previously been composing.

The experience of writing "(Won't You Be My) June" was exotic and haunting and strange.

And I loved it.

When I initially wrote the song, I was really proud of the fact that I managed to weave in so many Johnny Cash allusions – everything from his cotton-picking days in Arkansas to the name of his backing band to his drunken light-bulb-smashing incident at the Grand Ole Opry. With this song, I was propagating the romanticized image of the Man in Black with facts and details taken straight from his life, but (more importantly) I was also honestly and earnestly relating my own heartache. The rhetorical question posed by the chorus – *"Won't you be my June?"* – is aimed right at Lani. She was my fire, even if she was unaware of how much I burned.

To be fair, I know that my lyrics don't do much to dispel the illusory image that Cash crafted for his adoring public. He was a flawed man with a flawed life, not a superhuman renegade who stood taller than Paul Bunyan. That being said, "(Won't You Be My) June" isn't meant to be a factual retelling of Johnny and June's stormy start; instead, it's a vehicle for me to examine how I felt about Lani, using someone else's love story as a meticulously constructed metaphor.

At the time, I could only hope that Lani was as tortured as I was by our strange little love triangle. Even though she was just across the hall, she felt light years away. Unfortunately, I couldn't know how she felt. I didn't want to talk about it, and I purposely avoided all conversations that might lead her to say the words that I dreaded most: "I don't feel the same way."

Of course, she *did* feel the same way.

I just didn't know it yet.

CHAPTER THIRTY-EIGHT

"Mele Kalikimaka"

By the time that winter vacation rolled around, I was ready for a break – a break from school, a break from Lani, and a break from being "Brian." There's something alluring about returning to your hometown after being away so long; though my absence wasn't quite as extended as that of Odysseus, I still felt inexorably drawn back to my old life in the Ojai valley, away from the golden-skinned vixens of Los Angeles and the academic wilderness of Westwood.

"Brian" was going to stay at UCLA. For a few precious weeks away from school, I would go back to being "Brick."

Returning home was a surreal experience. It had only been a matter of months since I started college, but I felt like a new person: there was a confidence and certainty in my heart that hadn't been there when I left Ojai at the end of summer. While my parents welcomed me back with open arms and my old bedroom looked like an untouched shrine to my childhood, the home of my youth felt foreign and unfamiliar – like I was vacationing in an adolescent-themed hotel made up to look like my past.

When I was reunited with the boys in Caulfield, we slipped into the comfortable routine of the old days, chatting about girls and bands and movies. Yet, we also seemed to be moving apart: all of us shared gossip about new friends in our new lives at our new schools in our new towns. Ethan and Chunk had even been dating girls! How shocking!

The real test, however, came when I saw Serena. On Christmas Eve, Steve showed up on my doorstep, trailed obediently by Serena and a few of her friends (including Amy and Megan, who looked *exactly* the same as when I first met them the summer before sophomore year). Serena pulled me into a tight hug, the inflated layers of her Columbia jacket squeezed flat from the pressure.

"I missed you," she told me with a tender, vulnerable tone in her voice.

"I missed you, too," I echoed back quietly.

And yet, despite the fact that she lingered just a little longer than necessary in our embrace, I felt something new for Serena: apathy.

For the first time since middle school, Serena Rios didn't retain a near-mythical quality about her. I didn't swoon in her presence, nor did I feel the insurmountable tug of heartbreak when my arms pulled away from her. It was a strange realization: I was over the girl that had kept my heart under lock and key for the majority of my adolescent years. Suddenly, I didn't feel the familiar sting of longing for her.

So, what happened?

Lani happened.

In the months that I had been away from Ojai, toiling away in my darkened dorm at UCLA, I had somehow grown beyond my affections for Serena… and those feelings had, instead, drifted to the *Beautiful Girl from Heaven* who lived across the hall. Once again, I was romantically trapped by my circumstances; this time, however, there seemed to be a mutual feeling budding between the two parties involved. It wasn't like my one-sided romance with Serena. It was something new, something ripe with possibility for a real future.

But it was still frustrating.

The next day was Christmas, though I wasn't feeling too festive. Marina was back home from Northern California for the week – and this time, she brought her boyfriend with her. During her last year at UC Berkeley, Marina had taken an internship with an internet startup company in San Rafael (just north of the Golden Gate bridge); it was there, in the sterile, confining cubicles of a Marin County office building, that she met Reggie Matroos. Though Marina was relatively tall, Reggie towered over her: he was a colossal statue of a man, with thick, coiled hair that added another few inches to his imposing height. With mahogany biceps as thick and sturdy as tree trunks, Reggie looked like a college football player – which he *had* been, when he attended Berkeley a few years before Marina. As tall as *I* was, I still felt like a dwarf in his presence. So, while having Marina back home helped brighten my spirits, the presence of her new constant companion only reminded me how alone and isolated I felt.

Something was *still* missing from my life. Lani.

Even with the change of scenery, I couldn't stop thinking about Lani, about the constant stream of conversation that naturally flowed between us. I thought about her unfinished half-smile, the asymmetrical grin that she wore like a loose-fitting veil and that obscured the breathtakingly beautiful features of her face. I thought about the way she bit her lower lip when she studied and pondered and thought... and I couldn't help but imagine what it must be like to taste the sweetness of those lips under the glow of mistletoe. Alas, such was not meant to be this Christmas. I was resigned to that fate.

On Christmas morning, after the sacred ritual of wolfing down chocolate chip pancakes, the Smith children (and Reggie) lounged around the living room, watching old black-and-white movies on television while my mom tinkered away in the kitchen. Sometime in the early afternoon, as I sat sedentarily under the mantel that displayed our twin family heirlooms – the chipped wooden *matryoshka* doll and our weathered bronze menorah – I heard the telephone ring with its static, mechanical alarm. At the time, I thought nothing of it. I just assumed it was an unnamed distant relative from parts unknown, checking in on the California clan of Smiths and providing canned greetings.

I remember sitting cross-legged on the floor, plunging my hand deep into a bag of BBQ-flavored potato chips and doing my best to drown my sorrows in the grayscale glow of *It's a Wonderful Life* as it played on our bulky television set. It was hard to concentrate, though, with my mom talking a mile-a-minute in the background. Try as I might to ignore her, I could hear her cackling from the kitchen, the telephone wedged between her left ear and shoulder as she dried dishes with a cloth towel.

"Who are you talking to, Mom?" I finally asked, more out of irritation than curiosity. "Aunt Alyssa?"

My mom cupped her right hand delicately over the phone. "It's the most delightful young woman," she responded brightly. "One of your friends from UCLA. A girl named Lani."

I'm pretty sure that my jaw dropped to the floor just as my eyes widened in terror, because my mom's expression changed instantaneously. "Well, dear," my mother sang into the phone, "it's been a pleasure chatting with you, but I think Junior is anxious to speak with you."

It's not very punk rock to have your mommy talk on the phone with the girl you've been desperately trying to impress. If I ever doubted my mother's innate ability to embarrass me beyond repair, that moment in time reassured me of her nuclear talent to decimate my well-cultivated coolness.

As I quickly grabbed the phone from my mom and pressed my twitching lips to the receiver, my voice cracked. "Ummm…" I muttered. "Hi. Hey. How are you, Lani?"

"*Mele Kalikimaka*, Brian!"

Once again, I had that sensation that my uneducated ears were hearing nothing but Greek. Or Hawaiian, as it were. "*Melly* what?" I asked.

Lani laughed and repeated her greeting, slowly articulating each syllable. "*Me-le Ka-li-ki-ma-ka*," she enunciated. "It means 'Merry Christmas' in Hawaiian, you dork."

"Oh," I mumbled, unable to think of anything more eloquent than a monosyllabic response. "Merry Christmas to you, too, Lani. And happy Hanukkah."

There was an awkward pause on the line, but Lani continued undeterred. "You've never heard the old Bing Crosby song before?" She proceeded to sing a few bars of the melody in her sweet, slightly stilted voice.

"I've never heard that song before in my life," I admitted sheepishly. Right about then, a light bulb went off in my brain – a vague memory of a distant, hazy conversation. "Hey… isn't '*Mele*' part of your middle name? Are you a Christmas baby or something…?"

Lani just giggled. "My name doesn't have anything to do with Christmas," she said. "It's pronounced *Mele'kauwela*, and it's a combination of two words: *kauwela* means 'summer' and *mele* means 'song.' So, my middle name means 'summer song.'"

"That's beautiful," I mumbled. "But what does a *summer song* have to do with *merry Christmas*?"

"You just won't let up, Mr. Inquisitive!" Lani said. "Well, *mele* means song or chant or poem, but it's also used in lieu of the word 'merry' and even the name 'Mary.' I think it's just a phonetic thing, to be honest. But don't quote me on that."

"Okay. Wow. Well, thank you for the linguistics lecture," I said. "Your dad would be proud of you for retaining all of that knowledge."

I couldn't tell for certain, but I had a hunch that Lani must have been smiling on the other end of the line.

"So, now that we've concluded our unscheduled Hawaiian lesson for the day," she joked, "how are you on this fine Christmas afternoon?"

"I'm okay," I said, "although I am a bit horrified that you spent so long on the phone with my mom."

"She is *so* delightful," Lani told me giddily over the analog hum of our long-distance phone call. "I can see why you turned out so sweet."

"Oh, god," I mumbled, horrified. "Please tell me she didn't say anything embarrassing."

Once again, I heard the ringing sound of Lani's joyous laughter fill the telephone line. "Don't worry," she reassured me, "your mom didn't give me very much source material. If I'm going to dig up embarrassing stories about your childhood, I'll need to do some further journalistic investigation."

Though I breathed a melodramatic sigh of relief, I still couldn't shake the feeling that something was wrong. Why exactly had the *Beautiful Girl from Heaven* called? It surely wasn't for a linguistics lesson.

"So, is everything okay?" I asked tentatively. "I didn't expect to hear from you over break."

"Everything's fine," Lani said, a little defensively. "I just... *you know*."

"Know what?"

"I… I missed talking to you," she breathed softly into the phone. "That's all."

"Oh," I mumbled. "Okay." I sat there stunned, momentarily dumbstruck.

After a pregnant pause, in which I could hear the delicate static of her breath in the phone receiver, Lani plunged into conversation with her usual dramatic flair.

"So, what's the weather like back in California?" she asked. "Has the sunshine disappeared now that I'm no longer in the state?"

"*Obviously*," I shot back (only half-joking, of course). "The sun refuses to shine when you're not here."

"Admit it," she pressed on. "You miss me terribly and you're completely inconsolable."

"I do," I whispered. "I miss you."

"Well, then," she said, "let's not waste any time. Tell me all about your trip back home…"

We talked for an hour.

It was the best Christmas present that anyone could have given me that year.

CHAPTER THIRTY-NINE
"Leaving This Town"

After Christmas, I had a short window of vacation time before I needed to leave my childhood house and head back to my new home. It's a strange feeling when you're caught between worlds – not entirely unlike what Serena and Lani (and even Ethan) had shared with me over the years. Though *their* concerns were obviously about mixed heritage, I could still identify in a small way after trying to navigate the small channel of water between Ojai and Los Angeles. That sense of duality, of feeling torn in two opposing directions, is something I've contended with countless times over the years – and being away from Lani only exacerbated my loneliness.

Despite my deep desperation, I used my limited vacation time wisely: Caulfield scheduled a few band practices to see if we'd lost any chemistry (fortunately, we hadn't) and I found myself writing song after song in the confines of my old bedroom. After I put the finishing touches on "(Won't You Be My) June," I felt like I was unstoppable. The chord progressions and melodies and lyrics just kept pouring forth from my overstimulated brain.

Right around this time, I also started binge-watching my favorite TV show from middle school, *Twin Peaks*. After renting a box full of VHS tapes from the local video store, Video Tyme (a company with an awkwardly anachronistic old-timey spelling), I spent hours with Chunk and my dad marathon-viewing the old TV show that had defined part of my early adolescent existence. As I watched the show with fresh eyes, I was simultaneously awestruck by the finer, haunting qualities of the show and horrified at how dated some of the fashion had become.

Watching *Twin Peaks* again also rekindled my childhood crush on Audrey Horne – and the actress who played her, Sherilyn Fenn. Audrey Horne was precocious and beautiful and captivating. And she inspired me to write a song. One of Caulfield's signature songs, in fact.

Though I had already written dozens of tunes by that point, I think "Sherilyn" served as a watershed shift in my craft. The song was born from an innocent place – a childhood crush – and it paid tribute to one of my favorite pop culture cornerstones. To be fair, I'm not the first (nor the last) songwriter to compose a tune based on *Twin Peaks*; however, I feel like "Sherilyn" is one of the few David Lynch-inspired songs to move beyond mere plot summary or vague, sweeping references to his work.

Yes, I realize how conceited that makes me sound.

But that doesn't make my statement any less true.

When I was drafting the lyrics, scribbling line after line in my blue chicken-scratch pen marks, I did my best to weave in as many allusions to the show as I could. Directly or indirectly, I mention Dale Cooper, Laura Palmer, John Justice Wheeler, the Black Lodge, and the recurring stoplight motif; for good measure, I even threw in not-so-subtle references to Elvis Costello's "Watching the Detectives" and "Alison" from his debut album, *My Aim is True*.

Not too shabby for an eighteen-year-old college kid, huh?

Even now, a full twenty years after I wrote it, I would argue that "Sherilyn" holds up pretty well. Personally, I prefer the raw version from the *Bookhouse EP* to the more polished version that we rerecorded for our major-label album, *A Different Slant of Light*...

But, once again, I'm getting ahead of myself.

For those of you who don't have the lyrics memorized by now, this is how the song goes:

"Sherilyn"

Rich girl in a miniskirt, how did your heart get burned?
Did your fire walk with you?
I don't own a suit or tie, I'm not an agent for the FBI,
But my aim is true.

Sherilyn, where will this end?
In the chapel or the graveyard?
Were we better off as friends?
Sherilyn...

Princess in a raven dress, my damsel in distress,
I can't concede defeat.
You won't change without a fight: you're like a red stoplight
Swaying in the street.

Sherilyn, where will this end?
In the chapel or the graveyard?
Were we better off as friends?
Sherilyn...

The prom queen's in a plastic bag;
You just light up and take a drag.
You may think that you're on your own,
But you're not alone...
You're not alone...

Sherilyn, where will this end?
In the chapel or the graveyard?
Were we better off as friends?
Sherilyn...

If you reached through the screen,
Would you end up here with me?
Or in the lodge from Cooper's dream?
Sherilyn...

The first time that I sat down and played "Sherilyn" for the boys in Caulfield, they were speechless. It was like that long-ago summer day when I first played them "Time Bomb" – they were incredulous that your humble narrator could have written something so sophisticated and catchy. Part of me was insulted – *Why can't they see how awesome I am?* I remember thinking to myself – but that affront was soon overshadowed by their enthusiasm for my newest composition.

"We *have* to record this," Steve said with a spellbound look in his brilliant blue eyes.

Ethan and Chunk nodded in agreement, while I grinned proudly.

"You know," Chunk said, "I think my dad might be able to get us into a recording studio for a pretty cheap price. The Stuttering Surfers have been using Mountain Dog Musicworks – this new studio off Ventura Avenue in Oak View. The guy who owns it is trying to drum up business and is offering some pretty affordable rates."

What had once felt completely improbable suddenly seemed like a feasible possibility to us. Maybe we *could* record our songs in a real studio. Heck, maybe we could even put out a real CD! The four of us spent hours talking about what this might mean for our future: maybe we could parlay this into a lifelong career in the music industry or the beginning of a new musical legacy. Maybe, like our hometown hero, Johnny Cash, we could (*gasp*) become *rock stars*. The possibilities seemed endless.

And it was all because of a catchy three-and-a-half-minute punk song that I wrote on winter vacation.

In many ways, I think that "Sherilyn" is the song that reinvigorated, perhaps even *resurrected*, the band. Here we were, four college freshmen without any other responsibilities or duties, searching for a cause – *a purpose* – in our young lives. During our last few days of vacation, we practiced until blisters formed on our tender fingers.

We had come to a decision…

We were going to record an album.

Well, a *mini*-album, at least: an EP.

The *Bookhouse EP*.

The next few months seemed like a blur. I remember coming home almost every weekend, usually hitching a ride with my dad or my roommate; serendipitously, Victor's family lived a little further up the Central Coast in Santa Maria, and he was happy to give me a lift when he went home to visit his boyfriend. As I quickly came to discover during our long drives, my roommate wasn't just a dinosaur-obsessed cartoonist pursuing a Computer Science degree: he also had *great* taste in music. In many ways, Victor defied stereotypes left and right; he was a musclebound computer geek who obsessed over 1990s grunge (most notably Pearl Jam and Soundgarden, though he also worshipped Weezer), *and* he had played bass in a "Queercore" garage band in high school. Victor was my first openly gay friend, and he helped open my eyes to the prejudices and microaggressions that he encountered all too frequently – even at a progressive, prestigious school like UCLA.

Like Lani and Serena and Ethan (all of whom struggled in some capacity with their cultural heritage), Victor found himself balancing his strict, traditional Chinese upbringing with the more open-minded aspects of the gay community. A self-described "Gaysian," Victor talked at length about how it felt to be a walking contradiction, someone whose past and future were colliding in a present-day battleground.

"The world can be unkind to those living outside the dotted lines," he used to say.

Though it was impossible for me to understand what he was going through, I could imagine (on a significantly smaller scale, mind you) that my own struggles with depression and anxiety might have provided some clarity and insight. The isolation and solitude that Victor described sounded eerily familiar to the stresses of my own straining soul; if only for that reason, I think that he and I bonded more quickly than many of our peers in the UCLA residence halls.

When Victor dropped me off every other weekend, I usually found myself falling into the same routine: Friday evening dinner with Mom and Dad, followed by a late-night acoustic band practice; never-ending Saturday recording sessions that stretched from breakfast until dinner; and, finally, Sunday afternoon studying that culminated in a drive back home to

UCLA. As stressful as it was taking classes at a world-famous institution during the "working week," it was less daunting than the band's non-stop weekend recording regimen. And yet, as tired as I might have been in class on Monday mornings, I couldn't help but feel rejuvenated. Each hour that I spent with the guys in the band, at home with my family, and in the recording studio revitalized me – nourished my soul, as it were.

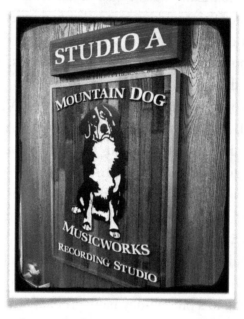

By the time that spring break rolled around, Caulfield's diligence had paid off: we had a seven-track EP of original compositions (all of which were written or co-written by yours truly) completely recorded, mixed, and mastered. Just like anything else, though, it took a village to create the album. While I was away at school, the rest of the band members would make their own visits home to flesh out the songs and add their own unique sonic textures. Frequently, I would only be around to hear scratch tracks and Chunk's drums; I would layer my ubiquitous bass guitar, an occasional electric guitar, and some light keyboard flourishes, but it wasn't until much later that I would get to hear the layers of guitars and vocals that Ethan and Steve were tracking in the studio.

For those unfamiliar with the process, recording songs in a studio track-by-track is a little like assembling LEGO bricks to build a tower: you start small with individual pieces, contributing in your own modest way to a much larger infrastructure. After meticulously placing brick upon colored brick, you end up with a delicate steeple comprised of interlocking shapes and colors and designs and orientations. Though such cleverly articulated displays might be fascinating to examine in depth, it's also important to remember that these building blocks can easily crumble. It doesn't take much for the towers to topple, the diminutive design dashed to pieces – just like any other human endeavor.

During those winter and spring months of 1998, Caulfield carefully constructed track after track in the confines of that cozy little recording studio on Ventura Avenue. Like an absent father, I would leave my songs – my artistic "children," as it were – in the hands of relatives... and pray that they were being raised right. Despite my reservations, it was remarkable for me to come home each weekend and hear the tracks that the boys layered in my absence. Even before I had my own children, I was a proud father.

Speaking of fathers, I should note that my dad and Uncle Jeff helped add some notable accouterments to our debut EP. Obviously, Ethan, Chunk, Steve, and I were the lead actors, but Dad and Uncle Jeff were always in the wings, making sure that things ran smoothly. Casual listeners might tend to overlook handclaps and tambourines and bells, but those small flourishes can transform demos into polished final drafts. In that sense, Dad and Jeff were channeling the spirit of Brian Wilson: they adventurously tackled the fine print of studio instruments, adding subtle layers and textures to the punk rock songs that the boys in the band tracked to analog tape.

And while they're not credited anywhere in the liner notes, my dad and Uncle Jeff really were the main producers of Caulfield's *Bookhouse EP*. The album merely says, "Produced by Caulfield," but that's a false proclamation: it should say, "Produced by Caulfield, Jeffrey Smith, and Brian Smith, Senior." In that regard, the fingerprints of Dad and Uncle Jeff feel like they've been wiped clean from the annals of history.

Hopefully, this page will help provide them with some of the recognition that they deserve.

Better late than never, I suppose.

CHAPTER FORTY
"California Girls"

C an we talk for a minute about how blink-182 saved rock and roll? For the record (no pun intended), I don't mean that in a facetious or condescending way: I wholeheartedly believe that during the late-1990s wading pool of mediocre pop music (think Britney Spears, the Backstreet Boys, and 98 Degrees), blink-182 was the only band capable of cutting through the ridiculously stagnant radio programming. Regardless of how you might feel about their potty-mouthed brand of pop-punk, this raucous band kept the spectacle of rock music alive in the popular vernacular. That's not to say that they're perfect, mind you; in fact, some of their more juvenile antics (the potty humor, the crass sexism, etc.) haven't aged well over the last few decades. However, that shouldn't diminish the fact that blink-182 was a guiding light of punk-rock optimism for many of us during our impressionable teenage years.

By no means am I a blink-182 super-fan. I don't have a "Loserkid" bunny tattoo or an arrow-laden smiley face bumper sticker or even a jade Buddha t-shirt. However, I will forever argue that the trio of Mark Hoppus, Tom DeLonge, and Scott Raynor (later replaced by Travis Barker) brought pop-punk back into the mainstream in a way that only Green Day or the Ramones had previously done. Those of us who watched blink-182 develop over time saw the band's exponential growth from the sloppy, lo-fi charm of the *Cheshire Cat* record to the pop masterpiece that is *Enema of the State* and the mature, brilliant self-titled record from 2003. Perhaps because they don't dominate the airwaves the way that they did at the turn of the century, we tend to downplay the importance of blink-182's contribution to popular music. People forget that pop radio was in a bad place twenty years ago: we were inundated with generic boy bands and prefabricated pop stars with pretty faces.

Then came blink-182... our pop-punk saviors.

All of a sudden, rock music was back on mainstream radio and on MTV. It crept up on the casual listener, first with the cavalry cry of "Dammit" and then onto the infectious "What's My Age Again?" and the bouncy "All the Small Things." If pop music had a candy-coated glass ceiling, blink-182 smashed right through it. For the first time in years, rock music – the kind with distorted guitars and pounding drums – was once again dominating the radio. Of course, just like the Seattle grunge explosion in the early 1990s, record labels sent out A&R (Artists & Repertoire) representatives to sign every similar-sounding band. Anyone playing fast-paced rock music was suddenly being courted with a contract.

And that's how Caulfield snuck through to the major labels.

Some might argue that we owe our entire career to blink-182. After years of small coffee shop gigs and talent shows, Caulfield's big breakthrough concert occurred on July 28th, 1998, when we opened for blink-182 at the Majestic Ventura Theater – a venue just a stone's throw away from our hometown of Ojai. Though we weren't originally slated to perform at the show, we managed to slip onto the bill after one of the opening bands cancelled at the last minute; apparently, Uncle Jeff had slipped a copy of the *Bookhouse EP* to one of his buddies at the venue's box office, and the nameless gentleman (God bless him) was so impressed that he offered us a last-minute opportunity to open up for the soon-to-be super-famous punk trio.

The lineup for the show was *unbelievable*. It was the first evening of a two-night residency at the Ventura Theatre (on blink's not-so-maturely-named "Poopoo Peepee Summer Tour"), and the opening acts included Jimmy Eat World, The Ataris, and Home Grown. What a bill! It felt like punk rock's Trinity test site, with a handful of nuclear bands that were destined to detonate on mainstream radio.

It was also a turning point in my life for a very *different* reason, but I'll explain that within the next few pages.

Anyway, we were clearly thrilled about the prospect of opening up for blink-182 (not to mention the three other bands on the bill), but we were also *incredibly* intimidated. Were we really "punk enough" to play a show like this? After the initial thrill wore off, the boys in Caulfield started to panic a little bit: our brand of rock and roll (I still hesitate to call it "pop punk," considering how many other genres we tackled) was pretty tame compared to the potty-mouthed dudes in blink-182 and the rough 'n' tumble charge of Home Grown. We might have fit snugly onto a bill with just Jimmy Eat World (considering their growing palate of styles and moods), but there was no guarantee that we'd be edgy enough to fit on the bill with the other acts. Heck, we started off playing Weezer covers – and Weezer in the late 1990s seemed quaint compared to the rabid fan-base that blink-182 had attained after the release of 1997's *Dude Ranch*.

To tame our trepidation, Caulfield practiced nonstop in the days leading up to the show. We had less than a week to prepare, and we used every spare moment to run through our songs, work out a carefully crafted set-list, and practice our punk rock posture. This show would be the ultimate test for us: were we cool enough to play side-by-side the giants of 1990s pop punk?

We would find out soon enough.

The day of the concert, we were all nervous energy. We had one last practice that morning, during which our normally overconfident frontman seemed surprisingly overwhelmed. It was strange to see Steve as anything less than impossibly, irritatingly arrogant; even Ethan and Chunk seemed concerned that one of our strongest assets (our indomitable lead singer) might actually be a hindrance.

Oh, how the tables had turned.

After practice, the guys disassembled their gear and packed it all up into Uncle Jeff's trusty minivan; it wasn't as extravagant or elegant as a professional tour bus, but at least it was *ours*. As we unplugged our instruments and wound up our cables, our anxious energy felt like static electricity: dormant and charged but ready to shock.

Somehow, to counterbalance Steve's moment of doubt, Ethan and Chunk assumed more aggressive roles. Even your humble narrator, normally a ball of nerves and anxiety, seemed strangely calm and collected. It didn't feel natural for us to unintentionally flip the script like this, but desperate times called for desperate measures. After a seemingly never-ending session of cleaning and packing, I bid my musical brothers-in-arms adieu, promising the guys that I would meet them at the theater in a few hours.

I had one more *very* important thing to do before then.

Despite the fact that I'd called Lani on the phone countless times before, I struggled to dial her number that afternoon. Try as I might to harness some bravery, I simply stalled. There was too much at stake.

After a few traumatic weeks of final exams, UCLA's spring trimester had faded into the recesses of memory. Summer, with its precious promise of freedom, was finally upon us. And, though school had been out for over a month by that point, Lani and I had been talking almost every single day. I assumed that she and I would drift apart like sailboats at sea after we'd been forced out of the dorms at the conclusion of the school year; instead, we found ourselves "rafting up" – tying ourselves together in tangles of telephone wire as we both anchored ashore in Southern California for the summer.

When we packed up our dorm rooms in Hedrick Hall, Lani had told me to keep her precious ukulele as a parting gift – she said that I might need it for something important later. I couldn't imagine what that might be, though.

"You never know," she said with a melodramatic sigh. "Surprises might be just around the corner."

After school got out, I retreated back to my family in Ojai. No surprises there.

Lani, on the other hand, had taken a professional plunge and started a summer internship at the *Los Angeles Times*. Her fantasies didn't revolve around castles or knights in shining armor; rather, the click-clack of computer keys and the industrial hum of a printing press constituted a "dream come true." Since she'd be stranded in Los Angeles all summer, Lani found a quaint, undersized apartment in Echo Park: a charming little pad that I visited every other week when I drove south to see her. While this internship meant that she'd be busy during our break from school, it *also* meant that she wasn't going back home to Hawaii for the summer.

This *Hawai'Irish* gal was quickly becoming a California girl.

When I finally mustered the courage to call her that fateful afternoon, I was surprised to hear the phone ring and ring ceaselessly. Lani wasn't normally the type to let the obnoxious trill of a telephone endlessly fill her apartment, but this time she didn't pick up. Weirdly enough, the answering machine didn't click on, either.

That's strange, I thought.

Just to be safe, I called back again.

And again.

And again.

Finally, after what seemed like an eternity, the phone receiver clicked.

"Hello," Lani's voice croaked raggedly into the phone. She didn't sound like herself. Her typically tireless boisterousness seemed deflated and defeated.

"Lani...?" I muttered tentatively into the telephone. "It's Brian."

There was a dead silence on the line.

"Hey, Brian," Lani said, sniffling into the receiver.

I waited for her to speak again, expecting some explanation for this dramatic shift in her personality. "Are you... are you *okay*...?" I asked.

Lani's breath heaved gracelessly into phone. "No," she sniffled.

"Do you want to talk about it?"

"Not really," she replied curtly.

I wasn't sure how to proceed. This unpredictable, irritable interaction was uncharted territory for us. "You know, Lani," I quietly spoke into the receiver, "I consider you to be one of my best friends. If there's anything I can do for you, you just need to let me know."

Lani didn't budge at first. I could almost hear the gears in her brain grinding as I waited for her to speak.

"It's just…" she started to say, before pausing.

"Just *what*…?" I asked tenderly, my voice softer and smaller than I anticipated.

The phone crackled with static, Lani's voice softly choking and aching but failing to produce any words. Then it all came pouring forth, like a cresting wave.

"He left me," she sobbed. Through the line, I could hear her heavy breathing punctuated by choking cries that stuck in her throat, her emotions exhumed with staccato beats. She didn't speak again for another minute, but her voice ached like a ghost in a deserted hallway.

I waited for her to speak, not wanting to intrude on this private moment, but reminding her that I was – and always would be – hers. "I'm here," I whispered.

The telephone line sizzled with tension. Unthinking, I twirled my fingers delicately around the coiled cord that stretched from the receiver to the wall.

"I should have seen it coming," she cried. "There were so many nights… so many times I would call. And he was never there. He wasn't there for me."

Not like I was, I thought to myself. *I was there for you.*

But I couldn't say that out loud. Not yet, anyway.

"When he finally came clean," Lani continued, choking up, "he told me that he's been seeing someone else. That he needed someone who was actually going to be *with* him. Physically and emotionally."

I listened.

"He said he was tired of being in a long-distance relationship," she continued, her sadness transforming into subdued anger. "Tired of having to be by himself all the time. He said he was tired of hearing about my 'L.A. boyfriend' and that he felt caged by having a ghost girlfriend three thousand miles away."

Wait, I thought to myself. *Who was this "L.A. boyfriend?" Had she been seeing someone without telling me?*

I was insanely jealous at first, but a realization slowly crept in and I mutely muffled the phone receiver. *Was he talking about me...?*

Like any lovesick teenage boy, I desperately wanted to ask her – but I also realized that this might not be an appropriate opportunity to interrogate the *Beautiful Girl from Heaven*. This was *her* moment of suffering; it wasn't *my* time to selfishly wallow in self-pity.

It was time to be there for the girl that I loved.

Even if she was nursing a broken heart from another boy.

For half an hour, I just listened to her talk. Occasionally, I would mutter some barely audible response into the receiver, a gentle *"go on"* or *"okay"* or *"sure"* that punctuated her meandering thoughts. But it was my job, in that heartsick moment, to just listen – to be the brick foundation that she needed for her quaking edifice.

She talked.

And I listened.

After a particularly dramatic rush of emotion that found Lani somehow chuckling and crying simultaneously, she sighed into the receiver. "I'm probably boring you," she half-laughed.

"Not at all," I reassured her. "I'm listening. I'll always listen to every word that you say, Lani. You know that."

Something shifted in the tenor and tone of our conversation. It's hard to describe how I knew, but things just felt *different* – like the tide had curled back from the shoreline and was receding gracefully into the ocean.

"Oh, *God*," Lani said, a lightbulb clicking on in her head. "Tonight's your big night, right?"

"Yeah," I whispered nervously. "But I totally understand if you can't make it, considering..." I left the sentence hanging mid-air, suspended by the weight of Lani's heartbreak.

But she surprised me.

"I wouldn't miss it for the world," she said.

I couldn't see her through the telephone, obviously, but I swear I could hear the smile in her voice. Even with everything that was happening in her life, even with the drama and heartache and tears...

She would be there for me.

The next few hours paradoxically dragged on forever and rushed by impossibly fast. Part of me dreaded the tremendous pressure and uncertainty of the evening that awaited me, but I couldn't suppress the anticipation of seeing Lani – and playing the concert, of course. It was like the feeling that I used to get in high school on Friday afternoon, waiting for the moment when the football team would step onto the field under the deluge of stadium lights. Appropriately enough, I would once again be following the quarterback into battle – but, this time, it would be on a wooden stage rather than a grassy field.

As the hourglass of the afternoon slowly trickled out grain after grain of sand, I couldn't ignore the feeling in my gut that this was going to be a monumental evening. Who knew what would happen?

Maybe surprises will *be just around the corner*, I told myself.

I should mention one other strange thing that happened that afternoon. As I stepped into the almost-empty garage, excavated and cleared of the boys' equipment, I saw my lonely bass rig tucked away in the corner. The rest of the band's instruments were gone, but my gear sat in isolation in the naked, uncluttered room.

It was an eerily prescient moment, one that would haunt me a few years later when everything went to hell. At the time, though, it just felt lonely.

While I packed up my bass guitar and pedals, the weirdness of the day hit an all-time high. Reaching to unplug my amp from the wall, I traced my hand along the waxy coating of the power cable and reached back to where the plug met the wall socket. As I grabbed the tip of the cable, I thoughtlessly placed my hand too close to the electrical socket and...

ZAP.

For a split-second, electrical current zipped up my arm, literally shocking me. It was a light, spritely jolt – more like an electric spasm than full-fledged electrocution – but I swear it coursed through my veins and arteries back to my heart and brain. I felt like Frankenstein's monster, lightning surging through electrodes and bringing me to life. I was stunned, but I was also somehow changed, as if that stray electricity had recharged my soul.

That moment was a precursor of things to come.

The night was going to be electric.

In more ways than one.

Rolling up to the theater an hour later, I was surprised and horrified by the fact that there were lines stretching endlessly around the block. Throngs of teenagers and young adults (with a handful of older punk-rock dudes in faded black t-shirts) stood in single-file, shifting weight from foot to foot as they waited for the evening's show. It was almost impossible to find a parking spot, but I managed to squeeze my dad's rickety old Buick Regal into a coffin-sized space a few blocks away from the venue. Thank God for parallel parking.

I had to make a couple of trips to and from the car to the theater, and I couldn't help but notice the awkward stares from people in line, many of whom glanced at me skeptically.

"Who's this big dude carrying all this stuff?" they must have wondered to themselves. Perhaps they thought I was a roadie or a crew member, doing the heavy lifting while the "real artists" waited in lavish, champagne-filled dressing rooms. I doubt that any of them looked at me and thought that the guy carrying the equipment was a sensitive singer-songwriter for a less-than-sensitive punk rock band.

The interminable hours of anticipation leading up to our time onstage felt excruciating. I remember lots of pacing up and down the halls, our Converse-clad feet creating a cacophony of squeaks on the wooden floorboards backstage. The boys all sought some semblance of solace as they waited, strumming on unplugged guitars and tightly tapping drumsticks against couches – anything that would help ease the pressure and the stress.

Five minutes before we were scheduled to go onstage, we huddled in the wings of the Majestic Ventura Theater for our usual pre-show pep talk. As I glanced around the group, I could sense Chunk's nervousness and Ethan's excitement, but Steve... well, Steve was a bit harder to read. He looked distracted, but there was an air of resignation in his eyes, as if he knew this could be his moment, his chance to reach up and grab the golden ring – or fall gracelessly to his doom.

For a fleeting moment there, I forgot all the drama that had besieged the band in the years leading up to the show. I forgot about Serena breaking my heart. I forgot about how crushed I had been when Steve seemed to steal my band away from me. I forgot about how nervous I was for Lani to finally see me play a show with Caulfield.

None of that mattered.

I was there in that pivotal moment with my musical brothers.

And I was ready for it.

As we waited silently for someone in the band to speak up – to say something, *anything* – I could feel the nervous energy threatening to turn dangerously destructive. For once, our effervescent frontman and fearless leader, Steve, was silent. His face betrayed him, as he turned paler than the coastal June fog that shrouded the Ojai Valley every summer.

Steve is going to blow this for us, I realized. *Our quarterback is on the verge of fumbling.*

Something possessed me to take charge, so I tightened my grip on the arms of Ethan and Chunk. For two and a half minutes, I reverted to my old position as leader of the band and I gave Caulfield exactly what it needed: a pep talk. My mind raced through the recesses of my memory for something to say before I had an epiphany. I remembered the words my father had spoken to me right before my graduation singer audition, words that spurred me on to play with every ounce of determination that I could muster.

"*Sing the hell out of it*," I yelled, reiterating my father's speech. "Let's play like we mean every word, every chord, every note. Because we do." As my voice echoed through the ancient backstage halls, I could sense a change in the air, could feel the atmosphere transform around us.

"Play fast," I continued. "Play like this is the last time that anyone will ever hear us. Play like we own this crowd and they are here only to see Caulfield... to see *us*."

I was stepping outside my designated duty as the quiet songwriter of the group. I'd been ousted from leadership that summer long ago at Serena's *quinceañera*, had my voice silenced (literally) and been relegated to a supporting figure in the group that I co-founded.

But I didn't care about any of that.

Call it a moment of clarity, a temporary lapse of bitterness... but it was exactly what we needed. Just like old times, we placed our hands together in the circle, counted off, and yelled "*Cooper!*" as loud as we could muster.

And then we hit the stage.

To call the show triumphant would be an understatement.

Opening for blink-182 that night was, hands down, the greatest show we ever played – no gig before or after could possibly rival the sheer exhilaration and joy that we felt during those twenty-five magical minutes on the well-trod stage of the Majestic Ventura Theater. It was our coming-out party, our declaration of independence. We were opening for our idols and for bands that would go on to create lasting masterpieces of the pop-punk era.

It was like ground zero for the rebirth of punk rock.

And we were the first band on the bill.

When we cautiously stepped out in front of the spotlights from our shaded spot in the shadows, we felt like ants under a magnifying glass. The floodlights stationed from the rafters magnified the heat and the blinding beams of a thousand suns – not to mention the invisible pressure we felt standing in front of countless cynical eyes.

We were being watched. And every movement mattered.

As usual, Steve swaggered to the front of the stage, stretched out behind the mic stand, and cupped the microphone in his right hand.

The crowd clapped unenthusiastically (aside from our well-placed ringers in the crowd), and a couple of jerks booed loudly from the center of the mosh pit.

"We are the Caulfield band from Ojai, CA," Steve announced with a smirk, casually running his fingers through his slicked-back bleach-blond hair. "And we are here to convert you."

Then, with a swift turn, he spun around towards us and screamed a countdown: "*1-2-3-4!*"

"*I wanna' be your time-b-o-o-o-mb...*" Steve howled into the mic. "*I wanna' detonate in your a-a-a-rms...*"

Within seconds, the mood in the theater shifted. It's hard to describe that mystical feeling when you know the crowd is yours – the way the air seems to resonate differently, and the volume of conversation drops as the audience refocuses its attention. I don't believe in magic or witchcraft or voodoo or Santeria, but I swear it was like Steve was casting

an incantation spell on the crowd below, captivating them with his curled
lips and crushing voice.

By the time that we hit the chorus of "Time Bomb," the mosh pit
was in full swing, bodies circling and smashing and crashing into each
other with reckless abandon.

We played the songs faster that day than we ever had before – we
easily upped the BPM by 20-30 beats – but we didn't feel rushed or
derailed. Instead, we felt liberated, like we had stepped behind the wheel
of a shiny new Camaro after years of driving in a secondhand Volvo. The
unbearable weight of uncertainty and anxiety was lifted from our
shoulders.

And we felt free.

When I glanced around the stage, I saw nothing but intense focus.
Chunk pounded the drums so hard that his sticks started to splinter, his
thumping rhythm propelling us forward. We were the passengers in a
throbbing locomotive, and Chunk was the conductor, hurtling us ahead
faster than Casey Jones ever could. On the far-left side of the stage, Ethan
palm-muted and slashed and wind-milled on his wine-dark Gibson guitar
like Pete Townshend in his prime. Immediately to my left, Steve locked
his gaze with the audience, spit darting from his lips as he belted melodies
into the microphone. Together, as one liquid unit, we moved so fast that
my fingers could barely keep up with the pace. Somehow, though, we
never fell behind the beat or lost our locked-in rhythm. I couldn't help
myself: a smile crept across my lips as I felt myself slip into a euphoric
state of equilibrium.

When we initially began our set, we found ourselves playing in
front of a relatively meager crowd – only a few hundred people, most of
them huddled hesitantly close to the stage. As was par for the course with
opening acts, we had exactly twenty-five minutes for our slot before the
next band was scheduled to take a shot at the crown. Needless to say, we
wasted no time in wooing the audience.

It was strange to watch from the stage, but I could see the crowd
slowly growing in size and energy – like an inverted cancer, metastasizing
with manic, positive energy. The sweet contagion swept the crowd, as the

cynical punk teenagers and pristine prom princesses and ironically dressed hipsters and discontented skater kids were drawn into our welcoming web, one-by-one.

I glanced around, trying in vain to make eye contact with any of my comrades in Caulfield. Were they seeing what I was seeing? Did they understand the magnitude of the moment?

But no one saw me. Steve, looking his rockabilly best with pomade-slicked hair and Levi's jeans cuffed above his spotless Doc Martens, focused his attention on the crowd; Ethan, sporting a trim-fitting Ramones t-shirt and faded gray-black jeans, kept his head low as he maintained a gaze adjacent to the aluminum shine of floodlights at the base of the stage; and Chunk just pounded away at his drum set, caught in a rapturous moment of religious fervor. It was unbelievable that this quartet of ambitious Ojai kids could be at the center of a musical maelstrom...

And we were playing *my* songs.

Unable to make eye contact with any of my bandmates, I scanned the crowd, frenetically looking for familiar faces. At first, it was hard to see through the blinding beams of spotlights that doused us in a swathe of artificial sunshine. As my eyes adjusted, though, I could see the *gathering of the tribes* below me, with Mohawks of every shade on the color spectrum punctuated by a diverse crowd of various suburban archetypes. I witnessed a true melting pot in that theater: every skin tone, eye color, age group, sexual orientation, and dogmatic affiliation represented. It was like the punk-rock version of Martin Luther King, Jr.'s "I Have a Dream" speech.

And it was beautiful.

In that moment, it didn't matter what seemingly insurmountable societal barriers had been erected around each of us: the crowd of disparate souls was united as one. Girls in their summer clothes – in short shorts and low-cut spaghetti-strap tops – were flanked by muscle-bound jocks with sagging shorts and tattered tank tops. But there were also plenty of awkward-looking kids like me, teenagers of all shapes and sizes, sporting braces and acne and bad haircuts and horn-rimmed glasses...

Like the vaguely Polynesian-looking girl in the third row whose flawless face I'd stared at for endless hours of study sessions, whose broken heart was not reflected in the sheer joy that showed in her uninhibited smile.

She was there.

Lani was there.

And she was looking right at me.

Though most of the audience was clearly in Steve's grasp, their attention focused on every curl of his lips and thrust of his hips, there was at least one person whose eyes were trained on me: Lani. I smiled at her, my lips quivering with elation and exultation – and she smiled right back at me.

Squinting through the darkness, I could make out a couple of shadowy figures on either side of Lani. I didn't recognize them at first; but, as my eyes adjusted to the darkness, I could see that Lani was flanked on either side by the familiar frames of my parents. Like Lani, they beamed with pride, with a sense of awe that their baby boy was part of something musically magical.

How many public-school teachers were at the blink-182 show that night? At least two: my mom and my dad. How's that for being punk rock in your old age?

It was a strange time to be alive, to be onstage – the crowd was a unique mishmash of young and old, of cool and ostracized, all blending together in a mass of sweating, steaming bodies in the poorly ventilated summer heat.

And I was somehow, inexplicably, at the center of it all.

By the time that we closed our set, after twenty-four of the wildest minutes in my life, we owned the audience. Just as Steve had proselytized, we converted that room of naysayers into devoted fans. Our lead singer was a rock-and-roll Billy Graham, baptizing the throngs of the willing into our church of pop punk. After an epic version of "Sherilyn" that saw us thumping and stomping and screaming our way through the familiar chord progressions, we stood there onstage listening to the rapturous applause of our audience.

Steve stepped back from the microphone, sweat dripping down his clingy white t-shirt, and appraised the remarkable scene before us. In a self-indulgent moment, he slowly strutted back to the center of the stage, curled his lips into a swaggering smile, and spoke into the mic.

"We are Caulfield," he croaked to the crowd. "Expect great things from us in the future."

And, just like that, we were done.

If my life was a picture-perfect rock-and-roll biopic, this would be the moment when the lights dim on the frames of the future rock stars, their silhouettes huddled together in the blinding lights of the stage...

But this was the real world. We still had to roadie our own equipment.

Even in the triumphant glow of the show's aftermath, we were acutely aware that the clock was ticking, and the eyes of the management were on us. Before we even had a chance to catch our breaths, we were gracelessly gliding across the stage, lifting our amps onto furniture dollies and wheeling them out to the van. Chunk, Ethan, and I grappled with our hefty gear, all the while grinning ear-to-ear.

Our lead singer, however, was suddenly, conspicuously absent. Good ol' Steve was back to his old tricks. Apparently, his momentary panic before the show had been replaced by the longstanding rock star entitlement that we had come to expect from him.

Lead singers, man... They're a breed unto themselves.

For the next half hour, I coiled cables, carted equipment through the halls, and repeated the trip until we were finally, completely packed up. Ethan, Chunk, and I felt victorious in the heat of the sweltering summer evening, marching through the halls like anonymous royalty.

Once the van was loaded with our amplifiers, guitars, and drums, we walked out to the front of the theater. Wordlessly, we glanced up at the yellow gleam of the venue's entrance. While our name wasn't on the marquee, we nonetheless felt a sense of ownership over the Majestic Ventura Theater that crisp summer night.

Like guitar-slinging warriors, we came, we saw, and we conquered. We were *veni vidi vici* vindicated.

Inside the theater, our makeshift merch booth was *swamped*. Uncle Jeff and Serena were frantically taking cash from customers, passing out shirts and CDs, while Steve posed for photos with giggling young blondes and doe-eyed brunettes. It was almost like an out-of-body experience, watching the entity of Caulfield exchanging money and requests for photos – all while ¾ of the band stood on the sidelines, conspicuously absent from the center of the storm.

I turned to Ethan and Chunk. "*This*," I told them, "is how rock stars are born."

We exchanged a conspiratorial glance before heading over to the booth to help Serena and Uncle Jeff with the long line of customers. Eagerly, we jumped into the commercial hurricane, exchanging cash for commodities; our proud lead singer, on the other hand, acted like a newly anointed celebrity, throwing his arms over the eager young girls who sidled up alongside him to pose for photographs.

It struck me at that moment that I was watching Caulfield's cellular division in action: the musical section of the band, the portion of the group that laid the foundation for Steve's captivating singing, was also becoming a barely visible presence offstage as well. Chunk, Ethan, and I shared a quick, knowing scowl – before we were immediately drawn back into the merchandise maelstrom.

But the band's rhythm section members were not the only ones feeling left out. Occasionally, I would glance over at Serena, Sespe Creek High School's own Helen of Troy; despite being a priceless prize claimed years ago by our lead singer, she wasn't sharing Steve's moment of glory, either. Instead, she looked on distraught while her boyfriend flirted with nubile teenage girls and exchanged fraternal greetings with football-playing friends. Serena looked like Helen, stranded on the shores of Troy, gazing across the waters with a watchful eye focused on Prince Paris.

She was not pleased.

We worked our way through a flurry of faces and arms and billfolds and wallets, each of us frantically flailing with handfuls of dollar bills to keep up with the demands of the crowd. It was surreal: these songs that germinated in the lonely confines of my dorm room and my parents' garage had been transformed into full-band orchestrations, captured to tape, reproduced on CDs, and then packaged into a commodity that was being sold at a rock show – opening for blink-182, nonetheless. I was barely able to look up at the customers raiding the merch booth, my eyes at waist level, handing over the green slips of paper that passed back and forth like leaves in the wind.

If only fifteen-year-old me could have seen this, I thought to myself. *He wouldn't believe it. I can hardly believe it now.*

I was so enthralled in the flurry of transactions that I didn't even recognize a familiar voice when it first floated across the table.

"I'd like a CD and a small woman's t-shirt," the voice sang sweetly.

When I looked up, my eyes locked with her smiling face.

Lani.

Without thinking, I reached across the table and threw my arms around her.

"You made it!" I yelled through the din and clatter of customers.

"Of course, I made it!" she shouted back, gently pulling away but keeping her arms draped around my shoulders. "Like I said, I wouldn't miss this for the world, Mr. Rock Star."

Her luscious lips creased into a knowing grin. I just stared at her, wide-eyed and beaming, grateful that she was there to share this historic evening with me.

"So... when are you off duty?" she asked, her voice competing with the conversations and orders swirling around us. More than a few guys nearby were lecherously eyeing the *Beautiful Girl from Heaven*, but I didn't feel threatened. Lani was here for *me*.

My eyes swept around the lobby of the theater, ignoring the lascivious looks of libidinous boys, and studied the throngs of concertgoers eagerly awaiting the evening's headliners. Though our booth was still swamped, I could hear another band (The Ataris? Jimmy Eat World?) hit the opening notes of their set, drums thumping and reverberating from the stage through the cacophonous corridors of the foyer.

And just like that, the waves of customers parted. Teenagers and young adults bolted straight for the vaulted confines of the theater's main room.

I turned to face Uncle Jeff, who had been watching me with his peripheral vision. "I got this, boys," he told us. "Go have fun. And don't worry about the merchandise."

Without thinking, I wrapped my fingers around Lani's wrist and pulled gently. "Do you want to get a bite to eat?" I asked.

Her face lit up like Christmas morning. "That sounds great," she said.

So, as Chunk and Ethan rushed inside to watch the soon-to-be-famous band onstage, I was leading Lani through the exit, weaving through the crowds of punk-rock kids as her arm looped around my elbow.

On our way out the door, I glanced back and saw Serena engaged in a heated discussion with Steve. Her face was flushed crimson and her arms were shaking wildly. Steve, on the other hand, just leaned back coolly against the stucco walls and smirked.

What a night, I thought to myself.

And this was only the antecedent of the tectonic hours to come.

CHAPTER FORTY-ONE

"Good Vibrations"

N ormally, I'm a stickler for sticking around until the end of the show. I'm the kind of obsessive music nerd who wants to be there early for the concert, eagerly listening to every hum and hallelujah from the musicians onstage. I want to see the opening acts and study their songs, their guitar-playing, their instrumentation. I want to watch wide-eyed as the headliners work their way through the greatest hits and the new songs and the covers. I want to see it all.

But there I was, leaving the concert without seeing a single band on the bill. On any other day, the chance to see blink-182 or Jimmy Eat World or The Ataris would have been a dream come true (let alone all three in one evening). That night, though, there were bigger dreams to consider. As I walked arm-in-arm with Lani down Ventura's bustling Main Street, I wasn't thinking about money or music or hipsters or crowds.

Some things in life are more important than rock and roll.

The seaside breeze drifted in from the coastline a few blocks over, exhaling a slight chill through the summer air. As sweaty and overheated as I was, the cool air felt like a reprieve from the surreal madness that I had just experienced.

As we walked, Lani gently draped her arm through the crook of mine, and our bodies bumped delicately against each other with each step we took. We must have looked like quite the anachronistic couple – like formal, Victorian-era suitors wearing casual California clothes.

What a weird night, I thought. *What a weird, weird night.*

As we ambled across the sidewalk, we peered into the windows of the restaurants lining Main Street. In each, we saw couples sitting side-by-side in booths, snugly sharing sweet glances. Hands covered hands; lips pressed against lips. As I tilted my head towards Lani, she looked up knowingly and smiled, sharing these voyeuristic moments without an ounce of shame.

Could this be us one day? I wondered. *Is this what my future has in store?*

Just as I was entertaining that fanciful idea, Lani gently tugged on my arm, stopping in front of one restaurant's large, clear windows. Alternating red and white stripes draped down from the overhang, while Coca-Cola crimson and vaulting vanilla squares checked the walls.

"How about this place?" Lani suggested. "It reminds me of the Hulabilly Diner back home."

I looked up at the glowing neon sign. *The Tiki Turtle Tavern*, it read, the letters flanked by an animated reptile with oversized sunglasses balancing atop a surfboard. We looked at each other, smiled, and nodded in agreement.

Just as my parents had trained me, I held the door open for Lani, the chill of the evening air suddenly clashing with the warm gust emanating from inside the restaurant. We were caught between worlds: the cold of the past and the warmth of the present.

The heat felt good.

Inside, Lani and I found ourselves crossing a threshold into a 1950s-themed world of soda pop, root beer floats, and jukeboxes. The hostess, a blonde high-schooler wearing thick silver braces and decked head to toe in spotless white clothes, greeted us with her metallic smile.

"Welcome to the Tiki Turtle Tavern," she said. "Let me seat you and a waiter will *turtle-y* be right with you." Her unfalteringly sunny demeanor told us that she was clearly immune to her own cringe-worthy pun.

Lani and I slid into a booth near the window, marveling at the array of memorabilia from a bygone era. Plastered onto the walls were old movie posters advertising Marilyn Monroe and James Dean flicks; clinging to the side of each booth's table was a miniature jukebox, populated with songs from Buddy Holly, Little Richard, Aretha Franklin, and Elvis Presley.

Like Michael J. Fox in *Back to the Future*, I felt out of space and time. There was something bizarrely fantastical about a venue like this, some remarkable feeling of being transported into the distant past. Walk through the door, and you left behind the fears of the new millennium – all the punk rock agony and late-90s angst that plagued teenagers and twenty-somethings across the country.

I realize that nostalgia is a beautiful liar. As I knew from my dad's old Beach Boys stories, the 1950s and 1960s were just as troubled as the 1990s. Despite that knowledge, it's tempting to imagine that there was once a simpler, more peaceful time in history.

A twenty-something young woman with almond skin interrupted my flight of fancy, handing us both tall, laminated menus.

"Hello," she greeted us, a smile cresting across her cheeks. "My name is Sophia, and I'll be your waitress tonight. Can I get you something to drink?"

Lani's eyes darted in my direction. "Will you think I'm completely immature if I order a strawberry milkshake?" she asked, her eyebrows knitted self-consciously.

"Not at all," I laughed, turning to the waitress. "Can we please get *two* strawberry milkshakes, Sophia?"

Our waitress nodded cheerfully. "Of course," she said. "And I'll be right back to get the rest of your order." She smoothed the pleated folds of her stark-white uniform and walked back to the kitchen.

"Thank you," Lani said, "for indulging my childlike sensibilities."

"You don't have to thank me," I told her. "We're *both* little kids, I guess."

Lani smiled.

Moments later, our milkshakes arrived, the pink hues mixing effortlessly with the soft, tender edges of the whipped cream that adorned the top.

"Here's to us," Lani offered, raising her milkshake in the air for a toast.

"Cheers," I said, focusing more on the sweet twinkle in her eyes than the sweet drink in my hand.

As I gently placed my milkshake on a Coca-Cola-themed napkin, it dawned on me that the tables at the Tiki Turtle Tavern looked like linoleum chessboards, checkered with black and white squares. I ran my hands along the smooth, lacquered countertop, wiping some lingering crumbs off the table.

Lani was nervously fidgeting with her fingers, picking at the edges of a hangnail and scraping her unpainted fingernails against her cuticles. She smiled at me, unusually silent and pensive, before reaching over to grab a saltshaker that sat mutely on the far end of the table. She gently batted it between her hands, watching the clear glass slide back and forth.

"Here we are," she whispered softly, her lips pursed around the plastic edges of her straw.

Flirting is a game of chess, I've come to realize. Each player makes strategic, meticulously planned-out moves in anticipation of the other party's choices. Sometimes, the players are equally paired, and the game becomes more complex, more psychological.

Lani and I had so much history by this point that I almost didn't realize that we had started the game – I didn't want to get my hopes up. On the other hand, everything else tonight had seemed magically kinetic, as if the sparks from that rogue electrical socket hours before had charged the evening with profound possibilities.

I started simply enough, with a non-committal pawn's move. "Did you see how many guys were checking you out tonight?" I asked, eyebrows raised. "You were quite the hot commodity this evening."

Lani lifted her eyes from the saltshaker between us and started fiddling with a thin paper napkin. "*Me...?* Are you kidding?" she asked incredulously. "Look at *you*, Mr. Rock Star! You just played a show in front of *hundreds* of people, and they LOVED you!"

I opted for a defensive move, a knight's swift jump forward. "Actually," I deflected casually, "they didn't notice *me*. They were staring at Steve." I tapped my fingers against the cool surface of the table. "You know," I added, "Mr. Lead Singer."

"Steve is just *eye candy*," she interjected firmly, parrying my move. Her eyes locked steadfastly on mine, and her hands crept up from her napkin to point an accusing finger. "*You* are the one with substance. A singer is nothing without a song, and you are providing him with the prerequisite ingredients to captivate the crowd."

I reached out to her flawless finger, suspended in the air, and gently pushed it back to the table. To be honest, I just wanted an excuse to touch her, to move the bishop diagonally across the board. The electricity was still there, crackling from my fingers – and I swear that she felt it, too.

"But no one cares about the songwriter," I grumbled. "No one will pick up a book to read it, if it doesn't have an attractive enough cover."

"That's where you're wrong," she countered quickly. "He's just a marionette, dancing along while you pull the strings. He's nothing without you, without the words and music that *you* write. That makes *you* the most important person in the band. Without you pulling the strings, the band is a limp and lifeless set of dolls. You bring them to life, my dear Geppetto."

She had me speechless. And she knew it.

"See?" she said. "You've got *nothing*. My thesis just beat yours." She giggled, sipped the strawberry shake in front of her, and shared a look of victory in her squinting chestnut-brown eyes.

Check.

That's one thing I'll give Lani. She's always been smarter than me – and a much better debater. There's nothing sexier (albeit more frustrating) than a smart girl. And she was the smartest girl I had ever met.

We ordered burgers and fries, like the spitting image of some 1950s Norman Rockwell caricature, and spent the next hour talking about everything that crossed our minds. She told me about her impending visit back home to Maui, about her internship in Los Angeles, and even about her breakup.

"So, if I might ask…" I gently prefaced, anticipating Lani's unpredictable reaction. "What happened between you and William?"

She sighed, deeply and despondently. "I wish I could sum it up simply," she offered, twisting her mouth into a half-subdued grimace. "I guess we just drifted apart. Long-distance relationships are hard in the best of circumstances… and these weren't the best of circumstances. I guess he wasn't patient enough to wait for me. And he just lost interest."

"I'm sorry," I reassured her. "I just don't get how he could lose interest in *you*."

Lani paused for a moment, a French fry dangling between her thumb and forefinger. She looked skyward, studying the ceiling of the restaurant as if it would reveal some grand truth to her.

"I guess if you stare at anything long enough," she sighed, "it no longer looks beautiful."

I reached my right hand across the table and placed it on top of hers.

"Some things will always be beautiful," I said gently, gazing deeply into her brown eyes. "And no amount of staring can possibly diminish that beauty."

Check.

An expression I hadn't seen before crept across her face. Her cheeks flushed bright red, perhaps with embarrassment, but there was something else embedded within the creases around her crinkled eyes… something more like eagerness. Or hope.

There's a time in every relationship when you realize you've crossed a threshold, entered an unprecedented territory full of unanticipated ambiguities. For once in my life, I took a leap of faith. I looked down at the checkered table, slid my empty milkshake glass forward like a queen across the board, and made my boldest move yet.

"When can I see you again?" I asked her, my breath catching in my pounding chest. "I know you're busy with your internship this summer and everything…" I paused, letting my sentence dangle between us – unanswered and incomplete.

"But…?" she prodded.

"But I miss this," I told her. "I miss just seeing you. And talking with you."

I took another deep breath. I prayed my parry wouldn't back me into a *zugzwang* corner.

"I miss you," I admitted.

I wasn't the only one meticulously plotting my words. Lani opened her mouth to speak, but stopped herself, choosing instead to fidget with her condensation-soaked napkin on the table. My words floated there like a child's balloon, wafting gently as they waited for the breeze to shift.

"Well..." she began.

Here it is, I thought, *the big rejection.*

But I was wrong.

"I'm pretty busy through the weekend," she said, keeping her eyes trained on the tabletop between us. "But I have a couple of free days in the middle of next week. Is there anything else going on in this charming beachside town of yours?"

She looked up at me and smirked. I took that as a good sign.

"*Well...*" I said, mimicking her intonation from moments earlier, "how do you feel about county fairs?"

"They're adorable," she said. "Why do you ask?"

"Because the Ventura County Fair starts next week," I told her. "You could drive up for the day, and we could... do the fair."

Lani raised an eyebrow at me inquisitively.

"You know," I explained, "do all the teeny-bopper stuff. Like ride the Ferris Wheel, eat cotton candy, knock over some milk bottles with a baseball. The usual."

She tilted her head to the side, placing a palm beneath her chin and studying my expression with squinted eyes.

"That sounds enticing," she whispered coyly.

"Plus," I added quickly, "they have fireworks."

"In that case," she said with an ever-widening grin, "count me in. Nothing competes with Ferris Wheels and fireworks."

My heart was exploding more intensely than any firecracker could ever muster. "Does Wednesday work for you?" I asked swiftly.

"It's a date," she replied, her lips pressed together in a full, iridescent smile.

A date.

A date.

After a long year of friendship with this gorgeous girl from across the hall – the *Beautiful Girl from Heaven* – I suddenly had the opportunity for something else... perhaps something more.

As the air between us crackled with an invisible electricity, a catalytic chemistry, the tender, melancholy intro of the song "Earth Angel" echoed through the restaurant. The song played in the background while Lani and I gazed at each other across the checkered tabletop, and I slouched into the scarlet vinyl cushions of the seats. I couldn't help but think about the sweetness of the scene, how perfect everything seemed at this precise moment in time. The serendipitous echoes of "Earth Angel" reminded me that there was a heavenly aspect to life on earth, even during subtle, unassuming moments like this.

Especially with the *Beautiful Girl from Heaven.*

Lani's eyes trailed wistfully towards the window. "No one ever writes songs like this anymore," she said with a placid sigh.

"What do you mean?" I asked.

"You know. Those sweet vintage slow-dance songs that are just pure, unadulterated adoration."

I paused, studying the dripping condensation on my empty milkshake glass. "Do you think people still feel that way these days?" I asked hesitantly. "That *'pure, unadulterated adoration'*...?"

She glanced over with a mysterious Mona Lisa smile. "I think so," she whispered with a wink.

Checkmate.

Right on cue, our waitress slid our bill across the black-and-white checkerboard squares of the table. "No rush," she assured us, "but whenever you're ready, here's your check."

CHAPTER FORTY-TWO
"And Your Dream Comes True"

After our notable dinner at the diner, Lani had to head back to Echo Park. Before she left, we talked some more, casually bumping into each other on the way to the parking lot, where her old, beat-up Nissan D21 sat unmoving between two thin white lines. And when she hugged me goodbye, it felt like she lingered for just a few seconds longer than normal.

Basically, it was wonderful. Once again, I felt like Cinderella at the ball, but with black Converse instead of glass slippers.

Lazily, dreamily, I walked back to the Ventura Theater, still reeling from the experience and the unexpected turns the evening had taken. The night had been surreal so far. And it was only going to get stranger.

As I finally crossed the threshold of the foyer back into the theater, I saw Steve chatting in a rapid-fire manner with an unknown, slightly older – but incredibly hip and well-dressed – gentleman. Ethan, Chunk, and Uncle Jeff stood around them in a semicircle, listening intently and intermittently nodding along with the conversation. Suddenly, Steve spotted me and called me over.

"Brick!" he shouted. *"Where have you been?"*

"I'm sorry," I told him. "I was out. At a restaurant. With a girl."

"With a *girl?*" he asked, arm thrown around my shoulder. He ushered me back to the semicircle like we were the best of friends, completely ignoring whatever friction might have come between us in the past. "You'll have to give me all the sordid details later. There's someone you need to meet."

Steve parked us right in front of the aforementioned middle-aged hipster. The man wore dark blue jeans, spit-shined Dr. Martens, and a vintage Depeche Mode t-shirt tucked beneath an immaculate, expensive-looking leather jacket. He looked impossibly cool, like the caricature of an aging movie star brought to life.

"This," Steve said, gesturing towards the fellow, "is Derek Schneider. He's an A&R man from Lowercase Records."

"It's a pleasure to meet you," Derek said with a gravelly voice, extending his right hand out to shake mine. A sliver of a tattoo crept out from the sleeve of his leather jacket and trailed down to his sun-wrinkled wrist. "You did a great job onstage earlier. I used to play bass myself."

"A fellow bass player!" I smiled. "Did you play with anyone I might know…?"

"Actually," he smirked with a Cheshire grin. "Are you familiar with The Autopilot Method?"

"Wait…" I stammered. "You played for *The Autopilot Method?* Like, the guys who did 'Break Me Off' and 'Sounds Like Ego' and all that synth-heavy rock stuff?"

"That was us," he said, puffing out his chest proudly beneath the fine layers of leather. "But I've got a desk job in the industry these days. It's much… *calmer.*"

He emphasized that last word, as if it was a mystery that he refused to solve for us.

Why would you ever want to leave a successful rock band? I wondered. *Why would you trade that in for a desk job?*

"I've been talking about a few things with your bandmates here and your uncle," Derek explained. His eyes twinkled with an almost mischievous glint. "And I like what you're doing. You fit nicely with what's coming up through the record labels these days. The industry is heading in a different direction – grunge is on its way out and the labels are ready for a seismic shift."

With every word and gesture, Derek held a captive audience. The boys in the band seemed to consider Mr. Schneider's words as gospel, intently focusing on his industry-insider knowledge.

"So, what's next?" Steve asked, posing the question that we were all thinking.

"Believe it or not," Derek said, "you're going to see two big, disparate threads in the next few years. Teenagers are the key demographic. They're the ones buying records and going to shows. The label is going to be pushing music *by, for*, and *about* teenagers."

"That makes sense," Uncle Jeff chimed in. "But hasn't it always been that way, though? Going back to the bubblegum pop of the 1950s and 1960s…?"

"*Exactly*," Derek affirmed. "We're going to have a big resurgence of teen pop music in the next few cycles. You're going to see the market flooded with young girls and boys trying to be the next Boyz II Men or New Kids on the Block or George Michael or Madonna. And while that's great for candy-coated pop radio, it's going to be hard times for rock and roll."

We all seemed a bit crestfallen with that last remark. Was he telling us that we had no chance, that we would never amount to more than an underground sensation?

"How is that going to work for *us*…?" Ethan asked nervously.

Once again, Derek gave us that Cheshire grin.

"Because there's going to be a violent reaction to that," he explained. "A massive, reactionary pendulum swing. There are going to be *other* kids – like yourselves – who will want real, organic rock and roll. That's what blink-182 and Jimmy Eat World are doing."

So maybe there was a glimmer of hope in the darkness.

"And you…" Derek continued, his eyes methodically making contact with each of us individually, "I think your band fits nicely with that target demographic."

"I agree," Steve said with a cocksure smirk. "I think we're exactly what you're looking for." Steve had always been the bold one, and now that unrelenting confidence was steamrolling us forward.

"I believe you may be right," Derek said. "But there's just one catch…"

"What's that?" Steve asked.

Derek pursed his lips and scratched at the faded tattoo on his wrist.

"I don't hear a single," he told us.

Ah, yes, I thought to myself. *A single.* The holy grail of pop music. That elusive, seemingly unattainable goal that distinguishes would-be indie bands from the big leagues.

"Here's the thing," he explained. "You guys have exactly what it takes to make it in the business. You've got a polished act and a contemporary, commercial sound that is – most importantly for the label – *marketable.*"

That last word seemed to be the key here. It wasn't just about *making* music; it was about *selling* music, preferably in that rare, scrutinized arena where art and commerce intersect. It was about the commoditization of cool, the way that vendors capitalized on the fringe (and not-so-fringe) corners of pop culture.

Derek continued his sermon. "You've got the sound. You've got the musicianship. You've got the handsome lead singer. You've got a collection of great songs." At this point, he held up a shrink-wrapped copy of the *Bookhouse EP* in his left hand. "If this record is anywhere near as good as what I heard tonight, I'm guessing you have the recording experience, too."

We nodded enthusiastically, like little kids in the presence of Santa Claus.

"But you don't have a single," he reminded us. Then, almost as an afterthought, he added one more word. "*Yet.*"

Everything Derek said seemed to be a confirmation of our success.

Until the end, of course.

It was at this point that Derek turned to me, his focus shifting intensely into a small tunnel, as if no one else in the room even existed. "Rumor has it that you're the songwriter for the band," he said, his unflinching attention trained on me.

"Ahhh…" I glanced around the group for some kind of affirmation. Ethan, Chunk, and Steve nodded, urging me forward. "Yes, sir."

"Get to work," Derek told me. "Give me a radio-ready single, and I can pass it along to the head honchos at the label. If you guys can write *the song...*" He paused, letting those two words sink in. "If you can do that, then I think I can make something happen."

Derek reached out his tattooed hand to shake mine in a firm grip.

"Yes, sir," I replied cautiously. "I'll see what I can do."

"Oh!" he barked, swinging back around to face the rest of the group. "One more thing. You need to change the name of your band. I've crisscrossed this country countless times, and there are a dozen different bands named after Holden Caulfield. You can't keep calling yourself 'Caulfield' and expect to get signed without a lawsuit or two."

We stared at him, shocked and dismayed.

"Why do you think *blink* added *-182* to the end of their name?" he said with a shrug of his slender shoulders. "It's not because they're mathematicians."

And with that, he disappeared out the theater's doors into the cool, dark night.

The boys and I stuck around for a little while longer, debriefing with Uncle Jeff about this unexpected development, about potential routes into the music industry and the path to career longevity. While it was a fascinating conversation, I felt my thoughts drifting away from music – the unshakable core of my universe for so many years – to a force even more powerful...

My heart.

Though this was the moment the band had dreamed about for years, I felt distracted. Here we were, teenagers essentially being offered a contract for a major record label, nearly living the rock and roll "*Star is Born*" dream...

But all I could think about was a girl.

The biggest thrill of the evening wasn't that we conquered a few hundred new fans, or that we got to open for our idols, or that we met an industry insider who all but promised us a major label contract. For me, the only thing that mattered was that Lani had been there.

It's hard to explain, but something changed between me and Lani that night. I went from being her best friend to something different. Something more. As a result, the future seemed limitless.

Of course, once the dust cleared and the crowds dispersed, the boys in the band had a chance to talk about everything that had transpired over the last few hours. As Ethan and Chunk attested, the bands after us had been stellar: blink-182, Jimmy Eat World, and The Ataris were all on the verge of mega-stardom, and here they were appearing right around the corner from our hometown. Of course, Steve recounted all of his unbelievable exploits from that night, hanging out with Mark Hoppus and Tom DeLonge from blink-182 and a bunch of other showbiz folk; he even showed me his autographed copy of *Dude Ranch* with a personalized signature – a raunchy one that I won't repeat in print, mind you, but a personalized one nonetheless.

He also pointed out, with great emphasis, that there were girls *everywhere*.

"It was like a buffet of hot chicks," Steve declared. "Blondes, brunettes, redheads… You missed out, Brick."

I couldn't help but wonder how Serena – the long-suffering sidekick to our fearless lead singer – might have felt about Steve's "buffet" analogy. Interestingly, she was nowhere to be found. Much like me, she must have vanished from the scene to attend to more important personal matters.

Some people spend years talking about their brief brush with fame – the night that they got to hang out with blink-182 and Jimmy Eat World, for instance.

I didn't get that chance.

I missed out on meeting some of my favorite bands because I was drinking strawberry milkshakes with the girl of my dreams.

And that was okay.

As my dad had told me years before, *some things are more important than rock and roll*. The night of the blink-182 show was proof positive of my dad's wisdom, a reminder that music – even *great* music – is only one monotone color in the broader palette of life.

CHAPTER FORTY-THREE

"Wake the World"

So, Lani and I had a date lined up. For a year – a long, *long* year – I had been breathlessly waiting for my chance. And, as you can imagine, months of breathlessness had left me emotionally lightheaded. For the first time since I'd known her, Lani was single and uninhibited by the bonds of a boyfriend. Like the Burt Bacharach/Hal David song, I was *"wishing and hoping and thinking and praying"* for a chance to redefine our relationship.

Lani was *clearly* out of my league. I knew that. And yet, despite that potentially crippling knowledge, I also recognized that we had some undeniable connection that transcended the typical rules of attraction.

Perhaps, if I play my cards just right, I thought, *I could elevate our friendship into the romance that would make my life complete.*

To pull this off, though, I needed to do something special – some grand gesture to prove to the *Beautiful Girl from Heaven* that she should descend from the firmament to take a chance on the earthbound boy from across the hall.

I knew what I had to do.

If you want a girl to like you, write her a song.
If you want a girl to love you, write her a *great* song.
That's what I did.

I couldn't stop thinking about our conversation at the Tiki Turtle Tavern on the night of the blink-182 show, and Lani's comments about the song "Earth Angel" kept replaying in my head on a relentless loop. She clearly had a soft spot for the earnest, sensitive songs of yesteryear – for the *"pure, unadulterated adoration"* of oldies radio. With that knowledge circling through my brain like some kind of crazed Cupid on the prowl, I thumbed my way through my father's old vinyl collection for inspiration, desperately searching for the perfect songs on which I could model this paean to Lani and all the things I loved about her. After an hour of painstakingly perusing Dad's old records, I found a handful of tunes that I thought might work: "Surfer Girl," "The Surfer Moon," "Your Summer Dream," "Keep an Eye on Summer," and "Girls on the Beach."

All the songs were, of course, by my father's favorite band: The Beach Boys.

What all these ballads had in common (apart from the co-writing team of Brian Wilson and Mike Love) was an aching, longing sentiment of young love. Because all five songs came from the early Beach Boys records, they capture an element of innocence alongside an innate sadness. Though Brian Wilson and the boys had recorded these songs years before Lani and I were even born, there was something timeless in the melodies and themes that resonated deeply – even to a new generation of lovesick adolescents, decades later.

How exactly do you replicate something like that?

The title was easy enough: "The Beautiful Girl from Heaven." Sure, it sounded a little archaic, a little melodramatic, but it was also the English translation of her given name, *Noelani.* Just saying *"The beautiful girl from heaven"* aloud had a musical quality, and a melody manifested without much effort. As I scribbled down ideas on an old yellow legal pad, I thought about the many details that drew me in: the scent of hyacinth and tangerines, her raven hair falling around her bronze shoulders, the simple smile that simultaneously knocked me out and lifted me up.

If ever there was a girl who deserved to be immortalized in a song, it was Lani. I just hoped that I could do her justice.

As I sat there, pen prostrate upon the page, I thought back (once again) to that moment months before – when we had almost kissed, when Lani draped her arms around me as she taught me how to strum her ukulele…

Her ukulele, I remembered.

I dashed to my closet, impatiently throwing aside clothes and books and guitar cables until I found it. I had almost forgotten about Lani's ukulele through the ensuing months of heartache and longing, but there it was – right in front of me. The delicate wooden instrument had been with me all this time, despite my best efforts to push it out of my thoughts. Even when I had tried to forget about it – forget about *her* – it had always been there, waiting for me to rediscover.

I had never written anything on a ukulele before, and my strumming felt relatively rudimentary, but it seemed apropos to write Lani's song on the instrument she had loaned me. I pressed my fingers to the strings, forming that familiar pyramidal *D* chord shape, which produced a different sound altogether on the ukulele, a *G* chord.

In those days, I tended to start most of my songwriting in the key of *G*, the so-called "people's key." I initially tried to mimic the traditional *I* to *VI minor* to *IV* to *V* chord progression that defined so many of the 1950s slow ballads, but I couldn't get the melody in my head to match the chords that my fingers clumsily formed on the ukulele in my hands. Eventually, I settled on an alternating series of *G*, *C*, and *D* chords with *Em*, *Bm*, *A7*, and *Am* added to the chorus and refrain. To the best of my abilities, I tried to emulate the mid-tempo, downward strumming of the summer ballads – something that would have made Brian Wilson proud.

Surprisingly, the song didn't require much heartbreak or frustration. Instead, it tumbled out easily, confidently, like a waterfall driven forward by the weight of inertia and gravity. After a few hours of diligently working, Lani's song came out like this:

"The Beautiful Girl from Heaven"

She might be the girl next door,
or just across the hall;
but when she smiles,
you'd better be ready to fall.

(Ooh-ooh) All I can do
(Ooh-ooh) is wait for you.
So I fall and I fall again
for the beautiful girl from heaven.

With skin as soft as hyacinth
and a voice like the summer breeze,
she'll lift you up above the sun
or bring you to your knees.

(Ooh-ooh) All I can do
(Ooh-ooh) is wait for you.
So I fall and I fall again
for the beautiful girl from heaven.

You must be, without a doubt,
What all the love songs are about.

(Ooh-ooh) All I can do
(Ooh-ooh) is wait for you.
So I fall and I fall again
for the beautiful girl from heaven.

So I fall and I fall yet again
For the beautiful girl from heaven.

Though the song wasn't easy to sing – it had a pretty challenging vocal stretch from the lower notes of the verse to the higher notes of the chorus – it captured the pure, innocent kind of love that Lani had swooned over that night at the Tiki Turtle Tavern.

It was simple. It was sweet. It was exactly how I felt about the girl from across the hall.

Noelani.

The Beautiful Girl from Heaven.

The first part of my mission had been accomplished: write a catchy song for the girl whom I thought was a catch. The only thing left to do was record it.

What people sometimes forget about songwriting is that composing the lyrics and chord progressions is only the first step.

Afterwards, you have to find a way to capture the magic of the melody with a recording that will actually do the song justice.

Fortunately for me, I had a garage full of newly purchased recording equipment that I could utilize – free of charge. You see, Dad and Uncle Jeff had been so inspired by our experiences at the Mountain Dog Musicworks recording studio that they shelled out a ton of cash – *thousands* of dollars – to buy a home studio's worth of equipment. Our garage, the de facto practice space of Caulfield (or whatever we were going to call the band in light of Derek's admonition), had been converted into a makeshift recording studio, filled with microphones, stands, cables, preamps, and an Apple computer with a brand-new software called ProTools. It wasn't Abbey Road or Sun Studios, but it would have to do. In any case, the rock and roll gods were looking out for me, their penitent priest of punk rock.

Because the house was eerily silent and still, all my movements felt awkwardly loud and clumsy. Every footfall across the wooden floorboards of the living room creaked and croaked, while my bare feet tapping on the tile of the kitchen resonated louder than I thought humanly possible. As quietly as I could, I crept through the halls towards the garage, careful to gently close the thick frame of the door without it slamming shut.

Humming along as I moved across that familiar tangerine carpet, I assembled piece after piece of recording gear, booting up the bulky Apple Macintosh computer and plugging cables into various microphones strewn across the floor. When it was all prepped and ready to go, I sat myself down on an old barstool, the stuffing streaming out from a tear in the center of the seat. For a few seconds, I picked at the stark white cotton batting. Things were unraveling and unfurling, but that left the possibility for new worlds, new relationships, new futures…

A new me.

I clicked the blinking red "record" button on the console and let it roll.

Over and over, I softly strummed the familiar chord progression, brushing my fingers gently against Lani's ukulele as if I was caressing her velvet skin. The nylon strings silently stretched with each finger positioning, the X-Y microphones picking up the echo of the ukulele in stereo and relaying the sound to my battered headphones. I tracked the song a few times, ultimately layering a fingerpicked acoustic guitar and a lightly-arpeggiated tremolo Telecaster on top of the softly strummed ukulele. It wasn't a dramatic orchestra-driven pop song. It *definitely* wasn't *Pet Sounds*. But it was simple. Sweet.

All the while, I was consciously aware of how late the night had become, the monotonous revolutions of the silent analog clock rotating around and around without hesitation.

12:00...

1:00...

2:00...

And counting.

I thought I had been so careful, turning the amp down as close to the "zero" demarcation as possible, but it was still apparently not quiet enough. Midway through my tenth take of the arpeggio on the bridge, I heard the familiar creak of the garage door swinging open and a rather audible clearing of the throat.

"What are you working on at this late hour?" my dad queried sleepily between yawns.

"It's... a song," I said.

"I can see that, smart-ass," my dad shot back, his eyes squinting in the dim light. "But what's the urgency for recording it *in the middle of the night...?*"

I didn't want to get into a detailed explanation about the love triangle that had haunted me for the last year, so I kept it simple.

"It's for Lani," I mumbled.

"Oh," he whispered back, knowingly nodding his head as another yawn escaped his lips. He ran his hands through the wispy remains of his hair and clicked his tongue against the roof of his mouth. "Just try not to wake your mom, okay?"

"Okay," I grinned back. "I promise."

My dad reached for the doorknob before turning back towards me.

"And Junior…?"

"Yeah, Dad?"

"If this is a song for a remarkable girl like Lani, then you better make it magical."

"Yes, sir," I smiled up at him.

He closed the door smoothly, soundlessly, as he left the room.

And then, once again, I hit the record button.

CHAPTER FORTY-FOUR

"Wouldn't It Be Nice"

After what seemed like eternity, the big day arrived: Wednesday, August 5th, 1998. I'm sure that nostalgia has tempered my memory a little in the last twenty-two years, but no hazy, dreamy filter can mar what was one of the best days of my life.

I woke up early that morning, unable to stay asleep with my heart skipping in nervous anticipation. For two hours, I performed trivial tasks around the house to keep myself busy: rearranging my CD collection, tidying up my overflowing bookshelves, making and unmaking and remaking my bed, etc.

It had been only a week since that night at the Ventura Theater and the Tiki Turtle Tavern, but so much had happened in the interim.

I had written her a song.

I had recorded it.

I had driven my "brand-new" – albeit *used* – 1985 Ford Mustang (purchased with savings from my part-time gig at the Ojai public library) to the post office, where I nervously handed my package to a teller who guaranteed that the first-class mailing would arrive shortly before our date.

Gasp.

Our date.

Lani and I had talked endlessly on the phone almost every evening, but she hadn't mentioned anything about the song. Had it reached her in time? Did the U.S. Postal Service fail to deliver its most important package? Did the dictum that "neither snow nor rain nor heat nor gloom of night" also apply to expedient matters of the heart?

The seconds and minutes and hours crept by until the agreed-upon meeting time of noon *finally* arrived. I won't tell you just how early I showed up to our rendezvous point at the Ventura County Fairgrounds, but let's just say it was enough time for *Pet Sounds* to play a few times – in its entirety – on my car stereo in the parking lot.

Five times, to be exact.

In the glaring summer heat, I watched the incoming cars with a hawk-eyed intensity. With every passing Corolla and Camry and Civic and Chevrolet, my nerves throbbed and my heart raced. All were false alarms, though, until I saw the familiar faded red of Lani's Nissan pickup truck cruise into the graying asphalt of the parking lot.

Showtime.

Slowly, methodically, I exited my Mustang and walked towards Lani's truck, my hands stuck deeply into my lint-filled pockets. As I got closer, I saw the driver's side door swing open and two gorgeously tanned legs reached out onto the ground.

It was like watching Venus emerge from the ocean atop a clamshell.

But, you know…

With clothes.

Lani beamed when she saw me, her eyes coolly hiding behind a pair of wine-dark sunglasses, her emotions betrayed only by the sheer grace of her unrestrained smile. She slammed her car door and raced up to meet me, throwing her arms up and over my shoulders. Something was different between us then: I sensed a hint of timidity in her gait as she strolled beside me, as well as a newfound tenderness in her voice.

Could this really be happening? I wondered.

It really was.

The whole day at the fair was magical. We walked around for hours, visiting the various vendors and the art exhibits and the gardens. We rode Ferris wheels and carousels. We ate cotton candy and popcorn. We talked and talked and talked about anything and everything.

I remember sitting in that creaky Ferris wheel seat, swaying back and forth as our metal carriage dangled precipitously from rocking hooks and straps. I was higher than I had ever been in my life, the clouds in the sky nearly within reach and the land visible for miles around us. Palm trees flanked the sides of our pod, their branches shifting gracefully in the breeze, fronds gently arching aloft towards the heavens. Though it was hard to pry my eyes away from Lani, I glanced seaward and saw thousands of rippling waves caressing the ocean in the distance.

It was when I was lost in thought that I suddenly felt her smooth golden-shaded arm slip gracefully through my own and pull me in tighter. I turned to face her, and she giggled, nuzzling her cheek against my chest.

Life can't get any better than this, I thought to myself.

Except it did.

The best part of the Ventura County Fair? The fireworks. At 10:00 PM sharp during every night of the annual two-week run, the world pauses and flowering lights punctuate the steady darkness of the evening sky.

Needless to say, I planned accordingly.

As the guiding light of the daytime firmament faded into the sweet haze of twilight and then recoiled into the comfort of darkened skies, Lani and I made our way back to the parking lot, our arms tightly wound together the whole time. The world seemed smoky, dreamlike even, as we collected coats and blankets before making our way to the nearby beach. Arm in arm, we strolled across the ageless concrete promenade to the soft silken sand and then to the ancient wooden pier that bridged the stable land and the aching sea just beyond the shore.

The beach was packed with other likeminded folks: giggling teenagers, googly-eyed couples, tittering drunkards, and festive families all staked their claim to spots on the sand. As we dodged children and lumbering adults, we clung tightly to each other and searched for an open section of sandy real estate to claim as our own. Eventually, we found a nice spot sandwiched between a tranquil elderly couple and a trio of hippy high school kids. Lani and I huddled together under a woolen blanket, keeping each other warm with our arms locked together.

In the light chill of the summer air, the evening seemed infinite and full of possibilities. But I felt myself trembling – not from the cold, but from my close proximity to Lani. Just as on the first day that we met, Lani smelled like tangerines and hyacinth blossoms, an intoxicating perfume that drew me closer and closer to her silky black hair.

Right at 10:00 sharp, we heard the pop and fizz of fireworks being launched skyward. Within seconds, the sky above us exploded in neon shades of red, orange, blue, and green, as a bouquet of colors illuminated the sky.

BOOM.

"This is quite a sight, isn't it?" she asked.

But I wasn't looking at the sky. I was looking at her face, illuminated in the staccato flash of the fireworks above us.

BOOM.

"Yes," I whispered. "It's the most beautiful thing that I've ever seen."

BOOM.

For a second, Lani looked confused. She cocked her head to the side, eyes still glued to the sky, before turning her attention to me. When she looked at me looking at her, she blushed and smiled before retreating under the folds of the blanket that covered our shoulders. I panicked, wondering for a moment if I had overplayed my cards, if I had misread her signals. That old, familiar fear of rejection started to creep up from the bottom of my chest.

And then she reached for my hand.

BOOM.

I felt her soft fingers slide delicately into my own, intertwining gently with mine. Her skin was so gentle, so soft, I figured that this was as close to heaven as I would ever get.

It's hard to describe the monumental importance of such an innocent, affectionate act, but holding hands for the first time with a girl you love is sweetly ceremonial. The interlocking fingers, the gentle caresses of palms and wrists – it's a beautiful moment of pure, unchained bliss. When adults think about such seemingly trivial events, it's easy for them to get cynical and jaded. In a world of lust, the gentle act of holding hands is a forgotten art. To a teenager, though, it can mean the world.

BOOM.

We sat in silence for a few minutes, just enjoying the sweet stillness of each other's company. It felt so honest and pure and perfect, I didn't want it to end. I wanted to scream that I loved Lani – had loved her for months and would love her forever – but I didn't know if I had woven myself into her heart the same way that she had infiltrated the trenches of my own.

So, I settled for a gentle declaration instead.

"The waves... the sand... the fireworks..." I casually remarked, tracing lines on the palms of her hands. "This is the perfect place for you and I."

BOOM.

Lani kept her gaze trained on the horizon, staring at the dusty fallout of sparkling detritus as the fireworks evaporated in the night sky.

"It's actually '*you and me*,'" she said.

"What's that?"

"Well," she sighed contentedly, snuggling into me as I lay my cheek on the top of her head, "It's supposed to be 'you and *me*,' not 'you and *I*.' You should know that, being an English major and all."

I laughed quietly. "As long as the two of us are together – *you and I* or *you and me* or *me and you* – I don't really care about grammar."

BOOM.

"Speaking of grammar," she continued, undeterred, "it's like in my song. When you sing, '*You must be without a doubt what all the love songs are about.*' You ended a sentence with a preposition. That's a venial sin in the world of journalism."

So, she *had* listened to the song. But what did she think?

"Seriously?" I remarked, squinting my eyes and frowning at her. "A guy writes you a song and pours his heart out to you, and you're going to correct his grammar?"

"I've got to keep you on your toes, Mr. Rock Star." She winked at me, her cheeks scrunching up into adorable smile lines.

BOOM.

"So…" I began, my heart thumping harder and harder, "what did you think of your song?"

She paused, running her pinky along the indentations on my wrist.

"In all seriousness," she admitted, "I cried."

BOOM.

"You cried?"

"Yup. Tears and everything."

"Good crying or bad crying…?" I asked nervously.

"Good crying."

BOOM.

"So… does that mean you liked it?"

"I *loved* it," she said.

BOOM.

She smiled up at me.

BOOM.

She nuzzled deeply into my chest and gently traced her hands along the back of my neck.

BOOM.

BOOM.

BOOM.

We sat there and held hands on the beach, watching the pyrotechnics above us crackle and detonate until the display culminated in a climactic blast of escalating explosions. Just as the whole day had been building up to this one critical moment, the fireworks mirrored the catalytic chemistry blossoming between us.

Once the last faded embers of the final firecracker dissipated in the blackened sky, we stood up from the sand and walked back to my car, holding hands the whole way. I made a grand gesture of opening the passenger door first and letting her into the car; Lani giggled and scooted into the gray leather of her seat, and I closed the door behind her.

As I walked around the back of the car, my heart thumping nervously with anticipation, I watched her reach across the expanse of the front seat and unlock my car door. My dad's words suddenly echoed through my mind: *"a girl who unlocks your car door for you is considerate and thoughtful – she's the kind of girl that you don't let go."*

I must have had some goofy, transparent expression on my face as I crawled into the driver's seat, because Lani studied me like a cryptic textbook she was trying to decode.

"What are you smiling about?" she asked, eyes squinting and mouth puckered.

"You unlocked my door," I told her.

"Of course, I did," she said. She raised an eyebrow quizzically.

"I've been waiting a long time for a girl to lean over and unlock my door for me."

Lani offered up a puckish smile and started singing. *"Ooh-ooh, all I can do... ooh-ooh, is wait for you..."* she cooed, before shooting me a flirtatious look. "Maybe you've waited long enough."

I turned the key in the ignition slightly, just enough to power on the radio, and felt a warm blast of air gust forth from the heater. At the same time, the stereo came alive with the whimsical accordions and chiming guitars of "Wouldn't It Be Nice."

I turned to Lani. "I've spent a lot of time looking for the perfect girl," I told her, the words tumbling out of my mouth.

Lani leaned towards me. "Maybe she's right in front of you," she whispered.

We inched closer and closer, our noses touching.

For a split second, the world stood still.

And then we kissed.

CHAPTER FORTY-FIVE

"I Can Hear Music"

A lot can happen in a year.

Three hundred and sixty-five days is enough time for a boy and a girl to cultivate a relationship, to transition from best friends into lovebirds. It's enough time for them to whisper their way through the twilight honeymoon phase of dating into something more substantial, more permanent. It's enough time for the boy to memorize the taste of her lips, the sweet waxy texture of cinnamon and cherry Chapstick. It's enough time for a girl to realize the boy's many flaws and insecurities – his ugly feet and bitten fingernails and slowly thinning hair – and to develop deep affection for him anyway.

It's enough time for the two of them to fall in love.

That night in the parking lot, Lani and I began the next chapter of our lives. Brian Wilson's entreaty in "Wouldn't It Be Nice" – that every kiss might be never-ending – felt like an invocation, a poetic page quickly turning into the long-awaited climax of the book.

Pet Sounds is a 35-minute album. That night, in the cool comfort of my Ford Mustang, we listened to the entire album. Twice. We kissed and we laughed and we cried and we talked, all while the Beach Boys serenaded us on what we would eventually declare our first official date.

It was the beginning of the rest of my life.

Three hundred and sixty-five days is also enough time for three trimesters of college to fly by, for two ambitious UCLA students to start investigating new hobbies and passions and career paths.

It's enough time for a girl to finish her internship at the *L.A. Times*, to start writing for the *Daily Bruin*, to build connections in the storied spiderweb of the Los Angeles journalism industry.

A year is also enough time for a band to hone its craft, to experiment endlessly with home-demo recording techniques, to master the intricacies of performing live and to gig all around Southern California.

And it's enough time for an ambitious young songwriter to compose several albums worth of songs.

Over the course of twelve grueling months, I submitted demo recordings of new songs to Derek Schneider every other week. And yet, for all my best attempts, every single song that we sent to Derek came back with a rejection.

Try again, one e-mail read.

Close, but no dollar bills, stated another.

A few times, Derek simply responded with a single, two-letter response: *No.*

Clearly, we had quite a distance to travel before that coveted major label contract would be ours – truly and unconditionally.

Despite the flurry of rejections and plateaued progression, we did have one monumental change: we renamed the band. Taking into account Derek's comment about the dozens of other indie bands with the name Caulfield (clearly, hipsters loved – and *still* love – *Catcher in the Rye*), we got a little creative, maintaining the momentum of the name we had used for the last few years while adding a slight twist.

We changed the name of our little rock and roll band from *Caulfield*...

To... (*drum roll, please!*)

Call Field.

It was, my father reassured us, the "greatest use of a homophone in rock and roll history."

Only Dad could come up with such a gratuitously nerdy remark.

For the next twelve months – through the rest of 1998 and into the autumn of 1999, when my sophomore year of college eased into my junior year – my life was just about perfect on all counts. I was dating the *Beautiful Girl from Heaven*, school had become a manageable routine, and the band was really starting to gain some traction. After that life-changing blink-182 show, we found ourselves sharing the bill with a bunch of notable bands from Ventura and Santa Barbara counties, including No Motiv, Army of Freshmen, Nerf Herder, and 8Stops7. We were even invited to play the SoCal stop on the Warped Tour the following summer, taking the stage at the "local" Southern California venue – which, for the record, was still a two-and-a-half-hour drive away from Ojai.

Though it was mind-blowing for us to see the band elevated to such eminence, I was now equally focused on cultivating a happy life with Lani. After waiting for so long, Lani's fate had become intertwined with mine – and music, for all its magical powers and obsession-inducing tendencies, was taking a second-tier position in my heart. My dad's wise words kept echoing around in my skull: *some things are more important than rock and roll*. With Lani, I finally understood the underlying truth of that simple phrase.

I remember standing on the Warped Tour stage in San Bernardino, thumping away on my bass guitar in front of hundreds of people, simply searching for Lani in the crowd. Of course, she was there near the front row, looking on fondly as her boyfriend (*me!*) played on the same bill as blink-182 (again), Eminem, Pennywise, and the Vandals. There we were, jamming away on an industrial-looking stage, the scaffolding exposed for all to see and sponsorship banners waving proudly in the wind. For others, the banners fluttering behind us might just have been background decorations; but for Call Field, it was a brutal reminder that big-time rock and roll was only possible through a corporate sponsorship.

We hadn't made it to the big leagues. Yet.

But we weren't just playing live shows. We had also been diligently working on our recording chops, spending countless hours in the Smith family garage fine-tuning our skills. Every demo that we sent to Derek got progressively more polished and cohesive; we were growing, steadily and surely, even if we didn't have a million-dollar contract to prove it.

As the band toiled away in semi-obscurity, my father suggested that we record an acoustic EP. As Dad continued to remind us, the heart of any song is the pure, unadulterated incarnation that's exposed when you strip away all the stomp and distortion of electric instrumentation. As our back catalog of original compositions grew from a paper-thin folder into a thick binder of words and chords, it was clear that we were in the middle of something really special. At some point, we made the decision that even if we couldn't secure a corporate deal with a major label, we would release something independently. The indie record label that had pressed and distributed the *Bookhouse EP* offered us some decent cash for a follow-up, and we were banking on that (literally and figuratively) to save us if band resources reached a point of depletion. So, we strummed and sang and smashed into microphones over and over again, working and working and working until we were happy with the songs.

Yet, despite our best efforts, we still hadn't produced *the single* that Derek wanted – the musical holy grail that would propel us into new, unexplored waters. In the fall of 1999, we still felt stranded on the shoreline, aching for the touch of the tide against the bow of our band.

That is, until the night before Halloween.

The night that I wrote "Incomplete."

CHAPTER FORTY-SIX
"Love & Mercy"

I t must have been strange for Brian Wilson to wake up in Northern California that Halloween weekend in 1999 and adorn the costume of a healthy, fully functional rock star. In the two decades prior, he had battled mental illness, lawsuits from bandmates, and the abuse of his psychiatrist – as well as the loss of his parents *and* both his brothers. And yet, for all the damage and destruction, Brian was on a career resurgence, making a comeback with 1998's *Imagination* album and the accompanying tour.

One of the stops along the way? Neil Young's annual all-acoustic Bridge School Benefit Concert at the Shoreline Amphitheater in Mountain View, California – which would be held Halloween weekend of 1999.

For my dad, this was a perfect storm of musical convergences. A completely "unplugged" affair (appealing to Dad's acoustic sensibilities), the concert would feature some of the greatest acts from his youth alongside some of the best artists of the 1990s. The awe-inspiring lineup included Neil Young, Pearl Jam, The Who, Sheryl Crow, Green Day, Billy Corgan & James Iha of the Smashing Pumpkins, Tom Waits, Lucinda Williams, and (most importantly)…

Brian Wilson.

For my dad, this concert was a gift from the rock and roll gods. Not only was this a chance to see his hero in action, but it would be an all-acoustic set. Though the Beach Boys' definitive works (like *Pet Sounds*) obviously benefitted from the lush orchestrations and arrangements that were their specialty, the Bridge School performance was going to be a once-in-a-lifetime opportunity to see Brian Wilson in a stripped-down environment, a la MTV's famed *Unplugged* series of acoustic concerts.

In true fanatic form, my father bought tickets for everyone – himself, my mom, Marina, Reggie, your humble narrator, and even Lani. And, since Marina was still living in the Bay Area after graduating from Berkeley, it was also going to serve as a small-scale family reunion. So, on the last weekend of October in 1999, Lani and I hopped into a car with Dad and Mom, slid onto the northbound 101, and headed straight towards San Francisco.

I should probably back up just a little bit here. I've neglected to talk about Serena and Steve for quite a few pages, so I need to fill in some blanks for you, my dear reader. Though Call Field's rock and roll Adonis and his Aphrodite had quite a few *seemingly* perfect years together, there was definitely trouble on Mount Olympus that autumn. Steve had, somehow, grown inexplicably handsomer... and found the fairer sex perpetually fawning over him – punk show groupies and random girls on the street, alike. For Steve, life was a bustling buffet of beauties beating down the doors. As you can expect, his long-suffering girlfriend wasn't thrilled.

Serena, ever the dutiful partner, tolerated the flirting and fussing at first. However, a relationship can only handle *so much* temptation. The little sideways glances from Serena's hazel eyes, the semi-permanent scowl that adorned her otherwise flawless face, the rigid posture that she wore whenever Steve was in the company of other girls – these were all warning signs that something had gone very, very wrong with our lead singer and his girlfriend.

So, when Serena cornered me the day before the Smith family left for San Francisco, I was backed into a bit of a compromising position. I was sitting unaccompanied in Ojai's Littoral Café, a French *boulangerie*, scribbling away on a beaten-up notepad and scratching out lyrics with a sharp black pen. Apart from the muffled sounds of the staff cleaning the kitchen, the otherwise-empty coffee shop was eerily still. Lani, my constant companion, was noticeably absent. I was so engrossed in my work that I had completely missed the chiming bells and the shrill breeze that swept through the shop when the front door opened... and Serena stepped into the café.

"Hello, *handsome*," she said, crossing her arms and tapping her flip-flop-adorned right foot inches away from me in the deserted café.

WARNING SIGN NUMBER ONE: when your kind-of ex-girlfriend calls you "handsome."

"Hey!" I replied, standing up and pulling her into an impromptu embrace. As she hugged me, it felt uncomfortably comfortable, paradoxically wonderful and problematic. I started to relax my arms and pull away, but she didn't let go; in fact, it seemed like she lingered against my chest just a *few* seconds too long.

WARNING SIGN NUMBER TWO: when your kind-of ex-girlfriend hugs you for a little bit longer than she should.

"Do you mind if I join you?" she asked, gracefully sliding into the chair opposite mine.

"No," I hurriedly replied. "Not at all."

WARNING SIGN NUMBER THREE: when your kind-of exgirlfriend wants to sit with you while neither of your significant others are present.

So, Serena and I talked.

For a long time.

A *very* long time.

An hour into our conversation, Serena heaved a massive sigh from her slender frame and started tracing cryptic shapes on the faded wooden tabletop between us, like she was crafting coded messages with invisible ink.

"Can I…" she started to say. She didn't finish the question, though. Instead she let the words linger vacantly in the space between us.

"Can you… *what?*" I prompted.

"Can I ask you… something?" Her eyebrows scrunched up in a furrowed brow and she warily ran her tongue between her flushed lips.

"Go ahead," I told her.

She glanced down at the folded hands in her lap, carefully rubbing the empty space on the ring finger of her left hand.

"Do you still think about me?" she asked quietly. Serena's eyes betrayed an earnest vulnerability as they skittered back and forth between the table, her hands, and my face.

WARNING SIGN NUMBER FOUR: when your kind-of exgirlfriend asks if you still think about her.

GET OUT AS SOON AS POSSIBLE.

GET. OUT.

I wasn't quite sure how to respond. I cocked my head at an angle, breathing deeply through my nostrils and letting my chest puff in and out with each calculated breath.

"What do you mean, exactly?" I asked.

Serena's perfect teeth gleamed from between her lips, but she didn't immediately answer me. Something sparked a thought between those sharp eyes, though, and she reached into the inestimable depths of her tan leather purse, flipping through keys and crumpled papers until she found what she was looking for. She pulled the slim plastic square from her bag and placed it delicately on the table between us.

It was a copy of the Call Field (née Caulfield) *Bookhouse* EP, the case cracked and scratched and worn out from years of devoted use.

Great, I thought to myself nervously. *She brought props.*

Serena sighed again and took a deep breath, exhaling through the side of her mouth. "Do you still think about me? I mean, like the way you used to?" She gestured to the CD in front of her, flipping open the worn plastic and slipping out the CD's thin booklet of liner notes.

She delicately traced her hands along the song titles printed on the booklet. "I've been looking at this recently," she admitted. "A lot. And as I'm studying the notes here, as I'm looking at the song titles... *'Time Bomb,' 'Canaan Road,' 'Photocopy'...* They're all about me, aren't they?"

Without thinking, I blushed deeply. "Muses don't normally ask about the artwork that they inspire," I told her. "I don't know if I'm prepared to answer that question."

Her eyelids clenched into thin knives of irritation. "You wrote 'Time Bomb' for me years ago, for my *quinceañera*. For so long, I thought it was something Steve had written. But it was *you*. You're the one who wrote that for me. And you never said anything about it."

Her face relaxed, the frustration subsiding into something softer, something kinder and more forgiving.

I, on the other hand, could feel my muscles tightening, tensing up uncontrollably as she spoke. "That was a long time ago..." I whispered, unable to complete a thought beyond this obvious statement of fact.

"I understand that," she breathed back forcefully. "But the things you said about me, that you wrote about me... *Do you still feel that way...?*"

How does one respond to that kind of question? How does a young man, barely out of his teenage years, confront this kind of question from a former paramour? Despite the obvious signs, I had a hard time believing that I was being backed into the vertex of a new love triangle. Was Serena, the girl of my high school dreams, actually pressuring me into some kind of romantic entanglement?

Ultimately, I did what any right-minded kid would do. I told the truth.

"I used to," I finally admitted. "I used to think about you. *All the time*. You were like a specter haunting me for years. And some of that wove itself into the songs."

She smiled brightly, her lips spreading into a glowing crescent.

"*But*," I countered, "your ghost has dissipated since then. I'm with someone now. I'm dating a girl who is brilliant and beautiful and talented and patient. And she loves me. Maybe more than anyone has ever loved me. And I can't walk away from that."

Serena's expression changed immediately. Though she maintained the semblance of a smile on her pursed lips, the hope that had shimmered in her dazzling hazel eyes faded to a soft watery blur.

"She's a lucky girl," Serena whispered. "A lucky, lucky girl."

"I'm a lucky boy," I whispered back.

But Serena wasn't done just yet.

"I mean," she clarified, her eyes cattishly narrowed to slits, bitterness tugging on her razor-sharp lips, "I don't even think she's *that* pretty…"

"But I love her," I interrupted.

"*But you love her*," Serena echoed, a hint of mocking sarcasm in her vulnerable voice. "And if she makes you happy, then I'll have to live with that."

She fumbled through her purse, indelicately tossing in the plastic case of the *Bookhouse EP*, and pulled out a crumpled Kleenex. As she swiped the corner of her nose, she averted her gaze, intently studying the contents of the jangling bag in her hands. Suddenly, though, an idea took ahold of her and she glanced up in my direction. Slowly, she reached her right hand across the table and settled it on my own nervously tapping fingers. Gently, she squeezed my hand, her palm tensing against the tops of my knuckles.

"If anything changes," she said, "know that I'm here. If you change your mind, or if she breaks your heart…" She let her words trail off as she stood up from the table and released my hand.

As her stance hardened and her eyes grew tight, the old Serena – the confident soccer player who swaggered across the field in high school – returned. She swung on her heels and proudly marched out the door, turning her head back to me one last time while she stood halfway shadowed in the dimming light of the sunset.

"Remember, if you need *anything*, Brian," she said. "Anything at all…"

She half-nodded to me, a conflicted smile on her lips, and let the door swing closed behind her.

So, you can imagine the mental maelstrom I was facing on October 30th, 1999, the evening of the Bridge School concert. I was at a crossroads: stay with Lani – the girl who understood me and loved me and transformed me – or take a wild gamble on the girl of my high school dreams.

What in the world was happening to my happy, humdrum life?

Despite my romantic conundrum, I carried on with Lani and my parents as if nothing had happened. The drive to the San Francisco Bay Area was unremarkable: we took the 101 north for hours on end, stopping in San Luis Obispo, King City, and San Jose along the way. For most of the journey, my parents prattled on nonchalantly in the front seats about students and administration and all manner of work-related issues. Lani and I, in contrast, held hands and cuddled in the back of the car, quietly admiring the scenic cityscapes and idyllic country visions that breezed by our windows. Though I was undoubtedly distracted by the labyrinthine love triangle that was twisting my brain into pretzeled knots, I was able to pass it off as fatigue or boredom. Or so I thought.

When we finally arrived at Shoreline Amphitheater for the big event (several hours early, I should add), we stretched our numbed arms and legs in the crisp October afternoon. Despite our early arrival, we were nowhere near the first folks there. Before us, we saw thriving lines of ex-hippies and contemporary hipsters, flanked by nondescript human beings of every imaginable age, size, and demographic. Despite the sharp variety of worlds from which we came, we were all united together as one throbbing mass of music aficionados… none more excited than my father.

I could spend hours and hours – pages and pages – describing the extraordinary concert that we saw that day. Though more than twenty years have passed since then, I can still feel the electric buzz of that eight-hour event and all the musical magic we witnessed. I remember The Who thundering through "Pinball Wizard," Green Day galloping through "Geek Stink Breath," and Sheryl Crow revving up the crowd with "If It Makes You Happy." There were some truly tender moments, too: Eddie Vedder strumming "Elderly Woman Behind the Counter in a Small Town" while Pearl Jam swayed through the song behind him, Tom Waits crooning "Tom Traubert's Blues" to a mesmerized crowd, and Neil Young brushing his bare fingers against the strings of his Martin guitar on "Harvest Moon." It was flawless, beginning to end.

Through it all, though, I was distracted and emotionally dismembered. On one hand, I had Lani, the dream girl who had helped me evolve in immeasurable ways over the last two years… but I also felt the strange, familiar tug of Serena, my first puppy dog crush, pulling me back into the romantic recesses of my past. A sharp pain pierced my chest during Green Day's performance of "When I Come Around," and I was suddenly reminded of Serena's *quinceañera* from just a few years earlier, when I weakly warbled my way through the same song in front of an indifferent crowd.

Why was I thinking about this ghost girl from the past, the temptation of this false idol, when I had everything I needed right in front of me? The heart is a strange mechanism, and what it wants is not always what you need the most.

In the midst of this inner turmoil, just as Neil Young was humbly hammering his bronze guitar strings on "Heart of Gold," something funny happened: Lani tugged on my flannel sleeve and tilted my face towards hers.

"What's going on?" I asked, one eye angled towards the distant stage.

Lani reached into the seemingly bottomless abyss of her oversized canvas purse, her fingers filtering through jangling keys and coins and bracelets until she found what she was looking for.

She handed me a bottle of sunblock.

"What's this?" I asked.

"It's for you," she said, forcing the bottle into my pale hands. "The last thing I want is for you to get burned."

This seemingly inconsequential offering hit me hard. It was a simple action, not a grand romantic gesture, but it resonated deeply. Here I was, weighing the value of the two most attractive girls in my life… and Lani was thinking only of me.

I felt like a jerk.

"Thank you," I murmured, my voice sheepish and small.

"I'm always looking out for you, Brian," she said, smiling back at me. "Whether you know it or not." Coolly, calmly, she leaned over and kissed me on the nose.

I blushed.

As she turned back to face the stage, Lani hooked her slender arm through mine and leaned her head against my shoulder.

Hours of incredible, breathtaking music gently wafted through the afternoon air, surrounding and enveloping us in its comforting embrace. We were enraptured by Lucinda Williams, half of Smashing Pumpkins (Billy Corgan & James Iha), and Green Day – though, like I mentioned earlier, I must admit that hearing "When I Come Around" did sting a bit. And then it was time for the main attraction (for us, anyway)…

Brian Wilson.

When he first awkwardly stepped onto the stage, I was shocked to see that Brian was no longer the goofy, sun-kissed young man of the 1960s that I had always envisioned. His once strawberry-blonde hair had faded to salt-and-pepper gray; even more jarring was the fact that he seemed to have so little affect, his hands stationary on the keyboard like lifeless paperweights, his face seemingly paralyzed, and his crooked mouth only emitting sound from one side of his curled lips.

Lani turned to me after his quiet, nervous introduction. "Did he… did he have a stroke?" she asked, echoing my own thoughts.

My dad leaned over to us, his awestruck smile casting a soft glow over the pallor of the struggling figure onstage. "I don't think it's a stroke," he dutifully informed us, his eyes never averting from the stage. "I'm pretty sure it's a drug-induced paralysis thing. If I remember correctly, it's some kind of palsy, from when he was overmedicated by Dr. Landy in the 1980s."

"Oh," Lani and I muttered in unison.

What a heartbreaking world we live in, I thought to myself, *when the heroes of our youth grow old and wilt before our very eyes.*

During the first few notes of Brian's opening song, "California Girls," that swirling, twirling strain of classical melody that defied simple surfer soundtracks, the audience erupted into wild applause. Clearly, despite his frailty, Brian Wilson was a beloved figure that night. For all his flaws and all his weaknesses, Brian was being embraced for the beauty that he had created over the course of his tragic lifetime.

What was it like watching a Brian Wilson show in 1999? Imagine, if you will, going to see Michelangelo's statue of David. Perhaps, as a child, you saw the sculpture and marveled at its perfection, the sheer smoothness of its slopes and the flawlessness of its features. In this state, the statue never ages, never shows the assault of wrinkles and lines and weight that accompany the accumulation of years.

The *Pet Sounds* album is the statue of David.

Brian Wilson is Michelangelo.

While that magical set of recordings he made in 1966 indisputably stands the test of time, defying the inevitable burdens of decline during the intervening decades, Brian Wilson grew up and grew old. His voice was not the soaring, goosebump-inducing instrument it used to be. Instead, his voice, like his deteriorating frame, seemed weighed down by the insurmountable gravity of his past and the enormity of his legacy.

Remember *Weekend at Bernie's*, that ridiculous 1980s movie? The one with the young dudes propping up the corpse of the title character and maneuvering him through a series of farfetched adventures? Seeing the Brian Wilson band was a little bit like watching the musical version of *Weekend at Bernie's*: Brian was a stiff figure, fighting against the forces of rigor mortis, and his remarkable band carried him through song after glorious song that night. It might sound cruel, but I mean it in the most loving way possible.

Anyone expecting a note-for-note recreation of those classic 1960s Beach Boys hits with a 23-year-old Brian in the spotlight was bound to be disappointed. Sadly, Brian's once-angelic voice had fermented into something more earthly and mortal. Whereas his vocals once evoked a heavenly aching, they now crumbled with a tender humanity.

And yet, there's something ennobling in that imperfection.

For Brian Wilson, the mere act of standing onstage (literally and figuratively) took a tremendous amount of effort, a level of bravery that few of us can understand. Between his stage fright, depression, schizoaffective disorder, and complicated history with performing, it's a miracle that Brian even made it onto the stage at all. To criticize that bravery would be a heartless act, one taking for granted the many years of suffering that the eldest Wilson brother faced.

I realize that, objectively, Brian's set that evening was nowhere near his mythical 1960s heyday. His arching, aching falsetto was long gone, destroyed by years of mistreatment and neglect. Yet, despite his imperfections, there was something noble – and ennobling – about Brian's trembling voice reaching for the rafters, lovingly lurching forward into the night sky.

It was a strange paradox: a fragile man creating gorgeous music, surrounded by a fleet of polished musicians. To be perfectly honest, it wasn't a flawless experience. At times, Brian's weaknesses and flubbed notes (including some botched lyrics during "Surfer Girl") were hard to watch; and, since Brian was the only Beach Boy onstage that evening, the set threatened to plunge at times into karaoke parody. Even with the shimmering acoustic guitars and clever keyboards that artfully imitated soulful sounds from decades past, the show still felt like an unfinished jigsaw puzzle — and the absent Beach Boys were the missing pieces that Brian needed to complete his vision. It was awkward and imperfect and incomplete.

And yet...

Regardless of the faults and flaws that might have distracted a casual listener, there was something incredibly moving about seeing Brian Wilson back onstage. Here was a man who had survived truly hellish experiences and emerged from the pain scarred – but still determined to keep fighting. Not to sound pretentious or melodramatic, but it occurred to me that night that the arc of Brian's life was not unlike Joseph Campbell's *hero's journey*: the protagonist proceeds forth on a rock and roll adventure, passing into the threshold of artistic and financial stardom, before plunging into the abyss of despair and transforming into a resurrected version of himself.

It was also an arc that my own life would imitate within just a matter of months...

But I digress.

During Brian's performance, my father sat with rapt attention, hanging on every last word, syllable, and utterance that the beloved singer made onstage. As Brian worked his way through Beach Boys highlights from the 1960s and underrated gems from the 1970s, as well as solo songs from the 1980s and 1990s, we knew we were witnessing something special – imperfect, of course, but special, nonetheless. After a rousing rendition of "Good Vibrations," which seemed like a surefire closing number, Brian chose to quiet things down for one final tune.

The last song Brian played that night was "Love & Mercy" from his self-titled 1988 record. Whereas the original recording on the *Brian Wilson* album is a heavily produced, synth-saturated track, the version he performed that crisp October night was a tender, understated prayer. The instrumentation for this arrangement was nothing more than Brian, a piano, and a choir of angelic voices…

It was magical.

For the three minutes that Brian and his band played the song, you could hear a pin drop. Even with more than twenty thousand people at the sold-out venue, there was a deafening silence from the crowd.

I will never forget that moment in time. While Brian played, I sat transfixed. The world simply stood still, and one of the most remarkable musical moments I have ever witnessed flowed around us like an ocean of comfort and healing. Unlike his performance during the evening's earlier songs, Brian's voice didn't seem shell-shocked or broken; rather it was a delicate murmur, a signifier of his suffering and a reminder that recovery – for even the most damaged of souls – is possible. It was a simple song with a simple message, but it transcended time and space to connect with twenty thousand people on one cold autumn evening. While there was sadness in his voice, a melancholy weight wrought from years of emotional scar tissue, there was something else.

Hope.

The Pandora's Box of Brian's soul might have been opened decades before, but the crowd that night was witnessing the hope that remained behind – hope that outlasted even the most profoundly horrific torment and suffering.

I won't lie. I felt a lump in my throat, a sting in the corners of my eyes, and a chill down my spine. I'm not too proud to admit that I got choked up watching an aging rock star play a quiet ballad at an oversized amphitheater. In fact, I've never felt more moved by a piece of music than I did that night. And I wasn't alone, either. As Brian played, I glanced around the crowd and saw hundreds of faces mesmerized by his performance. With every trembling finger he placed on his piano and every wavering note that left his lips, Brian became more and more human to us – a mere mortal delivering a prayer for peace.

While I could try to describe that tear-jerking performance with a litany of adjectives, there is nothing I could say here that would do it justice. In this restrained rendition, "Love & Mercy" was a plea, a prayer – a valediction and convocation. It was a sweet, sincere song, searching for a simple sentiment of understanding amid the chaos and confusion of a mixed-up world.

During the last thirty seconds of "Love & Mercy," just as Brian seemed to have finished his fragile message, his backing band swooped in like a troop of angels trumpeting wordless vocal refrains. When people have religious experiences in church – when they see and feel the presence of God in every refracted ray of light – I assume it must feel something like the sense of clarity, heartbreak, and transcendence that I experienced while watching Brian Wilson sing "Love & Mercy" that cold autumn evening.

And then it was over. Brian stood up from his piano, thanked the crowd, and awkwardly shuffled offstage. When he exited, the applause was deafening, the crowd fervently thanking the former Beach Boy for his divine, otherworldly performance.

Through the clapping, my dad turned to me with glistening eyes and a broad smile. "That's the song," he said, "you want someone to play at your funeral."

He didn't know just how right he was.

CHAPTER FORTY-SEVEN

"Meant for You"

That night, I couldn't sleep.

There was a lot to think about – my first time seeing Brian Wilson live, my flourishing relationship with Lani, the tormented love triangle with Serena, the general awkwardness of growing up – and my brain felt like a conflagration of confusion. Seeing stripped-down performances of those old, venerated Beach Boys songs (which normally required ornate orchestration) reminded me of my dad's old mantra: "*Any song worth its salt needs to sound complete with just an acoustic guitar and a voice.*" I never envisioned the piano-playing Brian Wilson writing his songs on an acoustic guitar, but it seemed possible, even *plausible*, that he might have composed a few songs late at night, locked in his room with just a Martin D-21 guitar.

While almost everyone left the Bridge School Benefit Concert that night reminiscing about the reunited version of The Who that closed out the evening, my father and I were still perseverating on Brian Wilson's performance. Hurriedly walking back to the parking lot in the frigid, goose-bump-inducing cold, my father and I prattled on and on about the musical magic we had witnessed; meanwhile, my mom, Lani, Marina, and Reggie just exchanged pained looks that seemed to say *these boys are so ridiculous.*

We didn't care, though. We were riding high on the crest of the musical surf, and nothing – *nothing* – could knock us off that wave.

By the time that we arrived at Marina's house in San Rafael after an hour-long drive, everyone seemed exhausted and ready to pass out.

Everyone, of course, except me.

Save for the thrumming pulse of the heater, the house was eerily quiet that night, even though there were more than half a dozen snoring bodies scattered throughout the rented rambler-style ranch house that Marina and Reggie called home. My sister and her boyfriend, both of whom were making excellent money working for a Bay Area tech startup company, had lucked their way into renting a beautiful, expansive – but relatively inexpensive – 1950s rambler situated off Lucas Valley Road in San Rafael. Fortunately for *us*, the house was perfect for a gaggle of visiting guests. Lani and my parents each had rooms to themselves, while I was able to snag the rather posh sofa that adorned the north wall of the meticulously decorated living room.

As I tossed and turned on the flawless fabric of the upholstered couch that night, something caught my eye: Marina's acoustic guitar. And, though it was the middle of the night, I quietly crept across the lacquered wooden floor to the expensive-looking Martin HD-35 guitar that hung decoratively in the living room. When I first lifted the guitar from its holster on the pure, eggshell-colored wall, I was self-conscious about strumming a borrowed guitar in the middle of the night. But, as the flickering analog clock on the wall reminded me, 3:00 AM was an awkward time to be awake.

Screw it, I thought. *What else am I going to do at this hour?*

Intuitively, I ran my fingers along the dusty strings of the Martin. Clearly, based on the musty layers of film that had accumulated on the fretboard, the instrument had not been played anytime recently. After flipping the guitar on its back and softly tracing the lines where the Rosewood merged into the Sitka Spruce top, I turned it right-side up and tucked it delicately under my arm. There, in the safety of Marina's living room, with the loud vibrations of the heater muffling my indiscriminate sounds, I huddled in the far corner, facing away from the bedrooms, and started strumming.

At first, it wasn't anything fancy or unique. I just softly strummed a shuffling beat on a *D* chord with my bare fingers muting the humble sounds that emanated from the guitar strings – something vaguely along the lines of "Help Me, Rhonda" or "Little Saint Nick." As I played, I tried to envision warm California days and the hazy summer afternoons evoked by the best Beach Boys songs. And yet, I couldn't escape the fact that my own life had never been so clean or dreamy as those nostalgic 1960s recordings.

California hadn't been kind to me as a child or a teenager. It had been taunting and tantalizing, but never sweet. It had been vicious. It had been hurtful.

It had been cruel.

And the first line of a new song – which seemed to emerge fully formed from the head of Zeus, miraculously harnessed from the ether – appeared on my lips.

"California can be cruel in the summer…"

I stopped cold. The line gave me chills. I thought about the hard alliteration of the first few words and this twisted take on the tropes of the California dream. It was almost perverse, toying with the Beach Boys' motifs like that, but starting a song by inverting a listener's expectations – sort of like the lyricist Tony Asher had done with the first line of "God Only Knows" – thrilled me.

California hasn't been kind, I thought to myself through the hazy fog of my sleep-deprived mind. *It's been* cruel. *And I can't be the only one who has ever felt this way.*

The seed was planted.

I remembered high school, that traumatic trial of my life in which I felt like a sailor endlessly adrift on the open seas. I thought back to Serena and those cold, isolated days of my teenage years, when I felt so lost and confused and alone.

Like that fateful summer day on the beach, when Serena had quelled whatever nascent chemistry had been developing between us… When, under the deceiving cover of a gray sky, my skin had been scorched by the seemingly absent sun – just like my fragile teenage heart had been burned by Serena. And yet, for as consumed as I felt, Serena had seemed to emerge unscathed, not a single singed scar on her flawless skin.

Girls will give you sunburns with a grin, I thought.

Nothing about that summer afternoon with Serena half a decade earlier had been remotely close to a frivolous California love song. In my case, California *wasn't* always a golden land of freedom and opportunity; instead, it was a gloomy coastline full of false promises. Those gorgeous California girls – like Serena – could just as easily scald you as warm your heart.

I learned that the hard way.

"The girls will give you sunburns with a grin," I sang to myself. Under the cover of a forebodingly gray summer day, Serena left me cold and aching for light.

And the gray skies can be colder than December, I thought to myself. *When all you want is sunshine on your skin.*

The first verse was complete.

For as effortlessly as the first verse had come to me, though, the chorus seemed maddeningly just out of reach. It would have been easy to mount the guitar back on the wall and place my weary head on a borrowed pillow, but something pushed me on despite my fatigue. I took the melody, which was rooted in a *D* chord, and moved the chorus to a *G*, emulating that familiar *I-IV* chord progression so commonly heard in folk songs – like the ones that my dad and I played in the garage when I was still living at home. As I experimented with chord progressions, toying with guitar scales, I hummed an escalating series of notes to myself, the melody slowly taking shape from the late-night fog of inspiration.

I droned a wordless refrain of *"Ba-da-bum-bum-bum"* over and over, dozens of times, desperately wracking my sleep-deprived brain for something that could carry the song forward with the momentum of a rushing river. The opening lines had conjured a paradoxical place of cold sunburns, that simultaneous exultation of passion and despair…

But what had saved me? What had lifted me from the darkness of depression to perpetual paradise?

The Beautiful Girl from Heaven.

Lani.

If Serena had been the cold summer sands shrouded by the overcast sky, Lani was the sweeping tide edging me past the safety of the shore into the powerful ocean. I had been lost – lost in a world of self-pity and isolation and meaningless pop punk music.

For so long, I had been *incomplete…*

Lani – that *Beautiful Girl from Heaven* – had completed me.

But there was more to it than that. In my own way, I had completed her, too. The incomplete half-smile that had haunted Lani during our freshman year at UCLA had faded over the last fifteen months that we'd spent together.

Together, we were something more than the sum of our parts.

Together, we were *complete.*

I grabbed a chewed-up pencil that had been lying on the coffee table next to me and desperately searched for a scrap of paper on which to write. *My kingdom for a scrap of paper,* I thought to myself. Marina had an old copy of *Rolling Stone* sitting on the tabletop, so I flipped through its tattered pages until I found enough space to scribble notes. Frantically, I scrawled words onto the margins of the magazine, composing lines and crossing off phrases until I had something resembling a chorus.

> *I get lost sometimes in the melodies of my mind,*
> *Where I've tried to find what I need.*
> *But the crashing tide has swept me off my feet,*
> *And left me incomplete for a while…*
> *And it's just like your smile.*

Lani had completed me – had quieted the distracting melodies in my mind – and helped me to stand on my own two feet. She *believed* in me, and that belief had transformed me into someone new, a man whose weariness had been washed away in the waves.

But I wasn't a simple romantic parasite. Lani and I had a spiritual symbiosis, supporting each other and building a towering infrastructure that achingly reached towards the heavens above us. I might have been a *Brick*, but Lani was mortar – binding and sealing and stabilizing everything around us. Though we weren't perfect, we were perfect for each other. And that's all that mattered to me.

It looked like I had made my choice, after all.

In the bizarre *Archie-Betty-Veronica* love triangle that was my life at that critical crossroads, I had made my decision.

I had chosen Lani over Serena.

And I would never look back.

Though I had started by writing about the cruelty of adolescent heartbreak, this new song was turning into something else: a tribute to the comfort and completion that I had found in Lani's arms. It wasn't a requiem for an unrequited desire or a lament for a lost love; it was a song reveling in the revelation of romance.

And, as I progressed through the writing of the song that night, I realized that I wanted the lyrics to show what Lani meant to me, how she had saved me from a life of sadness and boredom and loneliness.

I thought back to our first kiss, that night in the parking lot of the fairgrounds. Though more than a year had passed, I could still feel the warmth of her lips and the music of her voice on that dreamlike summer evening. As my aching eyes blurred in the late-night chill, I knew that I had to put her *in* the song, to place her as a character in the lyrical narrative.

Serendipitously enough, there was a common thread that linked my past, present, and future: The Beach Boys. This was, after all, the night of the Brian Wilson concert, and it seemed an uncanny coincidence that *Pet Sounds* had been the soundtrack for our first kiss the summer before. Of course, considering how much Brian's music had served as the soundtrack of my childhood and adolescent life, the statistical probability was pretty high... *But still.*

So, I wrote about it, taking those autobiographical threads and weaving it all into the tapestry of the song, inadvertently making my life as transparent as an insect trapped in amber.

> *"Pet Sounds" was playing in my Mustang*
> *On the night we shared our first kiss.*
> *Suddenly, I didn't feel so lonely:*
> *I found salvation when I touched your lips.*

Yes, I *do* realize how melodramatic that last line sounds. In fact, I'm confident that a part of me recognized it then. Even at that time in my life, when I was barely twenty years old, I understood that *salvation* was a loaded word, ripe with hyperbolic religious connotation. Regardless, the love that Lani had shared with me *felt* like salvation. The *Beautiful Girl from Heaven*, imperfect as she might have been, was the only girl with whom I could imagine spending the rest of my life.

I had two verses and a chorus, so the only thing left to do was to compose a bridge. I was almost done with the song.

I thought about watching the fireworks that August night, the sheer thrill of wrapping my arms around Lani for the first time, the way that everything felt so blazingly raw and sweetly innocent. The ghosts of the past seemed to be exorcised for those precious hours together, banished to a far-off shore from which their voices only faintly echoed. And, though Lani and I had to say *"goodnight"* like the lovers in "Wouldn't It Be Nice," it didn't feel like the end of something. It felt like the beginning.

> *As specters sang from faraway horizons,*
> *Fireworks exploded in the sky.*
> *We watched it all from underneath the pier,*
> *Before we had to leave and say goodnight.*

And it was done.

I glanced up at the clock, my eyelids stinging and sore. *5:00 AM,* the clock read. The denizens and guests of the house wouldn't be stirring for another hour or so. Quietly, I snuck through the dim living room into the shadowy kitchen and grabbed the cordless telephone from its station on the wall. Tiptoeing back through the house, I knew I had one last thing to do: preserve the song through a makeshift recording, lest I fall asleep and forget the whole darn thing.

Fumbling through the fog of my sleep-deprived state, I dialed our Ojai phone number, knowing perfectly well that no one would be home to answer the late-night/early-morning phone call. After the static staccato voice on the answering machine finished warbling, I heard that familiar, elongated beep beckoning me to leave a message.

Like a runner at the starting line, I immediately dashed into the song. For three and a half sleepy minutes, I strummed and sang my way through this brand-new tune. My voice was quietly craggy and my strumming was shamelessly shaggy, but it didn't matter. It was all for posterity's sake, anyway. I didn't think anyone would ever hear this late-night makeshift work tape. I just needed to capture the song before it disappeared forever.

When it was all done, I hung up the phone, mounted Marina's guitar on the wall, and crawled over to the couch. I closed my eyes and slept the slumber of the dead.

I had almost forgotten about the song entirely when I woke up, sleep-deprived, three hours later. Lani was slowly shaking me awake, an oversized mug of coffee cupped between her thin, graceful fingers.

"Wake up, Sleeping Beauty," she whispered in a singsong voice.

She held out her hands, inviting me to take the steaming coffee mug from her. The fluid inside was a creamy beige-colored concoction, and it smelled like cinnamon.

Lani must have noticed me half-dazedly gazing into the drink. "Your dad doused it with creamer and sugar and spices," she explained. "He said something cryptic about life and coffee…"

"'*Life's too short to drink your coffee black*,'" I murmured back. "Yeah, I've heard that one a few times before."

I sipped from the steaming porcelain mug.

My dad was right. The coffee, like my life at that precious moment, was delicious.

Though it was Halloween, we encountered no ghosts or goblins on the long drive home. The closest thing to a movie monster was me: a sleep-deprived zombie. Exhausted from my long night, I felt dizzy and delirious – but also grateful for all the gifts in my life.

Like the *Beautiful Girl from Heaven* who sat by my side.

By the time that we pulled into our place on Lago de Paz Court back home in Ojai, I had spent hours humming my intoxicating new melody from the night before.

"What's that song?" Lani had asked, her coruscant brown eyes reflecting the twilight haze of the setting sun. "It's catchy."

"*That,*" I told her, yawning away my exhaustion and threading my fingers through hers, "is the song that's going to change my life. That's going to change *our* lives."

Of course, as we shuffled off our baggage in the living room of our Ojai home, I wasn't thinking about money or fame or major label contracts.

I was thinking about the woman who had saved my life, the raven-haired girl across the hall who had given me the strength and confidence to make something of myself.

Lani.

Noticing the frantically flickering light on our answering machine, my mom drowsily strolled over to the kitchen and pushed the big silver button on its surface. A mechanical voice informed us that we had one new message. Through the tiny, tinny speakers of the answering machine, I heard a crackling analog fuzz and the distorted strumming of a guitar emanating forth into our empty living room.

The four of us – Mom, Dad, Lani, and I – stopped and listened to the song.

California can be cruel in the summer –
The girls will give you sunburns with a grin.
And the gray skies can be colder than December
When all you want is sunshine on your skin.

I get lost sometimes in the melodies of my mind,
Where I've tried to find what I need.
But the crashing tide has swept me off my feet,
And left me incomplete for a while…
And it's just like your smile.

"Pet Sounds" was playing in my Mustang
On the night we shared our first kiss.
Suddenly, I didn't feel so lonely:
I found salvation when I touched your lips.

I get lost sometimes in the melodies of my mind,
Where I've tried to find what I need.
But the crashing tide has swept me off my feet,
And left me incomplete for a while…
And it's just like your smile.

As specters sang from faraway horizons,
Fireworks exploded in the sky.
We watched it all from underneath the pier,
Before we had to leave and say goodnight.

I get lost sometimes in the melodies of my mind,
Where I've tried to find what I need.
But the crashing tide has swept me off my feet,
And left me incomplete for a while…
And it's just like your smile.

I got lost sometimes in the melodies of my mind,
Where I tried to find what I need.
And the crashing tide swept me off my feet,
But you've made me feel complete now for a while,
And it's just like your smile.

When it was over, and the last seconds of static faded from the speakers of our answering machine, a hush fell over the room like a muted magic incantation. No one moved or said anything. Instead, we just stood there, breathing in the musical aroma of what we'd all just heard.

My dad was the first one to break the spell.

"That was incredible," he muttered, more to himself than to me. He turned in my direction, his jaw gaping open. "And *you* wrote that?"

I sheepishly and sleepily nodded.

My father just about lunged for me, grabbing my shoulders with his big bearlike hands. "*That* is the song, Junior. *THAT. IS. THE. SONG.*"

From her vantage point in the kitchen, my mom beamed. "That was *really* impressive, Rick," she said. She shivered and rubbed her arms up and down, her fingers tracing the goosebumps that seemed to appear out of nowhere. "I am *really* proud of you." She walked over to me and pulled me into a gentle embrace.

From over my mom's slender, sun-damaged shoulders, I could see Lani grinning widely, her scrunched-up eyes twinkling. "I love you," she mouthed silently to me.

"I love you, too," I whispered back.

Life was just about perfect.

For now.

It might sound utterly unbelievable to say that – at the ripe old age of twenty – I wrote what would later become a hit song. However, it's much less impressive when you consider the fact that Brian Wilson had two complete albums released (including six hit singles) before he could legally drink alcohol. Brian was barely 20 years old when Capitol Records released *Surfin' Safari* in October of 1962, and the record label released *Surfin' U.S.A.* only five months later. Even more mind-blowing is Brian's claim that his very *first* original song was "Surfer Girl" – a song he conjured from nothingness when he was still a high school student.

That's right. Brian Wilson composed one of his masterpieces, one of the best songs of the entire decade – nay, the *century* – when he was just a teenager.

By that grading scale, I was barely scraping by with passing marks.

However, the fact that this brand-new song, later titled "Incomplete (Just Like Your Smile)," poured out of me so quickly was a big surprise – even to me. Sure, I'd written dozens and dozens of songs by that point, but it was often a stressful endeavor, complete with hair-tugging, frustration, and endless rewrites. In sharp contrast, writing "Incomplete" felt almost effortless, like I was channeling the vision of an already completed sculpture rather than trying to mold a statue from wet clay.

It reminds me of that afternoon years ago, as my father and I stood before the mirror in our Ojai home, the old man teaching me how to tie a necktie.

It didn't take me just ten seconds to tie this necktie, he had told me. *It took me decades of practice to be able to tie this piece of fabric in only ten seconds.*

Just like the old folktale about the emperor's portrait that my father had retold to me that afternoon, what people *don't* see is the time and effort that preceded the creation of this song.

It didn't take me just two hours to write "Incomplete." It took me twenty years of life and fourteen years of playing in a band and six years of writing songs to be able to compose "Incomplete" in just two hours.

When you look at it that way, it doesn't seem all that improbable, does it?

I should add one more important detail – a *dénouement* for the scene, if you will. Later that evening, an hour or two after we listened to the static-filled rendition of "Incomplete" on my parents' answering machine, I walked Lani out to her truck. It was a brisk Halloween night, and light precipitation drizzled from the heavens like tender weeping from the angels.

"What a whirlwind of a weekend," Lani sighed, popping open the passenger-side door of her Nissan pickup truck.

I handed her the suitcase she had packed for our trip to Northern California, and Lani meticulously tucked it into the passenger seat. She lovingly arranged the luggage on the faded leather cushions, even pulling a frizzy seatbelt across to lock it snugly in place.

"But at least I got to spend it with you," I said. I smiled and swayed in my spot, my hands plummeting deeply into the front pockets of my fraying jeans.

She gently closed her passenger-side door and turned back to me, a mischievous smirk creeping across her lips.

"So…" she began, draping her arms over my shoulders. "Who is the girl in the song?"

I stared at her for a second, my eyebrows raised and lips pursed.

"I thought that it was pretty clear," I said.

Lani pulled away, lowering her arms and hooking her thumbs in the belt loops of her jeans as she swayed deferentially in place. "*Well…*" she murmured. "I just want to hear you say it out loud."

I reached out and placed a finger delicately below her chin, tilting her face towards mine.

"It's you, Lani," I told her. "It's always been you."

Her eyes welled up a little bit. If I'm being honest, so did mine.

Lani wrapped her fingers around my wrist, stood up on her tippy-toes, and leaned in towards me. She quickly pecked me on the lips and then let the weight of her body melt into my own, resting her head against my chest as she planted her feet back on terra firma.

"I was just thinking…" I started to say, my cheek resting placidly against the top of her head.

"About what?" she asked, her voice a soft, purring murmur.

"Your middle name. *Mele'kauwela* …"

"What about it?"

I kept my eyes trained on the constellations above us. "The first part, *Mele*… It's the Hawaiian word for 'song,' right?"

"That's right," she said softly, brushing a rogue strand of hair from her cheek.

"Well," I said sleepily, "I just thought…"

"Thought *what*…?"

"*You* are the girl in the song," I told her. "*You* are my *mele*."

Lani pulled her head back from my chest and looked up at me. "Oh, God. You're not going to start calling me *Mele* are you?" She raised her eyebrows skeptically. "That's what my *dad* calls me."

"I was thinking about it," I told her with a sheepish shrug. "Is that weird?"

"*Ugh*," she groaned, rolling her glistening brown eyes. "Yes, it's weird."

In my sluggish state, I pressed on gently. "What about something shorter?" I asked.

"Shorter than *Mele*…? You can't get much more concise than two syllables, Brian."

I half-closed my tired eyes. "What about *Mel*…?" I suggested.

"That makes me sound like a *haole*," she whined. "I don't know…"

"It's got a nice ring to it," I reassured her.

"I'll think about it," she sighed complacently. "But I make no promises."

A smile crept across my lethargic lips. "It'll grow on you," I said. "Trust me."

"I guess we'll just have to wait and see," she grumbled, scrunching up her nose with a wincing wink of her eyes.

"Just consider it shorthand for the *Beautiful Girl from Heaven*," I told her.

"Well, when you put it like *that*," she assented with an impish grin and a theatrical roll of her chestnut-brown eyes, "I guess I can cut you some slack."

And that is how *Noelani* who is *Lani* became *Mele* who is *Mel*.

We swayed there in the mild moonlight for a few precious minutes, calmly content together in the cool California night. It was everything I had ever wanted. After so many years of longing – of feeling incomplete – the arc of my amorous life had reached its apex.

With Lani's arms wrapped around me like a comforting cocoon, everything in the world seemed just about perfect. Every breath, every sigh was a delicate reminder of how far my life had come since those lonely days of my childhood. I wanted that moment to last forever, to remain engraved in the channels of my memory like the etched grooves of a vinyl record.

But it was getting late.

After one particularly ostentatious yawn, Lani straightened up and propped her chin against my chest. "You know, *salvation* is a pretty loaded word, Mr. Rock Star," she grinned. "That's a lot of responsibility for a simple little island girl from Maui."

"It might be loaded," I said softly, "but that doesn't make it any less true. You saved me. And I'm in this for the long haul. Salvation implies eternity."

"Eternity is a long time," she said with a smirk, pulling me closer to her.

"Is that too long of a time for you?" I asked.

"If it means that I get to spend it with you," she said, pressing her lips against mine, "count me in."

If you want a girl to like you, write her a song.
If you want her to love you, write her a great song.
If you want a girl to *marry* you, write her a hit single.
It worked for me.

CHAPTER FORTY-EIGHT
"Getting Hungry"

The next Saturday, Call Field reconvened in my parents' garage. It was an unassuming autumn afternoon, the forgettable kind of November day that could have easily been wasted away with frivolous shopping or napping or reading.

Instead, Call Field gathered together to hear "Incomplete" for the first time.

When I initially ran through the song for my bandmates, I felt a weird sense of déjà vu. It reminded me of the summer before our sophomore year of high school, when Steve had just joined the band and I played them "Time Bomb" for the first time. I had written *that* song for Serena, the girl who had broken my heart and chosen the lead singer/football star over the humble, nerdy bass player.

Half a decade later, here we were, gathered together again in the same modest suburban garage, reenacting the ritual of learning a new song. This time, though, it was a different song for a different girl. And it would have a *very* different outcome.

From the opening riff, I could tell that Chunk and Ethan were smitten with the tune. The vintage shuffling rock-and-roll rhythm must have resonated with them; perhaps it was all the Beatles and Beach Boys tunes that we had studied over the years, all the way back to that middle school band class in which the Bookhouse Boys first met. The excitement that I saw growing in Chunk and Ethan was palpable; it almost seemed ready to manifest in a twinkling haze of corporeal magic before our eyes.

In sharp contrast, Steve simply leaned against the wall, skeptically examining me with half-closed eyes. Our lead singer just stood there, emulating James Dean with his tight shirt, cuffed jeans, and emotionless face. When the song finished, he sighed condescendingly and thrust his hands into his back pockets, his chest protruding proudly before him.

"I don't think it's the song that's going to break us through to the major labels," he finally muttered, bitterness curling from his lips like cigarette smoke.

His reaction was so far removed from that of Ethan and Chunk (and Lani and my parents, for that matter), I couldn't help but feel shocked. However, whereas the *old* me would have sheepishly bowed to Steve's opinion, the *new* me took an alternate route. I was angry. My musical masterpiece – which I *knew* was really good, damn it – had been dismissively forsaken by our cocky lead singer.

"You don't have to *like* it," I sneered at him. "You just have to *sing* it."

A darkness fell over his face, a scowl that I would come to know all too well in the next year. We were at a stalemate in this pissing contest of a working relationship, but I refused to budge. Steve stared me down with a glacial expression in his crystal blue eyes.

"Fine," he said. "I've got a notebook full of better ideas, but I suppose we can make time for this little... *trifle*." His eyes were thorny and piercing, but my skin was as thick as concrete that afternoon. "Let's just record it and move on to something better," he added.

We spent a few hours learning the song that afternoon, as I channeled my inner Brian Wilson and led the boys through the riffs and fills and refrains that I had envisioned. After so many years of playing together, the pieces of the puzzle came together rather easily – even our skeptical singer managed to digest the melody and replicate it within a matter of minutes. Once we had the song down, we set up our equipment, positioned ourselves in front of the microphones, and hit record.

And we played the hell out of it.

By the time that we finished a rough mix, burned the song to a CD, wrote an explanatory note to Derek, and placed it all in the custody of the United States Postal Service, a few days had elapsed. We figured it would be a week or two before we heard back from Derek with his usual rejection e-mail. So, when we were mid-practice the following weekend, we were surprised to see my mom urgently rushing into the garage.

"You need to stop!" she yelled at us. "Right now! You've got a phone call from Derek Schneider, and he says he needs to speak with you. *Immediately.*"

Almost comically, we looked at each other, threw our instruments to the ground, and ran to the cordless phone cradled in my mother's hands. Steve surreptitiously snagged the receiver from my mom and raised it up to his ear.

"Hey, Derek," he cooed casually into the phone. "What's happening?"

Steve nodded his head, listening to Derek's voice chiming through the other end of the telephone. Intermittently, we heard louder expressions surging through the receiver's speaker, while Steve's eyes grew wider and wider.

"Okay," Steve whispered into the phone. "We'll get back to you soon. Thanks, Derek."

Steve, looking like he'd been slapped in the face by an angry girlfriend, turned to us. He didn't say anything.

"*Well...?*" Chunk asked, his voice a barely restrained yelp.

"That was Derek..." Steve said, gazing off into the distance, refusing to make eye contact with any of us.

"We know that!" Ethan interrupted. "What did he *say?*"

Steve's eyes trailed up to our faces, a grin gradually creeping across his lips.

"He loved the song," Steve told us, his smile widening exponentially. "And his label wants to sign us."

And that's how my love letter to Lani led Call Field to a major-label recording contract.

It was the beginning of the end of my childhood.

I could never have predicted what would happen next – or the darkness that lay in store for us.

SOLO

CHAPTER FORTY-NINE

"From There to Back Again"

I glanced up at the clock. The second-hand continued to sail smoothly in a circle, circumnavigating the face of the timepiece, but hours had passed since I'd first arrived on the doorstep of the Jones family. During that time, I'd laid bare the most sensitive details of my childhood – the fractured pieces of myself that only my family knew. Like it or not, Veronica Jones had schemed herself into that tight circle of confidantes. Though no deep, dark, dirty secrets had been revealed – *yet* – I still felt like a walking open wound, a throbbing gash of emotion that threatened to stain everything around me.

"I'm afraid, Veronica, that we'll have to stop here for the night," I told her. "It's getting late, and I've got my wife and daughter waiting for me at home."

Veronica's jaw dropped to the floor. "Wait, wait, wait… You can't end on a cliffhanger like that!" she commanded, throwing her hands in the air like a traffic cop. "That's not the end of the story, right?"

I turned my attention to the darkening sky that loomed through the panoramic windows of the Jones family's living room. The foreboding clouds that formed in the distance threatened rain, and little droplets were already appearing on the patio outside.

"It is for now," I told her.

Veronica's normally calm composure gave way to a distressed determination, her flustered face reflecting her frustration.

"But there's so much you haven't told me yet," she said with a surreptitious scowl, her eyes darting around to see if her parents were within earshot. "What happened next? Why did the band break up? When did you and Mel get married? What happened with Steve and Serena? And your big album? How did you go from all of that to *teaching high school English?* You didn't answer *any* of those questions…"

I let out an exasperated chuckle, an honest admission of my exhaustion. Stretching my arms heavenward, I yawned and felt the muscles in my chest tensing up. "Those are a *lot* of questions, Veronica," I told her. "And the answers would take a few more hours to explain."

"But I didn't get to hear the full story!" she protested, eyes ablaze.

"This was the story of a *song*, Veronica. And you *did* get the narrative that you needed for your assignment, right? You now know how I wrote a one-hit-wonder pop song and made a few extra dollars for a few years. That should be sufficient for your Economics teacher."

I was hoping, praying that Veronica would act out of character and just let it go.

Of course, she didn't.

"Yeah, yeah, sure," Veronica said, frantically fiddling with her fingers. "But I want to hear about the *good* stuff. Clearly, something happened that altered the trajectory of your life."

"You're right," I admitted. "But *that*, kiddo, is a story for another day."

Before Veronica could protest any further, I stood up from the dining room table, and smoothed out the wrinkles on my plaid shirt.

"Thank you for taking an interest in my personal life, Veronica," I said resolutely, extending my hand out towards her. She begrudgingly took it and gave me a terse handshake, creasing her eyes into bitter slits.

"We're not done yet, Mr. Smith," she told me. "I'll get the truth out of you somehow."

I stepped towards the door, my shoes echoing on the tile floor, but I turned back to face Veronica one last time. "We'll see about that," I told her. "But, like I said, we'll have to save the rest of the story for another day." And with that final dismissal, I made my way through the portal of the past into the cool, dark night – gently caressing the door behind me as I passed through.

Right foot. Left foot.

Right foot. Left foot.

Repeat until the story's over.

Veronica trailed me with her eyes while I walked down the cobbled pathway towards the sidewalk. As I stepped towards the silent street where my car was parked, I turned back to her and waved a curt goodbye. I ambled forward, further away from her porch, and turned my attention to the firmament overhead. Behind me, I heard Veronica close the front door, but the distraction couldn't deter me from staring up at the sky above.

I flipped my collar up against the bitter chill of the shoreline's cutting wind and plunged my fingers deep into my pockets. The saturated clouds above me appeared ready to burst at any second, threatening a deluge of biblical proportions. And yet, for all the bleak blackness that surrounded me, I looked up and saw the illuminating shape of the moon – that singular, solitary figure that hovered high above the horizon – lingering like a trapeze artist on an invisible tightrope.

We are all darkness and light, I thought. *Storm clouds of grief and moonlight aching overhead.*

Veronica was right: my story was far from over.

But I wasn't ready to talk about it yet.

I wasn't ready to climb above the clouds and claim my rightful place beyond the tempest.

I wasn't ready.

Though I would be…

Soon.

When I was a kid, my parents used to have a *Matryoshka* – a Russian nesting doll – placed casually on the mantel above our fireplace. It was a family heirloom, an artifact of my ancestors' times in Europe before they made the long, perilous voyage overseas to America. Though faded and chipped from decades of wear and tear as it matriculated through generations of the Smith family, the *Matryoshka's* labyrinthine layers of shells remained intact. I used to run my fingers along the splintering edges of each shell, marveling at how one piece fit inside the next; it seemed almost preordained by some higher power that they should molt like little wooden butterflies inside a larger chrysalis.

It occurs to me now that we are all Russian nesting dolls, hiding layers of ourselves coiled together beneath superficial masks and costumes and flesh. The childhood version of you is concealed in your preteen incarnation which hides inside your adolescent shell – all of which is obscured by the adult façade that you share with the world. We stack each part of ourselves underneath coats of maturity and folded skin and wrinkled hands; deep down inside, though, there's still that vulnerable child cloaked behind layers of yearning years and emotional evolution.

I might be *Mr. Smith* to Veronica and the rest of the outside world, but beneath that I'm *Brian* and *Brick* and *Richard* and *Rick* and *Junior*. While Veronica could see my surface as clearly as translucent film, the other photonegative layers had been obscured by decades of denial and anxiety and grief. Even though I'd opened myself up to this precocious student, peeled back the layers of identity that comprised my emotional epidermis, there were still pieces of me that remained hidden.

I realize there are several layers that you, dear reader, have yet to see. I assure you, those secrets will all be revealed in time. For now, though, I need to take a break and turn my attention back home – to my wife and daughter. Gravity is dragging me back from the unpredictable weightlessness of the outer atmosphere, and I can't resist its pull.

It's time to go home.

Many, many years ago, I learned a very important lesson from a wise man. It took me a long time to figure it out, but I understand his words now.

Some things are more important than rock and roll.

END SIDE A

Brian's story will continue in

INCOMPLETE SIDE B:

A Different Slant of Light

ACKNOWLEDGEMENTS

My father once told me that every person has a book inside of them, waiting to be written. Though he was a stubborn, solitary soul, I've taken that creed and turned it into a basic tenet of my life. We all have books inside of us; we just need to devote the time to writing them. I owe a debt of gratitude to Mark Levin for teaching me that vital life lesson.

First and foremost, I want to thank my mother, Marion Levin-Welch, who has guided me for four decades with one unwavering principle: *love will always win*. Her life's had more plot-twists than any Dan Brown novel, but she has always put the needs of her children and her students before her own. I've spent ten years as a parent (and eighteen years as a teacher) emulating her compassion and dedication.

To my siblings, Richelle Feldan and Matt Levin: thank you for all those years of late-night conversations, *Star Wars* marathons, and once-in-a-lifetime concerts. Marina and Chunk have got nothing on you two. I'm also thankful for the additional family members that I've inherited from you: Max, Ashley, and Dillon. I love you all.

Thanks to Richard Feldan for providing me with an irreverent (but honest) template of what true fatherhood looks like. His wit, candor, dedication, and humor (*yada, yada, yada*) set him apart from most of the mild-mannered adults in my life. I'm grateful for his lifelong wisdom and guidance... even if he does live a hundred miles away in the boondocks of Santa Maria. Let the *airing of grievances* begin!

Though California is obviously quite a distance from Kansas (geographically and otherwise), my Jayhawk family is never far from my thoughts. My aunt and uncle, Murray and Julie Levin, are two of the most incredible, inspiring people I know. Equally impressive are the next generations of their brilliant, compassionate family: Paris, Alan, and Hazel Levinovitz. *Rock Chalk, Jayhawks!*

I'm eternally grateful that I inherited the best in-laws in the world, George and Edie Stassi. Not only did they raise my wife to be an upstanding, loving, compassionate woman, but they're also remarkable grandparents. My daughters are beyond blessed to have a *YeYe* and *PoPo* as amazing as them.

I didn't have a large, expansive family growing up, but my wife's clan has embraced me and welcomed me into the fold over the last twenty-two years. Thanks to them, I've benefitted from the benevolence of new branches on my family tree: Grandpa Sal Stassi; Aunt Susan, Uncle Galen, and Julie Onizuka (along with Nathan and Maia, of course); Johnny, Trevor, and Nicole Wu; and Karen, John, Madden, and Jackson Blomquist. From all of them, I've learned the joy, loyalty, camaraderie, and exaltation of extended family. That's worth more to me than any musical instrument or record collection.

Mahalo to Nani Edgar and Danny Carvalho. Little did I know that a single summer interview at Coffee Bean would blossom into a wonderful friendship and collaborative partnership. It's been an honor writing songs with Nani and Danny (a.k.a. Kailua Moon), and I'm incredibly proud of the music that we've created together. Nani and her *'ohana* (Lowell and Sylvia Edgar) have been incredibly generous with their time and insight into *Hawaiiana*, and any errors about Hawaiian culture solely reflect my own mistakes and ignorance – not theirs.

I'd like to give a shout-out to my book club: Marilyn Beal, Brooke Gant, Dawn Maloney, Cheryl Wheeler, and Amie Lyans. Thanks for endless hours of love, laughter, and literature – and for serving as my badass beta readers. They were the first folks to read *Incomplete*, even during its various stages of completion (or *Incompletion*, as it were). Their notes, suggestions, and guidance have helped strengthen this novel into a more polished, professional product. I wouldn't expect anything less from this cool, classy coterie of retired English teachers.

Annie McGavren (the best human being I know) has been a tireless cheerleader, and her words of encouragement have kept me afloat more than she might realize. My personal mantra in life is *"WWAMD?" ("What Would Annie McGavren Do?")*, and I know that I'm a better person for following that stricture.

Kevin Downey, my musical partner-in-crime at Buena High School, has been an unceasingly devoted supporter of this book for the last six years. Together, we've spent countless hours recording music for the BHS Choir; and, during that time, he has perpetually inspired me with his dedication, passion, and attention to detail. Kevin provided copious notes on the penultimate draft of *Incomplete*, and gave me a much-needed confidence boost during the eleventh hour of the novel's construction.

Although various beta readers supplied valuable suggestions and guidance, no one provided me with better feedback than Christine Young. This passionate public school librarian (and former AP English super-student/TA) read through multiple drafts of *Incomplete*, and gave me vital recommendations for my final revisions. Brian has Veronica to push him out of his comfort zone; I have Christine Young.

For years, I've been a super-fan of Chris Jay (and his band, the Army of Freshmen). Though we tend to float in and out of each other's lives, I always appreciate his machine-gun fire of conversation and his lyrical prowess. Chris's feedback and notes helped add additional credibility to the novel – especially his insight into the inner workings of the music industry and his guidance fixing my antiquated boxing metaphors. If I'm Rocky Balboa, Chris is Mickey Goldmill: the tough-as-nails coach who pushes me to transform my literary jab into a full-fledged uppercut. *Incomplete* is more of a "contender" thanks to him.

My favorite Hogwarts professor, Alissa Charvonia, plowed through a draft of the novel in less than a week and left me pages of in-depth notes and thoughtful marginalia – which is truly remarkable, since she did so without Rita Skeeter's Quick-Quotes Quill. With her keen, discerning eye, Alissa helped me work through some of the more sensitive subject matter addressed in the novel.

Theresa Olivier is one of the brightest students to have ever walked the hallowed halls of Buena High School. When I first met her, she was a precocious, preternaturally mature eleventh-grader in my AP English class. Much like Veronica Jones, Theresa challenged me and motivated me to become a much more effective educator. Sixteen years later, I'm still learning from Theresa: her "unbridled praise" and "food for thought" helped me refine *Incomplete* for its final draft. Fun fact: Theresa shares a birthday with William Shakespeare. As the Bard might say about his B-day doppelgänger, "How far that little candle throws [her] beams! So shines a good deed in a weary world." Because of Theresa, I was a better teacher for future Buena Bulldogs – and a better writer for *Incomplete*. A beaming candle, indeed!

The last – but certainly not least – of my beta readers is my former super-student and current dentist (yes, you read that correctly), Dr. Stephanie Hwang Kroll. Stephanie read *Incomplete* **four** times in various drafts, and her incredible insight helped me with credibility and continuity. Though we started with a teacher/student relationship fourteen years ago, we evolved into doctor/patient and friend/friend. I'm incredibly proud of her and everything that she's accomplished in her life.

Stephanie's husband, Bryan Hwang (another favorite former student), provided key feedback on the novel's cover art. Bryan's suggestions for fonts and layout helped me invoke some of my favorite 90s bands, lending era-appropriate authenticity to *Incomplete*.

Muchas gracias to Emmet Cullen, teacher extraordinaire, who used his award-winning photography skills to take my "About the Author" headshots. If Emmet can make *me* look presentable, then you know he's talented. In all seriousness, Emmet is a true hero (inside *and* outside the classroom), and I'm blessed to work alongside him at Buena High School.

Much love to the many, many high school students with whom I've worked over the last two decades. Thank you for inspiring me and teaching *me* about life, loyalty, friendship, and duty. I only hope that you learned as much from me as I learned from you.

I've encountered a variety of "Veronicas" over the years – those remarkable, awe-inspiring overachievers who surprise you with their creativity, commitment, and depth of character. The fictional Veronica shares DNA with some of my favorite former students: she inherited the tenacity of Aricka Wilde, the brilliant mind of Nick Jones, the dedication of Danielle Pelkola, the hipster musical appreciation of Allison Knight, the sharp wit of Jeff Dunne, the musical collaboration of Brenna Neri, and the compassion of Alexandria Jason – as well as the determination and dental career of the aforementioned Stephanie Hwang Kroll. Veronica's character borrows a little bit from each of them (and many more), in the same way that a baker's recipe samples a variety of ingredients. No matter how great Veronica might be, though, she still pales in comparison to all these fantastic non-fictional folks.

Thanks to Eli Barnes and Bret Colman for the last-minute consultations about football jargon and gridiron logistics. Like the high school incarnation of Brian, these two brilliant young men have continually defied expectations as introspective, high-achieving, multitalented football players. Any reader who doubts the veracity of Brick's character has clearly never encountered Bret and Eli.

While I never made it to the major label contracts and upper echelons of rock stardom that Brick experiences in the novel, I have been lucky enough to know a few future rock stars before the throngs of adoring fans adopted them: Jeffrey Jacob Mendel (In the Valley Below), Donovan Melero (Hail the Sun), and Cole Citrenbaum (Opia). I am so proud of these three gentlemen – not only for their musical successes, but for their development into wonderful, inspiring human beings. All three have endured trials and tribulations during their musical journeys, but they've crafted remarkable melodies in their stratospheric ascent through the music industry. I admire them all.

Much appreciation goes to my own rock star public school English teachers (in chronological order): Betty Whitney, Julie Simshauser, Susan Edgar, Brooke Gant, Marilyn Beal, Mary Hill, Steve Pollock, Virginia Cotsis, and Chris Mathers. Though teaching can be an exhausting, overwhelming profession, they all made it look so easy. Over the course of their professional careers, these phenomenal teachers have inspired me – and countless others – to change the world for the better.

Many thanks to my colleagues, coworkers, and compadres at Buena High School. In particular, I'd like to thank Jaime Jones, Heather Arrambide, Kelly Herrera, Frank Davis, Bobbi Powers, Karen Rodrigues, Katherine Loughman, Bethany Wood, Lynne Barnes, Kathleen Olivier, and Cindy Randall. They've made Buena seem less like a day job, and more like a home away from home. *Go, Bulldogs!*

To my bandmates in Far From Kansas and the Briar Rose Ramblers (Matt Levin, Danny McDermott, Frank Cruz, Diana Essex,

Mark Pohl, Chris Dixon, Natalie Leichtfuß, Willie Makiling, Jon Crocker, Devon Hammond, Jeff Dunne, Josh Brock, Jason Dinkler, Mike Cromie, Jordan McWethy, Samantha Perkins, Jamie Allen, Brittany Oliver, and Nani Edgar), I thank you for two decades of collaboration and friendship. I've tried my best to be a benevolent Brian Wilson, and I'm grateful that you've been my musical "messengers." Thank you for the many lessons you've taught me – onstage *and* offstage.

For the last two decades, Dr. Frank Eugene Cruz has been one of the most inspirational figures in my life. Frank produced my first proper solo album, *Lo Fi Angels*, and co-produced Far From Kansas's *The Ghost Inside of You;* both of those records pushed me to grow as a singer/songwriter and I'm grateful for the innumerable hours that Frank invested in our musical pursuits – and our friendship. *Go, Bears!*

Though I've had many bandmates over the years, I consider Devon Hammond to be my musical righthand man. Devon has produced or co-produced every album that I've made since 2006, lending his piano, organ, guitar, and bass to many, many Far From Kansas and Briar Rose Ramblers recordings. His incomparable musicianship and production skills have been an absolute godsend, and I'm incredibly lucky to have him as my go-to musical collaborator.

When I first started working with John Cabral, I was stretching my wings beyond the mellow confines of folk-rock into a heavier, more complex full-band sound. John co-produced the first two Far From Kansas albums, and over the course of those projects, he became a dear friend and confidant. Although he has since moved to the southeast coast of the country, I will always be thankful for his friendship.

Fate serendipitously brought Jeff Dunne into my life – first as a student in my AP English class, and then as a musical collaborator. Before he even set foot in my classroom, my colleagues and students warned me that Jeff was an "old soul" with whom I would inevitably bond. Little did I know that this precocious musical prodigy would become the co-producer of the final Far From Kansas albums and a longterm collaborator. I'm truly blessed that our paths crossed and that this genius producer invested so much time, energy, and talent into our shared musical projects.

My gratitude goes to three strong, independent women who inspired me in subtle and not-so-subtle ways. To Anna Levy: I was grateful for our friendship in high school when we were two tie-dyed teenagers, and I'm just as grateful for our resurrected friendship today. Props to Meghan Clark, my favorite "Hawaiian Okie," who shared her real-life experiences and helped illuminate what life was like growing up in Ojai in the 1990s. Thanks to Melissa Guerra for all of our standing Saturday morning chats – even though I lost countless productive hours of writing, our conversations were worth it.

I would also like to thank Shekinah Pugh-McGlocklin for her generous guidance during a critical juncture of this novel's journey. I took her advice and "lit a fire," finishing off *Incomplete* much earlier than I anticipated. I would be remiss if I did not also give a shout-out to my favorite real-life superhero: Shekinah's older brother, Zachary Levi. His inspiring work with Operation Smile and his brave honesty in discussing mental health make him much more remarkable than any caped crusader or spandex-sporting superhero. You've made the world a better place, Captain Sparkle Fingers – far beyond the confines of the silver screen.

Toda raba to Rabbi Lisa Hochberg-Miller, Robin Faigin, Marisa Schrier, and Danielle Stoyanoff. It was an honor to write and deliver the Beach Boys-themed *Midrash* at TBT's "Good Shabbat Vibrations" event. Who knew that Moses and Brian Wilson had so much in common?

Although I don't personally know any of the famous bands who fictionally appear and/or are discussed in *Incomplete*, I feel like my life has been enriched by the work of Neil Young, Elvis Costello, blink-182, Jimmy Eat World, The Ataris, Green Day, and the countless other artists whose music is referenced in this novel – especially, of course, Brian Wilson and the Beach Boys. Please support them by buying and legally streaming their music. Just like any other occupation, artists need income to make ends meet. Art without commerce is an injustice to the artist.

I've benefitted greatly from the many movers and shakers in the Ventura music scene, most notably Brian Parra, Mike Kohli, Jan Peyton, Bill Locey, and the Hogansons (Polly and Steve). These remarkable human beings have kept the music alive in our hometown for years, and I can't thank them enough for giving me multitudinous opportunities to play shows in Ventura – particularly at Zoey's Café, the Livery Theater, Rock City Studios, and the Garden Village Café. If not for their wonderful work curating, booking, and hosting shows, I wouldn't have any insight into the inner workings of the music business. Although most of those valuable venues have since shuttered their doors, the many memories of life-changing concerts will always remain.

Merci beaucoup to Todd Winokur for giving me his blessing to use Café Voltaire in one of the novel's key scenes. I had my very first sip of coffee at the venue a quarter of a century ago, and I played my first CD release show there, too. I hope that *Incomplete* does justice to Todd and his coffee shop. R.I.P. Café Voltaire.

Thanks to Tim Frantz at Mountain Dog Musicworks Recording Studio for graciously giving me permission to use his business as a setting for the *Bookhouse E.P.* recording sessions. Tim has been a staple of the Ojai music scene for several decades, and I've spent many hours at Mountain Dog mixing and mastering tracks. I'm thrilled that I could place Caulfield's recording sessions at such a meaningful local institution.

A huge portion of this book was written in the foyer of the MacKinnon Dance Academy in Oxnard, while my daughters rehearsed in the mirrored rooms adjacent to the hall. Thanks to Susie Eskridge, Sarah Trotter, Kaitlyn Herrera, and Joy MacKinnon for teaching my daughters how to move and groove – and for giving me space right outside the studio doors to write *Incomplete*.

Thank you to Eddie Raburn, Martha Benavides, and the Cal Coast Strength & Conditioning team for helping me on my health transformation. The forty-five pounds that I've lost these last few years mean much less than the confidence that I've gained.

A few published authors (including one famous one) offered me vital guidance for publishing my first novel. Thanks to Wendelin Van Draanen for her encouragement and feedback during our brief encounters. Mick Brady gave me priceless insight into self-publication, and I sincerely appreciate the time that she spent talking me through the process (especially for pointing me in the direction of IngramSpark). Finally, I'd like to thank Claire Laminen, who inspired me with her own debut novel, *Across the Formidable Sea*, the pages of which I saturated with the bleeding ink of my blue editing pen.

One of my best and oldest friends, Keith Flores, has been an inspiring and supportive presence in my life for almost thirty years. We met in a seventh-grade science class, roomed together in the dorms at Berkeley, and have remained friends in spite of geographical roadblocks. Thank you, Keith, and the rest of your family (including your children and your wonderful wife, Sandy).

My good friend Rich Letus was a bold, supportive ballast in high school, even as I struggled to find the light and wind during that dark era of my youth. During those formative years, we bonded over cross-country, theater, and The Rolling Stones. In the years since, Rich has become a passionate and dedicated teacher – not unlike the protagonist of this novel.

When I was a wee little Levin, I was blessed with the world's best babysitter, Peri Froedge. Before she became a lifelong elementary school teacher, Peri instilled a love of literature and a passion for reading in one particularly precocious preadolescent. I credit Peri for teaching me how to read and inspiring me to become a comic book aficionado.

Thanks to Ron and Amanda Vogelbaum for almost forty years of love and friendship. The time that I spent with their family was a pivotal piece of my childhood, and I will always have a special place in my heart for the Vogelbaums. In my mind, Brian's Ojai home is modeled after their loving residence, where so many treasured memories were forged.

I am forever indebted to Nicole, Shamus, and Gabriel Auth, for friendship and emotional support. You three are more than friends: you're family. 'Nuff said.

I wish I could somehow send transmissions to the afterlife, so that the surrogate mothers and fathers I've lost could read this novel. Thanks to James Welch, Diana Vogelbaum, John Young, and Carol Duran for loving me unconditionally, supporting me in obvious (and not-so-obvious) ways, and teaching me what it means to be a parent. I miss you all, and I wish you could have read this novel before you passed on.

To my wife, Kathleen: it's no coincidence that Mel borrows some... *ahem*... *many* of your characteristics. "Salvation" *is* a loaded word, but it's not an exaggeration to say that you saved my life. I can never thank you enough for that.

For my daughters, Alexandra and Charlotte. Some things are more important to me than rock and roll: *you*. Thank you for completing my life. I love you.

READER'S GUIDE

READING GROUP DISCUSSION QUESTIONS

(Because Book Clubs Are Awesome!)

1.) Music plays a pivotal role in *Incomplete*. How has Brian's life been shaped and informed by his passion for music?

2.) Brian and his father are self-professed "Beach Heads," obsessed with Brian Wilson and the Beach Boys. In what ways has music impacted or enriched your life? Is there a singer, artist, or band whose work is as dear to you as the Beach Boys are to Brian and his father?

3.) Second only to music references, literary allusions are abundantly scattered throughout *Incomplete*. What authors and pieces of literature seem the most important to Brian? What novels, stories, and poems have had the most profound effects on your life?

4.) What significance is embedded in the names of the novel's characters and settings? Take another look at the names of supporting characters and locations (perhaps with the help of Google Translate). How do the names of these characters/locales reflect their roles in the story and their relationship to Brian?

5.) In the "First Verse" section of *Incomplete*, Brian discusses his life as a "mild-mannered English teacher." Were you surprised at all by Brian's childhood and adolescence, as he describes it to Veronica in the "First Chorus" section? In what ways has Brian grown up and evolved from his younger years? In what ways is he virtually the same?

6.) Just before he reveals the story of his youth to Veronica, Brian warns her that he might be an "unreliable narrator." How credible do you think Brian's accounts actually are? Has he misinterpreted or misjudged any of the events in his life? Has hindsight revealed any truths to Brian during the intervening years?

7.) Although Brian doesn't recognize it until his senior year of high school, his father is a widely celebrated teacher. How has Brian's life been shaped by having two teachers for parents? In what ways have the careers of your family and friends impacted you?

8.) Early in the novel, Brian paraphrases Bruce Johnston's quote about the Beach Boys and compares teachers to "surfing Doris Days." Despite Brian's assertion that teachers are inherently "uncool," it's clear that he and his father are inspiring figures for their students. Are teachers ever *really* cool? Have you had any "cool" teachers in your own life?

9.) How are Brian's romance with Lani and his relationship with Serena different? What qualities in Lani and Serena does Brian find attractive? What key differences do you see in Serena and Lani?

10.) A recurring theme throughout the novel is feeling "caught between two worlds." How has this sense of feeling torn – between past and present, personal and professional, modern and traditional, etc. – informed the lives of the different characters in the novel? Have you ever encountered anything like these experiences?

11.) Throughout *Incomplete*, Brian hints that he's so traumatized by his experience with Call Field that he's reticent to revisit his youth and adolescence. What trauma(s) has Brian encountered so far? What might have happened to Brian in the summer of 2000 that has left him so scarred?

12.) In the last chapter of the novel, Brian compares himself to a *matryoshka* doll, with various layers reflecting different aspects of his identity. How do his many names and nicknames reflect this analogy? What layers of identity do you see within yourself? Does your exterior "shell" reflect the person that you feel you truly are at your core?

13.) The presence (and absence) of water is a not-so-subtle motif in *Incomplete*. What does water symbolize for Brian and the other characters in the novel? How does Lani's life as a "double-island girl" reflect Brian's own complicated relationship with water and dry land?

BIBLIOGRAPHY

Anderson, John, and Joe Thomas, directors. *The Beach Boys: Doin' It Again*. Brother Records, 2012.

Boyd, Alan, director. *Endless Harmony: The Beach Boys Story*. Brother Records, 2000.

Carlin, Peter Ames. *Catch a Wave: The Rise, Fall & Redemption of the Beach Boys' Brian Wilson*. Emmaus, PA: Rodale, 2006.

Dillon, Mark. *Fifty Sides of the Beach Boys / The Songs That Tell Their Story*. Toronto, Canada: ECW, 2012.

Fusilli, Jim. *Pet Sounds*. New York: Continuum, 2005.

Gaines, Steven. *Heroes and Villains: The True Story of the Beach Boys*. Da Capo Press, 2002.

Hilburn, Robert. *Johnny Cash: The Life*. First Edition ed. New York: Little, Brown, 2013.

Leaf, David. *The Beach Boys and the California Myth*. Grosset & Dunlap, 1978.

Love, Mike, and James S. Hirsch. *Good Vibrations: My Life as a Beach Boy*. Blue Rider Press, 2016.

Morgan, Johnny. *The Beach Boys: America's Band*. Sterling Publishing, 2015.

Sánchez, Luis. *Smile*. Bloomsbury, 2014.

Stebbins, Jon. *The Beach Boys FAQ: All That's Left to Know about America's Band*. Milwaukee, WI: Backbeat, 2011.

Was, Don, director. *Brian Wilson: I Just Wasn't Made for These Times*. Lionsgate, 1995.

White, Timothy. *The Nearest Faraway Place: Brian Wilson, the Beach Boys, and the Southern California Experience*. Henry Holt and Company, 1994.

Wilson, Brian, and Ben Greenman. *I Am Brian Wilson: a Memoir*. Perseus Books, 2016.

Wilson, Brian, and Todd Gold. *Wouldn't It Be Nice: My Own Story*. Harper Collins, 1991.

SOUNDTRACK PLAYLIST

*I*ncomplete is a book that leans heavily on a listener's knowledge of popular music, with particular emphasis on Brian Wilson and the Beach Boys. Although a purist's complete playlist would be at least eight hours long, this condensed list of songs (in chronological order of the novel's events) will provide you with a *fun, fun, fun* soundtrack for your reading. Enjoy!

"Sail On, Sailor" [Live in New York, 1973] (Brian Wilson, Tandyn Almer, Van Dyke Parks, Jack Rieley, & Raymond Kennedy) — The Beach Boys, *The Beach Boys in Concert*, 1973.

"So You Want to Be a Rock 'N' Roll Star" (Roger McGuinn & Chris Hillman) — The Byrds, *Younger Than Yesterday*, 1967.

"Veronica" (Elvis Costello & Paul McCartney) — Elvis Costello, *Spike*, 1989.

"In My Room" (Brian Wilson & Gary Usher) — The Beach Boys, *Surfer Girl*, 1963.

"Time of the Season" (Rod Argent) — The Zombies, *Odessey and Oracle*, 1968.

"California Girls" [Live] (Brian Wilson & Mike Love) — Brian Wilson, *Brian Wilson and Friends*, 2014.

"God Only Knows" (Brian Wilson & Tony Asher) — The Beach Boys, *Pet Sounds*, 1966.

"Surf City" (Brian Wilson & Jan Berry) — Jan & Dean, *Surf City and Other Swingin' Cities*, 1963.

"Pipeline" (Brian Carman & Bob Spickard) — The Chantays, *Pipeline*, 1962.

"Help Me, Rhonda" [Live in New Jersey, 1972] (Brian Wilson & Mike Love) — The Beach Boys, *Made in California*, 2013.

"Smells Like Teen Spirit" (Kurt Cobain, Krist Novoselic, & Dave Grohl) — Nirvana, *Nevermind*, 1991.

"Undone - The Sweater Song" (Rivers Cuomo) — Weezer, *Weezer (The Blue Album)*, 1994.

"When I Come Around" (Billie Joe Armstrong, Mike Dirnt, & Tré Cool) — Green Day, *Dookie*, 1994.

"Ball and Chain" (Mike Ness) — Social Distortion, *Social Distortion*, 1990.

"Blitzkrieg Bop" (Joey Ramone, Dee Dee Ramone, Johnny Ramone, & Tommy Ramone) — The Ramones, *Ramones*, 1976.

"Over the Rainbow" (Harold Arlen & Yip Harburg) — Israel Kamakawiwoʻole, *Facing Future*, 1993.

"Hanalei Moon" (Bob Nelson) — Jerry Byrd, *Steel Guitar Hawaiian Style*, 1976.

"Surfer Girl" (Brian Wilson) — The Beach Boys, *Surfer Girl*, 1963.

"Dammit" (Mark Hoppus, Tom DeLonge, & Scott Raynor) — blink-182, *Dude Ranch*, 1997.

"Earth Angel (Will You Be Mine)" (Curtis Williams, Jesse Belvin, & Dootsie Williams) — The Penguins, *Earth Angel*, 1954.

"Wouldn't It Be Nice" (Brian Wilson, Tony Asher, & Mike Love) — The Beach Boys, *Pet Sounds*, 1966.

"Surfin' USA" [Live in Mountain View, 1999] (Brian Wilson & Chuck Berry) — Brian Wilson, *The Bridge School Concerts: 25th Anniversary Edition*, 2011.

"Love and Mercy" [Live in Mountain View, 1999] (Brian Wilson) — Brian Wilson, *The Bridge School Collection, Vol. 2*, 2006.

A NOTE ON THE TYPE

The principal text of *Incomplete* was composed in Times New Roman, 12-point font. Duh. You can take the boy out of the English classroom, but you can't take the English classroom out of the boy.

ABOUT THE AUTHOR

J.D. Levin is a mild-mannered librarian by day… and a mild-mannered rock & roller by night. He has worked as a public school educator for almost two decades – first as an English teacher, then as a Teacher Librarian. Outside of the classroom, he's written songs for The Briar Rose Ramblers, Far From Kansas, Kailua Moon, and Grammy-nominated slack-key guitarist Danny Carvalho. Levin is a graduate of UC Berkeley (BA '01), Stanford University (MA '02), CSUN (MA '09), and CSULB (TLSC '15). He lives on the central coast of California with his wife, two daughters, and cluttered collection of musical instruments. *Incomplete* is his first novel.

LEARN MORE at **www.notsosilentlibrarian.com** |
CONTACT: **notsosilentlibrarian@gmail.com**